THEY ALL CALLED JACQUES

HILARY NEWMAN

BY THE SAME AUTHOR

The Man at the Gate

THEY'RE ALL CALLED JACQUES

HILARY NEWMAN

COMBIS PRESS

Published in 2024 by Combis Press

Copyright © Hilary Newman 2024

Hilary Newman has asserted her right to be identified as the
author of this Work in accordance with the
Copyright, Designs and Patents Act 1988

ISBN Paperback: 978-1-8381129-2-9
Ebook: 978-1-8381129-3-6

All rights reserved. No part of this publication may be reproduced,
stored in a retrieval system, or transmitted in any form or by any
means, electronic, mechanical, photocopying, recording or otherwise,
without the prior permission of the copyright owner.

All characters and events in this publication, other than those clearly in
the public domain, are fictitious and any resemblance to real persons,
living or dead, is purely coincidental.

A CIP catalogue copy of this book can be found in the British Library.

Published with the help of Indie Authors World
www.indieauthorsworld.com

IndieAuthors
World

To George whose enthusiasm and passion enabled us to restore a 17th Century Chateau in the Gers, and to spend many happy days there for over 20 years.

CHAPTER 1

JANUARY 2004

Winter started that year in early January. The months leading up to Christmas and the New Year festivities had been mild and sunny, so the citizens of Toulouse were startled to be greeted by a cold wind blowing from the South and snow laden skies as they stepped onto the streets. Annie Scott on her way to work, and passing the bakers, was tempted by the scent of warm bread. Holding her coat tight to her chest, she paused before joining the queue that snaked from the door to the busy counter. A man pushed in behind her and an icy blast followed him in. There was a chorus of complaint. The queue shuffled slowly towards the large, rosy faced woman behind the counter, whose plump arms and bosom evidenced a life of good bread and cakes. Annie edging forward looking at the display; delicate patisseries, fruit filled tarts, almond tuilles, glossy chocolate eclairs, cheese straws. Her mouth was watering, as she finally reached the front, 'Une tarte aux pommes, s'il vous plait. Celui la! She pointed. It would be a treat for supper after a cold day. It was swiftly boxed and she moved aside to pay the young girl at the till, whose bored expression discouraged any friendly greeting. Annie hardly noticed, Mondays in January were always difficult and the draught from the door, which repeatedly opened and closed, would have put anyone in a 'mood'.

As she continued her walk Annie thought of Charlie, her young son, who had certainly been in a mood at breakfast. He now insisted on a café crème with his baguette and croissant, which she thought was an affectation, suspecting that it was the caffeine that made him edgy and grumpy. The teenage years are on me, she thought, inwardly groaning, and remembered how rude and unhelpful she had been at that age with her own mother. Holding the boxed tart carefully and clutching her heavy bag of books, she weaved her way down the cobbled street, thinking back to her previous life in rural Kent; married in her early twenties, she had lived with her husband Ralph and Charlie in a cottage on the outskirts of a small village. They had not been easy years, money was tight as she sought to combine part time work with rearing her small son. Slowly the marriage fell apart built as it was on weak foundations. She and Ralph had little in common apart from Charlie whose birth had prompted the marriage in the first place. Her relocation to Toulouse when Charlie was eight was a gamble that had mostly paid off; she had well paid and interesting work in the City and Charlie had settled well at school. They lived in a large slightly shabby apartment in the heart of Toulouse, on the fourth floor of a 19th century building. She loved her apartment and was proud of it, proud that she had bought it with her own money and made it into a home for herself and her son.

Turning into the Staff Only gates of the University, where she taught classes in horticulture, and flashing her security card, she nodded at a colleague and put Charlie out of her mind. She focused on the day of teaching that lay ahead.

*

Some minutes after the departure of his mother, Charlie was also walking through Toulouse, but he didn't stop at the boulangerie for he was very hard up, having spent his small allowance on new trainers. He had ignored his mother's advice at breakfast, 'Wear your winter anorak and take a scarf, it looks ready to snow. She had said, before slamming the door and running down the stairs. Charlie had gone out in his favourite black cotton jacket, so was soon thoroughly cold and his temper was not improved by stepping into some dog's poop at the crossing near the school. 'Merde! He swore.

'Oops! A voice behind him called out.

Charlie turned and saw a girl laughing at him. He flushed.

'You'd better change those smart trainers when you get inside, she said, moving away towards the big entrance gates.

'Yeah, he muttered, 'Thanks.

He knew the girl, but not well, her name was Anya and she had long black hair and a fringe. She was in his year and was clever, in top sets for most subjects. He was not, except for maths where he quite simply shone. He looked at his new trainers and swore again, quietly, and followed her into school, looking for his friends, with whom he could have a moan. Charlie had been feeling unsettled since his return from spending part of Christmas and New Year in England with his father Ralph and then Annie's parents. Ralph had met him on his arrival at the airport and driven him back to the cottage in Kent where he was living with Edna his new partner. Charlie liked Edna, previously his holidays with Ralph had been chaotic and confusing, but now he felt part of an ordered life, his father working every day and Edna cooking regular meals. She was kind and funny and had a matter of fact approach to life. He enjoyed his days in their cottage next to the village green. He had made friends during his stay in the summer with some of the local 'lads' as Edna called them. Boys of varying ages, they all had nicknames, Spike was nearest him in age and owned a newish bike and there was a big chap called Jock who had taught him to bowl overarm. Charlie was nicknamed' Frenchie' which secretly pleased him. The 'lads' were a gang, using the ramshackle cricket pavilion as their meeting place and roaming about in a haphazard but satisfying manner.

Charlie liked the freedom of his holidays in Kent, he could open the kitchen door and just wander out, down to the shop or across the Green. Ralph had given him a bike for Christmas, not new of course, but it had gears and good brakes and he happily rode it around the lanes that led out of the village. Exploring, Edna called it waving him off. Sometimes he rode with other boys, but often on his own and only once did he get lost. He was late home and Edna was waiting for him.

'Your lunch is in the oven, a bit spoilt! Where did you get to?

Charlie was relieved that she wasn't cross and tried to explain, but Edna was not a great one for detail and went to find the crossword. They had a pattern of doing the puzzle together over lunch. They finished it every day, timing themselves. If they did it quickly Edna reached for the box of chocolates that Annie had put in his case as a gift.

His father took him out on his last evening, he was moving to stay with his grandmother the following morning. Edna was visiting her sister for a 'girl's night out' as Ralph described it. They went to the pub, the Cricketers and settled at a table next to the fire.

'Lots of my mates drink here. Ralph confided. It was almost empty.

'Every one a bit short after Christmas, he explained. There was a pause, whilst Ralph swallowed some beer and Charlie sucked his fizzy drink through a straw,

'So you still enjoying life in Toulouse? Plenty of friends? Charlie assured him that everything was fine.

'You could come back, you know. Ralph leant forward, 'Good school nearby, where all the local kids go, and, well, Edna and I would love to have you. To live with us. Think about it.

Then as encouragement, 'There would be cricket in the summer. They say that you're a promising bowler.

*

No more was said and Charlie moved on to stay with his grandparents. He tried not think too much about what his father had said. How could he leave Mum? On her own. And what of his friends? But the idea lingered in his thoughts and for the first time he saw the advantage in having parents who lived in separate countries. He was developing a somewhat romantic view of what life would be like, if he moved back to England.

CHAPTER 2

On that same morning Mme. Marthe le Brun set out from her apartment in Collioure to drive home to Les Palmes, her home outside Toulouse. It was a bright sunny day but the skies to the south were leaden with snow and there was a cold nip in the air as she loaded her car. She had been in Collioure since the middle of December but her holiday had not been a great success. Many of her favourite restaurants were shut, and she was too much on her own. Even the sunny walks along the Promenade had not lightened her mood, the town so lively in the summer had a desolate feel. Her friend Patrick, whose company she had enjoyed in the summer was not to be found, and she realised that she had been foolish to assume that he would return in the winter.

Marthe was a widow, now in her sixties. Some years previously she had taken the bold decision to move from Paris where she had lived nearly all her life, and start a new life in the Gers in what had once been the home of her father, Bertrand. It was called Les Palmes and had been in the family since the mid 19th century. 'I have been under the influence of others all my life, she had explained to her son and only child a bemused Felix, 'my mother, my maternal grandparents and for the last nearly forty years your father. Now I can live for myself, make my own decisions and this is one of them.

Felix thought of his father Xavier who had so recently died and wondered what he would have thought of this move. He made a slight attempt to dissuade her, but there would be advantages; it would be easier for him to look after his mother, keep an eye on her, if she was living only a short drive from Toulouse. His own relocation to this southern city had occurred several years earlier and had been successful. Besides, he thought, she would enjoy the warmer climate of South West France and the challenge of making a new home for herself at Les Palmes.

*

So Marthe had moved and had been there for more than a year when she met Claude, Count of Soulan. It had started as a business relationship but had quickly developed into a warm friendship and then become much more.

They had met by chance when she stopped on the road to Auch, the capital City of the Gers department. Her eye had been caught by two large stone dogs which guarded the entrance to Claude's business. He sold antique garden furniture; urns and statues and fountains and benches anything that could decorate a garden. During a long summer, as Annie Scott redesigned the long neglected garden at Les Palmes, Claude had visited regularly in his battered van selling her various items and as they chatted in the garden (Claude carefully positioning an urn or an old stone seat) they realised that they had much in common and became friends. He took her to Toulouse where he had friends in the art and antiques communities, and they attended the opera and went to cinemas and concerts. He met Felix. Then on an early Autumn holiday in Collioure, they became lovers, and Claude spoke of marriage. He had not pressed her and the suggestion was left in the air.

*

Marthe enjoyed her holiday with Claude by the Mediterranean and began to spend increasing amounts of time in Collioure. The town offered her an alternative way of life, and as the grey days of late Autumn settled around Les Palmes, she was attracted increasingly to the freedom and life style of the little town with its leisurely atmosphere. She bought an apartment there and whilst her Christmas holiday was somewhat disappointing she had much time to reflect on Claude and his marriage suggestion and made the decision to end her relationship with him. She feared being 'taken over' by him and becoming too reliant on his friendship, she was wary of losing her independence (so recently gained) and, whilst it was an extreme step, during her drive home she planned her letter to him stating that.

*

As she approached Toulouse she considered driving into the City and calling in at the apartment of her son, Felix. He was often working at home, writing or teaching. She had not seen him for a while, they might have lunch she thought. But the traffic was slow as a wet snow fell and the roads became tricky. The light was becoming difficult, so she ignored the Toulouse exit, pressing on for home. A decision that she later regretted.

After a quick lunch, she sat at her desk and wrote the letter. It was brief and she hoped made clear her reasons for her decision. Finally it was finished and she placed it on the hall table before walking out into the garden. Snow was falling, there was a heavy grey look in the sky and she returned indoors to find her warm coat and hat. Setting off again she was soon caught up in the loveliness of plants and shrubs with their dusting of snow. It was the first time that she had seen snow at Les Palmes, it was a rare occurrence, the climate generally warmed by the warm winds off the Atlantic. Today's snow came from the South and East, from Spain and over the Pyrenees, it would last all day. Marthe walked through her garden along the paths that had been laid the previous year, and stopped under the three palms that marked the focal point. Her garden designer, Annie, had assured her that they would thrive here in the Gers and looking at them now with snow on the tall branches, she hoped that they had not been a rash choice. They looked magnificent, against the darkening sky. She walked on towards the far wall and found the gate, which was kept locked. Lifting the key from its hook, she pushed it open and snow fell onto her arms and shoulders, giving herself a shake she turned onto the tow path. Already the path beside the river was snow covered and she stared at the fast flowing water.

'That'll be cold! She thought. It was all very white and beautiful and silent. She stamped her feet, grateful for the warm boots which her husband had bought for her several years ago on a skiing holiday in the Alps. She thought about him with sadness and affection, Xavier had been a kind and loving man and the purchase of these boots reminded her of that. At the time she had scoffed at the purchase, thinking them an unnecessary luxury, but they had turned out to be very warm and she had worn them frequently. Even in Paris.

She turned towards the nearest town of St.Girou, it was half a mile away and she could easily walk there. It would clear her head after the drive up from Collioure.

*

The snow was beginning to drift at the foot of the willows that bordered the river, and also against the high brick walls behind which other houses stood. None of these were as old as hers, and though she passed them frequently, either in her car or on foot, she had never spoken to any of the families who lived in them. The previous summer Marthe had opened her garden to visitors. It was a celebration of the transforming work of Annie, an opportunity for the local community to see the many changes that had taken place over the course of one year. Annie had turned an over run garden into something new and modern. It was now a garden of Mediterranean plants, specially selected for their tolerance of hot dry summers, with little need for watering. The open day had been a great success but had not led to Marthe receiving invitations to visit the homes or gardens of the many people who had enjoyed their visit, who had walked the paths, admired the palm trees, sat on the benches, put their hands in the water of the fountain or eaten an English tea. The local towns, there were two within a short walk, were small and traditionally suspicious of strangers. Marthe was an outsider having settled so recently, though it was known that she was the daughter of the Du Pont family, who had once employed many men and women in the brick works near Toulouse.

*

The snow was falling more heavily now and she could no longer see the spire of the church of St Girou, so Marthe turned back towards home. Her hands and nose felt cold and she was thinking about supper and some hot soup. Suddenly she slipped on the root of a willow tree, lost her footing and fell heavily onto her hands. A sharp pain caused her to cry out and she feared that she had broken her ankle. It lay on the snow, twisted at an odd angle. Unable to maintain her position, she collapsed onto her side. Marthe knew that she was now in trouble, there was no one about, nor had she met anyone on her short walk. The locals, as she thought of them, would be indoors keeping warm and stoking their fires and preparing the evening meal. Marthe felt sick with a combination of pain and fear. Trying to keep calm she slowly and cautiously turned herself around and sat up. The ankle was horribly painful and the cold was seeping into her. Snow had managed to creep down her neck and inside the collar of her coat and up the sleeves too.

Beside her was a high brick wall and she looked for a gate, leading into a garden and a house. She considered shouting for help. Further along the path was a discarded fencing post and she began to inch herself towards it, believing that she might use it to hoist herself up. Her ankle was now excruciating and she wondered whether she should try and remove her boot, but she could not bear to touch it for the moment and the boot kept her foot warm. After several minutes she reached the post and holding it firmly tried to heave herself up, but the angle to her body was wrong and she had insufficient strength.

'Help! Help! Oh someone please help! She called out loudly.

Marthe now became truly afraid, the snow was settling on her head and despite her woolly hat she felt her hair becoming damp whilst her shoulders and coat and trousers were white. She was wet, very cold and quite alone. She put her head in her hands, curled up and wept.

CHAPTER 3

Warm and dry in his apartment in Toulouse, Felix was browsing the estate agents' lists of properties for sale. He had decided that he needed more spacious accommodation than his present apartment, airy and delightful though it was. He was always restless at the beginning of the year, eager to make changes and set himself fresh challenges. Finding a new home was part of that. At present he lived in a chic modern apartment, very near the City centre, it overlooked the Garonne and on a clear day he could see the Pyrenees. Felix was 36. He had lived all his life in Paris where his father Xavier was music professor at the Conservatoire, but Felix had moved to Toulouse some four years ago with Valerie, his girl friend, and they had chosen this home together. Felix was tall and slim with dark slightly long hair, popular with both men and women. Highly gifted musically, a talent that he had inherited from his father, Felix had been encouraged from a young age to pursue a career as a concert pianist. But after years of study and hours of practice he had failed to succeed in that competitive world, and now, in Toulouse, supported himself by writing a music column for the regional newspaper and teaching the piano. In many ways Felix was a fortunate young man; he was the only son of loving parents and enjoyed a substantial income from a trust fund set up many years ago by his grandfather Bertrand. He quickly became a familiar figure in Toulouse, attending concerts in his role as a music critic, and was regularly to be seen in restaurants, bars and galleries. Valerie was no longer part of his life, she had been drawn back to Paris to pursue her career in accountancy and in truth the relationship had run out of steam. They had become bored with each other, and Felix was in no way heartbroken. He rearranged his apartment, throwing out items, vases and pictures and decorative bowls that reminded him of her, and got on with his life.

*

Marthe silently feared that Felix, her much loved only child was something of a dilettante, a bit of a playboy, with his pretty girl friends, frequent holidays on sunny beaches and ski resorts, and his love of fast cars. He had always been closer to his father and there was often a coolness between mother and son as Felix felt her silent criticism. He hoped that Marthe's move to Les Palmes would give them a better understanding of each other and his growing friendship with her gardener Annie, a woman whom Marthe greatly respected, had certainly added a new dimension to the relationship of mother and son.

Appearances are deceptive. Felix had another side; underneath the glamourous life style that he presented to the world, he often lacked confidence, a result of the disappointment that he, and, worse, his father had felt, over his failed attempt to succeed on the concert platform. Somehow he could not forgive himself for that. Furthermore, the recent death of his father, had profoundly shocked him. It was so unexpected and sudden. For the first time in his life Felix understood the precariousness of life and what a gift it was. He began to appreciate the many advantages that life had given him, and became eager to take more responsibility for what he made of that life. He began to think of his future, a future that he intended to share with Annie Scott and her son Charlie. For the first time in his life Felix had fallen deeply in love.

*

There were two possibilities on the property list and, after several phone calls and a short walk, he was standing next to a very pretty agent in a large spacious and sunny salon. It was very grand. He was in one of the tall brick houses that had been built near the Cathedral of St. Sernin, in the heart of Toulouse. It was in the old quarter, approached down a narrow, cobbled street, lined with similar houses. 'A merchant's house, the agent was reading from her file, 'dating back to the 17th Century, with additions of the 19th. She eyed Felix, 'Fully modernized in the last twenty years.

. There were three floors and storage rooms at street level, where the merchants had kept their goods, and a large cellar. The house had retained many of its original features, heavy wooden doors, tall casement windows, and some large fireplaces with fine mantels. The ceilings were high. The agent sensed Felix's interest and went into her selling mode; she emphasized the flexibility of the accommodation, the updated kitchen and the presence of bathrooms on the upper floors. Felix tried to ignore her and turned aside, he was envisaging living there; where his music room would be, and which of the large bedrooms would become his (their bedroom). For it was to be a home for Annie and Charlie, he wanted to tempt her to live with him, and this house was perfect. He thought of Annie busying about, leaving every room untidy, cooking supper in the large kitchen, and working in a room that would be 'her space' a proper study for her work. How could she resist? And Charlie! He could live on the top floor in a much bigger bed room, opposite what he had decided would be his music room, the two men of the house set slightly apart. It was sunny and light at this level, as it looked over the tiled roofs of the houses opposite. A very different aspect from his present apartment but quiet above the stir of pedestrians below. He leant out of the window and saw to his right the spire of St. Sernin...how could she resist!

'I'll return with my partner. Felix said. His phone rang, a number he did not recognize. 'Hello'. It was the hospital in Toulouse, they were talking about Mme. Le Brun. His mother. She had been admitted in the last hour, an emergency. A suspected broken ankle and hypothermia. Felix did not hesitate, he ran down the stairs, shouting a farewell to the young agent, slamming the heavy entrance door behind him. She locked up the house, disappointed and confused, yet confident that she had secured a sale.

Felix's afternoon and evening passed in a whirl of confusion amid the sights and smells of the hospital. Marthe lay sedated, her eyes closed and one leg raised. She was very pale and wrapped in heavy blankets. Her ankle which the nurse said was the main problem would be operated on the following day. Felix peered in through a small window, there was nothing he could do. She was unable to speak, so the doctors had as yet little understanding of what had happened to her, but her life was not in danger. Reassured, Felix finally left the hospital and took a taxi back to his apartment, he felt anxious and shaky. Holding a large whisky he stood on his balcony, and for the first time realised that the tall brightly lit building on the other side of the river was the hospital. He had never noticed it before. It was an ugly white concrete building too high for its surroundings, he must have subconsciously blotted it out. 'Somewhere in there, he thought, lies my mother. What had she been doing, when she fell? Where was she found? He turned away, shutting out the cold night air and walked across the room and sat at the piano, he played a piece with which his last pupil had struggled. He checked the fingering and after some time, finally tired he went to bed. He had forgotten all about the house on the cobbled street with a view of St.Sernin.

*

Marthe lay in the hospital in a sedated state, she was pale and spoke softly and hesitantly. Annie, an early visitor, was shocked at her appearance as was Charlie who had come too. He had never been in a hospital before and was eager to see Marthe of whom he was very fond. He envisaged her sitting up in a bed, surrounded by flowers and smiling nurses in crisp white uniforms. The reality was very different. There was a large and cumberson plaster on her leg, and she was wearing an ugly gown. She didn't smile but lay with her eyes nearly shut, her right arm was horribly discoloured. The smell was overwhelming, disinfectant, Annie explained. And something else which he couldn't identify. He sat tentatively on a chair well way from the bed and tried not to stare. Annie sat nearer and quietly stroked a hand that lay on the sheet, but conversation was impossible as Marthe drifted in and out of sleep. It was a short visit.

After four days Marthe was thought to be ready to leave hospital. Her ankle, diagnosed with a severe sprain, was now in a lighter plaster, but was very uncomfortable and she complained of constant pain. Felix was advised to hire nurses for the next few weeks, though he intended for the moment to move into Les Palmes. Marthe looked at him helplessly, 'How will I manage? Those horrible crutches! They stood near her bed and she found them ungainly and heavy. 'I'll never get up the stairs, will I? I can hardly walk to the bathroom at the moment.

She had given an incoherent account of the accident, unable to remember anything after her fall. Felix was given the name and address of the neighbour who had called for an ambulance, but he did not know them. Over supper in Annie's apartment, the day before Marthe's release, Annie and Felix discussed how the next few weeks could be managed, and Annie tried to be encouraging, 'You'll have to stay for a while at Les Palmes, maybe a week. I know you've got the nurses organized but Marthe will need you as well. It's not going to be easy, Felix, but she'll be back on her feet quite soon I'm sure. You know how determined she is! She gave his hand an encouraging squeeze, he smiled bleakly.

'And what about Patricia? Annie continued, 'She's such a good friend, I'm sure she'd come and help out? Phone her... and phone Claude, he'd keep her amused, and he's close by.

Annie slowly raised Felix's mood, as she continued, 'Who found her? You've not said. Whoever it was, he saved her life didn't he!

Felix didn't answer, he hadn't thought about that. He had a name somewhere in an envelope in a pocket, but had hardly glanced at it. He was thinking about the house in Toulouse which he hadn't yet had the opportunity to discuss with Annie. Marthe's fall had pushed that to one side. The agent, Delphine had left several messages but he had been too preoccupied with the hospital and Marthe to respond. Now seemed a good moment to tell her about the house, which he had found.

'Can we talk about something else? He asked.

Annie turned in surprise, she was stacking the plates in the sink and preparing to call Charlie who was delaying going to his room for bed. He had a new habit of hovering, hoping for a quick game of chess with Felix.

'What?

'Well, I've been thinking about you and me and…

'Oh Felix! Please not now! I'm tired. It's been a long day and…

He looked at her, 'When isn't it a long day? His voice was overlayed with tones of frustration. There was a silence and Annie, now taut and unsettled, turned back to the sink. Felix stood up from the table. He too was tired, but also angry and hurt. He had been looking forward all day to telling Annie about the house and his plan for their future, his temper, generally so mild, flared, 'I'll leave now, he said, 'and see myself out. Picking up his jacket, he strode to the door, calling goodbye to Charlie, who, sensing trouble, had retired to his room. Annie could hear his steps as he ran down the stairs and later the slam of the street door, she felt terrible. She knew that she had been thoughtless and insensitive. Felix was overwrought and needed kindness and support, she had given neither. But she believed that Felix wanted to discuss their long term future, and in one word…marriage. It was a subject that she desperately wanted to avoid.

*

Felix returned home, walking briskly and ignoring other people on the narrow pavements. It was still cold, but the snow had melted and there was grey slush in the gutters. His shoes were wet and he kicked them off at the entrance. The apartment was warm and he poured a large whisky and stood at the window. It was dark and the river ran blackly, there were lights in the houses on the far bank and he thought of families gathered together, preparing for bed, calling goodnight to each other. Families! His anger returned and he went to the piano and after a moment's thought, began to play some Chopin. A Nocturne. Slowly he became lost in the music, he played for a long time until he felt tired enough for sleep. It had, as Annie had said, been a long day. And for Felix a disappointing one.

*

The following morning to keep himself busy and put aside his row with Annie, Felix began to make preparations for Marthe's return. He drove out to Les Palmes. There were patches of snow lying on the fields and the air was cold, but the house was warm and he unpacked the fresh food that he had bought in Toulouse. He stared at Marthe's garden from the landing window, it looked forlorn, with snow under the hedges and not a tree, shrub or plant seemed alive. The countryside, he thought, how desolate it can be. He was reminded of Annie who had worked here all the previous year transforming it into a beautiful and interesting garden. He remembered driving out on Sundays, to have lunch with Marthe, and eager to find an excuse to search Annie out. She was always deeply engaged in whatever she was doing, planting, pruning, planning her next task, sometimes up a tree perched on a ladder, quietly humming. Slowly he had fallen in love with her, which was unexpected, for she was so unlike the other women with whom he had been involved. Unlike Valerie and the girls who had taken up his time in Paris. Annie was not over conscious of her looks, though she was very pretty, and her work clothes were unashamedly practical. She was also very recently divorced, with a lively twelve year old son. And she was English. She was interested in music and she made him happy. They laughed a lot together. He had taken her to concerts and bought her some clothes, he was good at that, and they had enjoyed a walking holiday together in July in the

Pyrenees. Which had cemented their relationship, they had become lovers. He had met her mother, Claire and Claire's partner Tony, and most importantly Felix had built, without even trying, an easy relationship with Charlie who came every Sunday to play in the garden whilst Annie worked. They shared a love of chess and 'boy's stuff'; fishing and cars. Since their week walking in the Pyrennees, he had moved between her apartment and his, it led to complications, and he was tired of it. Now he quite simply wanted to marry her and live as a family. In a large house in Toulouse. Was that too much to hope for?

Felix finished checking Les Palmes, he had secured several shutters and ensured that the boiler was set correctly. The house must be really warm for Marthe's return. He walked through the hall, picked up his coat and a letter that lay on the table beside the door. It was addressed to M. Claude de Vigne, le Compte of Soulan he would post it on his way home as he drove through St.Girou.

CHAPTER 4

Marthe was confined to a day bed in the salon, she could not walk without crutches and had been unable even to go down the shallow steps to the two rooms she used most often, the kitchen and her favourite little sitting room that faced the garden. A team of nurses were in charge, administering the pain relief on which she was reliant and checking her bruised arm and heavily strapped ankle. They were competent and strict. Felix had established himself in a bedroom and did what he could to keep her cheerful; playing the piano which stood in a corner and had recently arrived from Paris, reading the daily paper out loud to her, and encouraging her to rest and sleep. The days were long.

She had plenty of time for reflection as she lay on her cushions and many of her thoughts were very discouraging. These low spirits lifted with the arrival of Patricia, her dearest friend, who had come from Paris to help care for her. She was accompanied by her little poodle, Gaston and walked in clutching lots of delicious treats, magazines and a bottle of champagne. It was opened immediately.

'Not to celebrate your poor ankle, she said, pouring two large glasses and putting a plump cushion behind Marthe's back.

'That's better now, sit up or you'll spill it. It's to say how pleased I am to be here again. She looked around the salon, it was a lovely room papered in a cream and green pattern, 'Zoffany? Not waiting for an answer, she continued, 'You've had the piano moved from Paris, Felix must be pleased! Lucky him. But you still play don't you? Patricia took a deep sip from her glass and walked to the fire place, turning to address Marthe, she said,

'Let's move your bed nearer to the fire and turn you to look out of the window. Staring at four walls is depressing and you'll be able to see out to the road. Not very interesting but that's the best we can do. We'll have to wait for Felix's help for that. Or maybe Claude? Whoever comes first!

After lunch, a rather mediocre meal Patricia thought, both women rested and Marthe woke to find Gaston had settled himself at her feet, he was warm and comforting. The nurse brought in tea, glancing at the dog and Patricia came down looking refreshed.

'I'll take Gaston out into the garden if that's all right. I'm interested to see how it looks in the winter. Last summer it was so splendid. That does seem a long time ago! Later you can tell me about your winter in Collioure, goodness how I did envy you!

Later Felix, who, now that Patricia was installed had returned to his apartment in Toulouse, arrived and they had supper together, eating off plates on their knees. The meal had been prepared by the night nurse, though Felix would have preferred to cook for his mother himself. 'I must be patient, he thought as he opened a bottle of red wine in the kitchen, whilst watching the nurse preparing the dishes, 'things will settle down.

He and Patricia move the bed after supper and set it at an angle to the fire but allowing a view across the room to the drive and the trees that lined the road.

'Not the best outlook, but you'll get the afternoon sun,' he said. They talked for a while and then Felix returned to Toulouse.

'He seems preoccupied,' Patricia commented. 'He's had a lot of worry with me, that's all.' Marthe replied. 'I'll keep Gaston tonight if I may, he's company. It feels lonely sleeping down here, silly of me.' But later the night nurse removed him when she came to settle Marthe and give her some pills to help her sleep. She put Gaston firmly in the kitchen with the door closed.

*

'How's Claude?' Patricia asked the following day as they were having lunch by the fire. Marthe was already looking brighter and her appetite was much improved. Lunch was greatly enhanced by the cheeses that Patricia had brought from Paris; a creamy Brie and a round Reblochon, and there was also the pork and pepper terrine that she loved. Patricia had opened a bottle of white wine.

'I've not seen him much,' Marthe replied, carefully.

'Well, you did rather abandon him, going off to Collioure for the Christmas holidays. Maybe he's a little put out! I like him, you and he are good together.'

They went on with lunch and no more was said. But Marthe had been thinking about Claude a great deal, remembering their close relationship of the previous year; days in Toulouse, its shops and galleries and cinemas and the good restaurants where Claude was well known. She had enjoyed those days and his contribution to the garden with his stone ornaments was an almost daily reminder of their time together. She thought of the letter that she had written too and could not remember if she had posted it. She was already deeply regretting it.

*

Whilst the two friends were lunching at Les Palmes, Claude was driving home from Bordeaux in driving rain. The bad weather had swept in overnight from the West deluging the narrow streets and Claude regretted his decision to leave that day, he could have lingered longer. He was angry with himself as he negotiated the busy Autoroute for the journey took him longer than he had planned and he walked in tired and hungry. His home, a wing of the Chateau de Soulan, stood some ten miles north of St. Girou on a hill facing towards the Pyrenees. The chateau was built of brick, it dated from the early eighteenth century. It had once been very fine and grand. But the passage of time and the free spending of his ancestors had taken their toll and the chateau now looked neglected and the large estate that surrounded it run down. It had been the home for many years of his aunt, the dowager Countess, an elderly, gentle person, content to live very simply. She had married young but it had not been a success and before any children could be conceived her husband, the Count, had died in a hunting accident. She had grieved little, taken the occasional lover and then settled into an isolated widowhood. She was fond of Claude, the Count's nephew and heir who had inherited the title, the Chateau and the land but Claude had made no attempt to take over the running of his inheritance and so things continued much as they always had. They lived separate lives meeting only occasionally when matters regarding the estate needed a resolution. They saw little of each other even after Claude had moved into the South wing when his marriage ended. He loved living there; steadily transforming his wing into a stylish home filled with paintings and an eclectic mix of furniture, lamps and rugs. He had an extensive collection of books, which were to be found on tables, shelves and the floor. In the heart of the large salon, was a long oak table which could easily sit up to twenty people. It was invariably covered in letters, magazines, bills, books and the occasional coat or hat.

He lived there alone, though his sons, he had two, were frequent visitors and often stayed overnight. He liked to let them come and go, enjoying the company of young people. These family evenings, frequently extending to include their friends, often lasted late into the night with supper, talk, arguments, music and wine. And dancing, they all loved to dance in the summer on the terrace and in winter in front of the large fire. Claude was cosmopolitan, hospitable and a popular figure in local society.

Sighing with relief that his journey was done, and ignoring the cold, he opened the windows and pushed back the heavy shutters, letting in the strange grey afternoon light. A fog was coming down, hiding the trees and blocking out the weak January sun. He was glad to be home and opened the fridge, unpacking the food that he had bought in the local Casino. Standing in the kitchen, he made a sandwich of fresh baguette, local sausage and tomatoes, and then finding the dry logs at the back door, he lit a fire. He watched it come alight, thinking back to the autumn days when he had carried in and stored these logs, grateful that he was still fit enough for heavy work. He poured himself a whisky, slipped an Ella Fitzgerald CD into his music system and wandered about, eating his baguette, humming to her beguiling, languorous tones. He plumped up some cushions and repositioned them on one of the two large sofas which sat on either side of the fire. The room grew warmer and he turned on several lamps. It was good to be home. He stretched out before the fire, drained his glass and fell asleep.

*

Waking an hour later, refreshed, he found the fire reduced to embers. He added more logs, 'I'm getting old, he thought, though in truth an afternoon siesta was a regular occurrence in his life, as Marthe knew. They had enjoyed many such in the previous year. Claude had spent Christmas and New Year in Bordeaux in a hotel near to the home of his exwife, Agnes. They had separated amicably several years ago, and Agnes now lived there with a retired doctor who was a widower. They had not married. Claude enjoyed staying in Bordeaux, it was an amusing city offering many things that his rural life did not; galleries, squares with bars and restaurants, a variety of shops and for him the opportunity to browse the premises of other dealers in antiques and garden statuary. In between the time that he spent wandering about and eating and drinking rather well, he ate occasionally with his wife and the doctor. They were joined for Christmas Eve by their two sons, Jerome and Luc, it had become an annual event which even the doctor enjoyed. Claude's holiday was enhanced further by time spent with Angelique, a dealer in antiques, with whom he had an 'understanding'. She was younger, had never married and was an amusing diversion for Claude. She ran a successful business and had no desire to make attachments.

But Claude, in spite of the delights of Bordeaux, had missed Marthe, and continued to be perplexed by her decision to leave Les Palmes for a long winter holiday in her apartment in Collioure. Without him. Was she bored with him? Had he been too demanding? This seemed more likely, for he had suggested that they might live together, if she wanted of course. Was it that she felt the need for what the young called, 'her space'? He had tried to put her out of his mind whilst in Bordeaux, but now he was home, his memories flooded back. He toyed with the idea of phoning her, but something held him back, his pride probably. He would wait for her to contact him, he decided, and then see how things went.

As he was preparing supper with a glass of wine in one hand, he glanced at the papers and letters that had accumulated whilst he was in Bordeaux. Bills mostly and some circulars, but a cream envelope caught his eye and handwriting that was vaguely familiar. Opening it he read the address at the top...Les Palmes. Sensing that something was wrong, he sat on the sofa in front of the fire and read it quickly. Then again. He was astonished, bemused and then angry. Whatever did she mean? She wanted to be independent! Why did that affect anything? Claude had enjoyed relationships with several women, some of them married, he had never demanded that they give up their own lives. He sought friendship and love, not control. Or did he? He sat for some time until, all his wine gone, and his supper ready, he stood up, poked the fire and with a sigh of disappointment sat down to eat. He slept fitfully still pondering Marthe's unwanted and unexpected letter.

CHAPTER 5

Claude was surprised to hear Felix's voice on the phone the following morning. Without any of the normal pleasantries, Felix launched into a rambling and incoherent account of an accident to Marthe, some days previously. Felix asked him to come to Les Palmes and pay her a visit! To cheer her up, he said.

'Has she asked for me then? To visit?

'No. But I know how much you mean to her. Your company would be the best thing... raise her spirits, make her smile! Patricia is here but they would both benefit from seeing you, I'm sure.

Claude struggled to collect his thoughts. He was not sure that he wanted to rush over and support Marthe, though he was concerned to hear about her accident. Part of him resisted Felix's request, he was not a faithful dog to be summoned when it suited, and what about the letter? Did Felix know of that? It seemed very unlikely.

'I'll come tomorrow, after lunch. He said and put the phone down slowly.

*

A week had passed and Marthe felt brighter. She was slowly moving around the ground floor rooms on her crutches, practicing going up and down the Hall. She stood at the foot of the stairs, looking up, 'I'll never manage those! She sighed. Patricia thought otherwise, 'You can hop up on your good leg, and come down on your bottom! Use the bannisters. It'll be fine. Try tomorrow and surprise Felix. It would be lovely to sleep in my own bed, Marthe thought, 'I'll try tomorrow, she said.

'Good. Now keep walking using your crutches, down to the entrance and back. You need exercise. Patricia had revealed herself to be a surprisingly determined carer.

The following morning, the nurse from the hospital arrived and Marthe was told to put her foot on the ground, and walk as normally as she could. Cautiously she did manage the stairs with Patricia beside her and stood at the top triumphantly. She hugged Patricia before descending equally carefully on her bottom. That night, finally, she slept in her own bed. Patricia urged her on to attempt more and more challenges, cooking was difficult but not impossible and getting in and out of the car was a slow process. She was walking tentatively without her crutches, using a smart cane that Felix had purchased in Toulouse.

'It makes me look old! She said waving it at him. He laughed, 'You're not old! Use it!

The nurses left and life felt normal. It was early February and the afternoons were lengthening, the sun was warmer and snowdrops spread through the orchard under the trees. Marthe ventured out walking carefully, delighted to be in the fresh if cold air, the garden smelt wonderful. She thought back to the summer days, when the garden was full of colour and life, and she ate outside under the wisteria, and took a drink down to the bench beside the fountain that Claude had chosen. Claude! His first visit, soon after her return home, had been brief, they found themselves uncomfortable with each other and wary of anything more than inconsequential chat; Claude avoided any questions about Collioure and Marthe did not want to talk about her accident. He had returned again the following week, and complimented her on her progress, but Patricia had interrupted them and any intimate conversation was impossible. Resting for long hours, Marthe had plenty of time to reflect on Claude and the likelihood that she would not see much of him now. She was full of regret, blaming herself for her folly in allowing a loving relationship to be jettisoned. Standing now in the February sun, Marthe thought hard, trying to think, yet again, whether she wanted to try and win him back. 'How nice it would be if he was here, she thought, 'If I could only turn and see him walking towards me with maybe a glass of wine and his gentle smile. What a fool I am! She was very angry with herself. She heard Patricia calling from the house, it was lunch time. Marthe returned to the house.

'You can't stay for ever! Marthe said, 'Though I would love you to. They had finished eating and, wrapped up in warm coats, were sitting outside on the veranda. 'The garden needs some work, she remarked, 'Annie hasn't been for a while. 'Oh? Patricia was surprised, 'Is she too busy?

'No. But in the winter there's not enough for her to do. Also her work here is complete now, I just need someone to keep it all going. I'll look around in the Spring, maybe someone more local. I rather miss her though!

Patricia had been worrying about leaving Marthe, but she was growing impatient to return to Paris, she missed her busy life there and her many friends. She still did not think that Marthe's decision to leave Paris and settle in the Gers had been a wise one, a view that the long dark winter evenings had confirmed. Winter walks were fine and a cosy fire burning was a comfort, but that was about it, she felt. It certainly didn't bear comparison with brightly lit streets, and busy shops. She longed to see people bustling about buying food, warm restaurants with delicious and enticing menus, the expectant queues outside the cinemas and the local parks for walking Gaston, which weren't covered in mud. She glanced at Marthe and tried not to sigh.

She feared that Marthe had few friends, even though she had now lived at Les Palmes for more than 4 years. Of course there was Felix, but he lived in Toulouse and had his own life and interests. He had been very good, visiting regularly and bringing flowers and lovely wine, but Marthe should not become dependent on him. Patricia looked at her little dog who was digging ferociously under one of the palm trees, maybe she could leave him behind as company.

*

'How's Claude? We haven't seen much of him! It was Patricia's last evening and they were sitting in the little sitting room. 'You and he were very compatible, that was the impression you gave. I didn't know him well, but I liked what I saw, he was amusing, intelligent and very charming. What's gone wrong?

Marthe had hoped to avoid this conversation, but the opportunity to unload some of her unhappiness outweighed her natural hesitancy. She tried to explain.

'I felt at the end of last year that I was losing my newly acquired independence. As you know, I married when I was very young, hardly out of school, I was just nineteen and knew nothing of life. Xavier rescued me from a life with my grandparents in a suburb outside Paris. He introduced me to a new and exciting world, not just Paris (though that would have been enough) but to music, and museums and supper parties after concerts. He encouraged me to cook and entertain, I even grew a little sophisticated. I learnt about clothes and travel. And we had a baby, Felix. My life revolved around them and I was devoted to them both. That was my life, I was a wife and a mother. Like thousands of other French women. But suddenly it all went! Firstly Felix moved away to Toulouse, then Xavier died, suddenly and unexpectedly.

I was overwhelmed but slowly life got back into some sort of order and I decided to start again, here, in my father's house. For the first time I had to live on my own and I began to value that independence. I'd never experienced it before, not deferring to anyone else, not having to plan my days around others. Pleasing myself. Claude was part of all that, we were well suited as you said, and he became a close companion, but I felt that my life was being contained by him. He suggested back in the autumn that we should try living together, but where? Here? Surrounded by my father's family portraits? I don't think so! And I cannot move to his family chateau, that wouldn't suit me at all.

Patricia interrupted her, 'So you have risked giving him up, in order for what? To bury yourself in Collioure? Or to live here alone? Marthe, you are 63, Claude was as good a man as you are going to find. Compromise, but don't lose him! She had spoken more bluntly than she had intended. There was a very long silence. Marthe spoke at last, 'Claude is delightful and I do miss him, but he is very strong minded, under his easy manner. I fear that he will take me over, even though he doesn't intend to do so. I don't want to be locked in…don't you see? And you? Don't you have several relationships on the go? You've been single for a long time now, and you're happy enough!

Patricia smiled, 'Yes. I have avoided commitment. I go to the cinema, supper, the opera and such like, but Paris is a big City so one can live more…

Marthe spoke, 'Exactly! You're free to come and go as you please. That's what I want. She poured the last of the wine, they had drunk a whole bottle. Patricia replied, 'Not so easy down here. This society is small, rural and everyone seems to know everyone, people are tolerant but do you want to get a reputation?

'I'm not going to be flinging myself about! Marthe responded quickly.

'Of course not. I know that. But think carefully, this is your home now. And Claude? He has lived here all his life, he can easily move on, he knows everyone. And he is a man, and that is different. Go gently Marthe. Or do you want to live, 'independently' for the rest of your life?

*

Marthe reflected on what had been said as she lay sleeplessly in bed. There has to be more, she thought, more than a house, family and friends. But I've no education, no career, nothing to offer! Nothing to build on. Lucky Annie, I envy her, she has her degrees and now an interesting career ahead of her. I missed my chance, I married so young. This generation have all the opportunities that were unthinkable for me. She thought of Felix whose apparent lack of ambition continued to worry her, was he wasting his life? His opportunity for fulfilment? His opportunities? Should she speak to him and offer encouragement? These questions were unanswerable and she fell into a fitful sleep, awaking tired and depressed the following day.

'One thing that you never told me, Patricia said as she prepared to carry her suitcase through the hall, 'and I keep forgetting to ask, who found you? On the towpath. Have you thanked them, or has Felix?

'It's all a bit confused. Marthe said, 'As I understand it, the family who live nearer into town took me to the hospital, they phoned for an ambulance but it didn't come. The snowy weather I suppose had led to numerous accidents. They gave their details to the hospital, and that information was handed on to Felix. Their name is Julienne, he's retired, a solicitor I believe. They were at home when a young man came and banged on their door, asking for help. This was the young man who found me.

'And who was he?

'That's even more confusing! He led them through their garden at the back of the house to the towpath, it was snowing hard and there I was. Lying in the snow. Semi conscious. They managed to lift me up and carry me into their house. The young man was in a hurry and did not give his name and they were so busy phoning for an ambulance and then putting me in their car that he just slipped away.

'How very unsatisfactory. Patricia said, 'Because he saved your life, didn't he. And you can't remember anything about him? Anything at all?

Marthe shook her head. 'Felix found the Julienne's house, that was easy, it's quite close, I must have been almost back home when I fell. He gave them a bouquet of flowers as a thank you.

'I'd try and track down that young man, once you're mobile. Patricia said. He must be local, walking home from the town I should think. He's a bit of a hero in my book.

Patricia left promptly after breakfast without Gaston. Marthe was more than pleased to have his company and it would do her good to have to exercise him every day. She settled into living on her own at Les Palmes for the first time in many weeks.

CHAPTER 6

Felix had calmed down slowly after his row at supper with Annie as he tried to tell her of the house in Toulouse, and once Marthe was settled at Les Palmes with her nurse and Patricia had arrived from Paris, he returned home to Toulouse and took up again his plan to buy the house and persuade Annie to live there with him. But he decided to tread very carefully. Annie, he knew, was making plans for herself connected to her career, they had been hatching in her head for some months. She had decided to follow up on the success of her work at Les Palmes by contacting the people who had shown interest in her garden design. Now that her ex-husband Ralph was in regular work, and apparently settled with his new partner Edna, his contribution to Charlie had settled into regular monthly payments and these enabled her to undertake some financial risk. She obtained a small loan from the bank and resigned her role with the Toulouse garden department. She kept her teaching post at the University, which paid for day to day expenses, and was a useful tool when looking for work. It impressed clients. She planned to work from home, and cleared a corner of the salon in the apartment to serve as an office. Charlie's many possessions were pushed into his bedroom, many ending up on the floor and under his bed. This working arrangement would be easy in term time, but the holidays would be more problematical. Still, she argued with herself, Charlie was expressing a wish to spend more of his holidays away from Toulouse with Ralph, a development which had come as something of a surprise. For the moment it suited her plans rather well.

In the early weeks of the year, as Marthe recovered from the accident, Annie organized advertisements in the local newspapers and sent out fliers. She made numerous phone calls recording each on her computer which now had its own space in her 'office', on the kitchen table. Annie was an optimist and ambitious, and looked forward to extending her career with this new project. It would be challenging and she liked that. Despite the gloomy weather there seemed to be many people interested in what she had to offer and Annie found her diary filling up with appointments and visits. It was very exciting and she was full of it as she shared supper with Charlie and Felix.

It was the first time Felix had been invited since the row and he felt tense whilst listening patiently to her plans, glancing at Charlie whose face reflected boredom. Annie continued her chatter, until Charlie interrupted,

'Can we talk about the weekend please? I want to stay over with Jean. Then we can set off early.

'Why? Where are you going?

Charlie stared at his mother, his face was flushed, 'I told you! We're going fishing. In the mountains, with his dad. You said it was ok! Can't you remember anything?

Annie apologised, but it was too late. Charlie, angry and disappointed, had stormed from the table and gone to his room, they heard his music. It was loud and untuneful.

Felix sighed, 'You're very self absorbed at the moment.
She sat silently, then rose to clear the table, 'Yes, I'm sorry. I

forget sometimes, of course my plans don't interest Charlie. But that was quite rude, banging out of the room like that.

'Can we also talk about something else? He tried to take her hand, this time there was no avoiding him, and she sat down and faced him. 'Yes. What do you want to talk about? She was trying to speak gently.

Looking at her, he said, 'I want to talk about us. Living together in a bigger space. I've seen a house near to the Cathedral, it has four floors and its own courtyard. I think it would be perfect; a study for you, which you certainly need now that you are planning to work from home, a music room for me, and a really lovely room at the top for Charlie with a view over the roofs to the sky. Out of ear shot too! Come and have a look with me, please.

Annie was more than surprised, 'I didn't know you wanted to give up your apartment. You love it! That lovely view of the river! Her heart was beating horribly fast, but she managed to continue, 'Of course I'll come and look, she said, 'But no promises. They talked for a little longer and Annie agreed to look at the house on Saturday, when Charlie was away fishing with Jean.

That night as she lay in bed listening to Felix' breathing, they had 'made up' which was good, she thought about the implications of what Felix was suggesting. She knew that for Felix this was a further step towards marriage and becoming a family. He had suggested this last summer, but had not pressed her. And again a few weeks ago which had led to a row. Felix would be a loving husband, but…why was there a 'but' in her head? She loved him for sure but…

Annie's first marriage had been a rushed affair, she was five months pregnant and they were both just out of college. It had ended when Charlie was six and though she and Ralph were less at odds with each other, nonetheless the years before she left him and moved to Toulouse had been unhappy and difficult. Marrying again was not something that she wished to think about, she had lost confidence in herself, fearing that a second attempt might also end badly. And she had to think of Charlie, he was a further complication. How would he react to another change in his family life? Having to share her more. Nor did she want to give up her apartment, it was the first home that she had owned, and she was proud of it and what it symbolized; it was the home of an independent professional woman, and her thriving son, both living busy lives in a foreign country. Lying on her back she looked up at the high ceiling, light was coming in from the street outside, making patterns, and she could hear voices in the street below. I don't want more than this, she thought as she plumped up her pillow, and I don't want to give it up! But how could she explain all this to Felix without upsetting him? He stirred in his sleep and turned towards her, his dark hair covering his eyes. Was she tempted? Just a little bit? Sighing Annie finally settled down, closed her eyes and matching her breathing to his, she fell asleep. 'Could she give it up? The question remained unanswered

*

Marthe decided to pay the Juliennes a visit, it would be good manners to thank them personally and she might get some information about the missing young man. I'll walk there tomorrow morning, she decided, it'll be good exercise and it's not too far, I'll take my stick.

Marthe walked slowly down the road that led into St. Girou, it was a cold bright morning and she wore her warmest coat, she was using her cane, it gave her confidence. She had left Gaston with a bone in the garden, he watched her go, chewing determinedly. The doctor had urged her to walk as much as she could, to use her still painful ankle, but it was difficult to ignore the ache that set in almost immediately. There were big piles of dry brown leaves that rustled beneath her boots from the plane trees above her head. She paused and looked up, they were very old, pollarded every spring, they had a stark appearance. It took her a little time to reach the iron gates of the Juliennes house. She pushed them open and walked to the door.

She and the Juliennes were soon sitting rather formally in the Salon. M. and Mme and herself. They were drinking coffee and talking politely. After a few minutes, Marthe asked the question that was the purpose of her visit, 'Please can you tell me who it was who came and told you of my accident and asked for your help?

'He was a young man, dark haired and strong looking. It was Mme. Julienne who spoke. 'He led us outside, it was such a cold morning, very unusual for this part of France and we were so worried. We found you lying just beyond our gate on the tow path, and there was another person there, a girl. She had covered you with her coat and was cradling you in her arms. To keep you warm. You were very still, unconscious I assumed.

'Goodness! Marthe was shocked, 'I didn't know that. Two people. And they helped carry me to your house?

'No. The girl stayed outside, there was a dog next to her, she stayed with the dog. They were twins, the boy and girl, I'm almost sure, they were very alike. The boy lifted you and we held your legs. Mme. Julienne looked down, a little embarrassed, then continued, 'We were very frightened that you were so cold, it was an alarming situation, for us all.

'And do you know them? Or did you ask their names? Marth leant forward, listening intently.

M. Julienne shook his head, 'No. We were so busy with you, finding blankets and phoning for the ambulance, which didn't come so we had to ask the boy to help us get you into our car. We left him behind and that was the last we saw of him. It was such a bad morning, the drive to the hospital was very difficult...Marthe sat silently, she felt quite weak at the thought of the danger that she had been in. They watched her, and Mme. Julienne said, 'But you have recovered I see. That is good. And now you must be more careful! She meant well but Marthe said impatiently, 'I had hoped to learn who my 'saviour' was. I want to say thank you!

M. Julienne replied, 'I would agree with Mme. that they were twins perhaps twenty years old, both dark and not tall. They were walking along the path with a dog, so they may live in St. Girou. He sat back, 'That's all I can say.

They talked a little longer and Marthe prepared to leave, her ankle was hurting and she was eager to get home. The Juliennes did not detain her, and M. guided her to the door. They shook hands and he smiled, 'Good luck with your search! He said, and then unexpectedly, touching his head, 'Oh! I remember something more. The dog, it was a big farm dog, long haired. The girl called it Jacques. Marthe listened and shook his hand, thanking him again for all that they had done for her.

The walk back was slower, but Marthe was deep in thought. 'Twins, they won't be hard to find surely. I'll take a taxi tomorrow into St.Girou and ask around. Two young people, maybe twins with a dog, that should be easy. It seemed a simple plan.

It took her less than half an hour the following day to realise that a simple plan does not always succeed. She began in the Pharmacy, then in the Tabac and then the check out girl in the Casino supermarket. The same question,

'Do you know of any twins, a girl and a boy, aged maybe twenty? Where they live or even their names?

A shake of the head each time followed her question, a smile and then a question about her fall and recovery. Gaston was having a fine time, as people patted him and asked his name. It seemed the whole town knew of her accident. That was kind and she felt better for it, but the problem remained. She finished her quest at the post office, but received the same answer, the post mistress ended by saying, 'They are not from here. I would know any local twins.

Marthe was tired and dispirited, she walked to the restaurant in the square and took a table beside the window. It was steamed up with the warmth from the kitchen. A hot meal will do me good, she thought as she pushed Gaston under the table and fed him little bits of bread. The owner approached her cautiously, he remembered the occasion in the previous year when she had stopped for lunch sitting outside under the mulberry tree. There had been an argument and Marthe had been assaulted, the first in a series of incidents, prompted by the local man, Henri, who had a grievance against Marthe's family. The owner had done nothing at the time to help Marthe and he avoided her eye. Marthe also remembered the incident and she maintained a cool manner as she ordered from the menu. But she enjoyed her plat du jour and a glass of red wine and, feeling rested, asked the Patron to call her a taxi. He did so with a small smile. It took several minutes and she waited at her table conscious of the glances of the clientele, locals, for whom she was still a stranger. After nearly two years, I'm still a stranger! She thought sadly. How long does it take to be accepted? The good effects of her lunch were wearing off as she eased herself onto the back seat of the taxi, tucking Gaston discreetly under her arm, and laying her stick beside her. The car smelt of cigarettes and she opened the window, the driver gave a hostile glare which she saw in the mirror. It had not been a very happy excursion.

Talking to Patricia later in the evening she recounted her attempt to track down the twins, 'Maybe you are looking in the wrong town. Patricia said, 'You were walking into St.Girou, they were perhaps walking away. They might live in the opposite direction. Marthe thought about that. 'Yes, that's possible. I assumed they were walking in the same direction as me, but you're right they could just as well have been walking away from St. Girou, That's why no one knows them, they don't live there. Why didn't I think of that! I'll have to try in S. Andre.

CHAPTER 7

In Toulouse Felix was in a foul mood, angry and disappointed yet again in Annie. It was Monday, and he was having breakfast in his apartment, a black coffee very strong and a fresh croissant from the baker's on the corner. The previous day, they had visited the house which he so wanted to buy and make their home. The Cathedral bells of St. Sernin were ringing out as they walked together down the narrow street, le Rue des Capuchins, which was busy with people hurrying to Mass. The bells felt like an auspicious welcome and Felix glanced at Annie whose expression gave no clues as to what she was thinking.

They walked around the house slowly and she had admired it a great deal, ignoring as much as possible the sales chatter of the agent. Felix escorted her through the rooms, starting on the first floor, where the kitchen and her study would be. Annie looked around with interest, or so Felix thought, and examined the kitchen with special care. 'It's certainly roomy, she had said. She had leant out of the window of the back room which Felix had said would be her 'study' and admired the courtyard below, 'Lots of space for pots, urns and chairs, Felix said, he was leaning out too. 'You can have fun there! Annie followed him up the stairs and listened as he explained how he saw them sharing the accommodation. The Salon was large and felt very grand despite the absence of any furniture, it had its orginal fireplace in maple. 'Their' bedroom, had two large windows and another wood surround fire place, and a dressing room off on one side and a bathroom on the other. 'Just for us! Felix said running his hand along the marble top of the twin basins. On the third floor, in the room that would be Charlie's, she opened the window and listened as the bells of St. Sernin continued to sound and looked up at the blue sky. She had turned to him with a smile and Felix was excited. They left the agent and walked to a nearby restaurant for lunch, they had eaten there before and Annie chatted to the owner as he took her coat. But Felix' dreams were soon exposed as just that, dreams. Annie quietly rejected the whole idea of moving into the house, so clearly that, thinking about it later, Felix wondered if she had decided in advance. That she had only looked at the house to please him. Or lead him along. They neither of them had mentioned the word, marriage, but they both knew that was what the house idea was leading towards. After she had finished speaking, Felix, flushed and angry, summoned the waiter and told him that they were leaving. The Garcon looked perplexed, and tried to protest, but Felix was on his feet and pressing some payment into his hand. Annie, embarrassed, did not dare to look at Felix. She followed him as he pushed his way through the tables and out onto the street, where she tried to take his hand. He brushed her off. At the Square, where they could separate each in a different direction she tried again, 'Please Felix, don't be so angry. He looked down the street towards his apartment, 'Oh Annie! You can't expect to have it both ways. To reject me and still have my affection, my love. It's impossible. He was pale, she thought, and she remembered Ralph and his parting words so many years ago. 'You only think of yourself, he had said, 'Everything has to be about you! What you want!

Was she so selfish? Thoughts flew around, as she watched Felix turn towards the river and his home.

'I'll pick up my books, clothes and music tomorrow. He said over his shoulder.

Annie stared after him, she had no words. Was this the end then? In a Square in Toulouse on a cold winter afternoon. She felt sick. As Felix walked steadily away she longed to run after him and put her arms around him and smooth his cheek with her hand, but she could not. She stood there for several minutes as people brushed past her, many arm in arm. Chatting happily. She could not believe that in a matter of only a few minutes her relationship with Felix was over.

*

Claude was back in Bordeaux, a business opportunity had come up, and he was happy to get away from the dull grey days in the Gers and return to a City which was lively even in winter. It was early March and the sun warmed his back as he sat down by the harbour, eating lunch, a delicious platter of fried fish with a green salad and a glass of white wine. The bottle still half full, rested on the table cooling in its bucket, he loved eating out of doors and did so whenever possible. Angelique was with him, eating enthusiastically, which was one of the many things he liked about her. They would repair to his hotel for the afternoon and then join some friends for supper. Claude felt more content than he had for several weeks.

The afternoon was turning chill as his phone rang. It was Jerome, his eldest son.

'Papa! I've been trying to find you! Are you in Bordeaux? You're needed here! Aunt Sophie is very unwell and the doctor thinks she may not have much longer. To live.

'How unwell? Is it her heart?

'Yes. Her heart is failing.

Claude sighed and stood up. He apologized to Angelique pressing some money into her hands, kissed her goodbye and returned to his hotel, the news was unexpected and inconvenient. Within three hours he had arrived home and walked to the main door of the Chateau. The next few hours were distressing. Aunt Sophie was failing fast and the doctor confirmed that she would not last long. They had never been close but she was the last of her generation and Claude had always respected her. He sat beside her high old fashioned bed, with its brocaded cover and thick mattress, and thought of very little. She did not speak and her eyes were closed, her breathing very shallow. He dozed, shifting in the high backed uncomfortable chair, Jerome came and lit a lamp beside him. He had never been in the room before and was astonished by the size of her bed and its ancient hangings.

'Do you want some soup? He asked, 'Or cold chicken? Maybe a glass of wine? Luc has arrived and brought food.

'Any whisky?

'Jerome smiled, 'Not here I think, but I'll fetch you some.

'No. Too much bother. A glass of red wine then, and a sandwich. Maybe two.

He ate and then dozed in the chair, rising occasionally to stoke the wood fire, the only heat in the room. It was not warm. She died in the early hours, as Claude slept and the fire burnt away. A quiet passing, much like her life, she had been undemanding. A gentle soul, known to few people. Claude did not weep. He went slowly from her room and down the wide staircase, it was cold and still dark, with only a single lamp lighting the large hall. He did not care to leave her upstairs alone, so he found a sofa in the salon and lay down pulling an old rug over him. He slept fitfully, and was glad to wake as a grey dawn ended the night, and he returned to his own apartment, where he phoned the funeral director.

The news of her death circulated slowly and messages of sympathy arrived in the following weeks. His close family and friends wondered how Claude would respond to his new role; he was now solely responsible for a large Chateau with all its outbuildings, lands, woods and farms. These brought with them challenges, responsibilities, and financial pressures. It also established him as an important local figure, a landlord with many people in some degree dependent on him. It was a world in which previously he had shown no interest, something that he now came to regret. But Claude had never been attracted to the role of a Count; he rarely entertained the local 'gentry', he did not hunt, did not own a set of guns, he kept no horses, the stables had been empty for many years. He had never attended the regular autumn or winter shoots, and indeed had little time for dogs or horses. He liked chateaux: their architecture, history, furniture and paintings but not their acres of woodlands and huge fields. As the days passed Claude became aware that he had a problem on his hands, a problem that he needed to address.

CHAPTER 8

The town of St.Andre was older than St. Girou but it lacked a weekly market and time had passed it by. There were some very old half timbered houses, clustered in a small square beside the church, most of them in poor condition, some with their windows boarded up. Several had been abandoned, their elderly owners having died and the next generation having no desire or means to restore them. The streets here were narrow and cobbled and very little sunlight entered. These houses were cold and dark even in summer. Beside the river which flowed behind the church there was an ancient wash house with stone scrubbing shelves and lines hanging from the high tiled roof for drying clothes. Marthe had seen women washing sheets there in cold river water, it astonished her that people still lived like that. But many did. Beyond the wash house there was a gravel path, bordered with willows leading to the river that connected the two towns, here dogs were exercised and children ran about. The river had once been an important thorough fare for barges, carrying goods down the valley from the Pyrenees to Toulouse, corn and wood and wine, but this commercial life was long gone and the river had silted up, though it still flowed swiftly after rain. It was the river that ran at the bottom of Marthe's garden, beside which she had fallen, but on this particular morning she had chosen not to walk into St. Andre, she had taken her car, driving somewhat cautiously. She was searching for the twins.

The day was sunny and bright, she parked in the old square, dodging the pigeons who had gathered there, they flew up noisily flapping their wings almost colliding with each other. Marthe was looking for the poste. She found it up one of the narrow streets, but the walking was difficult on the cobbles, with Gaston tugging on his lead. He sniffed about eagerly, looking for other dogs, and Marthe regretted leaving her stick at home as he stopped and started, nearly pulling her over. She was hot and bothered when she finally reached the poste. It was gloomy inside and there was a queue. She suppressed a sigh. Finally it was her turn. The woman behind the grille, dressed officially in a dark uniform, regarded her suspiciously as she asked her question. 'No. I can't help you, Madame, I'm sorry. I don't know the family you're looking for. Perhaps you should try in St. Girou, she was already turning her gaze on the next customer. Exasperated Marthe walked back slowly the way she had come and noticing a small café decided to enquire there. It was more of a bar and there was a strong smell of beer as she pushed open the door. A small group of men, clustered around the bar, stared as she approached, and almost reluctantly made a space as she asked for a café crème. The old woman, la Patronne, served her and Marthe asked her now too familiar question. The woman showed a flicker of interest, 'Twins you say?

'Yes perhaps aged twenty, or so.

'There are twins at the Moulin, it's about two miles out of town on the road south. The boy comes into town sometimes, for a beer. She handed over the coffee and turned back to chatting with the men. Marthe finished her coffee quickly and walked towards the door, as la Patronne added some directions.

*

'I hope this isn't a wild goose chase, Marthe thought as she finally turned off the road and down a bumpy lane, which if her directions were right, should bring her to the Moulin. It had a very pretty site, on a bend of the lane with pollarded plane trees framing a wide bridge which, after a pause, she steered carefully across. The Moulin was, like all the farm houses of the Gers, built of brick with a long sloping roof and small windows. She parked and climbed out of the car taking her stick for support. She was standing beside what was once the mill race, near the great wheel that once drove the water. It had ceased to work for many years and created a somewhat desolate mood. There was a sudden cacophony of noise and several dogs bounded from the barn to her left. 'Stay there! she said to Gaston who had shrunk down, he was not a brave little dog and buried himself under her sweater. There was much shouting and the dogs ran back towards an old man, rather bent, who appeared round a corner from the rear of the farm house. He stood watching her as Marthe, shutting the car door firmly, walked towards him. They greeted each other and Marthe asked if there were twins who lived with him. He didn't seem surprised and he said, 'Yes, my daughter had twins, a boy and a girl. Marthe felt a surge of excitement as he continued, 'They're working, he pointed, 'There! Marthe turned and saw another building, a smaller barn, further down the stream. She began to explain why she was looking for them, but he seemed quite unconcerned and turned away shrugging. She realised that he was more than a little deaf.

'May I talk to them? She asked raising her voice. He paused, 'If you can find them! He walked towards the house, but she sensed that he was watching her as she set off towards the second barn.

This barn emitted an overpowering smell, an odour both dry and sweet and there was a loud noise coming from huge ventilators set in the long tiled roof. A heavy wooden door prevented her entering, so she banged on it as hard as she could, calling out. And waited. No one answered. Having got this far she was not inclined to walk away, so shouting now she banged again. She could hear Gaston barking anxiously back in the car. The door opened suddenly, and Marthe jumped back, in front of her stood a young man, dressed in blue workers overalls, his hair was dark and his skin swarthy. 'Yes? he spoke cautiously. Marthe replied quickly, eager to get his attention, she feared he was ready to disappear back inside the barn, he had one foot inside the heavy door, keeping it ajar. As she tried to introduce herself, he interrupted, 'How can I help yo? He asked. Marthe forced herself to speak slowly and he began to listen. A brown dog had joined them, it stood close to the young man its tail wagging slowly, and Marthe remembered that M. Julienne had spoken of a hairy farm dog waiting next to the young girl on the snowy path. She felt more confident as she asked, 'Do you remember me? I think that you found me in the snow beside the river several weeks ago. You were with your sister? There was a brief silence and Marthe began to doubt herself then he said, 'Yes. It was us. We found you. There was a pause as he recollected, 'We were walking back from St. Girou, from visiting our grandmother, she's in the Maison de Retraite there. I remember...it was snowing. He stopped. Marthe tried to urge him on, 'And you found help in the house? He nodded.

'You saved my life! Marthe exclaimed suddenly. 'You and your sister! He looked at her, he was surprised and embarrassed, 'I've come to thank you both. She said, and pressing her point, 'I nearly died, and might well have done, if you hadn't helped. He shrugged, 'We didn't do so much, it was just that we were walking by.

Marthe finding herself frustrated by his response, said 'Can I speak to your sister please? Is she about? I want to thank her too.

'I'll see if I can find her. He said, and walked back into the barn. Marthe waited with the brown dog, who regarded her thoughtfully. The smell and noise from inside the barn were oppressive. 'You were there too! She said looking at the dog, 'Weren't you. He wagged his tail, impassively. A minute later, a young girl emerged, she was slighter than her brother, but they shared the same dark hair. She was in work clothes too. Marthe smiled and held out her hand, and explained who she was and why she was there. 'I would have come sooner, to thank you, but my ankle was sprained, when I fell and I couldn't drive. The girl stood listening awkwardly. Like her brother she was very unresponsive, and Marthe was beginning to feel that she was wasting her time. She tried another approach, 'Is this where you work? The girl eyed her, and finally spoke very softly, 'Yes. I look after the ducks. So that's the smell! Marthe thought. She's shy, she decided, and said 'Can I see?

The girl brightened a little, 'Yes. Madame. Stepping back towards the barn. she pushed the heavy door open, and said. 'I'm Agathe. I remember you! We were walking home and you were lying on the path, covered in snow. You were in pain. I waited with the dog and gave you my coat, you were very very cold and I lifted you up. Out of the snow.

Marthe shut her eyes, envisaging the scene, she wanted to hug this shy girl, 'Agathe, that's a pretty name, she said with a smile.

'It's my grandmother's name too. The one we were visiting.

They were now inside the barn. The sight, sound and smell were overpowering. Over a hundred ducks were housed there, side by side, each confined in its separate space and there was a shallow stone trough with water flowing in front of them. There were wires suspended from the beams above with beakers attached. 'I was about to feed them, Agathe said, tying on a dirty apron, Marthe thought how thin she was, no figure at all for a girl of twenty or so. 'Do you want to watch?' Then without waiting for a reply she swung one of the wires and began pouring from a large sack into the beakers. It was corn. Agathe carefully filled a beaker, then, concentrating, slowly poured the grain into a tube that she inserted down the throat of the duck nearest her. The fowls sat patiently waiting their turn, occasionally dipping their beaks into the flowing water. It was a slow process and the girl spoked quietly to each duck stroking their throats as they fed. Her tenderness amazed Marthe. Foie gras she thought to herself. She wished she had not seen this feeding ritual and having watched for a few minutes, turned away and walked back towards the door. Agathe did not look up. 'Thank you, Marthe called, and made her way towards her car. It really had not been a rewarding visit. The young man was there, 'I spoke to your sister, she said. He had an amused expression, 'She doesn't talk much, but she understands plenty. He said.

'And what's your name? Mine's Marthe, or Mme. Le Brun if you prefer.

He inclined his head, his hair falling across his face, 'Gregoire, he said and held out his hand.

'And do you work with the ducks?

'No, he grimaced, 'That's womens'work! I'm a market gardener. Come and see if you're interested. His stiff manner had gone and with a smile he invited her towards the back of the farm house. The dog loped along beside him and she asked its name.

'Jacques, he answered, 'they're all called that. It's simpler. Turning a corner, she saw several abandoned and rusty bits of machinery and stumbled slightly on a piece of iron, half hidden in the long grass. Her ankle was still annoyingly weak. 'You ok? Gregoire asked kindly. Marthe looked at him out of the corner of her eye, remembering his earlier kindness to her; she decided there and then that she liked this dark haired young man, he was shy certainly but there was something honest and sincere about him. He slowed his pace and offered her his hand as they continued to walk through the long grass. He stopped suddenly and pointed to a large area of cultivated land that stretched towards the woodland in the distance. 'That's what I do. His voice was proud. It was a very large plot almost a field, recently ploughed and the rich dark soil was shining in the sun. The air smelt fresh and there was light cool breeze. Marthe inhaled deeply the air was wonderful. She stood and stared, noticing now that the plot was divided into strips with paths in between. Nothing was growing that she could see, nothing green at all, but a sense of readiness was overwhelming. It was waiting for spring. 'All on your own? She asked, 'Or do your parents work here too? Gregoire shook his head, 'No, we live here with our Grandfather, just the three of us now. This land grows vegetables for market. Marthe wanted to ask more, but his words, 'Just the three of us now, seemed like a warning to enquire no further. They stood quietly for a while then he turned and led her back towards the house. Marthe felt an overwhelming urge to ask about Agathe, 'Is your sister happy, caring for her ducks? It seems a lonely life.

'She's shy, likes to stay here on the farm, not interested in going out. She loves her ducks. He spoke with affection. Gregoire walked with her back to the car and they shook hands, 'Thank you for showing me your land, Marthe said, 'and thank you again for what you did for me in January.

*

Marthe drove home, she had managed to thank each twin, which was why she had tracked them down, but that didn't feel enough. For some reason she wanted to help them both, they seemed so isolated with only an old man for company, working on the land and in that smelly barn. She shuddered at the memory of the ducks and the thin girl pouring grain down their slender throats. The day had turned cold and she was pleased to get inside her warm home, Gaston ran around barking, relieved to return to the comforts that he was used to. Marthe thought of her previous life in Paris, it was another world from life at the Moulin. She knew little of farming or rural life but was interested in how people lived, earned their money and survived the problems of weather and fluctuating markets. It seemed to her that it was a difficult life.

In the evening she phoned Patricia, who was returning to Les Palmes in a few days to collect Gaston and check up on Marthe's progress. 'I can't explain it. Marthe had been talking about her visit to the twins, 'They're just so cut off... on their own. No neighbours, just dogs and ducks and empty fields, and the sound of the mill race. I found it sad. Gregoire seemed more intelligent, but growing vegetables is his life and no sign of parents at all!

Patricia, ever practical said, 'A great many people live like that. Cut off and isolated. It's called farming.

'Don't laugh! Marthe was getting cross, Patricia did not say anything. Marthe said, slowly, 'I want to help them. I have so much and if it wasn't for them I might well be dead.

'Perhaps, Patricia interrupted.

'Oh do listen! Let me speak will you? These twins need help, they need options and possibilities. I can't help comparing them with Felix, and all the advantages that he's had; good education and supportive parents and life in a City and foreign travel. Don't you see? If I can help widen their horizons just a bit, with a little financial help…She stopped. Patricia hesitated to speak, she had always regarded rural life to be unspeakably dull, so Marthe's description of life at the Moulin was not a surprise.

'Marthe, she said, 'If you like we could go and visit the Moulin together, make some excuse, then I'll see for myself. But you would have to step very carefully, you can't interfere in another family, no matter how good your intentions. Country people are notoriously suspicious, and it's not as if you know them. Or they you. They're not family are they.

'Well I feel, strongly, that I owe them something.

'Ok, but that doesn't commit them to you for ever. Patricia had the last word.

CHAPTER 9

The funeral of the Dowager Countess had taken place, and she now lay in the ornate family sarcophagus, surrounded by other stone and marble tombs many of which dated back to the nineteenth century or earlier. These monuments, with their angels and trumpets and dates of lives lived, some short some long, made an impressive sight in the small local grave yard. Set on a hill, it had a fine view of the surrounding country side, but the church itself was small and on this occasion cold. Claude and his family stood silently as the priest said Mass and made a short address and Claude tried to concentrate, but it was a chill afternoon and he longed for his warm fireplace and a large whisky. He was aware of his two sons, their heads bowed and wondered what they were thinking. They did not linger.

Back home, with his whisky, he stood with his back to the fire and regarded Jerome and Luc. Since her death they had been talking about the future. Claude had held the title since the death of his uncle but now he owned the chateau itself, with all its contents, and lands and park and farms. And investments. His aunt had relied on an estate manager to run her properties, and a bank manager to look after her wealth. It had all ticked along quietly for many years, with a complete absence of any plans for the long term future.

'So, Claude said, 'You've both had time to think! Any ideas? What shall we do? Sell up? Or let out what we can! Or do one of you want to take over, maybe become a farmer. There was irony in his tone.

A lively conversation followed, they had different views. What was surprising was that they had never spoken before, never anticipated this situation, even though the Countess had been frail for many years. Claude might have been expected to have some incipient plans but he had not. He liked his life as it was; a business that supplied him with adequate funds, which enabled him to live as he pleased. He loved the countryside about him, but his affection was based on familiarity, he liked to look at the gardens and grounds outside his windows, but rarely went for a walk. He loved his Wing, it was full of character and style and he did not want or need more space. He had no desire to be Grand, indeed he disliked ostentation. But he was now faced with new and extensive responsibilities. The estate employed a number of people, they also needed consideration.

'There's Eric of course he will stay on as Manager obviously, he continued, watching Luc drinking his wine, 'he knows everything about the running of the place. We can trust him to deal with the tenants and farms. Also there are the farm hands, we need them I suppose. And gardeners. He was remarkably vague.

'If they'll stay, it was Jerome who spoke, 'Eric's getting on now for such a big job. He's only hung on out of loyalty. Claude looked at his son with horror, 'God! Don't say that! We need him. We'll offer him more money, that should persuade him.

'But can you afford that? Luc said. Claude didn't know, 'I'm off to the bank next week, now the funeral is over. I can get down to all these issues then.

They continued to talk as they prepared supper, Luc mainly in charge and Claude decanting the wine, a fine Burgundy, which he had brought up from the long neglected cellar of the chateau. He was anticipating spending several hours examining the wines that had been ignored for many years, some he feared were now too old to be drinkable. They ate at the long table and then sat before the fire. It was late in the evening and Claude became gloomy. He was tired and their lengthy conversation had resolved little. Luc regarded his father and said,

'There's something I've been thinking about for a little while, how about we turn the chateau into a hotel? A small one. Then it would pay its way, it might be fun and a challenge, and we could...well work together! The three of us, in different roles. There was a stunned silence.

'Are you mad? Claude said, 'We know nothing about running a hotel. And the state of the place, we'd have to spend a fortune, it's barely habitable. Besides who'd want to stay in such on old fashioned place! The décor goes back at least one hundred years and the bathrooms are quite ghastly. Not to mention the dire state of the heating, the wiring, and the drains. He finished the wine in his glass and stood up to fetch the whisky, barely looking at Luc. There was a silence.

'I think it's quite a clever idea. Jerome said, 'Lots of people like staying in old fashioned hotels, especially if they are chateaux, it's trendy and different. People are frightful snobs and it makes them feel connected to something grander than themselves. ' This summer I'm having a week in a chateau' that sort of thing. It's worth thinking about. He smiled at Luc, 'Well done! Claude said nothing. 'Obviously there would be a lot of work, Jerome continued, 'but the chateau is structurally solid and the roof was redone five years ago, I remember that.

It's got all the necessaries; heating, water supply and electricity, it just needs modernizing and upgrading. He stopped and there was another silence, Claude had found new glasses and poured them all a whisky.

'Who's going to run this hotel? He asked. 'And more importantly, who's going to finance this mad scheme? His face was a little flushed.

'You of course! Luc said, 'You've run a business for years, you know about making money. A hotel is just a business. And you're a natural manager, you are good at delegating, and balancing the books and so on. Also you'd be good at the hospitality side, welcoming guests and smoothing customers. I think you'd enjoy it. And it would be nice to see the chateau looking smarter, it's a very fine building, do we really want to let it go after so many years? Sell it?

'You'd have to smarten up a bit, as front of house, Jerome added trying to lighten the mood, 'a good haircut and some fancy jackets and ties. Claude protested at that, 'I always look good, he said but he was smiling and no longer looked tired. 'You're both sort of serious aren't you? But I know nothing about the hotel business and I am far too old to start a new career.

'But you know what makes a good hotel, you've stayed in quite a few. Jerome continued, 'think about what you like and enjoy, and create it here. The chateau could easily provide space for what fifteen bed rooms, or suites. And the main rooms could be splendid, though I haven't seen them properly for years. There's the impressive entrance hall and staircase, and the large salon and the dining hall which is spacious. And I remember a library full of old leather bound books which hadn't been touched or read for many many years. Of course it all needs lots of work, rewiring and decoration which would cause disruption and expense but we could be sitting on a gold mine. And we won't be living on site will we? He sat down opposite Claude and said, ' It's completely your field, choosing furniture and paintings and such, restyling places, you've been doing it all your life. You'd enjoy it you know!

Claude began thinking out loud, 'How would people know about us? We're not visible, the drive shuts us off from everyone.

Luc replied, 'Not a problem! I've been thinking about that; our location is excellent, we're half an hour from Toulouse and Auch, both interesting and historic Cities, with long established tourist reputations. We put a big board up on the road at the entrance and some advertisements in the local papers. And talk to the tourist offices, maybe try and tempt some journalists to visit and write about us. We would be perfect for a romantic weekend or a family holiday. We'd have to put in a swimming pool of course, everyone expects that.

'Children! I'm not sure about that. Claude had finished his whisky. He was trying to decide whether to have another one, the boys watched him. 'They do terrible damage to furniture, don't they. He was not convinced, but Luc had not finished, 'And weddings! They are real money spinners. You'd be amazed at what people spend. They can't be so difficult; a marquee on the terrace, lights strung in the trees, a band playing until dawn.

'Stop! Stop! Right now. This is a crazy idea, all of it. We would lose money and spend a fortune. Jerome saw his angry face, his father rarely shouted at them, 'Ok Papa, we've said enough for one night, but think about it. As for me, I would love an opportunity to work with you and Luc, it would be, he paused, 'Well, I guess, pretty special. The evening ended on that note.

*

Claude went to bed, leaving his sons to clear up the meal, he could hear them chattering and laughing, and finishing the whisky probably. He woke in the early hours, it was dark and cold and he was terribly thirsty. Stumping around in the bathroom, he thought about the previous evening, and his brief loss of temper. Was it a possibility? A hotel in the chateau? He didn't know the answer, but something aroused him. It was what Luc had said, 'It would be fun! A challenge. And Jerome's concluding words, 'An opportunity to work with you and Luc. He liked the idea of the three of them working together. A hotel would suit Luc, he could work and develop his skills in the kitchens, and Jerome needed to get out of his bookshop, where he locked himself away from the world, barely able to pay the rent. He climbed back into bed, 'I'll go and take a good look at the chateau in the morning on my own, calmly, he said to himself, and having made that decision he slept.

CHAPTER 10

Felix stood at the window of his apartment in Toulouse looking at the river, it was a grey damp morning and the river moved slowly. Barges moved into his view, all low in the water and on one a small white dog barked incessantly. Since the unhappy visit to the house in Toulouse and the disastrous lunch that had followed it, he had not returned to live in Annie's apartment. He had refused to respond to her phone messages but remained devastated by her rejection whilst accepting that their relationship was over. He struggled to put her out of his mind. Not very successfully. But Felix had made one decision, he had put his apartment on the market and agreed to buy the house with four floors near the Cathedral. The agent was delighted, she had judged him correctly, he was a wealthy man.

'But why? Marthe asked, she was serving lunch in the kitchen at Les Palmes, moving carefully about the kitchen, her crutches and stick now put away. It was a Sunday, his usual day for visiting his mother. 'It sounds very spacious for one person. And you love your apartment, I do too, it's so light and airy. She had listened to his description with something like amazement. 'What are you going to do with so many rooms?

He flared up, 'It's a bit like you then, here! So many rooms. He was more abrupt than he intended, and said quickly,

'Sorry I didn't mean that.

'Yes you did! But Felix I inherited this house. I didn't choose it. I know it's too big for one, but it's my family home. Where my parents lived and my grandparents. And it'll be yours one day. Maybe quite soon, if I keep falling over! Felix smiled, 'You're fine, you look well again. You'll be here for many years yet!

Marthe came and sat at the table, lunch was ready, she thought he looked tired and strained. She tried to change the subject, 'I miss Annie on these days, she was such a regular part of my Sunday routine, working in the garden with Charlie running about. I know there's nothing to keep her here now, the design is done, and she tells me that she's busy, setting up her new business. But I was sad when she gave me her notice. Felix ate a slice of roast veal, took a long drink from the glass of red wine in front of him, and said nothing. Marthe waited.

'How does Annie feel about the house? Will she and Charlie move in? It sounds ideal for a family. Inadvertently Marthe could not have said anything worse. She noticed that Felix had gone very pale, his hand was trembling, 'What is it? What have I said? Felix tell me, why are you so upset?

'I don't know where to start!

'At the beginning?

*

So Felix did start at the beginning. His first encounter with Annie in Toulouse, there had been a misunderstanding and she had accused him of abducting her son. Then an unplanned meeting a little afterwards in the street outside the cathedral of St.Sernin, she had been singing in a choral concert that he was there to review, they had shared a coffee afterwards and learning that she was a gardener he had had an inspirational idea, that she should work for his mother, here at Les Palmes. Then on Sundays watching her here working; her hair tucked into a woolly hat, as she cleared and dug and raked. He found her one morning up a ladder singing quietly as she pruned an unruly climber. From the house he watched her as she left at the end of her day with a haversack on her back, chatting and laughing with her son Charlie. 'She bowled me over! Her energy, her ideas, her …

'Yes I know! Marthe interrupted, 'She was so full of life, and pretty even in those dungarees. Felix stared out of the window, thinking back to the previous year, he said, 'I fell in love, and I thought, so did she. We shared an interest in music, she sings of course, and we went to concerts. I loved being with her and Charlie, we enjoyed simple things; supper in her kitchen, helping Charlie with his homework, and chess, lots of chess. It was like I became part of her family, I didn't need to worry about entertaining her, taking her out. We just did sort of ordinary things. He stopped.

'What went wrong? Marthe asked.

He tried to explain but could not elaborate, it was too raw. Marthe felt sad, very sad, 'So you will move into the house that Annie does not want to share, and then what?

'Make a life for myself there. It'll keep me busy! Move on! Isn't that what people do? He answered abruptly. Marthe didn't say anymore, Felix was normally so calm and content, she had never seen him so edgy and unsettled. She cleared the lunch and got up to make some coffee. Felix was drinking too much she realised.

'Go and play the piano for a while. I'll bring the coffee through, she said.

He stayed for some time playing on the piano in the salon, now emptied of the day bed and tables brought in during her convalescence. The piano had been his father's, they had played duets together often on Sundays after lunch, the memory was painful. He stopped playing and closed the lid, Marthe had been standing at the door listening, she could not think how to help him. 'Can I come and see your new home? She asked. He stood up, 'Of course, I would like that.

'There maybe something from here that you would like, I have so much furniture! It's old fashioned, but it might suit an older house. I'd like to give you something, it sounds as though you will have large rooms to fill.

Felix liked that idea, 'Yes something from Les Palmes would be welcome, a little family history coming with me. We can talk about it when you visit, thank you. They didn't talk anymore about Annie, and Felix left. Marthe had intended to tell Felix of her visit to the Moulin and her discovery of the twins, and her plan to 'help' them in some way but wisely decided not to. She understood that it was not a good moment to unsettle him further.

*

In the following week Felix cleared out the apartment and walked out without a backward glance. A young couple with a baby were to be the new owners. He left them a bottle of champagne in the fridge and some helpful instructions on the glass table which he no longer wanted. He was very busy for the next few weeks, settling into the house on the Rue des Capuchins, and at work, reviewing concerts and attending a festival for young musicians in Albi. He stayed two nights there, narrowly avoiding a fling with a violinist who lived in the City. He was drinking heavily. He felt free to indulge himself with his new home and a number of workmen were quickly set to work renovating and decorating the rooms which he found dated and shabby. The top floor was transformed into his music room; his own grand piano had been hauled up four flights of stairs and new shelves lined the walls. There was a modern desk where he could write and several chairs. It was a beautiful space with a view, not like his apartment of the river, but of roofs and spires and the sky. He immediately loved it and the quiet made him peaceful, high above the traffic and city noises.

For the rest the rooms were mostly large and empty of furniture. He began exploring the many antique shops in the narrow streets nearby which drew people into this part of Toulouse. He was looking for anything, furniture or paintings or objets d'art to furnish his home. Buying an eclectic mix, he placed his acquisitions carefully, changing their positions until he was satisfied, whilst music from his expensive music system drifted down from the top floor. He realised that he was able, by keeping busy and preoccupied, to escape from the complex emotions that Annie had evoked in him; they did not go away, but for long periods he was able to forget her.

One afternoon in March, he was inspecting a pair of antique lights, they had decorated bases in a Chinese style and he thought they would do well at the top of the stairs on the first floor, when he heard a familiar voice. It was Claude's. They were pleased to see each other. 'Don't buy those! Claude said, 'Over priced, and grabbing his arm, he continued, 'I'll show you some lamps at a shop opposite, nicer and cheaper. He led the way out of the shop, waving at the owner who seemed unperturbed at the sudden collapse of a sale. He clearly knew Claude well.

'Come with me, young Felix, he said companionably, 'And how are you? He talked rapidly as they pushed their way across the narrow street, and Felix realised that he had not seen him for many weeks. 'Do you live nearby? I hadn't realised. They entered the shop. Felix explained that he was now living in a house on the rue des Capuchins which required furnishing, and Claude moved into business mode. The afternoon passed in a whirl of buying, not just lamps, but rugs of varying size and two walnut tables and a magnificent oak coffer. Just when Felix thought they had stopped, Claude led the way into a gallery, Felix immediately spotted a large oil painting and quietly crossed the room for a closer look It was the most lovely landscape. A mountain scene; the Matterhorn, standing high, backed by a blue sky, there was snow on the upper slopes, and lower down a farmhouse, stone buildings, and red roofed barns. He stood silently, he knew just where he could hang it. In the salon over the mantel of the fireplace. Centre stage. Claude joined him and said, 'You like it. I can tell. Let me negotiate the price, for you, don't say anything.

*

Within the hour, Felix was showing Claude his new home. The painting was propped on the mantel, he would hang it properly later.

'This is a glorious house! You're a lucky young man, you've bought an absolute treasure, and right in the heart of the City. A perfect location! Claude had finished his tour, it had taken some time as he carefully inspected every room and looked out of every window, Felix accompanied him with some degree of nervousness knowing that Claude had a very critical eye. They were now in the salon sharing a bottle of red wine, and Felix began to relax.

'Have you seen Marthe? Felix asked, topping up Claude's glass.

Claude grimaced, 'Sadly no, not so much. She seems to want more, he said the word slowly, 'Independence'. Felix stared at him, 'Whatever does she mean? What is she saying? Claude looked at Felix and tried to explain the letter that he had received in January and Marthe's expressed wish to spend more time in Collioure, 'She wants to make new friends there, a new life and I don't seem to be part of that, he stopped.

'I think she'll be regretting that! Felix said, he was astonished and disappointed in his mother. He thought she had been very lucky to have found Claude and had noted the effect that he had had on her in the previous year. She had looked smarter and prettier with a sparkle that had been missing for some time. Since the death of his father of course.

'I think she'll be regretting that letter, Felix repeated, 'And there won't be any trips to Collioure for some time. She can only drive short distances still.

Please go and see her.

Claude shook his head, 'No Felix I can't do that. She was very clear in her letter. I visited after her fall, and as soon as she returned from the hospital when I was asked, but that has been that. He rubbed his head and said, 'It's my pride, of course! Rejection is hard to bear and we were a good fit. Love is never easy…I'll get over it. It's not the first time…I have some experience of women, my age you understand. I'm moving on. A silence fell between them, 'But you and I must remain friends, Claude said, 'I can't resist wanting to help you here with this exciting new home. Anyway let me tell you my news, I have become a land owner! He stayed until the wine was finished and he had explained his new position. He did not mention the hotel idea, it still seemed most unlikely to proceed. Felix listened thoughtfully, it did not seem an obvious direction for Claude whose interests were not those of a country man. Claude prepared to leave and Felix escorted him down the stairs into the entrance hall. 'I recognize that, Claude said, putting his hand on the large oak coffer that now stood at the foot of the stairs, 'That comes from Les Palmes, it looks far better here. It was too crowded before. A gift from your mother?

'Yes, she wanted me to have something 'family'.

'And does she like your new home?

'She thinks it large. But yes she likes it very much.

'I think it would look better, away from the stairs, more centred, Claude said, he had his hand on the coffer, 'What's in it? Is it too heavy for us to move a little? 'I haven't really looked, Felix stood next to him, 'blankets I think and rugs. Shall we have a try? They lifted it cautiously, it was heavy indeed, but they were both strong and Claude was used to heaving furniture and garden ornaments about. 'Yes, you're right, Felix said, 'Thanks, it's a handsome piece, looks much better now. He lifted the lid, there was a tartan rug on the top, but putting his hand further in, he found that most of the coffer was filled with old leather books. Claude peered in, 'You'd better have a look at those, he said, and always the dealer, he added, 'they could be valuable!

Felix showed him out onto the street, 'I think you may well hear from Marthe, he said, 'she's very impetuous and I'm sure is realising her mistake. Claude did not say anything, and they stood together looking down towards St. Sernin. There were throngs of people returning from the market, whose stalls surrounded the cathedral, many carrying bags of fruit, vegetables and meat; the market was central to the lives of those who lived nearby it sold such a variety of goods; food, shoes, cassettes, berets,buckets and books. One could find almost anything in that market. The afternoon light was fading, cafes were pulling in their tables, and turning on the lights for the evening. 'You're a lucky devil! Claude said, his hand on Felix's shoulder, 'All this on your doorstep. Let me know when you want to spend more money, I'll be glad to help! He walked off and Felix went inside, it had been an interesting, if expensive, afternoon.

He went up to his music room, he had a pupil that evening and needed to prepare. But he couldn't stop thinking of what Claude had said about his mother... about pride and rejection, and 'moving on'. Claude enjoyed a wide circle of friends and came from a long established family, now as the Count, more doors would open up for him. If he chose he could now play a wider role in local politics and the affairs of the Gers, though Felix thought this unlikely. Claude would be all right, Felix concluded, but his mother, what was she thinking of? Her position was very different! She was still seen as a newcomer in St Girou and her early years at Les Palmes had been difficult, but the apartment in Collioure...he saw that as running away, a foolish whim. He knew Collioure a little, he thought it a pretty little sea side town with an interesting history. Its society was fluid and a little 'arty'(it had in earlier times been the centre of the 'fauve' group of artists, and there were many galleries. It was quite normal to see easels set up in the narrow streets and along the Promenade, a hazard for the unwary. It was much swelled in summer by tourists and holiday makers. How did Marthe see herself there? Her background was urban, she was a Parisenne and her marriage to Xavier had revolved around musical soirees and concerts. Was she planning to establish herself in a different world of galleries and exhibitions, to put her previous life behind her? It seemed so, and Felix admired her in part for wanting to do that. She had always been in the shadow of Xavier, a loving and loyal wife and mother, her identity fused in his. It would appear that Marthe wanted something more. now that she had the opportunity, something new for herself. But what of Claude? In the past year he had introduced her to his wide circle of friends, they had been to parties and gallery openings in Toulouse, and she had joined him on buying expeditions. But maybe he had been a little too controlling? Was this developing into another relationship in which she was the partner who followed? Was this what she feared? Were these the reasons behind the letter?

These thoughts led Felix into a new anxiety as it occurred to him that Marthe might be planning to go further... to leave Les Palmes altogether and settle permanently by the sea. If so what were her plans for Les Palmes? Did she intend to sell? Surely not. That would go against all her insistence on the importance of family. Or give it to him? Neither prospect held any attractions. Felix felt unsettled, uneasy.

*

As he was tidying up after supper, enjoying the many cupboards that filled the kitchen, the phone rang, he picked it up as calmly as he could. It wasn't Annie! It was the agent who had sold him the house. She invited him for a drink. To celebrate his wonderful new home she said. A date! Felix was bemused. 'Moving on' Claude had said, he wasn't sure that he was ready, but he couldn't stay solo for ever. They agreed to meet up the following day, she was pretty he remembered and it was only a drink. He opened a bottle of wine a Chablis that he had bought on a visit to Albi with Annie, they had been to a concert together. He enjoyed it nonetheless.

CHAPTER 11

The first months of the year had passed quickly for Annie, but slowly things began to go wrong. The weather had been unfavourable for a landscape designer, a wet cold January had been followed by a grey damp February. And March was windy with brisk winds. Spring was late, the mimosas were not yet in full flower and the grass was dull and lifeless. The farmers were disconsolate, their cattle still housed in their winter barns, eating silage. Two of Annie's new clients had failed to materialize, despite their initial enthusiasm and a third was uncertain. 'They are keen until they see the cost! She said to herself, 'New gardens cost money. Had they not realized? She thought back to the previous year; Marthe had never questioned the price of trees and shrubs, she had given her a free hand and her employment at Les Palmes had been nothing but pleasure. She began to fear that giving up her City job had been rash as she sorted through bills and shouted at Charlie to turn his music down, and some of his lights off. She felt tired and out of sorts as the cold, or worst wet days, continued. Charlie had become difficult and argumentative at home, he was missing the company of Felix, grumbling that the apartment was boring without him. Annie could not explain his sudden absence from their lives, and Charlie's morose moods exhausted her. He wanted a drum set which

Annie refused even to consider, 'We live in an apartment! She shouted, 'Or hadn't you noticed?' There was a lot of door slamming. This and her other worries made Annie edgy, and there were some fractious arguments.

Charlie was returning to England to stay with his father for the Spring break and she was ashamed to realise that she was looking forward to his departure. Let Ralph deal with him, she thought, as she sorted his clothes for his backpack. 'Do you want to help?' She called out the day before his departure. He was watching football on tv. There was no reply, and Annie sat back on her heels and looked around his room. It was a mess. They were both untidy and she had recently ignored the chore of sorting it out. She thought of Felix who had shared their life in the apartment and tidied all the time. He couldn't believe the state in which she and Charlie lived, and under his care her home had become neat and organized. It had been a revelation: clothes folded and put away in drawers, toothbrushes in mugs, flannels drying on the taps, coats on pegs and shoes in pairs in a line by the door. And the kitchen and the salon transformed. She and Charlie had improved their ways to try and please him, but since his departure old habits had slid back and now the mess had returned. It had all gone down hill.

Annie felt a pang, she missed Felix more, much more, than she had expected. She missed his smile when she returned tired from shopping, the glass of wine he quickly handed her, his patience with Charlie, whose moods dated from his departure. She missed going to restaurants where the maitre d' recognised him and led them to a nice table. She missed sitting beside him in his expensive car, choosing music from his cd selection and singing loudly as he drove, always a little fast. She missed him in bed too, though she tried not to think about that. Annie slammed the door as she left his bedroom. Charlie stared at her, she looked cross, again. He turned back to the football, 'In two days I'll be with dad, he thought, and Mum can have this place to herself. Maybe that's what she wants. He felt sad.

*

But she quickly missed Charlie, the apartment felt quiet and empty and she could not settle. To her horror she was lonely. Ralph phoned once. Charlie had arrived safely, the weather was cold but sunny and they were spending time, after he finished work, having bonfires in the garden. There was to be a village barbeque on Sunday. It was great to have him, Ralph said, which made Annie feel worse.

On the Sunday, her mother, Claire phoned. She asked Annie the usual questions, work, weather, was she busy? Annie answered carefully, until, of course the questions she dreaded came, 'How's Felix? What are you going to do without Charlie? Are you off skiing?

Annie didn't know where to start. She had avoided telling Claire that their relationship was over and that she was, well, no hiding it, on her own again. Claire listened silently as Annie tried to explain. 'Why am I being so defensive, Annie thought angrily, as she heard herself talking. 'It worked for a while, and then it didn't. She said. 'It happens all the time. It's not the end of the world. She concluded by saying, 'Mum we weren't married! Felix and I just lived together. Like you and Tony, except you've managed it better and for longer!

Claire was shocked and disappointed, she liked Felix and had seen him as an ideal partner for her daughter. He gave her love and security, and was good with Charlie. What could have gone wrong? Claire was a firm believer in making things work, sticking it out, give and take. She had slowly accepted the breakdown of Annie's marriage to Ralph, but had not approved of the divorce, nor of Annie settling in Toulouse. Now having listened to Annie's attempt to explain herself, Claire accused her daughter of being selfish and unthinking, and more seriously of ignoring the interests of Charlie, who loved Felix very much. Annie sighed as her mother spoke on and on, finally asking,

'So, how's Charlie taken all this then?

'It's not been easy, he's going through a difficult stage, sort of teenager.

'Oh?

'Yes argumentative and challenging me all the time. Always wants to be with his friends. And angry that I won't let him play the drums.

'That's not surprising. He's upset. You make life impossible for him, first he loses his father and now Felix, he doesn't know where he is! Annie could hear the disappointment in her mother's voice. She sat down and stared at the phone, willing it to be quiet. She said.

'Charlie has not 'lost' his father, he's with him now and having a happy time. Things will work out Mum, just give me a little time. The conversation ended. Annie put the phone down and burst into tears.

*

'You look charming, my dear. The conductor of the choir had taken her elbow and was turning her around, they were at a post concert party, both standing at the bar. It was two days after the row with her mother and Annie was still feeling depressed. She faced him. His name was Jean, a tall man in his early fifties, unattached, predatory. A friend of Felix's, the two men were old friends, they went to concerts together and talked about music afterwards over long drawn out suppers.

She wondered if he knew that she and Felix were no longer together.

Did men discuss such things? Probably, why wouldn't they? Annie turned away as fast as she could, and began a conversation with a young girl who sang soprano, the girl was new to the choir, she was shy and nervous. Normally Felix would have been there, chatting to the singers, indeed she thought she had seen him sitting in the back row, his head bent over his notes. It was the first time she had seen him, since early January, and it had made her unsettled. The evening grew lively and Annie was drinking at one of the tables, her head felt light and airy, she was talking too much. The conductor suddenly moved to sit beside her and put his hand on her arm,

'Shall we leave together? He whispered. Annie was horrified, had she been flirting with him, without realising it? My God! She thought, 'He's propositioning me. She stood up and said, 'No I don't think so. Thanks.

Leaving soon after, Annie walked home. It wasn't far and the cold air helped clear her head. She turned into the Place du Capitol, and waited to cross the road, to her horror a familiar red car drove past. She shrank behind a lamp and watched. It was Felix and beside him a pretty girl, they were both laughing. They were heading towards the rue des Capuchins. 'Has he moved into the house? Is he taking her there? Her thoughts were in a spin as she stood very still as people pushed past her, she felt both angry and sad. 'Didn't take him long, she thought, as a wave of jealousy poured over her; she wanted to be the girl, laughing next to Felix. She felt ill and tired as she entered the empty apartment, perhaps things will look up in April, she said to herself, things could hardly get worse.

*

A week later Annie was back at Les Palmes. 'What are you doing here? She bent to stroke the little dog, 'It's Gaston isn't it? She was taking her coat off in the hall. Marthe smiled, 'He's been here for a little while now, he encourages me to walk, which is what I've been told to do, to help my ankle, get it strong. They walked down the stairs towards the kitchen, 'Ooh, something smells good! Annie said, 'I remember those Sundays all last year, when I was working here, there was always a delicious aroma drifting out into the garden. Charlie used to complain about that! Marthe went back to the stove and poured some red wine into the daube which simmered gently. Annie peered out into the garden, she hadn't seen it for several months, but there wasn't much to admire. 'I'm sorry the garden looks dreary. But give it a couple of weeks and you'll see some changes: snowdrops and buds on the trees, the mimosas are late this year, it's been so grey and cold. And the Judas tree, I can see that has lots of buds. Marthe poured some wine and they sat at her table. The smell of the daube de boeuf suddenly made Annie nauseous, and she drank some water, Marthe asked,

'How's work? Have you lots of clients?

'A little slow, I've had a lot of interest but no commitment. I am waiting for warmer days, then hopefully it will pick up.

'I'll be a reference, you know.

Annie who had not yet touched her lunch, looked around the kitchen; nothing had changed. She had always admired this room, with its wide fireplace and large dresser, where Marthe displayed her blue and white china. A classic look, which worked perfectly. The sun had struggled out, but the wisteria banged against the window, 'I'll prune that back for you after lunch, she said. Marthe nodded, Was the daube too rich? She wondered. Annie had barely eaten any. Marthe said, 'Let's have some dessert, it's apple pie with cream, Felix's favourite. There was an awkward silence, Marthe continued slowly, 'I know you and Felix are no longer together. I don't want to know why, it's nothing to do with me, but I'm sorry. You seemed happy together and Felix loved Charlie, he wanted to settle down, I thought. There was a long silence. Annie stared out of the window, she knew that the previous year had been difficult for Marthe, and she did not want to make this year troublesome. Nor did she want to explain her relationship with Felix. It was too complicated...and sad. Nor was she confident that she had acted wisely. The image of Felix with a girl in his car beside him had aroused deep feelings of jealousy which had made her very unhappy.

Avoiding Marthe's eye, she said, 'I can't really talk about it, I'm sorry. I know that Felix is angry with me and disappointed too. We wanted different things, that's all I can say.

She had eaten some apple pie and was feeling better, 'I'll go and prune the wisteria now, if that's all right, it looks like rain is on its way. Marthe watched her through the window, she wondered if Annie was suffering more than she let on, she had certainly lost her appetite. Having pruned the wisteria and put the long trails of growth on the compost, Annie checked the garden. She stood in the orchard and bent to touch the snowdrops, overwhelmed by selfdoubt. She longed to talk to Marthe, who had always been kind and thoughtful to her, but understood that this would be inappropriate. Marthe could not be expected to tale an objective view of her relationship with Felix and her own mother had already expressed her opinion. Annie felt very alone. She said goodbye and Marthe was sad to notice her pale face.

It had been a difficult visit for both of them and driving home and into Toulouse, Annie wondered if she would see

Marthe again. There seemed little reason now for them to meet. Marthe tidied up, feeling sad for Felix and for herself too, she was very fond of Annie and would miss her and Charlie. She put on her coat and called Gaston, 'Come on, we'll have our walk, she said, he jumped about as she attached his lead. There's nothing I can do about Felix, he's a grown man, she thought. But she could not ignore her concern, for this was not the first failed relationship that Felix had suffered in recent years. Before Annie there had been Valerie who had returned to Paris leaving Felix in Toulouse. What next? She wondered.

CHAPTER 12

Claude was in Auch, seeing his lawyer, he would then proceed to the bank. The purpose of these visits was to discuss the now growing likelihood that the Chateau would be converted into a small hotel. In spite of his early misgivings, Claude was now enthusiastic; he saw it as an opportunity to hold onto the chateau and hopefully ensure its financial future, whilst at the same time be a project which would bring he and his sons together. Having been a business man all his life he was not unduly daunted at the idea of owning and running a hotel. Since Luc's proposal, which at the time had seemed so astonishing, he had carefully examined every room, upstairs and down, assessing each in turn and making a note as he did so. A crazy idea had thus become a definite possibility. He had decided to invest only where strictly needed; to renovate the kitchens, all the bathrooms (and add some more), upgrade the wiring and decorate throughout. The public rooms as he thought of them required attention; decoration and some furnishings were needed throughout. He had not fully investigated the drains, nor the boilers, but felt for the moment they would do. He approached both the lawyer and the banker with confidence.

The lawyer listened carefully whilst expressing considerable surprise. He was an elderly man, who had known the Countess for many years, he had only once visited the chateau. There were several legal issues connected to the estate to be discussed and, having reviewed the will and the family trusts, Claude was able to get away. He stopped for a coffee and a croissant in the square in front of the cathedral, sitting at a table on the pavement and flirting lightly with the waitress who had seen it all before. but it was a windy morning and he moved swiftly on. The Manager at the bank was less than enthusiastic with Claude's proposal, he was a young man and eager to make an impression, but was overawed by Claude, who quickly ran out of patience with his objections. He stood up to leave, 'I have discussed this with my two sons, and we are agreed, to convert the Chateau into a hotel is the only way to keep it in the family. I am here to ask for a small loan towards the expenses of doing that. He spoke firmly.

'Have you looked at other hotels in the area? Are you able to compete? The manager knew he was losing control, but hadn't yet given up. Claude suppressed a sigh, 'We feel we can offer something special. The chateau has a long family history, it offers privacy and delightful accommodation. Our guests will be able to enjoy the lovely park and walks in the grounds. He rose from the ugly chair which had recently been purchased, it was most uncomfortable, the meeting ended soon after in a sour atmosphere. But Claude had his loan.

He walked swiftly to Jerome's bookshop, it was in the narrow street that led from the Square and the Cathedral to the open garden where the statue of D'Artagnan stood. It was a touristy street and busy with people. He found Jerome in a shop empty of customers. It was not an inspiring sight. Jerome was sitting at his desk reading, he had recently started wearing glasses, which gave him a professorial appearance. Jazz was playing quietly in the background. He looked up hearing the door open, smiled and asked, 'So? How did you get on?'

'Settled. We have the loan. But my God he's a miserable man! Come on, lock up, let's go and celebrate. The Hotel du France, I think. A glass of champagne or two.

Jerome followed him down the narrow street, dodging other pedestrians, as Claude strode ahead, his shoulders back, anticipating a good lunch. Jerome wondered what he should do with his book shop, which was not just his place of work but also his home. He had a small apartment on the top floor, it had views over the roofs of the Auch and was very old, with low beams and open brick work, full of character. He was very attached to it. Keep it going perhaps, in case the hotel plan came to nothing. Interesting times ahead, he thought. They had reached the Square and walked across to the Hotel, father and son, very alike in their stature. Claude took Jerome's arm as they entered, passing through the revolving door, 'Time to get him away from that failing business, he thought to himself, as he walked briskly into the restaurant.

*

Indeed interesting times were ahead. The chateau ceased to be the forgotten home of an elderly lady, in the next few months it became a place of work; plumbers, bricklayers, electricians, plasterers and painters swarmed all over it, dust and banging and rough voices filled the air, whilst vans, lorries and great piles of rubbish took over the driveway. The work was messy and incessant. Then, slowly, as Spring settled in the Gers, a new chateau emerged, not exactly a butterfly from a chrysalis, but something very different; the freshly painted rooms had new shutters and wall lights, there were warm bathrooms with modern fittings. A kitchen that would subsequently attract one of the best chefs, poached from a restaurant in Toulouse, had been installed. The staircase was stripped and polished, and the fireplaces swept. The cellar was now properly lit, and a laundry room created with large machines for washing and drying the sheets, pillow cases, towels and linen. This linen would be stored on the top floor under the sloping roof, whilst way below in the basement, new boilers and hot water tanks rumbled and gurgled. The bank loan was exhausted, as were Claude and his two sons.

*

Meanwhile Marthe returned to the Moulin with Patricia, who had driven from Paris to collect Gaston. She intended to use her stay to stop Marthe's plans for assisting the twins. It was a cold bright morning and the sun shone as Marthe parked next to the bridge, the willows were in full leaf and the Judas tree beside the stream was covered in deep purple blossom. Nonetheless, Patricia looked around with distaste; the Moulin seemed to her horribly run down and sad; brambles and nettles grew robustly in the area near the house which itself seemed on the point of collapse, with the north wall supported by a huge wood beam. Forlorn and rusty machinery, abandoned apparently, blocked the rough path to a large barn and there was a nasty smell pervading the air. Several dogs were barking somewhere and she was pleased that Gaston was safely tucked up in his bed at Les Palmes.

'Whatever is this place? She turned to Marthe, 'Do people really live like this? Marthe shrugged, 'Of course they do. They just don't have money for refinements, things that don't matter to them. She stood uncertainly, there seemed to be no one about. They walked slowly towards the barn where the girl, Agathe, kept her ducks. The smell intensified and Patricia stopped. 'Really Marthe, what do you intend to do here? You are a Parisienne, you know nothing of this world, she pointed at a pile of discarded tyres stacked untidily against a wall, 'This life! Nor will they thank you for interfering, if that's your plan. Marthe ignored her and called out as she approached the big barn door. A long haired brown dog came bounding out, Patricia who was several steps behind her, gripped her hand bag, 'I'll hit it if it comes closer, she decided. The dog stopped as a voice from inside the barn, shouted, 'Jacques! Jacques! And then the figure of a young man appeared. Gregoire came forward, he had recognised Marthe, and extended his hand, smiling courteously,whilst glancing at Patricia, who stared at him. Marthe, aware that they had come uninvited, spoke quickly, there were the usual pleasantries and Patricia was introduced, then Marthe said,

'I've been thinking of you and your sister a great deal and I'd like to help you both. As a thank you for what you did for me. We needn't go over it again, but you saved my life and I am deeply grateful. Blushing a little she continued, 'I'm a widow, with a little money to spare, and it would please me to assist you, give you a helping hand. Gregoire had not moved, Patricia was dumbstruck. Marthe was going much further than she had ever expected. Marthe continued 'Perhaps with new machinery or paying someone to help you on the land, to develop where you showed me on my first visit. She stopped and then added, 'And I would like to do something for Agathe too.

Gregoire was too shaken to speak, Marthe said, 'Shall we look around together and see if you have any ideas? Having taken control of the situation, Marthe was content to follow Gregoire as he led the way and they walked around the immediate area behind the farm house. Patricia in reluctant attendance. It was a market garden, she now understood, on land facing south and west on a gentle slope. Gregoire explained to them that the family had once farmed crops; flax, rapeseed and corn, but his grandfather for some years had been too old to work and so they had abandoned several fields and he had converted those they could see now, for growing vegetables.

He supplied the local markets and Toulouse. Marthe nodded, listened carefully and asked several questions. She liked this young man more and more, he was proud and enthusiastic about his work, and clearly loved his land.

'And your sister? It's Agathe isn't it? Where's she?

'Taking some of her ducks for slaughter. She doesn't do that herself, he said with a shrug. Marthe turned away, trying to block out the image of the swollen livers of ducks too heavy to walk, or raise themselves up. 'She won't be back till the afternoon. He said. This was disappointing, they turned back towards the car, and Marthe said 'I'd like you to draw up a plan, a proposal, of how I might help you. A business plan. Can you do that? I'll come back in ten days and then I'd like to talk to Agathe too. You can tell her of this visit and explain to her that I will assist her too. She must think carefully. I need just an outline for the moment. She buttoned up her coat, the morning had turned colder and a nasty wind had brought in rain clouds from the Pyrenees. Patricia was already back in the car, her face expressionless. There was no sign of life from the farm house, no grandfather had appeared and the dogs were back inside. Peace had returned. Gregoire opened the car door for her as Marthe concluded, 'I'm not wanting a partnership, but I do want a clear idea from you both of how my money could be put to good use, so as to improve your lives. They shook hands and Gregoire nodded to Patricia. It had all happened very fast and Patricia was quite speechless, but she was not so overwhelmed that she had not formed a strong opinion.

Gregoire stood watching them drive away until they disappeared over the bridge and down the rough track. He turned then and walked slowly to the house calling to the dogs, he was overwhelmed.

*

'Partners! I should think not! Patricia was pushing open the door at Les Palmes. 'Really are you serious? She bent to pick up Gaston who was fussing at her feet, he could smell Jacques. 'This is the worst idea you've ever had. And your most impetuous. You must discuss it with Felix before you do anything more.

'No. I don't need his advice. Marthe threw her coat on the hall table. 'It's my idea, and my money! Don't you see? I want to help them to make more of their lives. They're nice people Patricia. But they've had no opportunities. They're unable to see outside their immediate world; ducks and fields and rusty tractors and dogs called Jacques. Patricia had rarely seen her friend with such a stubborn face, she watched as Marthe walked through the hall and down the little flight of stairs and into the kitchen.

'Lunch? A drink? Marthe offered, as Patricia joined her. She was grateful to her friend for coming with her and eager to improve the mood of the morning.

'Both I think! I'm in shock. She paused to sip her wine, trying to calm down, 'you're going to do this, aren't you? She said.

'Probably. Yes. Let's see. Here, she held out her glass of wine, 'To whatever happens next!

*

Ten days later she returned to the Moulin, alone. She had carefully read the proposals from both twins and they were waiting at the bridge. They led her into the farmhouse. The elderly grandfather was there, sitting by the fire in a large dark room, it was the sitting room and was somewhat smoky and not warm. They introduced Marthe and he nodded. He was very deaf, in his eighties, Marthe thought, his shirt and thick jacket were old but clean and his slippers were very worn. They all sat down on the shabby chairs around the fire. Marthe had read their separate plans, she now wanted to discuss them, the old man listened as she spoke and tapped the floor with his stick when he was unable to understand. He coughed intermittently. Marthe found it difficult to concentrate. After nearly an hour they all stood up and shook hands, and Agathe disappeared into the back of the house, reappearing soon after with a tray, holding an old black bottle and four small glasses, handing the first to Marthe. Very solemnly she filled the other three and they each raised theirs. Grandfather struggled to his feet and gave a toast 'Salut he said and bowed to Marthe. There was a silence and then they all took a sip, 'Salut'. They echoed. It was plum brandy and very strong. The agreements were thus sealed. Marthe sipped her brandy cautiously watching the family, her heart was thudding and she wanted to get away. She needed to be by herself, she had just made one of her biggest decisions since the death of Xavier.

Agathe accompanied her back to the car. 'Why are you limping? Is your ankle still sore? She asked quietly. Marthe regarded the girl, 'Yes it is. It aches, when I walk. Agathe said, 'If you like I can help you! A little massage if you'd like. Marthe was surprised, she had thought Agathe rather a dull girl, her plan had been simple, some money to help improve the conditions for her ducks. She seemed to have low expectations for herself, she had asked for so little.

'Where did you learn massage? She asked. Agathe flushed and replied slowly, 'I've not been taught or trained, but I do it for my grandmother, she's arthritic and it eases her pain. Sometimes I give a massage to other elderly people in the home, if they ask. Many of them suffer with their joints. At the Maison de Retraite in St. Girou. I enjoy it.

'You like caring for others, don't you? Marthe said, 'Mme Cazeaux told me that when Gregoire led them to where you were lying, they saw that you had put your coat around me and lifted me off the ground, out of the snow. And I watched you feeding your ducks too, you were gentle with them stroking their necks as you poured the corn down their throats. Agathe was silent and then said,

'I had to when I was little, my mother was very sick, she needed nursing and I was the only person who could do that. Grandmother couldn't do much even then, her arthritis...

'How old were you? When your mother fell sick?

'Ten, but she was ill for a long time three years or more, she died here in the farm house.

Marthe did not ask about the girl's father, no one had mentioned him and she assumed that he was dead too. Agathe had brightened up when talking about caring for her grandmother, she had come alive and Marthe suddenly had a very new idea, 'Why not let me help you to train to be a nurse? It would suit you, I think.

Agathe turned pale and clutched her stomach as though she was in pain, 'Oh I can't accept that. It takes a long time to train, and it would be very expensive. Marthe felt like hugging this shy, unassuming girl who had so little in her life, and no expectations.

'Yes, you can! Accept, I mean. Nursing is a very good career and if you want to try, then go ahead. It's a really worthwhile profression. Go and find out as much as you can about where you could train. Ask Gregoire to help you.

'I don't need to ask him! I'll do it on my own. She spoke forcefully. Marthe patted her on the arm 'Good girl! I'll return in a week, and see what you have found out. She shut the car door and prepared to leave, winding down the window, she called out, 'Salut! Agathe did not linger, she was racing back towards the house, her heart was bursting with excitement.

Marthe drove home she would phone and talk to Felix about the twins that evening.

*

It was April and Annie was pushing her trolley up and down the aisles at Inter Marche. She didn't bother with a list, she always bought the same stuff, she could shop here with her eyes shut. It was all the boring things she purchased at the super market, meat and fish and bread and fruit and vegetables came from the market near to home. Today it was tins of tomatoes, cling film and kitchen foil, loo paper and toothpaste. Tampons, she reached up for the familiar brand and had a horrible thought, but I haven't bought any for months. Standing very still, her trolley now blocking the aisle, she calculated, not since…Good God! Before Christmas! Panicking she tried to remember when she and Felix had last made love. It was ages ago, the night that they had 'made up' following their row. So that was three months ago, or thereabouts. Could it be? Was it possible? A tall willowy woman brushed past her, an unusual sight, most women here were short and square, Annie recognised her, she was a fellow lecturer at the University, and not someone she wanted to talk to at this moment. She dipped her head until the woman had turned the corner and then dragged her mind back. That would explain the tiredness and feelings of nausea that had bedevilled her recently. 'I'm pregnant, she thought and felt like screaming. She swore under her breath, every foul word she knew. In English and French. Then ignoring the protests, she pushed her trolley towards the check out, paid and loaded her shopping into the back of the car. Sitting behind the wheel, she shut her eyes and tried to calm down, 'Pregnant... again. It was the last thing she wanted. The very last thing. Gripping the steering wheel tightly, Annie wept in great gulping sobs.

CHAPTER 13

Felix had come very near to sleeping with the house agent, Delphine. She was pretty and a flirt and more than happy to encourage him. He had twice invited her for drinks in his home and then they proceeded to eat in a nearby restaurant. Felix always paid. On their third date, he had cooked supper in his kitchen, anticipating leading her upstairs. She was more than ready, drinking carelessly and letting her blouse fall a little open. But the phone rang, an urgent work matter, he was needed at the printers, and that opportunity was lost. There would be others he thought as he showed her to the door, she kissed him there, pressing herself into him and walked away with a wave and a little dance.

*

Felix had continued to spend time furnishing his home and was particularly delighted with Marthe's oak coffer which he and Claude had positioned carefully in the entrance hall. He hung a new painting above it, a modern still life, it made an interesting contrast. One wet morning, returning from the market, he stopped and lifted the lid, and looked more carefully beneath the rug, that had been placed on the top. He recalled Claude's view that the contents might have value. Smiling at the memory, he leant in. It was dusty with a dry smell, there were some ledgers and leather bound books, opening one, he saw that it was a diary. Its owner, he had written carefully on the first page in an italic script was M. Bertrand le Brun. It was for the year 1939. He saw other diaries and bending down, began to lift them out. He piled them on the floor, there were five in all. The last was for the year 1944. Felix decided that he had found something that might be of interest. He next lifted out the ledgers, these were heavy in the same script, full of columns of figures and dates. There were nearly twenty.

Felix drew up a chair and examined the diaries, each one had been filled in meticulously, a page for every day of the year. Glancing quickly through he realised that his grandfather was clearly a man of great discipline, he recorded the weather, the state of his health, his appointments, his social engagements, there were also references to his business in Toulouse. All in the same neat hand. He never missed a day. Felix decided to look more carefully at the last, the year 1944, it was incomplete. He remembered that his grandfather had died in the autumn of that year, he had drowned in the river outside the garden wall of his home at Les Palmes. The diary stopped. He turned quickly to the last pages, his heart was beating fast; the last entry, had been written in the morning. His health was good, he had written, the day was cool and damp, he had a business meeting later in the afternoon, he was deeply worried about the war, in particular the allied bombing around Strasbourg, he feared further damage to the family's factories in that City.

It was cold sitting in the hall, Felix took all five diaries upstairs to the Salon, and carefully read the 1944 diary right through from the first entry. It took him an hour, as he paused regularly trying to take it all in. He read with growing interest, the diary was no longer a record of his health, the weather as before. Fetching a pen and paper, he began to take notes. Felix understood that this diary was important, very important. Absorbed in his reading, Felix ignored the ringing of the phone. It rang again some thirty minutes later, he ignored it. Thus Annie, anxious and tearful, was unable to tell him her news. She assumed that he was busy or away and did not try again that day.

*

Her anxious evening was interrupted when Claire phoned whilst she and Charlie were having supper. Annie heard it and nodded at Charlie who was always happy to chat with his grandmother. He told her of his oncoming chess tournament, managing to talk whilst at the same time lifting spaghetti onto his fork and putting it into his mouth. Annie frowned at him, but he kept going, now giving a long garbled account of his latest football match. Finally he handed the phone to Annie and went to fetch some more pasta from the stove.

'How are things? Claire enquired, she spoke cautiously, remembering their conversation about Felix. Annie, panicky and desperate, burst into tears. She turned hurriedly away from Charlie. 'Sorry, I can't hear you. Claire said.

'I'm going into another room, Annie said, and walked quickly into her bedroom, shutting the door.

She began to sob, shaking badly, and Claire asked, 'Are you crying? That's not like you! Are you ill?

'No, Annie replied, then speaking in a rush, 'I'm pregnant. I found out...just this morning. In Intermarche. Oh Mum! Claire was so surprised that she was unable to respond. She couldn't think what Intermarche had to do with it. 'I can't believe it, but I am...definitely, Annie sobbed, 'About three months I think.

Claire said, 'Have you told Felix?

'No. Not yet. He's not here you may remember.

'You're going to aren't you!

'Yes! Of course. Annie was no longer crying, she sniffed and said, 'He'll be delighted, thrilled, of course. She spoke almost angrily, 'It's fine for him isn't it! He won't feel tired and have to give up work and blow up like a balloon. She lay back on the bed, thinking of her earlier pregnancy,

'Are you still there? Claire asked, there had been a long silence. Annie sat up, as Charlie came bounding in, 'Can I watch the football? I've done the washing up. She nodded, he bounded out,

'Mum, sorry, I can't really talk at the moment. I'll phone you tomorrow, promise. You're pleased aren't you, another grandchild! Everyone will be delighted, except me! Claire tried to frame a tactful and kind reply but Annie cut her short, saying goodbye, as she lay back on her bed, thinking. The tv blared in the next room, as an excited French football commentator with an odd high pitched voice filtered through the closed door. She tried to assess the reality of the situation; it's not just about me and Felix, but Charlie too and Ralph, and work and finding space for a baby. She remembered the early years when Charlie was little; she and Ralph in a draughty cottage, as she took the responsibility of caring for a small person twenty four hours a day. There was no time for anything, and her incipient career which was really taking off was put on hold. She remembered too well a life of endless demands; breast feeding, then warming up little bowls of mushy food, endless washing and sleepless nights, teething, it had gone on and on. Claire had been a wonder supporting her and Ralph financially, and making regular visits; pushing the pram on cold afternoons, clearing up and tidying, shewing endless love and care for her grandson. There had been unfortunate, occasional rows between mother and daughter, Annie was very sensitive to criticism and she winced to recall some of the words that had been said. But she knew that life without Claire's help would have been much worse. And this was all about to happen again. Annie knew that her disappointment was selfish but for the moment she felt no joy in her second pregnancy.

She got up and washed her face, and Charlie looked up and grinned, as she returned to the salon, 'We're winning! He said, 'Come and watch! She joined him on the sofa, pushing his feet off, she looked at his face, absorbed in the football, and felt guilty about her recent negative thoughts. To his annoyance, she leant across and gave him an enormous kiss on his still youthful cheek.

*

The following morning, after Charlie had set off for school, she sat down and very slowly picked up the phone. Felix! The line was dead it was, of course, his old number at the apartment, the only one she had. Sighing she found her coat and prepared to find him at the house that she had visited in January. It seemed a long time ago.

'Pregnant! Felix turned pale as he gripped the counter of his smart new work top in the kitchen, 'Are you sure? We were so careful weren't we? Annie looked at him, 'Oh I'm not blaming you! She said, 'I was careless, simple as that.

'How many months?

'Three I think. We broke up about that time. If you remember. The irony escaped neither of them.

He crossed the room to where she was standing looking bleakly out of the window at the little courtyard below. She noticed that he had put some stone urns in a group in the centre, and wondered if he had planted them out.

Such irrelevant thoughts, she was unable to concentrate on anything. Felix was in turmoil, he wanted to take Annie in his arms and hug and kiss her, but her face was set in a resolute expression. He was astounded by her news, but overwhelmingly excited and happy. Pregnant, he said the word in his head, 'I'm going to be a father! He had joined her at the window, he was trembling,

'You are going to keep the baby aren't you?

Annie turned and her face softened, 'Yes Felix. I am. It's what you wanted isn't it? A child with me. It seems that you are in luck! There was a hint of bitterness in her voice, he stared at her and before he could respond she burst into tears, the whole wretched business wasn't to be avoided was all she knew. Tears poured out of Annie, Felix could not bear to see her so upset, so defeated, he did what he wanted to do from the first moment and held her, hesitantly at first and then tightly, very tightly, stroking her hair. Slowly, slowly, Annie relaxed and the tears stopped. Her face was red and blotchy, she sniffed. 'God, Felix, where do we go from here?

He guided her upstairs to the salon and she sat down, she looked pale and tired, he thought. 'Coffee?

Annie shuddered, 'No thank you. Can't bear the smell at the moment. Have you tea? Lemon or peppermint. Felix disappeared and Annie, trying to relax, looked about. It was the first time she had been there since her disastrous visit in January. The salon, she immediately saw, was now furnished and she thought it delightful. It was calm and restful, but also sophisticated and sort of grown up. Most of the furnishings were new, she didn't recognise them at all. And there were new paintings and rugs and lamps. She continued to look around; there was a pile of old leather bound books, some on the table beside her and more on the wood floor, they looked incongruous in this ordered room. She did not pick one up, but found herself thinking of pushchairs and high chairs, plastic toys and milky bibs, all the chaos and mess of babies.

And Felix, where would he be in all this? He had no idea what impact a baby had on one's life.

'This is a lovely room, she said as he gave her a lemon tea in a cup decorated with pink roses, 'It suits you, sophisticated and elegant. Rather like you! It was the first affectionate thing she had said for many months, Felix flushed. 'Claude helped, he said, 'he's very good at that sort of thing, spending other people's money. But he saved me a lot too, he's a terrific bargainer. You remember him? A friend of my mother. Annie did remember him, he was a great charmer, but nice all the same.

'And Marthe, how's she?

'Well, she has a madcap scheme to help the young couple who found her after her fall. They were twins it turned out, living in a Moulin on the road south. She wants to set them both up, give them money. I'm unable to dissuade her, we can't discuss it all. She has made up her mind.

'But why do you want to? If she wants to give a helping hand, isn't that something rather wonderful? Felix stirred his coffee cup, and Annie tried not to blanch at the smell. 'So, poor Felix, she continued, 'you've had some surprises. Your mother is taking over two strangers and I'm having your child. Her teasing touched him and he smiled, but he was wary of showing too much, Annie was unpredictable and he feared another rejection. He glanced at her as they sat quietly, he thought she looked tired and he longed to hold her, then Annie stood up, 'I don't think we need to make any decisions for the moment, there's no need to rush. I can keep working, and in the fourth month, which is soon, I'll start feeling less emotional. Less inclined to dissolve into tears. I have to tell Charlie soon, it'll be a huge shock for him too! And you must tell Marthe! I wonder what she will say! She looked at Felix, 'Are you ok? She asked and touched his hand, 'You went very pale when I told you.

'Well it's not every day you learn that you're going to be a father, is it? He said. 'It's astonishing and wonderful news Annie, I really cannot take it all in for the moment. Finally he hugged her lightly and she stood still enjoying the moment. It was a long time since she had been touched by Felix and she experienced a surge of love. It was unexpected and surprised her.

'This room is lovely, she said, 'thank you, I feel better…I'm glad that I found you. He was surprised, 'You knew where I was didn't you? I moved here in January.

Annie grimaced, 'Ah January! Not a happy month.

Felix looked at her, 'That's behind us. She made her way towards the door before he could say more.

After she had left, he thought about telling Marthe his news, there was also the other surprise which he had not yet mentioned, the discovery of the diaries and ledgers written by Bertrand. They would be as great a surprise to Marthe as the news that she was going to become a grandmother.

*

Walking home Annie thought about her morning, Felix's joy had lifted her spirits and the black cloud that had settled on her began to drift away. 'He'll be a fantastic dad, she thought, but, it raised the difficult question of another role… a husband? She had enjoyed being with him again that was certain, and he had been so kind and enthusiastic, it had felt normal sitting in his salon, chatting, she realised how much she had missed him. But a husband? That was another matter. She pushed it to the back of her mind and with an unexpected burst of energy set about tidying the apartment, a job she had spurned for several weeks. The phone rang later in the afternoon, just as Charlie burst in from school, 'I'm in the team! He shouted throwing down his bag and heading for the fridge, 'First match this Saturday! She held up her hand with a thumbs up sign, as she lifted the receiver, it was Claude.

'I have a proposition for you, he said. 'Come and see me. He gave her directions and they agreed that Annie would visit the Chateau in two day's time. Annie was intrigued. Could it be work, she wondered, opening the fridge door and searching for a pizza for Charlie's supper. What other reason could Claude have for inviting her to the Chateau? It was very unexpected whatever it was. Speculating about Claude distracted Annie from sharing her 'baby' news with Charlie, she needed to think carefully about how to tell him. She wanted to get that right, the timing and the wording, it was important to her that there should be no misunderstandings.

*

'So, what do you think? Claude asked, as he and Annie stood on the south facing terrace, in a brisk wind. She had been invited to the Chateau. He had shown her the garden that spread out on all sides, it was overgrown, long neglected. Where once there were lawns, flower beds and terraces lined with clipped hedges, there was clumpy grass, thistles and docks. Several tall trees had fallen and blocked the paths, which were almost invisible under moss and weeds. The orchard was overwhelmed with bramble to the extent that they were no longer separate trees and the kitchen garden, with its high brick walls, had been devoured by rabbits.

Annie hesitated, she didn't want to be rushed into saying anything that she might later regret, Claude was, it appeared, a possible client. The state of the garden appalled her, she had never before seen such a wretched site. She reached into her work bag, retrieving a pad and pencil, and staying calm asked, 'Perhaps the best thing would be for you to tell me what you are looking for. She moved to sit on a rusty chair, turning her back to the wind and Claude sat down beside her. He talked for some time and Annie scribbled away her note book balanced on her knee and finally stopped, 'A hotel! You have surprised me, she said as a young man joined them. 'This is my oldest son, Jerome, Claude introduced him. 'He'll be working here with me. He paused, 'On this mad project. Father and son grinned at each other wryly. 'So all the workmen that I saw as I arrived are converting the chateau I take it, Annie said.

'Yes, we've been going busily, and noisily for some weeks now. The garden we forgot about. Which was a mistake! It's as important as the inside, we were idiots not to realise that. Annie liked his honesty, 'Let me be absolutely clear, she said, 'You want to upgrade the whole garden that surrounds the chateau. 'Yes, Jerome interrupted, 'it's very...unattractive at the moment, hardly a garden at all really. Certainly not good enough for a hotel. We want a garden that will draw our guests outside, with areas where they can stroll and sit, and a terrace with tables for drinks, with pots and such. There will be a pool, over there, he pointed to the western side, 'we've started work on that, but we should make it sheltered and private. Trees and shrubs can do that can't they? We have this marvellous view. He stopped abruptly and looked at her. Annie noted his enthusiasm, she was experiencing mounting excitement, she responded, 'All that can be done. Though it's a great deal of work you realise. We're talking about flower beds and paths, trees and shrubs. It's a fairly windy site so

I would suggest a wind break, down the whole of the west side. Though that will take time to establish. But you can buy quite tall trees now, from specialist suppliers. Also some large shrubs to give a more intimate feel. This terrace, where we are now, is too narrow, it can be widened, with a retaining wall, and you need to build new steps down to the lower area, she pointed, which can be levelled and we can create a lawn. That's important, people like lawns, they give a sense of space and style.

'Luc is talking about growing vegetables and herbs, he's the chef in the family, home grown stuff looks good on the menu, doesn't it. Claude said, he was becoming increasingly enthusiastic, Annie kept scribbling, thinking about the walled garden as a perfect location for Luc's vegetables. She heard footsteps and looked up to see a woman coming to join them, she was carrying a tray with coffee and biscuits. Jerome brought up a rickety table and Annie realised how little this terrace had been used. 'This is Angelique, Claude said by way of introduction. The discussion continued, as Angelique handed the coffee cups around, 'No thank you, Annie said, 'Just a biscuit. Do you plan to serve meals out here? How far are we from the kitchen?

'Lunches maybe, Jerome replied, 'and drinks before dinner on warm evenings.

'Too far for dinner! Claude said firmly. He did not relish the prospect of serving his guests other than in the dining room, which had been refurbished and decorated at considerable expense.

'Unless we set up a BBQ. Families love those, its more informal. It was Angelique speaking, she laughed at Claude who had shut his eyes dramatically with a loud sigh of protest. 'Families are your market Claude, you need to attract them if you're going to make money. He sighed again, 'Really? I'd envisaged more, well...

'People like you! It was Angelique again, and Annie realised that she was more than someone employed to make coffee. Claude took her hand affectionately, 'I'll manage, I've had children, he said.

Annie prepared to leave, 'I'll return in a week if that suits. With an outline plan. I would need to return and do lots of measuring, if you decide to go ahead. But I've got enough to work on.

Claude got up to walk her to her car and said, 'I've seen Felix a little, helped him with his rather grand house. Is it just for him?

Annie answered lightly, 'Yes, as far as I know. I found it rather formal, a place to be admired rather than lived in. He was surprised at that, 'I'm sorry you felt like that, it'll change as he settles in, it needs a bit of love that's all. They said goodbye and Annie drove off. Claude stood thoughtfully watching her as she went up the drive and disappeared round the final corner, and then returned to the terrace. 'She's pregnant! Angelique said as he took the last of the biscuits. 'And don't eat now, Luc is preparing lunch. Lunch had become their main meal, cooked by Luc who, preparing for his role as a sous chef in the kitchens, he experimented daily on recipes with varying success. 'How was that? Too spicy? Would you want to eat it again? He quizzed them every day. Today it was to be chicken cooked with artichokes in a red wine sauce, followed by pancakes in syrup. Claude was putting on weight and had started to long for an omelette or simple risotto or a salad, 'However do you know that? Claude asked, quickly swallowing the biscuit.

'Refused coffee and had a sort of 'glow'. Didn't you notice? The two men looked at her in surprise,

'Must be Felix's, how interesting! Claude said, recalling his recent conversation with Felix who had made no mention of Annie sharing his life there in what he thought of as the grand house. It seemed an odd choice for a family with a baby, lots of stairs and, as Annie had commented, 'formal' in style. She certainly had not sounded enthusiastic about it.

*

Angelique had been staying with Claude for some time, she had arrived for a week and then just stayed. She was full of ideas and energy and had kept the family going as the building work threatened to wear them down, and the bills poured in. She could turn her hand to anything; advising Claude in choosing furnishings, and accompanying him on furniture buying expeditions. She chatted about books and jazz with Jerome and encouraged him to improve his accounting skills, an area which he found challenging, but would be all important if he was to help his father. She was often in the kitchen, dipping her finger into sauces, as Luc poured over recipes, and helped him in the cellar, sorting through the old bottles with their faded and dusty labels. Dressed in jeans and a variety of tshirts, she chatted easily with all the workmen and her informal manner fended off some difficult scenarios when Claude lost patience with an unexpected problem. She never seemed to sit down and Claude became almost jealous of the time she spent away from him.

That afternoon after Claude had enjoyed an afternoon siesta and kept his temper through a long discussion with the mason about fireplaces, Angelique said,

'Let's go and look at the garden now. You need to have your own ideas or Annie, if it's she, will take it over! Claude recalled the work that Annie had done at Les Palmes the previous year, she had certainly taken that place over! They walked outside and encountered Jerome who joined them.

'She's quite something, he said, 'Full of ideas! Hope we can afford her. Suddenly it seems like a huge undertaking. But if she's pregnant, does that affect our decision?

'She'll need help anyway, there's far too much for one person. Claude said,

'Is she the right person then? Jerome asked again, 'we're looking for a long term commitment surely.

'We'll ask her next week, I think, Claude replied, avoiding an answer, he had already decided that Annie was the person to take on the challenge. Claude took Angelique's arm as they walked across to the walled garden and peered through the rusty wrought iron gate, it really looked an impossible task and feeling intimidated at the size of the task ahead, Claude said 'Let's go back in, I need a drink! Another Luc supper ahead! Angelique said and Claude groaned.

CHAPTER 14

Annie was in a difficult position: the possibility of embarking on a new project at the Chateau was more than exciting. Claude had presented her with just the sort of challenge that she had been looking for; she would be able to create something from scratch, in a location that had all the elements that were fun and interesting to work with. Her head buzzed with ideas: new flower beds, a wide terrace, lawns and walled gardens could be made to create a harmonious garden, the design and planting would be a wonderful challenge. She sucked the end of her pencil and concentrated as she sat with her feet up on the sofa in the kitchen, drawing paper and soft pencils and books jostling for space. She was happy. Then reality struck. 'Was it wrong of her to accept the position (she was confident that Claude would offer it), knowing that she would be unable to work after the end of July? But Annie couldn't bear to let such a wonderful chance go, 'I'll be honest, I have to be, then it's upto Claude, whether he wants to employ me or not. Having decided that, she felt better and returned to her paper and pencils. She was still working there, when Charlie returned from school, I must tell him about the baby, she thought, but it needs to be the right moment. Their relationship was still fractious as he continued to miss Felix, yet at times he was fun and caring. She found his unpredictable moods difficult, fearing that her son was more like her than she had previously understood. She stood up and stretched, 'Supper? Or a sandwich now, and pasta later? 'A sandwich now, but I'll make it. Do you want anything? Charlie was walking to the fridge,

'A cup of tea, peppermint please. He turned, 'Is that a new fad? Are you on some kind of weird diet? Annie nearly spoke, but held back. She had missed her opportunity again.

*

It was the morning of Marthe's third visit to the Moulin. She was awake early and opening her bedroom window she leant out. It smelt of Spring, she thought delightedly, breathing deeply. An agitated blackbird flew low across the path beside the three palms, disappearing into the catmint, not yet in flower she noticed. The bird was looking for worms under the pale green shoots. Below the window, the pergola roof supported an old wisteria, whose buds were pale grey and velvety, a small bird hopped about in the dry branches, a sparrow or finch maybe. The garden was coming back to life. Marthe dressed and went down stairs, opening the big landing window as she passed, the air was cool. She was excited and hungry. Felix phoned as she was drinking her coffee, he asked if lunch tomorrow would suit her, he could arrive around mid day. She was pleased to hear his voice, he sounded different, he had something to tell her he said.

Agathe was waiting on the bridge as she arrived, she was smiling. She had tied her long black hair into a pony tail, and was wearing a dark green jumper. She looked neat and tidy, 'She's quite pretty. Marthe thought with some surprise and followed her towards the house, and in to the kitchen. Marthe could hear the old grandfather coughing in the adjacent room where the fire burnt in a haze of smoke. The large kitchen was dark and cluttered, there was a smell of soup. A huge loaf rested on the table, Marthe had seen these in the market in St.Girou, they were large enough to feed a family for a week. She had never bought one. Agathe took a blackened kettle from the stove and poured boiling water into a coffee pot as she indicated a chair. Marthe sat down looking about her, the kitchen was dominated by a large dresser crowded with china and a pile of papers and an old radio. There was a stone sink under the window and on the sill a line of jugs containing a mix of pens, pencils, cooking utensils and one of dried leaves. Huge cooking pots were stacked beside the stove, they looked very old and much used.

Holding her mug, Agathe outlined what she had learnt: she could start her training almost immediately at the Maison de Retraite. It would be a probationary period in which she would be observed and assessed whilst doing basic work like, bed making, washing the elderly residents and helping at meal times. An important task as many of the residents needed assistance. 'They know me anyway, she said, 'I visit my grandmother at least once a week and help out with other residents, when they're short staffed. And I give my massages to many of them. She spoke confidently as she enjoyed explaining to Marthe what her responsibilities would become. If that went well, she could then apply to the college of nursing attached to the hospital in Auch, where her training would last a minimum of two years.

'And that's what you would like, is it?

'It's what I've always dreamed of… to be a nurse! But we can't afford it, I have to work with the ducks, to help Gregoire and grandfather. Marthe asked, 'When did you first realize that? That you liked caring for others?

Agathe said, 'When I was looking after my mother, when she fell ill. They sat silently. Agathe spoke again, 'Then our father left the Moulin soon after she died. He hated farming, it was my mother's life not his. And he did not get on with grandfather. He's living in Toulouse now, and has a new family. She shrugged, 'We don't see him much.

'How old are you and Gregoire?

'We're just twenty. Marthe calculated quickly, 'So you've lived here without your parents for quite a time.

'Yes, our grandmother brought us up, but she's been in the Maison for several years.

Marthe thought about this, she had lost her father when she was four, and had lived in the home of her grandparents thereafter. Her mother had been a shadowy part of her life, but she had not died when Marthe was ten or eleven. She smiled at Agathe, 'I would like very much to help you, to train to be a nurse. That's what I want to do. You will be an excellent nurse I know. Agathe flushed and played with her mug, as Marthe, full of resolution, continued to talk. They talked about money, the cost of training, the loss to the farm of the income from Agathe's ducks. She would need transport, a moped possibly, the journey to St.Girou was nearly four miles, there was an old van, but Gregoire used it to take his produce to markets. Anyway she couldn't drive. Agathe listened breathlessly as Marthe calmly spelt out all that she was prepared to provide. 'There has to be some written agreement, so that you have security in case anything happens to me. I'll get a lawyer to draw something up. Otherwise I don't see any difficulty. Do you want me to talk to grandfather now? He must be told what you are planning.

'Can I tell him? He's very deaf but he's used to me. Marthe thought this a good idea, she didn't relish the smoky room and trying to talk to the old man.

Soon after, Marthe found Gregoire out behind the big barn. They talked at length, it was decided that the twins would come to Les Palmes in a week, and they would all sign an agreement drawn up by her lawyer. It had all been decided with surprising speed. Marthe drove home, she was thrilled to be able to spend some of her wealth on two worthwhile young people, to help them make more of their lives. She liked the fact that they were a local family, she would be assisting the local community, the community which finally she had decided to make her home. She thought back to her winter months in Collioure, where her days drifted by and nothing was achieved. It was a frivolous life there she knew and a waste of her time, she regretted her foolishness in thinking that was what her life should be. She would let the apartment go now, she decided, which would please Felix, he had never supported her plan to live there.

But with the twins she knew that she would have to tread carefully, she did not want to be seen as an interfering old busybody, dispensing charity. Largesse was an unattractive word. Her help would be discreet, as she hoped would be the behaviour of the twins, though the changes could not be hidden. All that remained was to tell Felix and Patricia.

*

'Pregnant! Marthe was astonished, 'Felix! This is so unexpected! She was serving soup in the kitchen, her ladle stopped in mid air.

'It is unexpected, yes. Felix said, 'And unplanned. He still felt uncomfortable with the word, it had such overtones and his awkwardness was evident.

'Are you thrilled? And before he could answer, 'How's Annie?

That was a difficult question and Felix replied carefully, he was still very uncertain, her moods changed all the time.

He had seen her for lunch the previous day. He had chosen their favourite restaurant in the Place du Capitol. It was Noon. He was overwhelmingly excited as he watched the tables slowly filling up, as menus were put before the customers, and bottles of wine and water appeared. He ordered a half bottle of white wine, and immediately regretted it, as he saw Annie weaving her way across the square, she was wearing a red coat and matching beret, her hands thrust into her pockets. He rose smiling and they kissed almost formally. He poured the water and Annie glanced at the menu, she knew it well. They began to talk. Felix was determined to take the initiative 'Everything has changed, we both know that. You understand how completely happy I am about the baby, he paused, thinking how often he repeated that word in his head, 'baby, baby', he looked at Annie, she sipped her water, her face impassive. Sighing inwardly, Felix kept going, 'I want to look after you more than ever now, to move you in to the house, where there's so much space, for you and Charlie. She sat listening, 'How does Charlie feel about this? Is he pleased?

'I haven't told him yet, her voice was flat. Felix was surprised, but didn't comment. It was Annie's decision after all. 'Please Annie, we should live together again, don't you think? Surely you can see that in makes…sense. He was about to say that he loved her, but the stubborn set of her mouth deterred him. He stopped.

Annie had expected this and had her answer ready. 'I know it makes 'sense,' you have all the space, and I don't. But the apartment is my home and I love it. It's what I've worked for since moving here, I own it. It's the first home that I've ever owned, and that's hugely important for me. It gives me stability and security and Charlie too. I can't just give it up! She was almost crying and Felix took her hand, 'Keep hold of it then. Let it, and move your furniture into store or in with me.

'It's not that simple, she said softly. 'I lose something if I live in your house. I shall feel dependent and sort of, grateful.

'Is that so awful? We are going to be more dependent on each other anyway. As I understand it babies are a joint effort! Annie smiled at that, 'I would feel like a sort of bargain had been struck, she said, 'I get to live in your house and you get to be a father. That's what people will think.

This made Felix angry, but he was stopped from replying hastily, as the waiter busied about them, putting bowls of soup and a basket of bread on the table. Annie picked up some bread, she was always hungry at the moment, and tore off a chunk.

'That's not quite fair, Annie. And who cares what people think. We wouldn't be doing anything more than all parents do, live under the same roof. Care for each other. I love you Annie, and I'm just asking you to let me love you and Charlie and…

Annie took his hand now, she knew that she had been talking selfishly, and she had relented as he spoke. 'I need a little time, she said, 'It's all happened so unexpectedly, I'm living in a whirl. Allow me some time please. Looking at him across the table she said, 'I love you too, I know that now, I really do, but I can't… move yet. I need to tell Charlie, and how he'll take the news, I have no idea! He's going to have to make big adjustments too, leaving his home and moving into your house. And it's all happened to him once before, moving and adjusting to a new situation. Her hand was trembling as she spoke. Felix leaned across and wiped away some soup that had dribbled down her chin, 'I can wait, he said, 'But surely sooner is better than later, I want you, us, settled, before the baby arrives. Do you know when that will be?

'In September I'll stop work in early August. Just when a really interesting project comes up, with Claude, equally unexpected! He glanced at her, she was smiling ruefully. For the rest of lunch Felix listened as she told him of her new project at the chateau. They separated in the square with a kiss, the first for many weeks, and Annie promised to tell Charlie their news. She felt better, believing that Felix better understood her reservations about moving into his house, and relieved to find that her feelings for him were still so strong.

*

So Marthe's question at lunch the following day was not easily answered. She listened as Felix gave her a brief summary, and said, 'Give her time! She's in shock, and sees her life being transformed. I know Annie, she's very strong willed and independent, and loves her work, which now has to be put on one side. Don't put pressure on her, she will accept what has happened...I really believe that she loves you. I expect that she is feeling tired too, the early months are like that. Give her some support, ease her load; invite her and Charlie for supper, drop by her apartment, offer to take Charlie out for the day, she'll appreciate that, and you haven't seen him for ages have you? Spend more time with her, your house is perfect for a family, she knows that, she'll come round. Be patient with her.

*

After Felix had left, a delighted and happy Marthe organized a bouquet of spring flowers to be delivered to Annie's apartment the following day, and then phoned Patricia with her news. She opened a half bottle of champagne, celebrating her, as yet unborn, grand child. She realised later that day that in the excitement of the baby, she had forgotten to tell Felix all about her agreement with the twns.

*

The presence of Marthe's bouquet at the apartment door as he returned from school surprised Charlie. Annie was driving home from the Chateau, so Charlie put the flowers in the sink, remembering at the last moment to add cold water. There was a label attached, Congratulations, he read, with love from Marthe. He didn't understand why Marthe should be saying that, and quickly forgot the flowers as he settled into making a sandwich, turning on his music and getting his school work out of his bag.

He glanced up at his mother came in carrying two bags of shopping. She crossed to the fridge and stopped, 'Where did they come from?

'They're from Marthe! Annie felt her heart miss a beat, 'She's heard about my new job, she lied. No more was said, but lying to her son was something that Annie had never done before. It took away the pleasure of the flowers. And she could not understand her reluctance to tell Charlie her news.

The next day was Saturday and Charlie's music filled the apartment, resounding into every corner, or so it felt to Annie who was struggling with plant lists at the kitchen table. Music was Charlie's new interest, fostered by friends at school, it caused tension between them. Annie was musical herself, she sung in a choir and enjoyed what she called 'good' music. It was an interest that she shared with Felix, they had met after a concert in St.Sernin, and she had loved listening to him playing the piano in his apartment. They had gone to concerts together and she had learnt a great deal from him. But Charlie's music was altogether different; it was loud and discordant and she struggled to find a tune. She had repeatedly refused his request for a drum set, but Charlie had inherited her stubbornness and persisted for many weeks. He gave up finally, but playing his music endlessly was, she felt, a way of punishing her. It was all more than tedious.

Annie continued trying to work. Her design for Claude had met with unquestioned approval, though he had added a rose bed under the dining room windows, and box hedging beside the steps leading from the terrace to the lawn. The rose bed had been Angelique's idea, he said, she was obviously very much involved, Annie realised.

The morning passed. Charlie came in and asked what they were doing in the afternoon, it was a warm day and he wanted to go out. She looked up, 'Are you ok? He asked, 'You look...

'Just tired, she said and was on the point of telling him her news, when the door bell rang. It was Felix. 'Come up, we're here, Charlie said and pressed the bell which opened the door. He walked in, wearing a dark sweater that Annie hadn't seen before. He looks good, she thought. 'Do you feel like a trip? Felix asked Charlie. 'I'm going to Albi, to collect some music. We could look around, if you like, grab a burger. Charlie did not need to think twice, 'I'll get my jacket, he said, going to his room. 'Turn the music off, please, Felix said, calling after him, 'Your mum's trying to work. He smiled at Annie, she looks exhausted he thought. 'You ok? You're a bit pale. 'That's what Charlie just said, she stood up and kissed him. He smells nice, she thought. Annie grimaced, 'Do I look that bad?

'No, not at all. I always like the way you look. Have a rest, go on, we'll be out all afternoon. Have you told him? She shook her head, 'It never feels the right moment, sorry. Felix was disappointed, 'I will, I will! She said apologetically, 'Have a nice trip, it's kind. Oh, and please play some decent music in the car. He listens to this awful stuff all day! They left and Annie heard them chattering on the stairs, she was relieved to get rid of Charlie, and went straight to bed and slept for an hour. As she ate some soup with a ham salad and a hunk of yesterday's bread, she thought about Felix, and how pleased she had been to see him in the apartment, looking nice as always, though his hair needed cutting.

*

Charlie loved riding in Felix's car, it was red, fast and flashy. He hoped a school friend would see him as Felix weaved his way through the lunch time traffic. A pretty girl, waiting to cross at the lights near the market, recognised the car and bent down to wave. She was wearing a low cut blouse and Charlie turned away, embarrassed; Felix kept looking at the road ahead, he had seen that it was Delphine, the agent. She stared after the car and then with a toss of her head crossed the road. Charlie said nothing. As they set off down the autoroute, Felix said, 'Some music I think! He inserted a cassette, 'A bit of opera to sing along to. Charlie did not respond. Do you like Mozart? Your mum does, she sang his Requiem last Christmas in the Cathedral. He inserted the first track of Don Giovanni and began humming as the overture reached its climax.

'I was in England with Dad. Charlie replied, he was looking out of the window, the flat landscape was passing by very fast, he sneaked a look at the speedometer, the needle read 140, which was really fast he knew. They cruised up the motorway, overtaking every other vehicle, and Charlie found himself humming too, Felix drove with one hand on the wheel, keeping time with the other. 'I don't listen to music like this much, Charlie said.

'Well, that's ok, but keep an open mind, just because music is old doesn't mean that you won't enjoy it. Felix changed the cassette, 'Let's try some jazz now. This is Duke Ellington. Charlie sat back in his seat, he was low to the ground, it really didn't feel like going out with mum at all. Charlie liked the jazz and they talked about jazz for the rest of the journey. Felix thought he had made some slight headway on the music front.

They returned to Toulouse in the early evening, it had been a successful day; Felix had bought him steak and chips for lunch, and they had talked about chess and music and going fishing the previous summer. Conversations that had been a regular part of Charlie's life before Felix moved out of the apartment. A haphazard exploration of the old streets followed lunch, ending in a visit to the music shop, where Charlie found a CD of Duke Ellington, which he bought. Afterwards they went into the Cathedral, it was cold and dark, Charlie said he was interested in architecture, they studied it at school, and he walked slowly up and down the aisles. He picked up the information booklet, reading it as he went. Felix was impressed, he realised that he had underestimated the boy.

*

Annie was dozing on the sofa as they entered, Charlie crept across to the sink and poured a glass of water, offering one to Felix. They sat quietly sipping at the table. Felix did not know whether to leave, but decided to see if there was any wine in the fridge, it was nearly seven in the evening and it had been a long day. Annie woke up with a start, 'Hi mum, we're back. Felix is having a glass of wine do you want one? To Annie it felt like their life during the previous year as Felix and Charlie joined her on the sofa, a bit of a squash, but nice. Felix was thinking the same thing, and he caught her eye and smiled, 'No wine for your mum now, he said.

Annie knew the moment had come, 'I'm having a baby, she corrected herself quickly, 'Felix and I are having a baby.

In September. Felix reached along the back of the sofa and stroked her hair, as she said, 'We hope you'll be as pleased as we are. How awkward she sounded!

Charlie jumped off the sofa and stood up looking at them both. 'What? A baby? Is it a girl or boy? That seemed his main concern, but he added, 'Where will it sleep? A question he followed up with the statement, 'Definitely not in my room. Unless it's a boy. He walked about the room, glancing at Annie on the sofa, he was trying to be grown up, as he absorbed the news. She pulled herself up and went to hug him.

'So are you, Charlie spoke carefully it was a word he had never used before, 'Pregnant? I do hope it's a boy, then I can show him stuff. When will you know?

'Soon, in a month or so. Charlie asked, 'How? How will you know? Annie explained about a scan, how that gave a picture of the baby, he listened earnestly. 'Wow! I think this is great! He sat down again and Annie did too.

Felix just sat grinning, relieved and happy.

'Now tell me about your day. She said, 'Did you have fun? Felix had moved towards the fridge, he wanted some more wine, and she called out, 'There's a lasagne in the oven, it'll be ready in half an hour. We can have it for supper. I made plenty for three.

The evening passed and Felix prepared to leave, Charlie had gone to bed. 'That went well, he didn't seem at all upset, he said. 'Extraordinary, how children just accept changes. 'He doesn't know what's coming, that's why. Annie laughed, 'And nor do you!

'Yes I know! And I can't wait! He opened the door and Annie said, 'Perhaps bring your toothbrush next visit? He kissed her for a long time and ran down the stairs. Annie tidied up after he had gone, and saw his scarf on the sofa, she picked it up. It smelt of him and she held it to her nose. And made a decision. There and then. She and Charlie would move in with Felix, the apartment could be let and Annie would see how things went once the baby arrived. She would tell Felix the next day. And her mother.

CHAPTER 15

Marthe was back at the Moulin and the twins signed their agreements sitting at the kitchen table. 'Read it through carefully, she warned, 'Oh and I need your bank details, she said. They stared at her, 'You have bank accounts don't you? Gregoire glanced at his sister, and shook his head, 'No.

'How do you manage?

'Grandfather does the money, he gives us what we need.

Marthe knew that she had to tread carefully. After an awkward discussion, they finally settled on a plan; each twin would have their own account, handling their own money separately, and Marthe would avoid any complications with their grandfather.

'You must set these accounts up as soon as you can. Go and see the bank in St Girou, go together. It's in the square, next to the pharmacie. Then post me your bank details.

She prepared to leave, the awful smell no longer lingered near her car, and she said to Agathe who accompanied her, 'What has happened to the ducks?

'I sold them! They were ready anyway. I won't get any more now. We are going to clean out the barn, when Gregoire has time. He's delighted he can use the barn for storing his stuff. I can't do it, both the Maison and the ducks. What name shall I use at the bank?

'Whatever do you mean? Your own name of course. Marthe was surprised and abrupt.

'I ask, because, Gregoire and I use Grandfather's name, our mother's name, it was easier at school. Gautier.

'So, use that. Marthe was climbing into her car.

'But, my actual name is my father's. Rinaldi.

A shock so powerful, that Marthe clutched the car door passed through her. 'Rinaldi?

'Yes, my father is Michel Rinaldi. Agathe saw that Marthe had gone pale, 'Do you know him then?

Marthe carefully took her place in the seat of her car, 'No, I just know the name. Use that name as it's really yours please, and tell Gregoire the same. Let me know when you have set up the accounts. She smiled at Agathe, who had been startled to see Marthe go pale, without any explanation. Marthe left hurriedly, her heart was pounding unpleasantly and she struggled to breathe slowly.

*

Back at Les Palmes, she sat at her desk, searching in the top drawer for the letter from Jean Jacques Rinaldi. She had received it the previous year. It had given her an account of the death of her father, Bertrand, in August 1944 and the part played in it by members of the Rinaldi family. Her father was walking along the tow path in the early afternoon, the letter said, a walk that he took daily with his little dog. Two of Jean Jacques older brothers, Andre and Pierre were waiting for him; they wanted some sort of vengeance for what they believed had been Bertrand's part in the disappearance and subsequent death of their eldest brother Jean at the hands of the Nazis. (Such 'disappearances' had become increasingly common in 1944 as the Germans steadily lost control of South West France and used every method possible to intimidate the population.) The brothers believed that Bertrand had betrayed Jean, a man known for his active support of the Resistance.

The encounter on the tow path quickly became an ugly confrontation and a struggle occurred, two strong young men against a man in his forties. Bertrand was abused and struck and pushed violently, he slipped, lost his footing and fell into the river flowing fast towards St. Girou. As he was carried down stream neither brother moved to save him. His body was subsequently recovered, trapped by the stout pillars of the dam at the weir outside the town. He was dead, drowned with nasty wounds to his head.

The receipt of this letter had caused Marthe great distress. She had no memory of her father but to learn the details of his death was deeply sad. What a terrible coincidence if the twins and their father were part of that same Rinaldi family, who, according to the letter had been directly responsible for the death of Bertrand. It was nearly 60 years ago, and it seemed unlikely that, even if they were related, that the twins would know anything about the event. An event of which the Rinaldi family would surely not have been proud, and would have endeavoured to keep secret. Searching carefully she found the letter, carefully folded in a drawer, but not the envelope, and the letter itself had no address. 'Surely I didn't throw it away? She cursed herself, 'How could I have been so careless? She phoned Felix, he had read the letter, had he kept the envelope?

*

Felix was at home planning the arrival of Annie and Charlie, they were moving in to the house at the weekend. Marthe dispensed with the usual formalities and asked about the envelope, Felix said that he thought he had it. 'I remember seeing it when I turned out the apartment, it's probably still in one of the boxes in the cellar. I wouldn't have thrown it away. Do you want it? Why? Marthe explained. They had avoided talking much about Marthe's plans for the twins, which he did not support as he feared that it was an impetuous venture, which would probably go wrong. And Marthe was keen to keep him out of her new interest, fearing his opposition and disapproval. This new complication was not good news for Marthe. At all. He listened as patiently as he could, 'Are you sure you want to do this? It's raking up the past, again, and they may not be the same family anyway.

Marthe was not to be dissuaded, 'I'll track down their father, his name is Michel, he must know, if he's related to the letter writer Jean Jacques, she insisted. Michel may know something.

Felix sighed and changed the subject, a moment of guilt passed through him as he had also kept something from his mother. The diaries of Bertrand, which he was reading when time permitted. He changed the subject quickly. 'You were right about Annie! It was a question of time. She and Charlie are moving in on Saturday, join us for lunch next week end can you? We should have settled in by then. Also I've got some news for you, I'll tell you more then. And don't be disappointed if you get no further with your Rinaldi search, there's probably many families with that name in the Gers.

They rang off and Felix returned to sorting out the room that was to be Charlie's, it was full of music scores and magazines and newspaper articles. Charlie would live on the top floor, a room at the back, it was twice the size of his room in the apartment. It was also two floors away from the kitchen and Annie's future study. He could play his music more freely was Felix's plan.

Felix hoped that his mother's search would be fruitless. But on the other hand he was researching too; reading the diaries and registers of Bertrand which he had found in the coffer. It was hypocritical of him to spurn Marthe's quest for information about the past when he was studying that material on the life of Bertrand.

Meanwhile he needed to go down to the cellar and find the envelope, it was there somewhere he knew.

CHAPTER 16

After delaying as long as she could Annie told Ralph about the baby and her decision to move in with Felix. It would affect their financial relationship, she couldn't expect him to contribute on a monthly basis any more. Or less anyway.

'Really? Congratulations! That's great news! His voice was full of enthusiasm, Ralph liked babies and children.

'Felix must be dead chuffed, he continued, 'When's the baby due? Are you ok? No sickness? He remembered Annie's first pregnancy, she had never looked more healthy or lovely. Annie relaxed, she should have known that Ralph would be excited, and replied, 'September and thanks, I'm fine. Just filling out now, around the middle. They chatted about Charlie and the move into the house, it was an easier conversation than some in the past.

Ralph immediately told Edna, 'I wonder how Charlie will take it, she said, 'a little brother or sister. There's a huge age gap isn't there. That's never easy.

'It won't make much difference to him.

'Oh? She smiled at him, 'His mother permanently occupied with someone else! Not available for him twenty four hours a day. He'll notice a difference all right!

Ralph looked at her in surprise. he had loved the early months with Charlie; the milky smell as he held him on his shoulder, his incredibly soft skin, the funny noises as he slept, the clutter that surrounded them in the cottage had never worried him at all. He surreptitiously looked at Edna, how old was she? He wasn't sure, maybe forty? Was that too old? Ralph felt quite unsettled.

*

Boyed up by Ralph's response, Annie, and almost for the first time, began to look forward to the baby. Her mother was as enthusiastic as Ralph. They talked the day before Annie's move in to the house, and Claire put aside all Annie's fears about losing work, and possibly her career. 'Don't be silly darling, she said, 'Enjoy not working! Enjoy the pregnancy! Put your feet up in the afternoons. Claire had stopped working as soon as her first baby was on the way and had never gone back. She had devoted her life to her husband and her two daughters. Once her two daughters were in school and taking up less of her time, Claire had developed new interests, tennis and bridge and spending a morning a week in the Oxfam shop, but nothing stood in the way of putting a hot meal in front of her husband and girls at seven o'clock. Annie listened patiently to Claire's advice and smiled to herself, she had no intention of giving up her career, though she had not worked out how she would achieve this. They chatted for a long time and Annie felt better about the pregnancy and the move into Felix's house and, just as importantly, her new job at the Chateau.

*

The inside work at the Chateau was being driven along as fast as was possible, and the results were more evident every day. Whilst Claude's goal to start taking guests in July was the most daunting part of the challenge that faced Annie. She had taken on a local man, Paul, to do the heavy work; digging out the new beds and clearing and widening the terrace. He had a son who quickly joined him and together they prepared the kitchen garden and a small herb garden. The mason provided one of his men to work on the new steps down to the lawn and slowly the garden began to take shape. Annie concentrated on the rose beds, and planting the area inside the walls that surrounded the swimming pool. The soil that was excavated there she used to level out the end of the lawn, where a wind break of hornbeams was planted. She was working four days a week, it was tiring but she loved it; with Claude's support she had created on the East side a Mediterranean garden, a passion of hers, and the future she believed for gardens in the dry climate of the Gers. The weather was growing warmer almost by the day and the activity in the garden regularly drew Claude and his sons out to observe the changes.

*

'Aren't you a bit hot? Claude asked one morning. Annie was in shorts, a baggy pink tshirt and a wide cotton hat, her face was very pink. He startled her and she stopped her digging and looked up. 'Now you're here can we go and see what's happening in the herb garden? She asked. They walked over together, and Claude observed that Annie had left unfastened the top button of her shorts. 'I think we should add a brick path here, she pointed, 'to run through the bed, it would make it easier to cut the herbs and also if your guests want to wander. People love herb gardens, the scent with the sun on it is gorgeous and it has such a Mediterranean feel. They stood looking at the area and Claude agreed with her idea. 'It'll be a little expensive but it'll look smart and be entirely practical. She turned to Claude, 'You were there last year weren't you, with Marthe? In the Mediterranean. She immediately regretted it and blushed even pinker. Claude nodded, 'Yes. He was not put out by the memory, but it was still a little awkward. They began to discuss other matters and the incident was put aside. Annie returned to her work. Strolling back to the terrace, Claude thought of Marthe, he had loved her and he still missed her, though less acutely.

Time the healer, he thought to himself. His thoughts were interrupted by Luc, wearing his cook's apron now stained from preparing lunch, 'All well? he asked.

'Yes, Claude replied, 'Annie seems to think you'll have lots of vegetables and herbs for the kitchen! He cuffed Luc lightly, 'And I heard this morning that the chef we wanted has agreed to start a week before we open. Apparently he needs a week to prepare.

'I can't believe this is all happening! Luc said. It's all so fast! So much done!

'If you throw enough money at a project, you can achieve a great deal, Claude said, 'And we have worked very hard you and me and Jerome.

'And Angelique. Luc added.

'I've not forgotten her. Claude said. They went inside, it was cool and dark after the bright sunshine, Luc returned to the kitchen to prepare lunch, and Claude walked to the small office that had been created beyond the hall. There were several unopened letters, invoices mainly, awaiting his attention, sighing he opened them. Angelique had been great fun for all of them, and she had worked hard in almost every area of the renovation. But she was not a 'stayer, and now that Spring had arrived she planned to return to Bordeaux and open up her business in time for the return of the tourists. She had enjoyed her time at the Chateau, both the work and getting to know Jerome and Luc. Claude was deeply grateful, but her role was over and he understood that she wanted to return to her independent life. He would miss her in many ways, but it would not break his heart to see her leave. They would remain good friends and meet in Bordeaux from time to time. He decided to take her into Toulouse for a farewell dinner, before she left at the weekend.

*

Annie was pleased with the way work was progressing. Claude was an ideal employer, he gave her a free hand and did not interfere. In that regard he was similar to Marthe and she wondered again why the two of them had split up, it had happened over the Christmas holiday she was sure. 'Was it Marthe? Had Claude tried to push her in a direction that she didn't want to go? Perhaps asked her to move in with him? His position was very different now with the Chateau and all his lands and farms, but that wouldn't interest Marthe. Perhaps Marthe enjoyed her freedom too much. She had been married happily for many years, was now her time for a tilt at independence? And why had she rented the apartment in Collioure, was she not happy at Les Palmes? Annie thought of all her work designing and creating the garden there, it would be a blow to her if Marthe now moved away. And how would Felix feel about that? She thought about Claude again, he was such a charming and vigorous man, surely he was a good match for Marthe. She could not fathom it at all.

She thought about her own life as she drove home, her new home. So far everything was running smoothly; Charlie loved his room on the top floor, he pounded up the stairs as soon as he got back from school, throwing his jacket on the kitchen table and grabbing whatever snack was to hand. Felix had set regular times when Charlie could play the drum kit that they had agreed she could buy, a deal that satisfied them both. Really she thought he had taken the move in his stride and was noticeably more cheerful than he had been after Christmas and his thoughts about moving back to live with Ralph seemed to have faded. Her shorts felt uncomfortably tight as she walked in to the kitchen, she would need new ones soon, 'Pregnancy' she sighed. Felix was coming with her for a scan the following week, then they would have a more accurate date. An unexpected surge of excitement swept through her, 'Was it a girl of boy? She would soon find out. She walked in with a smile, the kitchen was silent, the chess board was set up on the table and Felix and Charlie were bent over it. 'I'll make my own tea then, she said. Neither of them looked up.

*

On Sunday Marthe came for lunch, it was her second visit and she was more than curious to see how Annie had settled in. This time the house felt different; there were boots lying untidily in the hall as she came in and an anorak had been left on the floor, climbing the stairs a welcoming smell of roast pork with something sweet, apple perhaps, filled the air. She walked in. Annie, in a red dress, was writing in a small book, with her feet up on the sofa under the window, Felix was leaning over the stove, stirring a pan, and humming to himself. It was warm a little steamy. She took off her jacket and handed some flowers to Annie. 'From the garden! Felix gave her a kiss and returned to the stove.

'How is it? The garden? Annie said as she got up to find a vase, 'I must come and have a look. They talked about the garden as Marthe sipped some white wine and Annie arranged her flowers. The atmosphere between them was very different from their last time together, the awkwardness had vanished. It was a typical family day and Marthe silently rejoiced as she watched Annie arranging her flowers. 'That's a pretty dress! Red suits you, I can't wear the colour at all, it makes me disappear! Marthe said. Annie smiled, 'Felix chose it, he's much better at clothes than me. He would buy me something every day if I let him!

'Lucky you, his father was the same. The memory sent a pang through her and she was glad to be distracted by Charlie, clattering down the stairs, 'Hello, he said, 'Are you here for lunch? Felix is doing it today! He joined her at the table, until Annie asked him to set it for lunch, which he did whilst chatting. All the knives and forks were put back to front and Marthe quietly corrected them.

After lunch, Felix left the two women to talk in the salon and went up to his music room, and Charlie set off for a chess match. Marthe looked about her with interest, it felt much less formal; there were two tall plants on either side of the fireplace, which softened the room and a soft blanket was spread over the sofa, to protect it, Marthe thought from Annie's habit of sitting with her feet off the ground. The Alpine landscape which Felix had bought with Claude hung over the mantel which now had a variety of glass vases, in various colours and sizes, placed on it. There were colourful cushions on several chairs whilst some lay on the floor. Annie had carried in Marthe's flowers arranged in a tall blue jug, placing them on a side table, sweeping away a scarf, which Marthe recognised. She had given it to Felix at Christmas.

'How are things? She asked.

'I'm well and still have lots of energy. But I do get tired and my waist is expanding! Felix watches me all the time at the moment, as though I'm ill or need to be careful. It's a bit wearing!

'Xavier was just like that! He would follow me about as though I was about to give birth. Felix will calm down, all this is very new for him. Annie sipped her tea, she realised how much she had missed Marthe in recent months, she had always found her easy to talk to, they were quite alike she realised.

'I think he likes having us here, Annie said, 'though we are all having to adjust; Charlie less noisy, me more tidy and Felix, well, it's what he wanted isn't it! Marthe smiled at Annie, 'He looks happy! He loves you, and that's all that matters.

Felix joined them, carrying some of the diaries. He explained where he had found them, and whose they had been and Marthe was immediately excited, 'Have you read them? What do they say? What years have you got there? Annie finished her tea and left them to talk, she wanted to check the work that she had been doing. She was planning the shrub roses for the Chateau garden, they needed to be scented, not tall and tolerant of a hot sunny position.

'I've found, Felix said, 'All the diaries that your father started in 1938 and continued during the war years. He was very methodical, most of them are a record of his daily life; his business outside Toulouse, the weather, his health, he was a regular walker, his wife of course. There are increasing references to the war, from the fall of Paris, to the division of France and the establishment of the Vichy government of which he disapproved. He supported the German invasion and subsequent occupation which... well it's obviously surprising. He seems to have admired the discipline of German society. He doesn't really explain why, but it's a diary, he was not revealing his thoughts to anyone. The last is that for 1944, which stops abruptly in August. The day he died.'

'Did he write anything that day?'

'Yes, look I have marked the last entry. He passed the diary to Marthe, who was surprised by its weight. She read the last entry slowly, once and then again. Felix watched her.

'Can I take them home?

'Yes, I think you should. I'll carry them down now. Your father was very meticulous, he never missed a day. But what with Annie and Charlie moving in, I've only glanced through most of them. There are some interesting revelations though. We may have to adjust our thinking about your father! There were also some work registers in the coffer, but I've not opened them. They're heavy, maybe leave them for the moment?

*

Marthe drove home, the diaries next to her, she glanced at them as she drove, wondering what revelations, if any, they contained.

*

At the Chateau life was buzzing. The army of workmen had finished most of the essential works and there was a huge clearing up process in full swing. The bedrooms awaited the last of the new furniture and there was a steady procession of men carrying in mattresses, headboards, lamps, tables, chest of drawers, frequently colliding on the stairs, as they manoeuvred their way up and down. Claude was ordered by Jerome to keep well away. A cleaning team, hired from Auch, accompanied all this, a cheery group of women whose chatter filled the whole chateau, they left a strong smell of pine behind them. Claude, sighing, opened every window, but he was relieved and excited to see the hotel, as he now called it, ready to receive the first guests. There was a large sign now on the road at the gates, Chateau de Soulan, it said in large letters, Chambres, Tout Confort. Restaurant. Piscine. Parc. And in red, Ouvert. He loved returning from his many trips to see it and delighted when people he met said they had noticed it as they drove by.

Angelique had left. She and Claude enjoyed a delicious and expensive dinner in Toulouse and talked over their weeks together, it had been a busy happy time for them both, but they were content to go their separate ways. The family turned out to wave her goodbye; Luc had made her some lunch to eat on her way home and gave her a cookery book, written by a friend. Jerome gave her a book on furniture. Now they were on their own and Claude, as he waved her away, felt a sense of relief. Finally it was just him and his two sons and the hotel.

Jerome left later that day for Auch, he had decided to sell the book shop and had found a buyer, a couple from Toulouse. He would sign the agreement before the end of the month. He was thirty in the autumn, still uncertain as to what he really wanted from life, but for the moment he would concentrate on helping Claude establishing the hotel.

Progress continued outside, where Annie, her assistant Paul, and his son were transforming the garden; the herb and vegetable plots were planted, the terrace, now much wider, had a border of pink roses which were in flower, their scent drifting in to the rooms above, just as Angelique had foreseen. Wide brick steps led from the terrace to the lawn, where benches and chairs had been placed for guests to enjoy the view. The hornbeam trees now in leaf were already providing a wind break. The swimming pool had been filled and a bed of lavender was in flower beside the surrounding brick walls. Large pots stood at the entrance to the hotel, bright, clashing scarlet and cerise geraniums, these pots had come from his own restoration yard, several were cracked and had been positioned carefully as Annie had noticed when she planted them out.

Claude walked around with Annie one morning, it was late June, already hot, 'What next? He asked. 'Keep going, much as we are, she replied, 'I'm disappointed with the terrace, I should have spread more gravel, and this grey colour isn't brilliant. She scuffed it up with her boot, 'See? It'll be fine as long as we don't have too much rain, otherwise it'll go muddy. It can stay till the autumn, then we can put down a better soft pinky colour. I used it at Marthe's on all the paths. Claude nodded, remembering. 'And you? When will you stop?

Annie eyed him, 'July. That's what I've promised Felix, though I will try and stretch it a little! Paul will be fine, he knows the garden and has good ideas and I can pop over if there's a real problem. But he'll need a full time assistant, best if he looks for someone right away. Unfortunately his son is ready to move on.

'Is Paul happy with that?

Annie grinned, 'He certainly is! Though he's sorry to loose his son but this is a dream job for him.

Claude returned indoors, he had decided to phone Marthe. It was an impulsive decision as they had not spoken since January. He was delighted to hear her voice and pleased when she said that she would love to visit the chateau. It was agreed that she would come to lunch at the end of the week.

*

Marthe was happy to have a distraction, having become engrossed in reading her father's diaries. He was a meticulous man, as Felix had said, writing, in a neat hand, and without fail, a record of his days. Much of the content was mundane; the weather faithfully described, the state of his health, he suffered from repeated colds and fevers, the exercise he took, at least one brisk walk a day. He wrote about his brick business in Toulouse, a thriving establishment that he had inherited from his father, and the books he was reading, history and biography and philosophy. There were occasional references to social engagements, events attended with his young wife, dinners with friends and visits to the opera in Toulouse. In the spring of 1939 he and Marie travelled to the Pyrenees on an energetic walking tour. It was to be their last holiday together as the war intervened.

Bertrand was evidently a serious and conscientious man, but he wrote little of his emotions or fears or worries. In the early entries for 1939 there were increasing references to international events: German rearmament, Hitler's rise to power backed by his supporters, the Nazis. Bertrand became steadily infected with the beliefs of Hitler, whose vision of a strong Germany, a state that upheld traditional values and strict morality, a state that encouraged and supported family values, echoed his own beliefs. Bertrand approved of order, discipline and a strong state, and like many French, he disapproved of the central government in Paris, believing it corrupt and weak. Bertrand expressed his dislike of the morals and hedonistic behaviour of French society; American music, 'modern' art, night clubs where women smoked and drank and danced, he deplored their cropped hair and short dresses, some wearing trousers in the cafes and bars of Toulouse. He hated and feared Communism, believing it a threat to France's economy, and banned any trade unionist from working in his factories. So he had no sympathy for the Spanish Communist refugees who sought refuge in France, fleeing over the Pyrenees, as they sought shelter from Franco and Fascism. As war became more imminent Bertrand was on the side of Hitler.

Though Marthe had known for some time that her father had supported the German occupation and was regarded as a sympathizer, nonetheless the diaries of 1939 were shocking, and difficult to read. These references to Hitler and Nazism sickened her. She felt ashamed. She worried about Felix, 'How would he feel? How far had he read into the diaries?

After the matter of Henri Carrere had concluded the previous year, Felix had been very clear that Marthe should put her father's role in the war behind her. Henri had run a vendetta against Marthe based on her father's support for the German occupation. Henri blamed Bertrand for betraying local men one of whom was his father. Five local men had 'disappeared' in the Spring of 1944 and, as it was subsequently learnt, taken to the German camp outside Paris, a holding place for hundreds of arrested men, some were members of the Resistance but there were also Jews and Gypsies and Communists. They were transported East for forced labour in the mines or inclusion into the German army that was suffering heavy losses on the Eastern front. These five had never reached their destinations, dying of suffocation in overheated cattle trucks outside Strasbourg. After the war they were commemorated with a plaque placed on the brick wall outside a local church. It was part of the history of the area and the name Rinaldi also appeared on the plaque.

*

Marthe had tried to put the knowledge of these events behind her: she found an escape in Collioure where her family were not known. She was running away she now saw; running from the house that was Bertrand's home, the garden where, following his death, her mother had burnt as many files and records as she could find, all the evidence of his life and opinions.

But running away was not a solution. Marthe had returned, the Collioure plan abandoned, and was now, without fully understanding herself, setting a new path: assisting the twins. The irony of the possible connection between the two Rinaldi brothers struggling with Bertrand beside the river and the subsequent death of the eldest Rinaldi, (one of the five) on the train at Strasbourg, and the young Rinaldi twins saving her life as she lay beside that same river...who would have foreseen that? If there was a connection that is. But it seemed likely: Rinaldi was not a common name in the Gers, the family had come from Northern Italy after the first world war, looking for land and settled there.

*

Marthe put the diary for 1939 carefully in the salon and decided to try and find the father of Gregoire and Agathe. He was a Rinaldi and might know something of the family history. Wishing to avoid asking either of the twins for his address, she drove into Toulouse, heading for the Poste. The man at the counter was more helpful than she had expected. He disappeared into a room at the back and returned after some time with a piece of paper, there were three Rinaldi families in the Toulouse area and one lived in the centre. His name was Michel, she wrote down the address, there was no phone number. It was a part of Toulouse that she knew vaguely, off the bypass, near the airport where there were tall apartment buildings dating from the eighties. Made of white concrete they jarred unhappily with the brick built city and were universally disliked. It was a poor district. After several attempts she located the address and parked. Young people were milling about on bikes, they watched her as she locked the car carefully and gave the children a glance as a football suddenly came close. Trying to ignore them she stepped over the ball and holding her hand bag firmly approached the entrance. There was a lift inside the dingy hallway but it smelt and she took the stairs, climbing up three flights. The stairwell was dirty and there was rubbish in the corners. She stopped outside the apartment, she could hear a baby crying and rang the bell.

The door was slowly opened by a young woman; she was North African and very tall, wearing a loose orange robe and a scarf over her head. She stared at Marthe. It was a difficult moment and Marthe quickly asked for M. Michel Rinaldi. The woman nodded but shook her head. He wasn't home she said. The baby cried more loudly and she was about to shut the door. 'Has he a phone? Marthe quickly asked. The mother turned and vanished back into the apartment, returning with a scrap of paper, and gave it to Marthe. 'Here she said. Her voice was low and husky. She shut the door.

Outside, the young people were grouped close to her car, she walked up and they moved slowly away, watching her, and continued to stare after the car as she drove off. In her anxiety Marthe took a wrong turn and found herself in a large estate of concrete towers, and tried not to panic. She found her way out with difficulty, passing groups of men who were lounging against the walls of the buildings, smoking they too stared at her. It was a stressful visit, but Marthe had the contact number in her handbag. She would phone in the evening.

*

He answered after a long time. Marthe explained who she was, someone who knew the twins and her interest in meeting him, their father. He knew her name, he said, Agathe had spoken of her. He was courteous and soft spoken. With much persuasion, he consented to a meeting in Toulouse at a café off the Place St. Christophe, near where he worked, at six in the evening, the following day. Marthe wrote down the details and tried to understand her excitement. Was it meeting the father of the twins? Or meeting a man who might be able to give her information about the Rinaldi family and their connection with her father?

She was not sure which was more important to her.

CHAPTER 17

'A girl? Are you sure? Felix leant forward staring at the screen. How could the nurse tell? The screen showed a tumble of lines and strange shapes in grey and white, with nothing very clear at all. He glanced at Annie who was transfixed, she asked, 'Is everything ok? The baby?

They left in confusion; excitement, happiness and something else, there was a new bond and they held hands as they returned to Felix's car, Annie lowered herself in. 'This is the most impractical car for a pregnant lady, she said, 'As for fitting a baby in, well, that's going to be impossible! She smiled at Felix, who was driving around the turns of the underground car park at some speed, 'Oh we'll manage, and we've got the Volvo, he said slowing at the kiosk, 'though we might think about getting a new one for you. He patted her on the knee, 'A girl! I wasn't expecting that. You'll have to tell Charlie, he's got his heart set on a brother.

Annie had already thought about that. She told him later when he was eating a slice of his favourite cake, a treat, deliberately chosen to show him how much she loved him. 'Ooh chocolate! He tried not to eat too fast. 'It's a girl... the baby. Annie sat down next to him at the table and cut a slice for herself, 'Felix and I were at the hospital today, they scanned me and, yes, it's definitely a girl. Charlie licked the icing from his thumb, thinking. 'So, a sister! He said, 'Will she be like you? Annie laughed, 'Would that be so terrible?

'No, not really. As long as she likes climbing and running about and being outside. No...dolls!

Felix had come in, 'Oh I agree. No dolls or pink things. Charlie smiled at him reassured, he stood up,

'I've finished, thanks Mum. I'll go and play my drums for a while. 'Home work? Annie asked, she was picking up the chocolate crumbs and eating them. 'Later, he said as he went for the stairs. 'I'll be up in a while, Felix said as he stood up, 'But keep the noise down. Your mother and I need some quiet. Charlie ran up the stairs, stopping on the way at the room which they all now called the nursery. He opened the door and went in; the room was full of clutter, mostly his mother's, it was much smaller than his own room, which pleased him. He looked out of the window onto the courtyard below, his bike was propped up against a wall, he was getting too long in the legs for it, and he hoped for a new one, well new to him. He looked at the room, imagining it, with a baby in a cot and one of those mobile things suspended from the ceiling. He felt excited, it would be fun to have another person in the house, someone he could teach and play with. He would help too, babies needed a lot of help he knew, and that would be ok too. He would be the older brother. Charlie shut the door and went up to his room, feeling grown up and responsible. He would tell his friends at school, that he would be busy in the autumn.

*

Marthe was waiting in the café in Toulouse, she had arrived early and was becoming impatient, endlessly checking her watch, she watched the door and sipped her glass of white wine. A group of men in work clothes were at the bar, drinking beer and watching the large television. A football match was on, but the sound was turned low. She recognised him immediately as he entered, Michel had the same dark hair as his children, and a hesitant manner which mirrored Agathe. Marthe stood up and he came over looking at her carefully, they shook hands and began to talk. She ordered him a beer. As they talked, his shyness gradually wore off, but Marthe realised that he was a quiet, unassuming man, bemused by her generosity to his children. She tried to reassure him that she sought only to thank them for what they had done for her. He did not appear to understand much about her accident nor his children's role in assisting her, but nodded his head as she spoke. 'It's a gift, and one which I am pleased to give,' she explained. He lowered his eyes and took a mouthful of beer. She looked at him, his hair was greying at the sides and his jacket was faded. He's poor she thought. He shifted his feet on the floor, and said, 'I don't see much of them now. The old man and I, we never got on and I'm not welcome at the farm. We fell out after my wife died, and that was that. Agathe comes to see us, she likes the baby, but I haven't the money to help her or my son.' They sat silently, and a sadness hit Marthe then, she thought of her closeness with Felix, to lose that would be… unthinkable.

She changed the subject and cautiously asked him about Jean Jacques Rinaldi, the man who had written to her the previous year giving an account of the role that the two Rinaldi brothers, Pierre and Andre had played in the death of her father. The letter had shocked her deeply. The mention of Jean Jacques surprised him and he looked at her. Marthe was reluctant to explain fully, 'I think we have a friend in common and I would like to see how he is.' She lied. 'Where can I find him?' She asked with a smile.

'Last I heard he was living in Auch, in an apartment. I can find his address.

'He's your uncle, Marthe said as though it was a fact, something she knew. He nodded, 'My father's younger brother. 'Your father's name was? She asked smiling again, it was an invasive question. He didn't seem to mind or notice, 'Pierre. Pierre Rinaldi. It was a difficult moment for Marthe, Pierre the letter had told her had been one of the brothers on the towpath that afternoon in 1944 and here she was sitting and talking with his son. She felt shaky, slightly sick. After a while, their drinks finished, they both stood up, 'Thank you for what you're doing for my kids, he said in a low voice, 'They've not had it easy. He didn't say anymore, they left the café and he said goodbye. Marthe drove home thoughtfully, reflecting on what she had heard but also sad for Michel Rinaldi, whose life had not been happy. She hoped his new wife and baby would help him forget all that he had left behind at the Moulin. Still it had been a useful meeting, she was beginning to understand the connections within the Rinaldi family.

*

Three days later the address of Jean Jacques arrived in the post, there was no letter. Marthe set off for Auch. She loved the drive; undulating hills turning a soft green with early wheat, fields shining yellow with rape, and cream coloured cows grazing on even the steepest slopes. The farm houses positioned high on the ridges, were full of activity; washing billowed on the lines, as tractors, their huge wheels muddy with the red soil, moved relentlessly across the wide fields and ducks, fat and listless, sat in whatever shade they could find. There were fields with horses tossing their heads against flies and orchards some still with blossom. It was a peaceful journey, with little traffic and Marthe tried to anticipate what she would fine in Auch. The address was an apartment in a small block on the south side of the City. The cobbled streets here were narrow and old and renowned for their steepness, running as they did from the river Garonne up to the Cathedral which dominated Auch, standing proud on a promontory overlooking the river. Ten minutes later, having climbed many steps and asked two people for help, she found the apartment. She was tired, hot and flustered. She sat on a wall outside the block of flats and gathered herself, then rang the bell for Jean Jacques Rinaldi.

Marthe waited for some time before he opened the door looking at her suspiciously, he was quite bent and his hair was white and sparse. As he stood holding the handle, she saw that he was wearing a hearing aid. Marthe spoke loudly and he almost shrank back, 'Monsieur, I am Madame Le Brun, you wrote me a letter last year, she paused, 'about the death of my father, M. Bertrand du Pont.

He seemed to hear, but she wasn't sure, 'Do you remember? Writing to me? He nodded and gestured with his hand for her to enter and shuffled down the narrow corridor ahead of her, leading the way into a small overheated room, where he sat down on a worn upholstered chair. She glanced out of the only window and saw the outline of the Cathedral which towered above, its strong presence gave her a feeling of comfort. Marthe took a seat on the only other chair drawing it as near to him as she could, its seat was not very clean and she tried to tuck her coat under her. He watched her. He was in his late seventies she knew, and his skin was grey and flaky, but his eyes were bright. She introduced herself again and he gave a faint smile. They talked for some time about what he could remember, which was very little as his memory was hazy and she saw him nodding off to sleep. She stood up to leave, and he raised his hand, 'He was a respected man, your father, but his ideas were wrong. What Pierre and Andre did…that was a wicked thing. Within the family it was never spoken of, but we all knew and were ashamed. It hung over us all. There was a long pause and Marthe thought he had drifted off again, then he continued, 'It was war time, bad things happened. The Maquisards were fighting for France, to get rid of the Nazis and all the Rinaldi family were Maquisards. And we had lost our eldest brother…taken away, 'disappeared' to die in a cattle truck outside Strasbourg, far from his home and those who loved him. His hands were shaking as he shut his eyes and muttered to himself, Marthe could not catch his words. He spoke again, 'They're both dead now, Pierre and Andre… She waited for several minutes, but he was asleep. Marthe rose, glanced again at the Cathedral and left the hot room and the apartment, quietly closing the door.

It had been a difficult visit and she wondered if he would forget all about it when he woke. She hoped so; it had been selfish of her to try and learn more about the past. To disturb an old man and urge him to relive an unhappy time. Driving home she knew that she had acted unwisely. Felix would be angry with her too if he found out. Marthe resolved that she would not tell him of this visit, nor of her earlier meeting with Michel in the café in Toulouse. And not telling either Gregoire or Agathe of these visits to their family, she felt shabby, and remorseful. Why had she been so impetuous?

*

Annie and Charlie flew to England for the Whitsun holiday, it was the first time that she had been 'home' for over a year. Felix took them to the airport, he was eager for her to have one last holiday with her mother before the baby came. He told her to have a good rest and instructed Charlie to look after his mother on the journey. He watched them as they walked together towards the Security gate, Charlie pulling the suitcase and holding their passports. He was pleased that Annie was not travelling alone. Annie was to stay with Claire and Tony and Charlie with his father.

Annie, following Felix's instructions took advantage of Claire's kindness; she slept late into the morning and came down in her dressing gown for breakfast, cooked by Tony. He believed in starting the day well, so she was spoilt with bacon and a choice of eggs and hot buttered toast. The radio played in the background and Tony read out the clues for the crossword, as Claire tidied and talked on the phone and chivvied the dog. The day continued gently; after eating her way through Tony's breakfast and relaxing in a leisurely bath, enjoying Claire's generous choice of bath oils, she sat on the sofa with the morning paper, Arthur the dog by her side, snoring. She joined them for an afternoon walk and then it was tea time. The weather was fine but Annie noticed how much colder it was in Kent. 'I've grown soft! She thought to herself and worried that she had not included Charlie's warm fleece in her suitcase. Returning home, Tony lit the fire and then it was some television, supper and an early night.

Felix phoned every evening, 'Still eating three large meals a day? He asked, 'Nearly four, she replied, 'You forgot tea! We'll have to buy more clothes when I get back, I am growing by the day! He was glad she was being spoilt, 'I'm seeing Ralph tomorrow when I collect Charlie, it's the first time we've met since I left England, and that's seven years ago. I'm quite nervous.

'Don't be. There's no reason. Everything has been settled between you. You've both moved on. Annie nodded as he spoke and hoped his confidence was not misplaced.

They met at a pub for lunch, both feeling awkward, Charlie was at home with Edna. Watching Ralph as he ordered drinks at the bar, 'Just fizzy water for me please, Annie thought that Ralph looked well; he had put on some weight, he had always been very lean, his hair was well cut and his shirt had been ironed. She was pleased that he had finally found someone to care for him. They talked about Claire, Charlie and his school, and the pregnancy. But there was an undercurrent, an edgeiness, and Annie slowly realised that Ralph was preparing to ask her something. As the pudding was served he put down his spoon, and looked at her hard, his eyes focused and direct. He wanted his son back in England, he said, to live with him and Edna. 'Not just these holiday visits, I want to be a proper father, see him every day, bring him up. He's my son, it's only right.

Annie felt sick as immediately the friendly atmosphere changed. They began to argue and their meeting turned sour. Ralph took a strong line, he had been preparing what he wanted to say, he continued forcefully, 'The schools are good and local, and there is a new 6th form college later on, if he wants. We have plenty of room in the cottage. He would be part of the village, with boys of his own age and lots of stuff going on. Cricket in the summer and football in the winter, all on hand. There's cycling and swimming in the river. It's a perfect place for a growing lad...fresh air and safe. I want him to have that, it's what I had growing up. Annie listened, a hard knot of stubbornness came into her stomach, a feeling she knew well and could not control. She plunged in with her arguments: Charlie was settled in Toulouse, he had lots of friends and liked his school, he was doing well there. 'He can decide for himself once he's sixteen, she said, 'but for the moment he stays with me, that's what we agreed when we separated. Ralph became angry, disappointed at her quick rejection of a plan that he had been thinking about for several weeks.

'And Felix? Is he the new father figure?'

'Don't be ridiculous!

'My son is living in his house now, how do you think I feel about that? And you're having his child.

'You said that you were pleased about that. Why have you changed? I still have my apartment and my long term plans... well, they're not settled.

'Still happiest on your own then? I hope Felix understands what he is letting himself in for! You don't change do you Annie? Still putting yourself first! There was a long silence, Annie could not look at Ralph. She pushed her unfinished pudding away and said quietly, 'I didn't come here to argue and your words are very unkind. Charlie loves you and looks forward to staying with you. You are his father. As I say, he can decide, in a couple of years. Let's not argue, it's bad for both of us. They both stood up and Ralph paid at the bar, then they stood outside in the afternoon sunshine, it was a pleasant day. Annie put her hand on Ralph's arm, 'It's not about me or you, we need to think what's best for Charlie at the moment. To uproot him now would be a terrible mistake. He's happy in the house in Toulouse, he has a large room with space for his drum kit and we no longer live on top of each other, and he's looking forward to the baby and a new role as a brother. Ralph did not reply, he knew that he had lost the argument and regretted losing his temper. They parted with a nod.

*

Ralph was suffering from jealousy, he envied Felix; his large house, his easy life and now the prospect of becoming a father.

He was jealous of the relationship between Felix and Charlie, who were now seeing each other every day, enjoying jokes and mealtimes and music, having fun together. Whereas he saw him only for holidays, which was more like a treat than normal life. Ralph feared that Charlie was growing more attached to his life in Toulouse, and that the baby would make the Annie/Felix relationship more permanent. They would become a family, the four of them. Seven hundred miles away from him.

*

Annie collected Charlie, avoiding Edna who was hanging out some washing in the garden. It was rude not say hello, but she was too upset to chat with a woman who she did not know. She thought about Ralph's hurtful words, but did they contain a ring of truth? They echoed what Claire had said three years ago when Annie announced her decision to leave England: 'Selfish! She had said angrily, 'You are only thinking of what suits you!

Claire was in the kitchen, making supper as she and Charlie returned to the cottage, he raced to hug his grandmother, glancing at the cake, cooling on a rack, and, very grownup, shook hands with Tony, who was marking a garden catalogue at the table. He had a pencil in one hand and a glass of wine in the other. They looked up, delighted to see him, as Arthur ran around barking, getting under everyone's feet. 'I'm going up for a bath, is that ok? Annie asked, she didn't want Claire to see that she was upset, near to tears. It was her last evening in England and, as she lay soaking in the bath, she stroked her tummy, 'Am I selfish? Please no...not with you! It seemed silly to be talking to a baby, she climbed out and prepared to pack her clothes which were strewn around the room, she was eager to get home to Toulouse and the comforting world of Felix.

*

Marthe was surprised to receive a phone call from Claude, they had not seen each other since January, when she was laid up on the sofa and he had brought her flowers. Felix had spoken of him as had Annie, so she knew of the changes in his life, the death of his aunt and his inheritance. 'Come and see what I've been up to! He said, 'And my son will cook us lunch. He sounded very cheerful.

She knew the chateau a little having spent several nights in his wing, but had never been inside the main building. She was delighted to have an opportunity to explore it, and to see Claude after such a long time. She dressed with her usual care and set off, it was late June and going to be a hot day.

Claude showed her the Chateau. Both floors were at last completed, furnished, painted and ready for guests. He was full of pride and enthusiasm, 'We open in two weeks, he clapped his hand to his head in mock horror, 'And there's still so much to be done! Marthe, a little overwhelmed by the size of the hotel and understanding what a large amount of work had been done, thought the hotel looked ready, she assured him that if she were a guest she would be more than happy. They both silently remembered their time together in the hotel in Collioure; the hotel on the rocks overlooking the Mediterranean sea, the gaily coloured flowered wallpaper in their bedroom and the balcony, where they had breakfast, just wide enough for two chairs and a round table. They had stayed several times. 'Now show me the garden, she said, 'I want to see everything!

*

Annie was working near the pool, trimming back the oleanders that grew near the wall, they were drooping onto the path and narrowing the access from the terrace. She was wearing a wide brimmed cotton sun hat but her face was pink and damp. Marthe was concerned, 'Should you be doing that? You don't want to get too hot! Claude agreed, 'Can you move into the shade please! Annie wiped her face with her sleeve and smiled at them, 'I'm fine! I've nearly finished and then I'll have some lunch in the shade. Honestly, work is not bad for me or the baby. And when I get home I shall do nothing, Felix is the cook now, and he insists that I have a rest before supper. Marthe took her hand, 'Well if you say so. But please don't overdo it will you? Let's sit down for a moment, she guided Annie firmly to a bench against the wall, where lavender was flourishing in the shade. Claude walked away, he was trying to understand the workings of the swimming pool, hoping to avoid paying someone to take care of it. The machinery was in an old barn, its shiny components in stark contrast with the dirt floor and rusty tools that had been pushed to one side. Claude watched as the water recycled in a large green container, shaped like a ball, it made a rushing sound. A loud pump worked constantly. There were plastic containers with chemicals and a lot of hoses, it looked very complicated. There was a thick manual, already stained, lying on the floor next to a huge coil of hose, he picked it up, a worried frown on his face. He decided to show it to Jerome, he had a more practical side, than either he or Luc.

Annie cooling down a little, took off her hat and began to explain to Marthe what she was planning for the garden, 'It's a new challenge designing for a hotel, I've never done one before. You have to be practical, providing for all ages, with steps and sitting areas. Also the site is quite windy so we've planted a shelter belt of fast growing trees, she pointed, there at the far end. Then Luc, I don't know if you've met him yet, he's the younger son and a cook, he wants lots of home grown vegetables and herbs for the kitchen, so we have set aside the walled garden for that. She spoke with great enthusiasm, and Marthe said, 'It's like last year when you were working for me, I remember how excited I was listening to you and imagining the plants and shrubs and trees. They were such happy days! And now I have the baby to look forward to…which is even more exciting!

'What do you think of the hotel? Annie asked, 'I've not really seen around, but it looks terrific from the outside!

'It's very smart. Someone has done an excellent job on styling all the rooms, quite a task. I wouldn't know where to start.

'He had help, Annie said, a friend from Bordeaux, she stayed for ages. Marthe was registering that as they were joined by Claude, 'I'll just finish here and then find some shade for lunch, Annie said, Marthe gave her a hug. Annie watched them walk back towards the hotel. It was nice to see them together, she thought, whatever their differences had been at the beginning of the year, they seemed to have been resolved. She regretted her reference to Angelique and hoped that Marthe had not been listening carefully.

Claude led her back to his wing where Luc had laid out lunch; a cold watercress soup, poached salmon with hollandaise and new potatoes, then a strawberry mousse. 'Goodness! Marthe said, 'do you always eat this well? It's delicious. She sat back and smiled at him, 'You do look very well…this hotel life suits you I think.

'We've not started yet! Wait and see how I look after a few weeks. But it has been fun, if exhausting. Now tell me, what would you change in the hotel? What have I missed? He looked at her expectantly. Marthe was not prepared for that, she thought carefully, 'Flowers! You need to fill the downstairs rooms with flowers, the hall and salon and dining room and the library. Especially the entrance hall, it's the first thing guests will see as they come in, you need a great bowl of flowers on the table, a glass vase with tall flowers, in striking colours. Guests remember something like that, first impressions are very important. Organize a weekly delivery for the moment, she continued, 'Until Annie can provide from the garden. There's an excellent shop in Auch, speak to them.

*

Claude was impressed, 'A feminine eye! He said, 'I knew you would help. Marthe was about to ask whether he had employed an interior designer but stopped herself, it's nothing to do with me, she thought to herself. He finished his wine, 'Shall we have coffee outside? Or is it too hot? I want you to see the view from the terrace again.

They sat under one of the new large sun shades, it was very quiet and there was a haze to the south where on clear days one could see the mountains. Claude silently admired Marthe, she blushed, aware that he was regarding her, 'And what are you doing at the moment? He asked. 'You look very well too, a smart dress and just your colour. Claude's charm came so easily to him that it was easy to miss it, but Marthe remembered how he liked to flatter and she smiled at him. 'I've been busy too. I have embarked on an adventure. Though it's very different from yours. And I hope, less expensive.

Marthe unfolded the story of the twins and the help she was giving them and her visits to the Rinaldis, the father in Toulouse and the old man in Auch. She was confiding in him and it was a relief to do so. He listened with mild astonishment, but he knew Marthe well, that she could be impetuous and enjoyed embarking on new ventures; her move to the Gers and the renting of the apartment in Collioure testified to that. 'I admire what you're doing, he said, 'Good luck! It's kind and generous, they sound a fine pair, and a very fortunate pair too! And if you can afford to give them a better start in life, to open some doors for them, then, he paused, 'Why not? I look forward to hearing how it all develops. He sat back and looked at her. She returned his look and said,

'Felix isn't so sure! He opposes my plans really, and I have not told him of my visits to the Rinaldis. Claude leaned forward, 'Well I think you should, it's bound to come out. Secrets in a family always cause trouble. Marthe listened and nodded her head, she knew he was right. Claude continued, 'Felix's never had to struggle in life has he? He doesn't know what it's like, not to be able to afford do something, to be held back by the need to earn one's living. Our children are spoilt in that respect, mine certainly are! They have, on the whole, lived as they pleased! Marthe was surprised at his tone, 'But your sons are very nice, they live and work with you, they don't seem spoilt. She recalled them both when she had stayed with Claude the previous year, both sons had often joined them for supper, and she had been somewhat jealous of the free and easy relationship that they all took for granted.

Claude replied, 'Well, thank you for saying that, but they don't know what life is like for people such as the twins. And nor does Felix. When I say 'spoilt' I am not being unkind, just realistic. Our sons have enjoyed parental support, which has enabled them to make career choices; Felix in his world of music and my two, well, they are still finding their way. That freedom was denied your twins, the boy went straight into working on the family farm and his sister also. He paused, 'So forget Felix's reservations, he'll be very proud of you in time.

The afternoon sun had moved round and the sun shade no longer protected her, Marthe stood up, she was hot, 'Thank you for lunch and my visit, it's very good to see you, the hotel will keep you busy now! Claude rose and she looked at him, he was still an upright figure though his grey hair revealed his age, 'I'll ask you again once we've settled in, he said and took her arm as they walked back to her car and they kissed lightly. Luc was watching from his attic room, 'Are they getting back together? He wondered. Neither Marthe or Claude would have known how to answer that.

CHAPTER 18

It was market day in St.Girou and the July sunshine had brought out many of the local population. There were signs of summer everywhere; the stalls had erected bright awnings and sales of dark winter clothes had ended. Now there were straw hats, dark glasses and sunny colours; red, orange and yellow dresses, blouses and shirts. People lingered and chatted, the children kicked the dust with their sandals and old men leant on the bridge, studying the slow moving river. The central square was close packed with stalls, it was the prime location and the vendors jostled for space around the fountain. A man in dungarees had set himself up there and was selling summer plants: marigolds, geraniums and nasturtiums, stuffing his pockets with notes and change, his wife worked beside him, watching and replenishing the stock from their battered farm van. The range of goods on sale through the market was bewildering: arrays of cheeses, bread, pastries, olives and dates, fat sausages, nuts and dried apricots from Spain, and pottery too, intermingled with berets, aprons, organic soaps, shoes, ladders and buckets. It was the weekly opportunity for gossip and the men gathered in clusters, smoking, they made much of market day, coming in from outlying farms, exchanging news; many had dogs at their feet, long haired working animals, grubbing for food. Babies in push chairs blocked the cobbled streets, made narrow by women with laden baskets. There was the occasional argument. The café on the corner was busy, men in berets crowded the bar, whilst on the pavement, the waitresses pushed their way impatiently through the tightly packed tables. Above the bar a television played pop music, adding to the hubbub in the smoke filled room, whilst one of the waitresses sung along as she carried her heavily laden tray out to the customers.

One of the smaller stalls had been set up by Gregoire, as a more recent trader, he had been allotted a site on a windy spot near the live animal market. It was his sixth week, he had left the Moulin early that morning, and was ready before the market opened promptly at eight. He stood leaning on one of the tables that displayed his vegetables as the animal traders arrived in their vans and lorries, parking to unload. Gregoire watched as chickens, ducks and geese were carried in, some in cages, others held by their feet, upside down. Young baby goats were driven forward bleating, their necks tied with tough rope, and there were soft baby rabbits held by their ears dazed and trembling. There were puppies and kittens in boxes and surprisingly a white parakeet. Screeching. The smell and noise were overwhelming, a pair of cockerels squawked loudly at the entrance, as if to welcome the people who pressed in as soon as a loud horn signalled the opening of trading. The captive animals waited their fate in their pens, cages and stalls.

Gregoire did a brisk trade, he was becoming a more familiar face and several customers returned to him. He smiled and did what he could to encourage people to stop and look at his produce. He did not have the banter of some of the traders; the man who wielded a sharp knife and cut off the outer leaves of his cauliflowers with a dramatic cry, nor the cheeky man selling olives and fresh figs with a wink and a leer. It was hard work and by noon many traders were preparing to pack up their goods, load their vans and return home. The noise at the bar was deafening and the waitresses were increasingly short tempered. The streets were now strewn with debris, cabbage leaves, squashed tomatoes, crusts of bread and paper.

Marthe was one of many enjoying the market, and was walking back towards the river where she had parked her car. Her shopping basket was full. She spotted Gregoire, he was talking to a customer, his face damp with sweat. She walked over as he began counting out some change taken from the large leather bag, hung around his waist. The customer walked away, carrying the last of Gregoire's carrots, and Marthe approached, she had not seen him for several weeks. He was delighted to see her and noticing her basket he said, 'I'll drop that off for you if you like. It looks heavy. Can I add anything? Marthe pointed to some courgettes, he put them on top of the basket. 'I'll see you back at Les Palmes then, she said, 'thank you for taking the basket, it was far too much for me.

Back at Les Palmes, she poured some lemonade and took it in to the garden. He wasn't long and they stood in the shade of the palms, it was Gregoire's first visit and he looked around with interest. Agathe had described the garden to him but it was bigger than he had realised, he wondered how she managed it. The lemonade was cool and refreshing and he drank it down quickly.

'I've an idea for you! Marthe said, it had come to her in the car as she drove home. She told him of Claude's hotel and the restaurant, 'You might find they'd be interested in buying from you. They're growing what they can, but it's early days and they are going to buy in for some time I know the family a little, and could introduce you if you would like. Gregoire had finished his lemonade and asked,

'But do you need any help here? I could come in the evenings, if you want.

Marthe was surprised, 'That's a kind offer, she said, 'Can I think about it? I do have help, but probably not enough. Let's walk around together if you've got time. Have some more lemonade? She poured a full glass, he smiled, 'Thank you, it's been a hot morning. They walked down the paths, stopping occasionally, she explained the planting design on which Annie had spent so much time; the hot colours near to the house and the cool blues and greys nearer to the orchard. Gregoire lingered in their shade, he knew about fruit trees, and saw that many needed pruning. 'I could help here, he said, 'though it's not a good time to prune. Maybe a fertilizer would help. You might plant a few more, these apples haven't got much life left and it would be nice to add some cherries too. He stopped, 'Sorry, I don't want to interfere!

Marthe was looking up at the sky through the branches, the blossom was over and the fruit was already setting, 'No! No! I want advice, she assured him, 'I love this orchard…I'm told it was my mother's favourite place, she liked to sit and read here. She spoke thoughtfully, wondering if she should tell him of the unfortunate connection between his family and hers. Gregoire brought her back into the present, 'Sorry I need to get home, grandfather likes his lunch at noon, so I'm already late. And I'll think about the hotel, it would be quite a commitment, so I need to be sure that I could meet their demand.

They walked back towards the house, though Gregoire was sad to rush. He was enjoying the garden and talking with Marthe. 'I'd love to help here, he said, 'but not for money. I think maybe a couple of hours once a week would make a difference. Marthe wrote down the address of the Chateau, he glanced at it briefly, then put it in his pocket. They walked to his van, 'Thank you for the courgettes, she said, 'Why don't we try you working here once a week? I would like that very much. And the evenings would be fine.

Gregoire drove back to the Moulin, where grandfather was waiting impatiently. It had been a good morning, he had picked up more work, helping out in Marthe's garden and supplying the hotel. It was going to be a busy summer.

*

After lunch Marthe took the diary for the year 1940 out into the garden and sat in the shade of the orchard, the diary for 1939 had distressed her; the references to the war and Bertrand's support for Hitler and Germany. On this afternoon she determined to read on. Bertrand continued writing as before; the weather, his health, his exercise regime, references to his young wife made each entry very similar, but the war had taken on a greater significance in his life. He welcomed the fall of Paris in June 1940 and the new German led government, now established in the Capital. He began meeting with other sympathizers who hoped to extend the German occupation throughout France. He despised the government in Vichy. He recorded meetings in Toulouse where Nazi propaganda was spread, and wrote of plans to set up a local cell of support.

He was looking forward to the birth of his first child, Marthe, born in the summer. The diary began to include details of his daughter; how she was feeding, her sleep patterns, her first smile. She resembled her mother, he wrote, having fair hair and an oval face.

He had set himself the task of reading more history, starting with a translation of Gibbon's history of the Roman

Empire, the first volume, (there were seven) absorbed him for several months, then he pressed on with the second. Marthe read the whole diary for that year, it was late afternoon before she closed it and sat back. It was a strangely intimate experience learning of the private life of another person, knowing that Bertrand had almost certainly not intended that anyone else should read it. Most disappointing for Marthe was that he revealed so little of himself; the diary was essentially a factual record, he did not write of his emotional life at all. Marthe thought about this, was he so reserved that his emotions were of no importance to him? Or was he so private that he could not express his feelings? Even her own birth was recorded as a fact, alongside the weather and his health. What was the purpose of it? Thinking further, the next question was, 'Did she like this man? She did not share or understand his political opinions, his pro German stance was horrible to her. He lived a strangely isolated life, there were few references to local life and friendships. What sort of a husband was he? What sort of father?

*

Marthe stood up, she was tired having read for so long, and overwhelmingly depressed. She wondered if she should put the diaries aside; she had learnt nothing of the inward life of her father, and felt ashamed of his support for the Nazi occupation of France. Perhaps Felix was right, she should try and forget all about him, put the past behind her. But the remaining diaries waited for her in the salon and she knew that she would not be able to ignore them.

*

Charlie found it difficult to settle after his visit to England and spending time with his father, he realised that Ralph wanted him to return and live with him and Edna, he had spoken of it and that his parents were arguing about this, and that made him unhappy. His mood affected his school work, he had become inattentive and careless. His teacher threatened a meeting with his mother, to discuss his general behaviour, which upset him even more. The novelty of living in Felix's house (he still didn't think of it as 'home') had worn off and Charlie now lamented the constant pressure to be more tidy and quiet. He missed the chaos of the apartment and his mother's undivided attention. It was Monday, supper was late and everyone was cross. Felix had missed a deadline for a concert review, Annie had found that slugs had eaten most of the newly planted lettuces at the Chateau and Charlie's maths test was so poor that he had been threatened with a detention. It was Annie who started the argument with her son, he had come to the table with unwashed hands, a trifling matter which very quickly deteriorated into an unpleasant squabble. Felix observed them, reluctant to interfere. After a few minutes a red faced Charlie jumped up from the table, his meal half eaten and walked towards the stairs.

'Come back! Annie shouted, 'Don't walk away like that!

'I've finished, he replied, 'Anyway I've got work to do. You're not the only person with problems, you know. He was half way out of the door, Annie stared after him. She stood up and called to him as his feet could be heard stomping up the stairs. 'Please Charlie, come and finish your supper. He did not reply. Felix said, 'Let him cool down, don't follow him. I think he's had a bad day at school. 'How do you know? Annie had returned to the table. 'Because I asked him when he got in. I always do. He comes up the stairs and I say, 'How was your day? And usually he says 'Fine. But today he was flushed and shrugged. He didn't say anything. They cleared the table together and then Annie climbed the stairs, she could hear Charlie's music as she approached his door and knocked and having no answer knocked again, and walked in. He was sitting at the table under the window with his shoulders hunched and his head in his hands. A picture of dejection. A text book was open in front of him, 'Maths? She asked gently. He nodded, 'But that's your best subject. Charlie sighed, 'Not anymore, I failed the test today. She didn't speak for a moment, 'Anything else, getting you down? He did not look at her, 'Come on, Annie tried to coax him. He continued to sit with his back to her, then said, 'You're always busy. Or tired. We never do anything together, just you and me. The weekends are boring; last year we always went to Marthe's on Sundays, I really liked that, the train ride, and buying a tart at the bakers in St.Girou, and mucking around in the garden, and then catching the train home, looking forward to supper in the apartment. I miss all that, he stared out of the window. He sounded very forlorn. 'And Felix is the same too. I used to do stuff with him, but now he's always teaching or writing and I have to be quiet. He was near to tears and stopped.

'I see, Annie said, 'we've been forgetting you. Is that it? Charlie nodded. 'I thought you had your friends, she continued, 'and were happy doing things with them. I know I've been busy with work, I'm trying to get as much done as I can before I have to stop.

He turned around finally, 'It's Dad too! He talked about me living with him and Edna, and I don't think I'm ready for that. It's all a muddle. Annie drew closer and ruffled his hair and placed her hands on his shoulders. She felt terribly sad, 'Well, the first thing is to change things around a little here. I've taken you for granted, which was wrong. I'm really really sorry. She looked around his room, 'How about we paint this and put some posters up? You could choose them. Shall we make it more a boy's room? We'll do it together. Charlie perked up, 'Can we? And can I choose the colour? I'd like it green, dark green. And shall we choose, just you and me? Felix has grown up tastes doesn't he.

Annie smiled at him, 'Well I look forward to doing that. And don't worry about your Dad, there is no way you are leaving here before you are, at the earliest, sixteen. At that age you can decide for yourself. I've told Dad that, of course he's disappointed, but he accepts it. Charlie got up, he was feeling much better, 'And can you ask Felix if I can bring some friends over to play music at the weekend. We're trying to form a band.

'No I won't do that for you, you ask him yourself. He is very reasonable you know. And loves you dearly.

*

Felix was reading when she came down the stairs, sitting under a rather grand lamp that Claude had delivered earlier. There was a glass of whisky next to him, Annie looked at it wistfully. 'Is the lamp new? It's very smart! I like it. Annie said as she touched it with her hand. 'Art nouveau or something?

'Is he ok? Felix asked as Annie joined him on the sofa putting her feet on a cushion with a sigh. It had been a long day. Felix took her hand. She leant on his shoulder and shut her eyes, he smelt nice and his sweater was soft. 'Yes. the problem is he feels left out, by both of us, we're always busy and…Felix cut her short, 'Well we are. He's right. You were hardly here last week. When does your teaching stop?

'Next week, they're into exams then, so I won't be going in.

'And next year? Felix asked.

'I've got a year's sabbatical. He sat silently, knowing that to press Annie about her work would provoke her.

'Has living here become a problem too?

'No, but Charlie wants to paint his room, make it more boy friendly. More Charlie and less Felix.

'What himself? Felix looked startled.

'I'll help, we can do it together. I think it's a good idea. He wants posters too. I promised to help him choose the colour, he's thinking green, which would be fine. Felix nodded, 'And while we're talking about that, Annie continued, 'what about the nursery?

Felix jumped to his feet, 'Please not pink!

'No! Too obvious! A warm cream, what do you think? She stood up,

'I have to check the new pots in the courtyard before it's dark, she said, they need watering. Coming?

They stood together in the courtyard, 'Where did you buy these? He asked, his hand on one of the larger pots. 'From Claude, she said, 'Have you ever been to his reclamation site?

'No I spend enough money with him here in Toulouse.

'It's like an upmarket junk yard, or that was my first impression. But as you get to explore, it's interesting. Claude is a very good sales man, he lets you wander around then quietly asks what you're looking for. Most of the pots and urns are old and many are damaged, chipped and cracked. But I like that. It's like you and your furniture, things with a past.

'Do we need any more pots here? He asked.

'Well I think a stone table would be interesting, a big one, something square or oblong, to offset all these round shapes. Felix walked into the centre of the courtyard, 'About here?

Annie nodded, 'Yes. We'll ask Claude to find us something, shall we?

'I think he's preoccupied with the hotel, Felix said, 'the business has been put aside for the summer. He was looking up at the house as he spoke, there were lights on in the kitchen and he could see Charlie moving around. He felt happy to see the boy there. 'Does he like living here? Is he ok with it?

'Yes, he is. But he's adjusting, so we have to give him time… and more attention. I have been selfish, preoccupied with work. Annie sighed. She returned to the question of the table for the courtyard,

'We can wait for Claude, these pots are fine for the moment but maybe we could ask Charlie to take over the watering soon, it's a bit of a chore for me now. Felix thought that was a good idea, he was eager to involve Charlie in the house as much as he could, he was wondering how else he could make life better for the boy.

Annie lay in the bath, one of her favourite places now, it was the smartest bathroom that she had ever had, soft lighting and pale grey walls and tiles. There were lots of cupboards for what Charlie called her 'stuff' and mirrors to create an illusion of space. She soaped her stomach, avoiding looking in the mirrors, she looked tired she knew, and slid down below the surface to wet her hair. Felix came in as she rose to the surface and sat on the low chair beside her. 'All ok? He put his hand on her bump, there was a tiny kick. Felix jumped back, nearly falling, 'My God Annie, did you feel that? Annie put her hand on her bump and was rewarded with a kick. 'How exciting! She's just said hello to us. She grinned at him, 'Can you help me out please? Felix helped her out and wrapped a towel around her, 'Come on Mum! He laughed and gave her a gentle hug. Annie tried to be very matter of fact about the tiny movement, but she was thrilled. In bed she hugged Felix, 'Wow Felix, that was a good sign. He turned 'Wow indeed! They made love.

CHAPTER 19

Claude was so tense that he couldn't sit still, he walked around the Chateau, checking every room; twitching curtains, moving chairs and rugs and puffing up cushions, rearranging the flowers in their vases. Luc had banned him from the kitchen where the chef, normally phlegmatic, was also on edge. 'Please go outside, you're in every one's way and making us all nervous! He said and propelled his father out through the entrance. Claude stood gazing up the drive, disturbing the gravel that had been raked earlier. He decided to distract himself and phoned Marthe, she was in the garden and not pleased to be brought in doors. 'Isn't this your opening day? She asked.

'Yes, our first guests arrive about now.

'Shouldn't you be checking things? Marthe continued, and dropped her trowel. 'Are you ok? Claude thought she sounded breathless, 'I was in the garden! Marthe answered, 'Look, go and attend to your guests and phone me later. Relax! It'll all be fine. As she spoke an estate car appeared on the drive and Claude put the phone away, he hurried back inside.

These first guests were steadily joined by other families and within a week the hotel was buzzing and nearly full. It immediately felt very odd for Claude and his sons to see strangers walking about what they now felt was their home; sitting in the salon, reading magazines or drinking coffee, their voices filling the rooms and drifting up the stairs. Wandering in the garden, sitting on the new benches as they admired the view, gathering in the hall, it all felt very busy. To be regarded as a servant was the least enjoyable part of Claude's new life, some guests were very demanding and he had to hold back several times from answering rudely. But others were charming and appreciative and they were a pleasure to have.

Claude was startled early one morning as he walked in from his wing, to find two children playing at the foot of the stairs, they were waiting for breakfast. He greeted them but they only nodded politely and went on with their game. It seemed to involve cards. They had no idea who he was he realized. Later these two were joined by other children, in a game outside, hide and seek or something, it involved a great deal of running about and shouting. The restaurant ran smoothly and the chef proved to be an excellent choice, Luc was happier than he had been for several years and Claude was delighted to see him so. There was nothing but praise for the food and the service. Jerome had taken on the role of supervision in the dining room, the 'maitre d'' as he now called himself, a role that he had not initially wanted. He welcomed the guests and showed them to their tables, keeping a look out for potential difficulties. Fortunately in that first week there were few. He presented the menus and wine list with a flourish, extolling the local cuisine and talking about the wines of the region. Watching him through the square glass window in the kitchen, Luc was amazed to see such confidence in his brother, hitherto the shy member of the family. Jerome moved smoothly amongst the tables, straightening chairs and adjusting napkins, even his father was impressed.

On warmer evenings, the noise at the pool continued till late, and Claude regretted its position near the terrace. 'Can we do anything about this? He was speaking to Annie, it was nearly her last week and her head was full of other matters; the roses which needed attention, some had black spot, and the vegetable garden which demanded constant watering. She had drawn up a long list for Paul. who was eager to be in charge. She had met Gregoire who was supplying vegetables, as Claude explained, until the Chateau produce could meet the demands from the kitchen. There seemed to be some connection with Marthe which Annie had not bothered to try and understand. Annie was not paying attention when Claude spoke, so he asked again, 'The noise what can we do? She had not noticed it, 'It's a pool, she said, 'we can't move it! Claude was surprised at her tone, Annie had always been so polite. He paused, 'Annie are you all right?

'Sorry that was rude, she quickly apologised, 'But Claude this is a hotel now and your guests are on holiday. Most of them will not mind a bit of noise, it's coming from their children isn't it? Claude saw the logic in that, 'You're quite right. I need to adjust, it's sometimes feels like an invasion! Annie felt sorry for him, 'Adjusting is difficult, she said. 'We're having the odd bad day in our new home, Charlie can find it difficult. But things do settle down, in time. Perhaps in the Autumn we could create a quiet area for you? That would be a good challenge. You've your own terrace, maybe an area there with a hedge.

'Are you coming back then, in the Autumn? Annie had not thought about that when she spoke, 'Well, probably not, Felix is very keen that I stop all work for a while, but I could design it and someone else could do the labouring. If you'd like? Now I need to finish here or I'll never get home.

*

Claude turned back towards the Chateau. He was mollified by Annie's words, but he saw what an outspoken woman she could be, he wondered how Felix managed. He was stopped on the terrace by an elderly couple, who had arrived that morning. They were on a touring holiday of the Gers. They had driven down from their home in Normandy taking several days, and were interested in learning something of the history of the area and the chateau. They sat on the terrace and Claude invited them to join him for a drink, they were the first guests to ask about local history and he was delighted. Jerome brought out a tray with olives and nuts and a chilled bottle of wine, it was very pleasant and Claude forgot his earlier complaints. He sipped his wine and talked. Claude explained his family's history and the role the chateau had played in the community for many years. 'And in the war? What happened then? The man asked, 'Did your family stay here?

'My uncle lived here then, he was head of the family, the Count of Soulan. A leading figure in the area. Like several Chateau owners, he was taken hostage by the Germans. He was removed to Albi, denied a travel warrant and kept in close confinement. His survival depended on the good behaviour of this part of the Gers, and especially his tenants. His wife, my aunt fled to Spain I think, they were separated throughout the war. 'And the Chateau? The man asked.

'Left empty, locked up. There was a guardian for a while but he was taken away under the forced labour scheme, so it was pretty much abandoned. And several of the farms too, there just weren't the men to work the land. This part of France was not occupied initially, so there was no German presence as such, but strict laws were enforced. In time a local Resistance developed, the men called themselves

Maquisards. It was extremely dangerous as the Germans introduced special police, 'the milice' charged with tracking them down. The Maquisards became increasingly active as the war went on, blowing up bridges and hiding those who the milice were hunting...Communists and Jews of course. Bt 1944 they controlled the more remote areas of the Pyrenees, having established safe routes for those trying to flee France. It was highly dangerous, there are several memorials to men who worked for the Resistance, those who lost their lives. I can direct you if you're interested.

The couple listened attentively, the history of Normandy was similar but worst; their province had been under strict German occupation and life had been harsh and dangerous and subject to constant bombing. Civilian deaths here had been some of the highest in France.

Claude paused and topped up their glasses as they all sat thoughtfully reflecting on the past.

'And did your uncle, the Count, return in 1945?

'Yes and my aunt, but their lives were very difficult; the farms on the estate had been neglected, the fields taken over by weeds and the ditches clogged. There were few animals, all ill fed and the barns were in disrepair, and most difficult of all there was a much diminished labour force. There was little fuel for tractors so working the land was hard and laborious. They lived very simply. Claude shrugged, 'I didn't know my uncle, he died soon after, strain and the harsh treatment in Albi I believe. They had no children, it was my aunt who brought the estate back to life...it was her life's work. She reached a great age and died earlier this year.

*

After dinner, Claude saw them again, they were in the library, leafing through the guide books and chatting together. Claude watched them thoughtfully, he had checked the hotel register, their surname was Zeigler, and he realised that they were Jewish. Maybe they were hoping to discover the history of family members, there had been many Jews in this part of France, in the cities of Toulouse and Albi and Auch. Their history was tragic compared to that of the Count and Countess, he felt humbled. The couple stayed for two more days and were delightful guests, appreciative of everything, friendly to the staff and Claude was sorry to see they had left. He had not spoken to them again after that first evening, and he wondered what they had learnt. He wished that he had said goodbye.

Running a hotel was full of unexpected incidents, and increasingly Claude found excuses to remove himself from the daily routine, and the complaints. One morning he drove into Toulouse, he had spotted a pair of 18th century water colours in a gallery on an earlier visit and had purchased them for Felix. He wanted to deliver and hang them. It was a hot summer's day, early August, and the fields were busy with tractors ploughing the straw into the soil. A dusty haze filled the air which had a pleasing scent of dry grass and straw. He relaxed as he approached Toulouse, paying at the toll booth and making his way confidently into the centre, the road was busy with traffic. He parked in the central square and walked down the rue des Capuchins.

There was a delicious smell as he entered the house, Felix was cooking risotto at the stove. Claude peered into the pan, 'Pea and...

'Courgette. Felix said adding some stock gently, 'Annie is on a healthy diet! Lots of green! How are things? Fun being Le Patron?

Claude stood back from the stove and sat at the table, it was very untidy and he smiled to himself, it was clear that Annie was in residence.

'It's all rather strange, to be honest! Having strangers in your house, well, it's not my house, I live in the wing, and thank God for that! One guest, yesterday, a man twenty years younger than me, paid his bill and handed me the keys of his car. 'Get the car round to the front would you? He asked, and then added, 'The bags need bringing down. You can put them on the back seat.

'And did you?

'Yes, slowly. But I didn't get a tip! He had a very fine car, English. Just the thing for you! I have two pastoral paintings for you, that's why I'm here, can you leave that cooking and help carry them up the stairs?

Claude stayed for lunch, he was thoroughly enjoying being away from the chateau. Annie joined them, she had stopped working now and Claude thought she looked much less tired.

'What are you up to? He asked.

'I've been helping Charlie, we're painting his bedroom. I do the lower bits and he stands on the ladder. It's fun but bending down is difficult! And Felix has even helped a little.

'Yes, I do all the worst bits, the cornices and such like, Felix said, 'We seem to have finished the risotto, cheese and fruit now? After lunch he and Claude hung the two paintings in the salon, Annie privately thought them a little old fashioned, but she kept that to herself. Her tastes were more modern and she liked vibrancy, the posters that she had helped Charlie choose for his bedroon were bright and colourful, set off by the dark green paint which she loved. Claude looked about noticing the changes in the house; there were Annie's family photos on the walls leading up the stairs, and tartan rugs on the kitchen sofa, some modern cushions had infiltrated the salon and there were books on the floor. Felix's house previously a setting for his furniture, paintings and art (much chosen with Claude's help) now was filled with objects that reflected a more cosmopolitan taste.

Felix was still trying hard to adapt; his instinct to tidy, to fold clothes and put them in cupboards, to pick up newspapers and magazines, to throw out fading flowers, became slowly a thing of the past. He wondered what life would be like when a baby added its own chaos. Annie tried hard to meet his high standards, but it was a losing battle. They had hired a cleaner.

*

Having hung the paintings, Claude left. He was pleased with his visit; Felix and Annie appeared happy and settled, he continued to be envious of the house, which he found even more desirable now that Annie and Charlie were living there, he wondered if she was planning to make it their permanent home. He thought of his sons; Jerome was now installed in a large bedroom on the top floor of the second wing of the Chateau. He had his own staircase and a bathroom, which gave him privacy but he was on hand if needed. What did he plan long term? Claude had not discussed it with him, but working permanently in the hotel now seemed a genuine possibility, he was taking on the role of manager with growing confidence and the quiet book shop in Auch seemed a thing of the past. That interested Claude; that Jerome seemed prepared to embark on a new career so easily as if he now saw the hotel as his future. After all the whole idea was that the hotel should be a family business, and Luc had certainly grabbed the opportunity with both hands, working long hours without complaint. His two sons appeared equally committed.

*

Thinking about the months ahead Claude planned to keep the hotel open until mid October by which time the tourist season would be over; the Gers was too far from the Pyrenees for visitors who were planning a skiing holiday or a walking tour. Whilst the nearest Cities, Toulouse and Albi, provided long established hotels for tourists who were interested in museums and galleries and music. Claude had to decide whether if they shut down in mid October, would they then reopen for Christmas and New Year? Then close again until Easter? That did not seem like a good idea. Either way there would be several months every year in which both of his sons would be unemployed. And also staff would be laid off for long periods. It was a problem, for all hoteliers in rural France.

On the bright side there were bookings for several weeks ahead and nearly all the rooms were full. As he drove in, he had to avoid a family setting out for a walk, they were tanned and lightly dressed with sun hats. He stopped and asked, 'All well?' The two children hopped up and down, they were dressed in tshirts and matching red shorts, 'We've been swimming, one said, 'Now we're going exploring! Claude smiled at them and tipped his straw hat, they grinned at him. 'Have fun! He said. The parents smiled and the mother took one of the girl's hands, 'They love the pool, she said, 'particularly this one!

Claude smiled at the little girl, she was about eight he reckoned, with all her life before her, he was pleased that she was so enjoying her holiday. It made it all worthwhile, the work and the noise and the whole business of running a hotel.

*

Luc saw his car and came out from the kitchen, he had free time in the afternoon and often walked over to the wing for a change of scene. Claude led him in, the salon was cool and dark, the shutters closed. Luc lay on a sofa and shut his eyes, he had had little free time since the opening day and he was tired. Claude sat opposite him and waited. After quite a few minutes, Luc stirred, stretched and glanced at his father, 'A siesta! He said, 'Now I understand! Claude laughed, 'Oh yes. A siesta is a wonderful thing! They stood up and walked to the kitchen, Claude made a pot of lemon tea and Luc watched, 'Have you thought about the winter? Luc said. Claude put a cup of tea in front of him, 'That's extraordinary. I was thinking about it this afternoon as I drove back from Toulouse. So yes. What are your thoughts?

'Well, Luc paused, 'I suppose we'll shut in the Autumn and reopen for Easter. I'll look for work in a ski resort. Either the Pyrenees or maybe the Alps. I can offer experience now, and, hopefully, someone'll be interested. Claude listened, pleased that Luc was planning to continue as a chef. In the past Luc had lacked application and drifted from one form of work to another. 'Sounds good, Claude responded, 'And you like the mountains, skiing and such.

'The night life is fun too! Luc tapped Claude on the shoulder, 'You can come too! You'll need a holiday after all this hotel business.

'What about Jerome? Claude said, 'Have you talked to him? Luc shook his head, they both knew that Jerome was cautious and disliked change, 'He's a man, Dad, let him work it out. They left it at that, though Luc had firmed up Claude's decision to close for the winter.

*

Annie was now at home all day, for the first week she was restless and fretful, finding pleasure mostly in the courtyard, an outdoor space that she had so missed in her apartment. Following up her conversation with Felix, she wanted to add a good sized table to her pots, and asked Marthe to accompany her on a shopping trip to Claude's business site. Les

Palmes was en route. It was a Saturday afternoon and at the last moment Charlie decided to accompany them. He missed Marthe and wanted to see how she was. He also hoped to meet Claude who he much admired. Charlie thought him 'stylish'.

Annie took the familiar route, and Marthe admired the countryside as Charlie chatted in the back. She pointed to a group of creamy white cows lying in the shade of some old oaks, they were peacefully chewing whilst one stood gazing into the distance. 'Are they Limousins? Marthe asked. Charlie, who had been surreptiously eating an old toffee that he had found on the back seat, leaned forward and said, 'No. I don't think so. I think they're called, he swallowed, 'Les belles Dames. Marthe looked at them as they passed from view, 'I like them, they look so docile. If I had a cow I 'd have one like that!

Charlie laughed, and Annie said, 'Well we will save up and buy you one! Which made all three of them smile.

*

Annie strolled around Claude's yard looking carefully at what might be a possible purchase, she had included the possibility of adding to her existing pots, confident that one could never have too many. The pots and urns were old and many were damaged, chipped or cracked. Some she could use and she checked the prices. She intended to negotiate with Claude. The tables were less promising and she realised she might have to forgo that plan. Meanwhile Marthe and Charlie were sitting with Claude in his cramped office having tea and cake, it was where Claude brought his prospective clients when he thought he had a sale, he was a shrewd man when it came to business. Charlie looked around and asked 'Where do you buy all these things? Claude explained that many people only wanted new things in their gardens and threw out or sold what was old.

'Not like you Marthe! Charlie said, 'Your statues and urns are really old. She laughed, 'Don't you like them then? Charlie tried to back track on his comment which he now realised could be seen as rude. 'Oh no, I love your garden, he said hastily, 'especially your fountain with the two stone ladies. They are fun! They were interrupted by Annie who came in looking somewhat hot, 'Come Charlie! See what you think, come and look around with me. He jumped up and they went outside together. Marthe watched them go. Deep in her heart she was jealous of their close relationship and Claude sensed this. He had observed Marthe and Felix together and noticed the slight formality which existed between them. It was not uncommon. He tried to change the mood, 'How are your twins? We see Gregoire regularly now, he's a pleasant young man and my goodness he works hard

'Good that's worked out then. And you? How is the hotel?

'In full swing! It's a pleasure to get away like this, though I'm not sure if I can manage the two businesses at the same time. The hotel is very demanding! Anyway it's good to see you, perhaps we could have another lunch?

*

An hour later Annie was driving back into Toulouse with Marthe beside her. On the rear seat was Charlie, two urns on either side of him, both carefully wrapped and behind in the boot other pots of varying size. 'I hope Felix likes them, Marthe said. They were driving down the narrow street which led to the house. It was late afternoon and busy with shoppers. Parking was strictly forbidden. 'Oh he will! Annie said, and when I plant them up, he'll like them even more. She reversed carefully outside the house, ignoring the complaints of the pedestrians. 'Go and get Felix! She said to Charlie. He disentangled himself and ran in.

It took some time for Felix to unload the car aided by the café owner opposite, a stout but strong man. Felix gave him a note, watched by Charlie, 'Twenty euros' he thought to himself, 'That's a lot of money for lifting some pots. The courtyard was in partial shade now and Annie's purchases seemed very much at home, Felix moved them around until Annie was satisfied, 'I'll plant them tomorrow, she said and took his arm. 'Marthe how about a glass of wine? Then Felix can take you home.

As Felix drove back to Les Palmes, slightly faster than Marthe liked, she asked him how he was. Felix took his eye off the road, as he turned to glance at her, 'Fine thanks, life is good. I've never been happier. Life is busy, demanding and noisy. A tractor pulled out from a farm track and slowly manoeuvered its load towards them, he slowed abruptly and then accelerated through the gap. 'Sorry! he said. Slightly perturbed, Marthe settled herself, 'And Annie?

'Well you've seen for yourself, she has stopped working for Claude but gets tired. Things are good, we've done some decorating and Charlie is cheerful. And the baby has started kicking which is exciting. He didn't expand further.

'Claude will miss her, though he seems happy with her replacement, I think he's called Paul, Marthe said, 'But Annie's done wonders there. Felix nodded, they were back at Les Palmes. Before climbing out of the car, Marthe said,

'I've been reading the diaries, there's a lot to digest... to follow. Some of it is repetitive, his health and so on, but I've read as far as 1941. The war and his response to the fall of France, the occupation of Paris and the appearance of Germans in Toulouse.

'Yes I read as far that, it's about where I stopped. Felix said.

'It's distasteful. His support for the new regime, his clear admiration of Hitler, it makes difficult reading. But I will keep going, I have to understand or try to understand him.

'Don't let it upset you. They were difficult years, who knows how we would have felt. Many thousands of French responded as he did, supporting the new government, others stood back in a position of neutrality accepting what had happened and not wanting to be involved. And some became actively opposed, ignoring the dangers. There was a silence then Marthe said,

'I need to finish reading them all, right through to the last entry. She leant across and kissed Felix lightly, 'Thank you for bringing me home, I've had a lovely afternoon, Annie and Charlie always brighten me up.

*

Felix drove home thoughtfully, he hadn't asked her about the twins which is what he had intended. He still felt very much in the dark as to her long term commitment to them, whilst Marthe realised that she had again not been fully open with him. She had not told him about her trips to Toulouse and Auch in search of information about the twins' Rinaldi connections, and remembered Claude's advice to avoid having secrets within the family.

CHAPTER 20

In Toulouse Charlie had fully settled into life in what now felt like home, and there were no further problems at school. He loved climbing the stairs to the top floor, and his dark green bedroom, an airy space with long views over the roof tops. He began leaving his bedroom door open, listening to the lessons taking place inside Felix's music room, he was learning to enjoy the music that drifted across their shared landing. Now that his room was painted and his posters were on the walls, he began inviting his friends back after school. Four of them were forming a band. They took tea up with them, laughing as they climbed the stairs, holding cake, biscuits and fruit, anything they could purloin from the kitchen. They were allowed an hour of practice by Felix who generally retreated to the salon or the kitchen when the music got loud. But it was sometimes too much for him, 'Keep it down! He would shout. But on the whole life on the top floor was harmonius.

True to his word, Felix invited Charlie to join him on any excursions that were suitable, so weekends became more fun. They passed a long afternoon looking for a replacement for Annie's old Volvo and several in the local park kicking a football and eating ice creams. They also played a lot of chess. His musical education continued in Felix's car and

Charlie listened with more interest to the discs that Felix chose, though his preference was still jazz. The summer jazz festival at Marciac was an important event in Felix's diary, and Charlie longed to accompany him. It would mean staying over night or perhaps for longer, Felix had not mentioned his visit yet. 'Can you speak to Felix for me? Charlie was in the courtyard with Annie, helping her to water the pots. She found lifting the cans heavy work. She turned, 'Charlie you are old enough to ask him yourself. It means you staying away doesn't it? He nodded, carelessly pouring water over the cobbles, 'Take care! She watched him with a mixture of gratitude and impatience. 'School will be over, he said, 'I'd really like to go. He looked at her with his best smile.

'Talk to him then. Ask! They finished the watering and Annie said, 'Come on, let's have an ice cream, we've time before supper. Go and find my purse.

They walked out together, it was late afternoon and the narrow street was crowded with tourists on their way to visit the Cathedral or just wandering. They strolled towards the Place du Capitol, Annie at a much slower pace than usual. 'Are you ok Mum? Is the baby uncomfortable? She laughed, 'No, I'm fine. You were much bigger at this stage! Girls tend to be smaller. Charlie liked talking like this it made him feel close to his mother, 'And Dad? Did he help a lot, when I was a baby?

'Yes, he spoilt you rather! She corrected herself, 'No that's unfair, he was a brilliant father, a natural. He didn't mind getting up in the night for you and was oblivious to the mess and untidiness of the cottage. He loves children and babies especially. They had reached the Place du Capitol and Annie headed for a table in the largest café, it was crowded and she had to push through amongst the people, strollers, bags and baskets. 'You go and queue, she said, 'I'll have a vanilla please, but no extra cream. Charlie joined the queue, Annie watched him, 'He's growing tall and more like his father,' she thought. Things were still difficult with Ralph, the row in England hung over them; Ralph had not spoken to her properly ever since, though he talked regularly with Charlie. She heard them chatting and laughing over the phone. Annie wanted to restore some normality to their relationship but had not for the moment found a way.

They sat together eating their ice creams out of old fashioned sundae glasses, and she gave him her wafer. He dipped it into the ice cream and sucked the end. 'Not frightfully good manners, she protested. 'Mum! He looked at her, 'Can I ask you something? Annie stopped searching in her bag for her purse, 'Of course.'

'I've been thinking, can we ask Dad for a visit? I'm sure he'd like to see where I, well we, live and it'd be nice to see him this summer. I don't really want to go to England again, or not for a while. Annie took a breath, this was a very unexpected idea and she didn't want to get it wrong. 'Have you asked him then?

'No, I wanted to ask you first. And Dad could meet Felix too, which might be nice. He looked at her expectantly.

'Do you mean to stay with us, in the house?

'I hadn't thought about the details exactly, Charlie replied, 'Maybe a little hotel nearby? Nothing grand. And Edna might like to come too, you'd like her I'm sure. Annie thought carefully and said,

'I'll talk to Felix and if he agrees that it's a good idea, then I'll phone and ask Dad. Meanwhile you ask Felix about Marciac. She stood up and Charlie noticed that her dress was tight, he wondered how much bigger she was going to get.

*

Agathe had started calling in at Les Palmes on her way home from work at the retirement home. Propping her moped against the wall beside the back gate, she slipped in through the garden. She never came to the front door, shyness or modesty Marthe assumed. Marthe enjoyed these visits, and began making cakes and biscuits, Agathe was always hungry, but she was no longer so thin. Her appearance was slowly changing; the Retraite uniform with a crisp white shirt and neat blue skirt made her more feminine and her hair was now tied back neatly. She wore no makeup. They talked about her work and its new responsibilities, her training in feeding and washing the elderly inmates. She was learning about their medication and studying in the evenings for her entrance to the college in Auch, where if all went well she would start in September. Agathe became animated describing her day, and her pale face became pretty. She was a favourite of the old people Marthe was sure.

On this particular day, Agathe arrived clutching a piece of paper, 'See Madame, 'I've been accepted! Look! Marthe read it carefully: Agathe would start at the end of September, four days a week, the course would take two years, followed by a year working in a hospital. 'So you will be qualified in three years. Marthe said putting her hand on the girl's shoulder 'It's a long training.

Misunderstanding her, Agathe spoke quickly, 'I can try for a scholarship. Marthe kept her hand on Agathe, 'No, that won't be necessary. I'll support you as I promised. There are other girls who may need a scholarship.

Agathe looked down, unable to express her gratitude, and there was a silence,

'And how are you? she asked politely.

'I've been reading today, Marthe replied. She began talking about her father's diaries, Agathe listened attentively, 'It's a long time ago, the war, she said, 'We didn't learn much about it at school, were you alive then? Marthe smiled at her, 'Just about! They chatted on but Marthe could tell that Agathe's interest in the war was limited and after a few minutes she left, taking some cake with her for supper. Marthe heard the noise of the moped as she accelerated away, a whine that vanished as she turned the corner. It had been a good purchase and she felt pleased. As yet the money spent on the twins had not been great, and the satisfaction that she felt knowing how their lives were changing made it all worthwhile.

*

Her conversation with Agathe caused Marthe to reflect; the war meant little to Agathe, and, understandably, she had not really been interested in the diaries. 'Am I wasting my time?' She knew what Felix would have answered. But it was different for him, he was a generation away and the war had no great interest for him either. She took the diary for the year 1942, and walked out onto the terrace, it was a very warm late afternoon, and the palm trees stood motionless. It was still and peaceful. She sat under the pergola, moving her chair out of the sun light, and began to read.

The diary now felt familiar: Bertrand was a meticulous man who adhered to the pattern of recording his days. Marthe began skipping the passages about his health and that of his wife and child, the weather, his books. More interesting were the new problems now facing the family, as the war came to dominate their lives. The tone slowly changed as Bertrand witnessed the impact of the occupation on those around him, both in the brick factory outside Toulouse and in the local towns. Change became formalized in November 1942, the Zone Libre had been renamed the Zone Sud and placed under military occupation; from then on German soldiers, many of them very young, armoured vehicles and military trucks became a familiar sight on the streets of south west France. Bertrand's family brick works continued to operate but now with new problems. There were difficulties in buying supplies, especially fuel, and there was a growing shortage of men, as many of his employees were taken to work for the occupying government, under the new law, of travail obligatoire. Local women replaced them, a circumstance that was inevitable but which Bertrand deplored, whilst the requisitioning of materials and regular transport disruptions undermined the daily routine of the business, and caused a steady fall in profits.

By 1942 Bertrand recorded, the south west of France had become subject to new draconian laws, already well established in the zone nord; a nightly curfew, the requirement for travel passes, food rationing and most unpopular the demand that two thirds of the farmers crops should be sent East to feed the German armies. Bertrand attended one of the public meetings in Toulouse where the new laws were explained and the penalties too, he sat silently. He did not like to see soldiers on the streets watching the people as they went about their daily lives, and he thought the milice, whose powers had been extended were a gang of thugs. He did not record attending any more meetings and by the summer of 1942 he seemed to avoid Toulouse as much as possible.

*

As she continued to read Marthe became absorbed in the difficulties her mother and father were experiencing throughout that year: Bertrand recorded the rationing of food, which resulted in a thriving black market, something of which he thoroughly disapproved. Many families in the towns were suffering great hardship, whilst queueing for even basic food, notably bread, had become the daily routine for most women. In the town of St. Girou and the surrounding villages, gardens were dug up and flower beds were given over to vegetables, the rearing of poultry became more widespread as chickens and ducks were now a valuable source of protein, and a pig, always housed secretly, was highly prized. Rabbits reared in cages were to be found in many barns and outhouses and the autumn hunting season took on a new importance. The family at Les Palmes were fortunate; they had a large garden, an orchard, and an elderly gardener, and Marie devoted much of her time to working out of doors on her vegetable patch, carved from her flower beds, an activity which was quite new to her. She was kept busy with a brood of chickens, and bottling the fruit and vegetables that would get them through the winter. Little Marthe watched as Marie chopped and boiled and strained their produce, her slight frame covered in aprons. The jars, carefully labelled, began to fill the pantry.

*

Travel passes were now mandatory and difficult to obtain, and Marie worried about her parents in a suburb outside Paris. The capital was suffering daily from allied bombing, and during that year civilian casualties would reach over seven thousand. Marie knew that life in the capital was hard, a strict curfew, food shortages and the overwhelming presence of German soldiers in the streets, bars and cafes intimidated the civilian population. Morale was low. Rumours rife. All these changes in their lives were recorded by Bertrand as was the long siege of Stalingrad, he commented that a German defeat there would have a monumental impact on the course of the war. Bertrand wrote like a historian, the diaries were detached and unemotional. This confused Marthe and raised many questions in her mind: 'Where did Bertrand's sympathies now lie? 'Was he still supporting Hitler? Was he unaware of the terrible suffering across Europe? And what of France? Did he continue to support the military occupation? He thought the milice were thugs but did he speak up against them?

Marthe was disappointed to learn nothing of his response to the growing strength of Resistance groups in the Gers though he referred to their activities. His journey to the factory had been made more difficult as the bridge at a local town had been blown up and he heard the rumours of dynamite hidden in barns and secret routes across the Pyrenees. It was dangerous work and men who were suspected of speaking or acting in opposition were taken and shot or deported North. Bertrand could not ignore rumours that were rife as those around him lived in fear of even their neighbours.

*

Marthe continued to read until she had finished the diary for 1942, it had taken her a long time, it was already evening when she put the diary down. Her reading left her depressed, sad and unsatisfied. There was so much about Bertrand that she had not learnt, he kept so much of himself hidden. She looked down the garden, imagining it dug up in the war, providing her parents with potatoes, cabbages, carrots, onions, with chickens pecking in the grass and her mother carefully selecting what she needed for the next meal. She walked down the path, through the orchard and opened the gate to the river, and onto the path where she had fallen in the winter. It was a lovely evening and she wondered if her mother had walked on the path perhaps even holding her daughter's hand. She had no memory of those days.

*

They're All Called Jacques

It was summer and school and colleges were on holiday. Charlie had left for a week's walking holiday with a friend from school, he was staying on a farm in the Massif central, the family had a dog which added to his general excitement. There was a nearby lake for swimming and canoeing and there would be picnics and barbeques, a perfect summer holiday for an active boy. Felix took Annie away, it was mid July and hot and Toulouse was crowded with tourists. They went to Collioure, to the hotel which Marthe had also stayed in, with Claude, the previous year. It was a small hotel, all the rooms were painted in the 'fauvist' style with bright colours on the walls and windows, the furnishings were also bright and the sun poured into their bedroom through a wide window. The hotel was perched on rocks on the southern tip of the bay and, leaning out, they had a view of the sea and harbour and light house. 'Perfect! Annie declared and threw herself on the bed, the drive had been long, with tourist traffic slowing even Felix down, and she was tired. He lay down beside her and put his hand on her stomach, hoping to feel a kick but the baby was tired too and he felt nothing. Felix planned to make this as restful a time as he could, aided by the fact that slowing Annie down was now easier than before. It was a treat for them to take a break, just the two of them, there wouldn't be many more chances in the time to come.

*

He rose from the bed, it was early afternoon, and looked out at the blue blue sea, 'How cold do you think it is? The sea? He said. 'Just what I was thinking! Annie had joined him and gave him a kiss, 'Let's take our stuff and find out. It was a short walk through the hotel, down some steps to a bathing platform, where there was a ladder. Felix tested it with his hand, 'Safe enough! You can manage that I think. He descended the rungs and held out his hand, Annie peered down, 'How deep is it?

'Very! He continued to watch her from below, half of him in the water, 'It's warm too! Annie took some steps back and then ran forward and dived in. Making hardly a splash she swam for several moments under the water, popping up some distance away. Laughing. The water was clear and salty and warm. It was the perfect start to a Mediterranean holiday. The following day, they ate a leisurely breakfast on their narrow balcony overlooking the sea, 'Heaven! Annie said, 'Pure heaven. Stop me eating too much please! He shook his head, 'I will not! You eat what you like, this is a holiday. Our last for a long time! Annie stared at the table, with the remnants of croissants, flutes, butter, honey and the basket of fruit, there was little left. She nibbled an apricot and said, 'I want to do absolutely nothing, just swim and laze and maybe wander into town.

On the second day Felix took her shopping. The promenade was busy with tourists and Felix took her arm to stop her being jostled. She kissed him in the middle of a cobbled street, 'It's so nice to get away. I love Collioure. A large woman in a flowery dress and straw hat, jolted them, muttering. Felix called out, 'Excusez moi! Anne laughed and tugged his arm, 'Let her be! She probably lives here and sees us as intruders. Look there's the dress shop. They went in. Felix had a critical eye and was an experienced shopper, he had been well trained by his previous girl friend,Valerie, whose passion for clothes drew them into the smarter shops of Toulouse most weekends. They had passed many a Saturday updating her wardrobe. He now began to trawl the rails. Annie drifted around rather aimlessly, she never cared much what she looked like and expensive clothes had not been within her budget. Felix was quickly selecting blouses, jackets and dresses, an excited young assistant in his wake. They emerged half an hour later, having agreed with the shop to leave their purchases there and pick them up later. 'So many new things! Annie crowed with pleasure, 'It's almost indecent! I would never have found so many! The red dress is going to be my new favourite, hope I can squeeze into it all summer. You have no idea how huge I'm going to be!

They had lunch in one of the small restaurants away from the sea, sitting at a table on the street in the shade. Felix had a beer and Annie grinned at him, 'I don't miss it at all. Alcohol I mean. But I'm really going to catch up once I've finished breast feeding. Felix jolted to attention, 'I didn't know that, no alcohol for ages then.

'No. There's a lot to learn about babies I'm afraid.

The days passed, it was sunny and hot and Annie understood why Marthe had rented the apartment there. They spent one day in Felix's car exploring the villages above the town, motoring up the foothills on windy narrow roads with occasional glimpses of the mountains to the south. It grew cooler as they left the coast passing through thick woods of cork trees and oaks, there was the occasional stream running off the mountains and Annie wished they had brought a picnic. Instead they had a leisurely lunch at a small table under the huge plane trees that gave shade to the square of the old town of Sagres. It was a jolly restaurant whose large patron seated on a chair in the entrance kept a sharp look out for possible clients amongst the tourists who lingered. It was where the previous summer Claude had taken Marthe. They were on one of his buying expeditions and had spent several nights in the hotel nearby in the square, and eaten in the same restaurant under the plane trees.

'Are you disappointed that Marthe gave up her place in Collioure? Annie asked. She had finished her truite aux amandes and was toying with idea of an ice cream.

'Not really. We can always stay in Collioure as we are now. To be honest I never know what she is going to do from one day to the next. This business with the twins, where did that idea spring from?

'Well, I think it's tremendous of her, giving two young people such a helping hand. I used to see Gregoire, up at Claude's, delivering to the kitchen, he seemed a really nice person, hard working too. Not everyone is born into an easy life. Her words were sharper than she intended and Felix was hurt, 'I think that's unfair, we don't choose our families do we? Regretting her words, Annie took his hand, 'No of course we don't, I'm sorry, but…the twins did something so remarkable for your mother, it's natural that she would want to repay them in some way. Maybe you should try and get to know them a little? I've never met the sister, she's a nurse I believe or training to become one thanks to your mother.

Sitting in the car as it swooped down the hillside towards the sea Annie dozed, and Felix thought about their conversation over lunch, he decided to take Annie's advice and try and meet the twins. He thought about his mother and her capacity to surprise him, she was enjoying her independence he understood after a long married life in which she had always taken second place behind her husband. He knew that was what Annie feared, deferring to someone, and wondered if it was an issue in all marriages, or whether some women accepted their lack of independence, did not seek for a career and a life away from their families.

His thoughts were interrupted as Annie jerked awake, he had cornered a little too fast and then braked. She glanced at Felix, 'Shall we have some music? she asked, opening the cassette box. 'Rossini, I think. He nodded, he glimpsed the sea ahead though it was still some miles away, it looked enticing. There would be time for a swim before dinner; the water had surprised them both, so warm and clear, the swimming had been an unexpected delight, and they dived in together each time, but Annie was neater, hardly making a splash inspite of her large round tummy. He turned to look at her as the music filled the car and his heart exploded with love, an extraordinary feeling of pure happiness. Oblivious and singing beside him, Annie was also thinking about a last swim in the sea. Their holiday was nearly over.

*

A week later Charlie and Felix were playing chess in the salon in Toulouse. The game was at a critical point, and, unusually, Felix was poised for victory. Charlie frowned with concentration, trying to ignore Annie who was talking on the phone in the kitchen. To Ralph. 'So you're coming here for a holiday, a visit? The surprise in her voice was heard by Edna, sitting next to Ralph at the kitchen table. It was a wet Sunday morning and the breakfast still had not been cleared. Edna tried vainly to envisage Annie, they had never met and she was mildly curious. Maybe she is fair like Charlie, and slim. She got up and began picking up bowls and coffee cups, wondering about a trip to Toulouse. It would be an adventure for her as she had never been a traveller. And France? She did not speak French and knew little about the country. She hoped that they would go. Ralph continued his conversation with Annie,

'That's the plan, Ralph said, 'Didn't Charlie say?

'No! Not exactly. Annie tried to keep the irritation out of her voice, she continued, 'On your own, or, with, she hesitated, 'Edna?

'Both of us. We want to have a holiday, the weather is dreadful here and my work has tailed off. Edna's never been to France, or abroad really. Annie wondered if Ralph expected to stay with her and Felix, and mentally tried to envisage them here in the kitchen eating supper.

'When are you planning to come?

They continued to discuss the idea, as upstairs, Felix quietly said, 'Check! He pushed his chair back, stood up and stretched, they had been playing for nearly an hour. Charlie stared at the board, pleased for Felix but cross with his own errors. Annie joined them, her face flushed and Felix thought how pretty she looked, 'I won! Felix said, he was really quite pleased with himself. Ignoring him, Annie walked up to Charlie who was still trying to understand his mistakes. 'You should have said, her voice was cross. Charlie continued to stare at the board. 'You should have told us! About your father coming here to Toulouse.

'Is he coming then? Is it agreed? Charlie looked up expectantly.

Felix stared at her, 'What? Ralph is coming here?

'Apparently Charlie and he discussed it over the phone. So yes, he and Edna. There was a silence and Charlie put the chess men in their box, perplexed by Annie's response. Felix said, 'I think that's great news! We should all get to know each other. How are we all going to fit in?

'They won't stay here, Annie said firmly, 'Ralph insists on that. They'll find a hotel and stay maybe for three or four days. Then they plan to rent a car and drive over the Pyrenees, Edna likes mountains apparently, and into Spain. In a couple of weeks. Ralph is booking flights.

'August. A hot time! Felix was putting the chess board in the cupboard as Charlie prepared to ask a question. Annie said, 'I reminded him of that, but it suits Ralph's work, it's a dead month he said.

'Can I go with them? Charlie interrupted, 'To Spain? I've never been either. He was excited at this possible development and relieved that his mother was less cross. 'I can help look after them too, shew them around Toulouse. You won't have to do anything Mum! Annie relaxed, 'Well that would be kind. I think it's going to be fine, and Felix is right, we should all know each other better.

Later she discussed it again with Felix, 'It'll be odd seeing Ralph here out of context somehow. And meeting Edna too, though Charlie says she's very nice. I think Charlie should go with them to Spain, we're not taking him anywhere this year. Things do work out don't they? Me and you, and now Ralph and Edna. Yes, it'll be fine I'm sure.

CHAPTER 21

Claude was seeing some guests to their car, he was glad to see them leave. They were a middle aged American couple, from Boston, and had been very demanding. They were 'seeing France', passing through the Gers en route for Bordeaux, where they were to go on a wine tour. They had not been impressed by the Gers and, despite a day in Toulouse, which Claude had carefully designed for them, and another day in Auch, commented that the area lacked interest for tourists. In Auch, encouraged by Jerome, they had spent considerable time browsing in the book shop, now under the supervision of a bright young girl, a student at the university. They had not purchased either a book or any of the jazz cds, but a couple of postcards of the wooden choir stalls in the Cathedral. Which as Claude pointed out were available everywhere.

They found the hotel cuisine too rich and the chef, Joel, had been asked to exclude all cream and wine from their food. This was too much for Claude who refused to serve them special meals and also rejected their request to have their supper served at 6.30.

He put their cases beside their car and prepared to say goodbye. 'Enjoy the rest of your time, he said generously as they sorted out their luggage. The wife had her nose in a large map as they drove off, neither had said farewell. Claude sighed, it was hard work being pleasant to some people he realised. His spirits lifted as he saw Marthe's car coming down the drive. It had to swerve to avoid the Americans. She was not expected.

He led her into his wing and found some wine in the fridge, Marthe watched him, thinking he looked tired and gloomy, 'Life difficult? She asked looking around and settling herself on a sofa.

'Is it that obvious? He passed her a glass and sat opposite her.

'I'll do us lunch here, he said, 'You'll stay? She nodded.

Claude began assembling a large bowl of salad.

'Is this from the garden? She asked. Claude nodded as he concentrated, pouring olive oil into his mortar and pounding the garlic, and cheered up, forgetting his difficult morning. The white wine did its work, that and the sight of Marthe at the table where they were now eating and the fresh food on the plate in front of him restored his spirits. They talked about the hotel, Claude said, 'On the whole it's going well, the chef is excellent and not too explosive and Luc is learning fast. Jerome has come out of his chrysalis and works wonders in the dining room and everyone enjoys the garden, the pool and drinks on the terrace. Marthe waited. 'The hotel is nearly full until September and we are opening to non residents for lunch and dinner next week. We've had lots of people turning up having seen the sign at the top of the drive, 'passing trade' it's called. My business relied on it!

'Can I say something? Marthe asked and then before he could stop her, she said 'You look tired and tense. You're doing too much, you've spent the whole year setting up this hotel and now you're living in the midst of it. You need to step back and start enjoying this new life. He stopped eating and looked at her. 'Can't you delegate more here in the hotel, and consider putting your other business on hold? She continued, 'The summer's not your best time anyway is it? Passing trade doesn't bring in so much, people wander around, express interest and leave. They can't put your lovely urns and benches and statues in the backs of their cars, can they?'

He knew that she was trying to help and smiled at her, 'Maybe you're right, I'll think about that, though the business does provide a bit of an escape, but the hotel is testing. We're learning all the time and I need to be part of that.

Lunch was over and they walked outside, Marthe immediately realised the extent to which Claude had lost his privacy. The Chateau garden was now a public space; there were groups of guests sitting under sunshades on the terrace, down the new brick steps to the lawn a game of croquet was underway and several guests were cheering the players on and a lot of noise was coming from the pool. Under the hornbeams, some children were playing with a ball and an argument was developing, there was an angry shout and then they heard loud screams. She didn't say anything but took Claude's arm, 'Let's go back to your wing, that'll be calmer!'

'I do enjoy some of this, he said, taking her hand, 'I've met some pleasant and interesting people, who appreciate what we have here and want to learn more about the history and so forth. And the chateau has come to life, I like to see the rooms full. They reached the little garden next to his kitchen door and he drew up two chairs, there was no lovely view from here but Annie had planted out some urns, it was calm and peaceful. Shifting in his chair to look at her, he said, 'The real test will be when we do our sums at the end of the season, if we haven't made money…well then I will really have to think again! Both Jerome and Luc need this work the hotel is meant to be their future. But that's looking ahead, for now it's hard work and occasionally fun.

Marthe left later in the afternoon, she had enjoyed talking with Claude and hoped to spend more time with him, but for the moment, she had no thoughts of reviving their affair. The awkwardness that had followed her letter had been put behind them, and she hoped she had given him good advice about putting his business on hold. Did they still have a future together? Time would tell.

*

On one of the hottest days of the summer Ralph and Edna landed at Toulouse airport, they were planning on staying for four days and then renting a car and driving down to the Mediterranean and into Spain. Heat was not a problem for Ralph who had travelled when young and spent time in Australia, but Edna was a little startled as she waited for the bus to take them into the City. She fanned herself, discarded the new blue linen jacket bought for the holiday, and looked for some shade. The bus arrived and there was a push and shove to board, to her relief the driver turned on the air conditioning and Edna revived, and holding tight to Ralph, there were no seats available, she stared out of the windows. It looked very busy and the buildings were tall and ugly, but as they approached the centre everything changed; tall brick houses, cobbled streets, shady plane trees and canals and the wide river. Her spirits rose as the bus stopped and they clambered out, the pavement was crowded and there was a delicious smell…it was lunch time, and there was a café right next to the bus stop. Edna led the way to a tiny table, pulled out a chair, picked up a menu, and observed, 'They've all got gorgeous black hair haven't they? And they're not tall, sort of stocky.

Lunch took a long time, not the quick snack that Edna had expected. There was melon or a cold soup, then roast veal or river fish, and finally vanilla ice cream served with a slice of apricot tart. Edna ate with enthusiasm, 'Do they always eat so much? She asked, she expected Ralph to know all about the French as he had stayed there before, 'If so, why aren't they fat? It was a question many many English people had asked before her. Ralph smiled, he had enjoyed his lunch and was delighted they were here in Toulouse, 'Don't eat the bread! He said. Edna was aghast, their bread basket was empty and she had asked for more. She resolved to be more careful.

They were joining Annie and Felix for supper at a restaurant near the house, and it had been agreed that Felix and Charlie would pick them up from their hotel. 'I don't know how this is going to work, Annie said, as she watched Felix getting ready. 'It feels odd Ralph here in Toulouse with Edna, who we've never met. Charlie overheard, 'She's really nice! You'll definitely like her!

'Of course we will, Felix said, 'It's going to be a great visit. Are you ready? They set off and having found the hotel, Felix left Charlie at the entrance to meet his father on his own. Charlie was in a state of great excitement, he gave Edna a hug and grinned at Ralph then set about exploring their bedroom and bathroom, examining the free shower products, pulling up the blinds and looking out of the window. He had never stayed in a hotel. He had brought with him city maps and tourist information, and a large sheet of paper, it contained his programme for their visit. Edna glanced at it briefly, her own plan was to sit in cafés, eat long lunches and wander about. And maybe a bit of shopping. Charlie clearly had other ideas, it seemed that there was a great deal to see and do in Toulouse; the Cathedral of St. Sernin, we live nearby he added, and churches, squares, markets and several museums and galleries. Edna wondered how many of these Charlie had actually visited, but she glanced again at his plan.

They arrived at the house a little early, and Charlie led them through the hall and up the stairs, calling out happily to his mother. It was the first time that Annie had seen Ralph since the row in the pub in Kent, and they were all a little tense. It was Felix who made the visit a success; he charmed Edna, enquiring about her life in England and shewed Ralph around the house explaining the changes that had been made. Annie and Edna chatted in the salon, and Annie quickly understood why Charlie had said, 'You'll like her she's very nice. Charlie could not decide who he wanted to be with and raced around.

In the restaurant Felix encouraged Edna to try something new, 'A cassoulet perhaps? He explained how this regional dish was prepared whilst pointing out the view across the river, where barges were easing slowly down stream. Edna became quite merry under the influence of wine and the delicious food, wondering if all French men were so delightful, and became quite flirtatious, to Annie's amusement. Annie liked her; she was unpretentious and easy going, and clearly fond of Charlie, who sitting next to her had benefited from the cassoulet which she found 'a little rich'. As the evening wore on Annie saw how happy Ralph was in her company, and wondered if they planned children of their own. She looked at Edna carefully, uncertain how old she was and decided that she had plenty of time still...if she wanted.

The next morning, while Charlie embarked on his tour of Toulouse with his father and Edna, Annie paid a last visit to the Chateau, she had tools to collect and wanted to check that Paul, who was now in charge, was happy. All seemed well in the garden, the hotel was full and Claude nowhere to be seen, Luc came out of the kitchen, his face was hot. 'He's in Auch at the bank, he said, 'Money issues! Annie grimaced, 'Is all ok? Luc shrugged, 'I think so, but it's Dad's area not mine. He's the business man. Can I get you some lemonade? Freshly made this morning. He gave her a tall glass and she sipped it gratefully.

On her way back to Toulouse, the tools in the back of the car and some courgettes, a present from Joel, Annie turned towards one of her favourite places, the convent on the hill. She parked by the pond and leant over the brick wall that enclosed it. The sun was hot on her back and the baby kicked gently as she rubbed her stomach. A nun was tending the garden, carefully raking the gravel path that led to the church. The path was lined with lavender and the scent drifted across to her. The nun wore a black habit and a dark overall, her head was covered. Annie watched her, it was very quiet and still. She stood there urging herself to enjoy this peace and put aside all the daily worries that engulfed her sometimes; worries about Charlie, was he happy in Toulouse? Was he doing well at school? Did he have nice friends? And then about Felix, did he enjoy them living in the house? How would he find life with a baby? and the baby was it growing properly? Was it healthy? And for herself, would she cope? With a new responsibility? And not working? This was a nagging concern. Annie liked to work, she liked to be independent, what if she couldn't work for a long time? She continued to watch the elderly nun who was wheeling an old heavy barrow now, she struggled on a tight corner, and the barrow nearly tipped on its side, she disappeared behind the church wall, there was no one else about. The other nuns were working in the fields or barns or kitchens she supposed, they were entirely self sufficient. Unlike me! She thought returning to her car, how her life had changed.

*

Felix enjoyed meeting Ralph, and similarly Edna; they were easy guests, very appreciative and friendly. Charlie had spent all his time with them, escorting them about, revealing a knowledge of the City which would have astonished his mother. Under his guidance they saw all the major tourist sites and walked what seemed to Edna several miles; along cobbled streets, through squares shaded by plane trees, beside the slow moving river and across bridges. They had visited the large indoor food market, where she would have happily lingered all day, smelling the cheeses and sampling the charcuterie, and just longing to taste the warm breads and patisseries. She needed frequent breaks, 'little stops' she called them, so they spent a fair amount of time in cafes and restaurants, resting their legs and observing other people. Charlie read the menus at lunch time, encouraging them to try the local food: the strong Toulouse sausage, the cassoulet,(not again thought Edna), the magret of duck, the soups made from fresh vegetables. Ralph listened to his son ordering their meals and drinks, noting that Charlie had quite a strong Toulouse accent, the boy was fluent. Edna loved it all; she happily ate terrines of hare, kidneys in mustard and foie gras with brioches, none of which she had ever heard of before. Ralph wondered how much weight she was putting on, but she was so happy and relaxed that he just sat back and admired her.

On their last evening in Toulouse, Felix suggested that they should all eat together at a restaurant next to the river, and hearing how busy they had been, he hoped that they would have a more relaxing time in the mountains, 'It will be cooler and less strenuous, he said, pouring Ralph a large glass of red wine. Edna said that she was not walking up any mountain, having only sandals and no waterproof. Charlie suppressed his disappointment, he had every intention of attempting at least one good hike. They chatted and Felix watched Annie; she and Ralph now seemed easier with each other, and the initial tension had gone, but Felix still found it hard to understand what had drawn them together. It was of course the arrival of Charlie that had forced them into marriage, even independent Annie had not been able to resist the pressures from her family. Times have moved on, he thought, attitudes have changed, Annie was quite happy now to bring a new child into the world, unmarried. He sighed.

Annie smiled at Ralph, 'Thanks for coming, she said quietly, I think we understand each other better now.

'Yes, I'm glad to meet Felix, you and he are good together.

'More than you and me?

'Well, we were good for a time but things changed. Life's not always easy and straightforward. The baby will bring you even closer.

Annie said, 'It'll be a change for Charlie! Having to share me. You remember how exhausting those first months were.

'I loved every minute! Lucky Felix, he's got it all coming!

Felix had left the table to pay and they stood up, Edna grinned at Charlie, 'So. We'll pick you up tomorrow. Be ready! She turned to Annie, 'Thank you for letting him come. We'll look after him! She turned and put her hand on Ralph, he gave her a smile.

Ralph and Edna arrived promptly the next morning and Annie watched as Ralph squeezed Charlie's ruck sack into the boot, they would be away for five days. 'Watch the drivers, the Spanish are worse than the French! And wear your sun hats all the time! She said. To her surprise Ralph gave her a hug, 'Thank you, he said and climbed behind the steering wheel. Annie watched him weave his way down the narrow street, turning at the end into the Square, they were soon lost to view. She was sad to see them go.

*

She decided to spend the morning tidying up the little room, now known as the nursery. It was full of boxes, scattered randomly, and some rolled up rugs leaning against the walls. A pile of photo albums, their covers faded and torn, had been abandoned in one corner and she opened one. They belonged to Felix. The photos were black and white; family gatherings on lawns and the seaside, ladies in large hats and nannies in stiff white uniforms, children in sailor suits or starched dresses. She looked closely trying to identify Marthe, but these photos were from an earlier age. Annie was overwhelmed with sadness, 'All these people…gone, forgotten. Forgetting her earlier plan, she wandered into the salon, and sat down, falling asleep as she now so often did. The morning passed.

*

Felix spent that morning driving to Carcassonne where he was to review a choral concert in the cathedral, it started in the afternoon. He thought about the evening at the restaurant with Ralph and Edna, it had been fun and emphasized to him that he felt part of the wider 'family'of Annie. He had driven too fast, and nearly missed the turn off for Carcassone and was forced to brake hard as he approached the toll booths. There was a long queue and he waited impatiently, changing lanes and hooting his horn. Felix was running late. The concert was thus well underway by the time he pushed open the door of the church, it was dark inside and after the bright sunlight he stumbled, almost falling. A woman hushed him and he ignored her, walking down the aisle and finding a seat. The choir were singing selections from their repertoire of songs of the Ardennes, Felix got out his notebook and sat listening attentively. There were not many people in the church and he wondered whether his visit was worth his time. His attention stayed focused for the next hour and then the concert was over. Felix decided to stretch his legs a little, find a café, enjoy a cup of coffee and then return home. His plan was interrupted by a former girl friend who called out and waved at him, she was sitting in the sun at a small bistro and he crossed the street to join her. They had dated for several months some years back when they were both newly arrived in Toulouse. She had left him for a journalist, Felix had not suffered greatly. He joined her and they spent some time catching up on their recent lives and Felix understood why he had found her attractive, she was fun loving and adventurous with glossy black hair and dark eyes. Claire began to flirt, teasing him about their past and watching him as he drank his coffee, fiddling with his spoon, a habit that she remembered. He responded slowly and then more openly, complementing her on her pretty dress and smiling. The time passed, 'Shall we have a drink? In the square? She suggested. 'Why not? Felix responded, and they set off. She took his hand as they crossed the road and Felix held it lightly. The square was crowded and they found a small table, forced to sit closely and he could smell her perfume, something spicy. The wine came and the temperature began to drop, it was very pleasant sitting there, watching people and drinking wine. But there was an unpleasant niggle in Felix's head, he knew that he wouldn't want anyone to see him there, it was not that the meeting had been planned, it was a coincidence, but he had not told Claire about Annie and certainly not that he was going to be a father. He became increasingly uncomfortable, but Claire was enjoying herself and chatted happily about her new work and her home in Carcassone, she had been living there for a year or more working in the tourist office. 'I'll make us supper! She announced, 'You always liked my cooking! And you must see my apartment it's very modern and chic. Felix jumped to his feet, 'No! No. I have to get back, he looked at his watch, 'I'd no idea it was so late. 'Late? It's not late Felix, don't rush off now! She teased and grabbed

his hand. Felix moved away, 'I'll pay the garcon, he said, and strode towards the bar. They parted outside but she had managed to get his phone number, which Felix knew was a mistake, he had always found her difficult to resist.

*

It was drizzling as he drove West out of Carcassonne, rain had settled on the Black Mountains to the North and was now spreading up the valley. He settled into the outside lane, weaving through the cars and lorries, as spray coated the windscreen, the road was wet and slippery. He was deeply regretting the time he had spent enjoying a glass of wine, or was it two? Oh please not three, in fact it was three, remembering that Annie had promised to cook supper. There was a delicious turbot in a cooler bag in the back that he had purchased before the concert, perfect for two people. The conditions deteriorated as he approached Toulouse on the dual carriageway that circled the city and the road was busy. Felix drove impatiently, using his horn and waving at drivers who sought to overtake him. Breaking hard he turned off the Toulouse road onto the exit lane for home, then saw in his mirror the flashing blue light of a police car coming up behind him. To his mounting horror it sped past, then pulled sharply in front, causing him to slow down and stop in a layby just before the toll booths. He had been caught. His guilt increased as the Gendarmes wrote down his personal details and issued him with a penalty fine, as did his sense of shame that he had wasted time on another woman, whilst Annie was waiting for him at home. The only relief was that the gendarmes had not breathalysed him, but the speeding ticket was substantial and they had referred to a possible careless driving prosecution.

He walked in looking harassed, 'What happened to you? Annie asked, she was lying on the sofa eating an apple, trying not to be cross, 'I didn't wait for you, I've finished yesterday's chicken.

He walked over to the sofa, 'The worst! The gendarmes stopped me for speeding and possibly careless driving. She sat up, angry. 'Good Lord! How many times have I told you to slow down. You and that car...She took a bite from the apple, 'I've no sympathy at all. There was a silence, 'Have you eaten? she asked. Felix shrugged, 'I'll make myself an omelette. He held out a bag, 'I bought a turbot, a treat. Annie didn't look at the bag, 'Put it in the fridge, you can cook it tomorrow. She lay back on the sofa and picked up some work, ignoring him.

Felix trudged off, he knew that he was an idiot, spoiling supper, disappointing Annie and earning himself a hefty fine. 'I can't behave like this, he thought to himself, as he beat the eggs vigorously, he loved Annie and had no business drinking wine with an old girl friend, and perhaps even leading her a long a little. All the pleasure of his day had gone, 'I'll sell the car and buy something more suitable for a family, he decided. This day had been a warning in several ways.

CHAPTER 22

Marthe had finished the diary for 1943 and had avoided taking up the last diary, fearing what she might learn. She kept herself busy in the garden, working outside in the cool of the morning and reading in the shade of the orchard in the late afternoon. Claude visited several times and they had been to the cinema in Toulouse and once to supper with Felix and Annie. Marthe talked to him about her father and he listened thoughtfully. He was careful to avoid being judgemental but was reluctant to express any opinion. He knew that Felix thought that she was unwise to continue her research into the family history and he silently agreed with him.

Agathe called in regularly and talked enthusiastically about her life at the Retraite, she was becoming more confident which was a pleasure for Marthe who was steadily growing more fond of the girl. She had no regrets about the support she was giving. Gregoire had also started to visit her at Les Palmes as he returned home from working at the Chateau, her house was on his route and he brought with him salad leaves and summer vegetables. Marthe appreciated the opportunity to get to know him better and recognised what a hard working man he was, the orchard at Les Palmes was already benefiting from the pruning work he had done. Gregoire never lingered long always eager to get on with the next job. Marthe grew very fond of him too that summer.

But finally she could put off the diary for 1944 no longer, and taking a pot of lemon tea she installed herself on the veranda in the deep shade of the wisteria and began to read. The afternoon was hot and sultry, a storm was on its way edging up from the Pyrennes and Marthe feared that she would end her day with a headache. This diary was very different Bertrand's mood had changed; he made the briefest of references to the weather, his health, the work at the factory, and filled the pages with recording the deprivations that all were now suffering. He wrote bitterly, angrily of the German occupation, describing its impact on the daily life of his family and on the local community. For the first time, he referred to the work of the local Resistance, recording instances when they had disrupted fuel supplies and transport. He approved of their bravery. In March he wrote of 'disappearances' that were unexplained, men taken from their beds at night, causing deep distress amongst local families. Marthe had heard of these but had no real understanding of what that word implied. The town of St.Girou seethed with rumours, he wrote, and on the occasions when he entered a shop or joined a queue, people avoided his gaze. He had become worried and unsettled, he wrote. At the brick factory outside Toulouse, the fuel shortages were disrupting production and Bertrand was forced to lay off some of his already diminished work force, many of whom were women. Making a living was, he wrote, 'impossible'. In early April, on a rare trip into Toulouse, where he had an appointment at the bank, he confronted the local milice, who were using batons to break up a group of angry women queuing for bread, outside the market of St.Georges. Their violence horrified him, these are mothers he wrote, French women trying to feed their families. He gave one of the milice, a young soldier in an ill fitting German uniform, a hard push as he tried to stop his baton wielding and was struck himself. He narrowly avoided arrest, but was forced to give them his name and home address. He was badly shaken with a nasty bruise on his cheek. Marie was angry with him he wrote for putting himself in such danger.

Later that month as Marie suffered with a bad chest, she probably had bronchitis, he recorded the absence of medicines and local doctors. Working men were in short supply everywhere, and all areas of life in and around St. Girou were suffering. Bertrand recorded the fall in profits at his factory, he feared that he would soon have to close down.

Marthe read until her eyes were sore, thunder was rumbling to the South and huge sheets of lightening lit up the sky, which was a strange purple colour. She closed the diary, marking her place carefully, the date was May1, as she did so the storm rushed in, gusts of wind and heavy rain swept through the garden, and she ran for the kitchen door holding the diary close to her chest. She determined to read on the following day.

*

But her plan was stopped as Claude appeared unexpectedly at Les Palmes. Marthe shewed him into the sitting room and prepared a pot of coffee, she listened to him walking about. 'Moving things, she thought to herself, 'he can't bear not to! She carried in the tray and sure enough Claude had repositioned a small water colour painting, it was now to the right of the mantel, she watched as he tried to readjust the angle of her chair, the much loved one that Xavier had found for her many years ago. In Collioure. She smiled at him. 'Sorry! He said, 'But paintings need space, it was too crowded before. Marthe stood back, still holding the tray, she looked, 'Maybe, she said, 'I'll leave it there…for the moment. Claude liked that about Marthe, she could be impetuous but she was generally thoughtful. She also spoke her mind. That morning she was wearing a blue jumper over a cream blouse, and a deep blue necklace that sat neatly below the collar, these suited her pale colouring. That was something else he liked about her, she invariably dressed with care, it was not as though she knew he was coming, yet she was more than pleasant to look at. Claude sighed.

'What? Marthe asked, pouring his coffee, 'Why the sigh? And the visit?

There was a silence, she waited. He sipped his coffee it was hot and strong, just as he liked it, something else that he liked…he nearly sighed again, but stopped himself. 'I've done what you suggested, he said, 'I've put the reclamation business on hold, I shall concentrate on the hotel till September, it was silly of me to think that I could combine the two. Marthe nodded, 'Good, and are you delegating more?

'Trying to! But living on site, as it were, makes it difficult. One sees a problem and is drawn into solving it. But I'm trying. Let's talk about something else can we? I've rather come here to detach myself, the hotel is very noisy this morning, a loud group have arrived and are staying for several days, guests at a wedding in Auch tomorrow, all very jolly! They make me feel old. They had finished coffee, but his low mood prevailed and Marthe stood up, ' Let's go into the garden shall we? We had a storm last night so the garden will be fresh.

They walked out into bright sunshine, Claude felt the sun on his back and moved towards the shade of the palm trees. It was a delightful morning and the garden was very lovely, he touched one of the urns with his hand, it was a stone one, old and weathered, he remembered selling it to her the previous year. She had planted it with canna lilies in red and orange, they glowed in the morning heat. 'Come and see the fountain, Marthe said, 'It's my favourite place on a sunny day. They walked on and stopped by the twin statues of Diana which stood on either side of the stone basin that caught the water as it flowed from the fountain. She put her hand in, the water was cool, she stirred it gently, removing a leaf which floated on the surface. It was calm and peaceful. Claude thought of the hotel, 'Had he made a terrible mistake? Why was he living surrounded by people he didn't know? People who threw their cigarettes in the flower beds, left their towels beside the swimming pool, and shouted at each other across the terrace. He thought of Luc, content to work all day and late into the night in the kitchen, laughing with Joel the chef as they prepared food, and of Jerome, welcoming guests with an ease that Claude had never seen in him before. It's working for them, he thought, they appeared more than happy. I am the one who is struggling.

*

Marthe had now taken a seat on the bench opposite the two statues, she motioned for Claude to join her. 'Can I say something? She spoke in a low voice, 'I want to apologise for the letter I wrote to you at the end of last year. I regretted it almost immediately! I was in a…she stopped, flushing. He waited. 'At that time I thought I could make a new life for myself in Collioure, away from here and the troubles that beset me last year, the Henri business I mean. I was… running away. I didn't realise it of course, and Collioure had entranced me. You understand that; it's sunny and colourful, the streets are full of charm and the promenade has cafes and those delicious fish restaurants. And the sea! I've always wanted to live where I could see the sea every day. My urban Paris background of course. But I hadn't understood that the town is only fun in the summer days, and that most people are passing through or leave when the winter sets in. There are very few permanent residents, apart from those who work in the fishing industry or run shops.

When I wrote to you, she continued, 'I hadn't realised all that, and so I saw your suggestion that we should make a permanent commitment as an obstacle to my new freedom, a freedom that I overvalued. I loved our friendship, it was one of the happiest thing that happened to me last year, and I was, she looked at him, 'A fool to throw it away. But I couldn't admit to myself that I had made a mistake, I had rented in Collioure for six months I felt I had to stick it out. There was Felix too, he did not approve of my renting of the Collioure apartment and I felt I had to prove him wrong. My pride of course.

'A life in Collioure away from me! He said very quietly.

Marthe stopped talking, she could not see Claude's face he had his back to the sun and was in shadow. 'Yes! Then I had that horrible fall and lay on the sofa, with my wretched ankle in plaster and feeling sorry for myself. I had time to reflect and think about what I had thrown away. Our friendship.

'Was it never more than that? He asked.

'It was! Oh!Yes. They both sat silently, then Claude said,

'We'd better start again then, he moved closer and put his arm around her shoulders. He did not kiss her yet.

'A new beginning, Marthe said turning to look at him 'I'd like that. She knew how fortunate she was, it was a second chance. 'Shall we go in? she suggested. He knew what she meant and they walked silently back to the house, climbing the stairs together, and entered the cool of her bedroom.

*

Claude drove home in the late afternoon, he was more than surprised at this turn in his relationship with Marthe. It would be different now, this new beginning as she called it. He would not rush her as he had before, he would play it much more slowly, play it 'cool' as his sons would have said. But he was happy too, he wasn't in love in the way of young people, but he admired and respected Marthe and found her company enhancing. He stepped out of the car at the Chateau, a group of the wedding party were setting off with much noise and laughter. He smiled at them, and they waved back, one of the girls called out, 'We're going for a swim in the river. He smiled again, she was very pretty, she flirted with him, 'Do you want to come? He shook his head, flattered, 'The water will be cold, he warned.

Claude watched them go, he was glad that they were having fun. I must try and enjoy our guests and not see them as invaders. He decided. What if they are untidy, thoughtless and noisy? They are on holiday, and we are here to help them to have a good time. He walked into the chateau and on into the kitchen, Luc glanced up, he was preparing vegetables and his face was flushed with heat. 'Where've you been all day? He asked. 'Oh, here and there, Claude answered. He walked to one of the great fridges and found a bottle of cold white wine, opened it and poured a large glass, 'Your health! He said. Luc stared at him, 'Good day then?

'Yes. Thank you. Anything I can do?

*

Felix had decided to make a shorter visit than usual to the jazz festival at Marciac, he went alone as Charlie had been invited to a chess tournament, an opportunity that he could not miss. He promised to take Charlie the following year, assuring him that they would stay for at least three nights. Thus satisfied Charlie set off with his team for a tournament in Bordeaux. He would be away for several days. Felix left soon after. Annie would have the house to herself, which she anticipated with pleasure. Felix had stocked the fridge, put the washing machine on and watered the pots, 'You'll be all right? Won't you? He asked her as he picked up his overnight bag. Annie was in the kitchen, 'Go! Go! She said, 'It's only two nights. I can surely manage that. Felix hovered in the door, 'Please Felix...

It made a lovely change to have the house to herself and Annie sat on the sofa, in the salon, her feet up, and closed her eyes. No noise! No piano, no drums, no voices calling out, or feet running down the stairs. Peace! The baby kicked, 'And you can be quiet too, she said, tapping her bump, which was now becoming more uncomfortable. A deep contentment spread over her. She dozed.

*

Marciac was hot and humid, there was a summer storm brewing to the south, and thunder rumbled around, whilst the festival filled the small town to overflowing. Felix worked hard, attending as many sessions as he could, scribbling away in his pocket book. He met several colleagues, and sat up late into the night drinking beer as the music echoed around the arcades of the central square. It was lively, tiring and fun. On the second day, after a full day of jazz and following an uncomfortable night in a stuffy bedroom in a cheap hotel, he decided to leave and return to Toulouse. It was well after midnight as he drove out, a slight rain was falling. Felix knew the road well and settled into his journey, if he drove fast, he would be home in less than two hours.

Rounding a sharp corner, in an area dark with trees, his headlights caught the eyes of a huge wild boar, its wet coat glistening. It was crossing the road. Felix braked hard, skidded and hit the animal full on the chest. The impact caused the car to shudder, it slid on the wet road and flipped into a ditch, landing on its side. The driver's side. The boar was killed outright, it lay on the edge of the road, bleeding from horrible wounds to its head and chest. Felix, trapped in the car, was unconscious.

Soon after a young couple, also returning from Marciac, rounded the same bend and seeing the red car in the ditch, made a hasty stop. The rain was falling lightly as they warily approached the car, horrified by the scene in front of them. Seeing Felix wedged against the steering wheel, his eyes shut, they stood together holding hands, uncertain as to what to do. The young girl said, 'You go and find somewhere to phone and I'll stay here. And put out our yellow triangle or someone will hit us! The man set off back the way he had come. The girl waited beside Felix's car, there was glass from the shattered windows both inside and outside and she reached in cautiously to touch him. He was warm and breathing, she stroked his head.

*

Within a remarkably short time the ambulance had arrived and with great care, Felix was lifted out, he moaned as they manoeuvered him through the windscreen, his eye lids flickering. He was taken to the hospital back in Marciac. In the morning the Gendarmes attended and Felix's car was towed away. The body of the boar was pushed from the road onto the grass verge, where it lay to be pecked at by birds, and gnawed by foxes. Its bones were soon scattered far and wide. Felix's car which had given him so much pleasure was taken for scrap.

In Felix's wallet, they found his address in Toulouse and a phone number, so Annie was the first to hear the news. She had got out of bed to use the lavatory, the baby pressing on her bladder, when she heard the ring. 'Charlie! She thought as she picked it up, her heart pounding, almost dizzy with apprehension. It was four in the morning, still dark, and the house was very quiet as she stood in her night gown, hearing a voice tell her of an accident to M.Felix le Brun. She was given the address of the hospital and told that M. le Brun would be in surgery first thing in the morning. No one could see him till later that day. His injuries were not life threatening.

*

Annie, numb with shock, sat on the sofa in the kitchen, staring at the courtyard and seeing nothing. At nine she phoned Marthe. They agreed to go to Marciac together late in the afternoon, and Annie would drive them. They spoke briefly, there was little to say. The morning passed slowly, Annie tried to keep calm but her mind raced as every possibility passed through it, she couldn't remember what the hospital had said. What were his injuries? Why was he needing surgery? How urgent was it? What had they said? She phoned the hospital, but was told only that Felix was in surgery, she could see him later if all went well.

His injuries were extensive. He had three fractured ribs, a deep gash across his face, which had only narrowly stopped at his left eye, but worst was the damage to his left hand, it had been crushed. The damage to his head, which had caused concussion, was not thought to be too serious. His seat belt and the strong shell of his car had saved his life.

For two days Felix, heavily sedated, moved in and out of consciousness. Marthe and Annie shared their time with him, talking to the doctors and encouraging him to open his eyes. It was exhausting and Annie tried in vain to persuade the doctors to move him to Toulouse, the journey there and back to Marciac, was time consuming. They regarded her sympathetically, noticing her pregnancy and shaking their heads. 'Maybe in a week' if he improves, was all they offered. She was overwhelmed with worry, he looked so fragile and pale, the black stitches near his eye, cutting across his face. On the third day the surgeon came to see Felix, Marthe was sitting quietly reading beside the bed; she had brought in a small CD player and he was listening to Chopin Preludes his 'good' hand moving in time. A long discussion followed. The damage to his left hand was serious: three of his fingers had been injured, and there were fractures to the wrist where several bones had been broken and these had now been set, it lay on the bed protected by a heavy plaster. The surgeon could not guarantee a full recovery of movement. Marthe gasped, 'He's a pianist! This can't be! Felix had turned pale and she looked at the surgeon in mounting horror, 'Can nothing be done? She demanded, 'Further operations? We could take him to Paris! The surgeon shook his head, 'That is your decision Madame, his voice was curt, 'I have done all I can. He left shortly after and they sat in silence, avoiding each other's eyes. It was devastating news.

*

Annie arrived later in the afternoon, Charlie would be home the following day, she had not told him what had happened, believing that it would distract and worry him and his chess tournament would be spoiled. Felix had been in hospital for four days now, he lay propped up on pillows and she listened as he reported the surgeon's news. 'No more piano! He said and she leant over and hugged him as he struggled to hold back tears. The full implications of the accident had finally overwhelmed him. There was not much that could be said, Annie stayed as long as she was permitted, helping him to eat his supper, with one hand, and opening the bathroom door.

She watched him walk shakily across the room, the plastered hand supported in a sling, and tried to hide her concern. She did not fool herself, the weeks ahead were going to be difficult and she feared that his life would now be very different.

*

Charlie did not visit the hospital but helped to prepare the house for Felix's return. He did not understand the gravity of the accident and Annie shielded him from any great anxiety, they planned Felix's return and went together to collect him. Charlie was shocked to see the plaster, the ugly scar and the shaven area around it, but he felt sure that Felix would soon be back to normal. He chatted happily in the back of the car as Annie drove home, telling them about the trip to Bordeaux, he patted Felix on the shoulder, 'You'll be better soon, he said, 'Don't worry, I'll be a help. You'll be able to pick up the baby, wont' you? He asked. No one had thought of that. Felix's stomach heaved and he felt sick, Annie looked at him briefly and answered, 'Of course. He'll be fine by then. But she was by no means sure, how would they cope? How would Felix? Driving slowly they passed the point of the road where Felix had crashed, it was marked by long skid marks, the damaged verge and some part of a bumper, rearing up out of the ditch. No one spoke. A moment of anger swept through Annie. Had he been driving too fast? Was that the explanation? They hadn't talked about the accident, as Felix could not remember any details, just the wet road and the boar and losing control of the car. Concussion had blocked out the rest. Annie wondered if she would ever know what had happened. A brief error maybe, yet, it now seemed likely, its consequences would affect him for the rest of his life. She wondered if he had thought about that.

*

The month of August in Toulouse was always difficult; hot days were followed by hot uncomfortable nights, the city was full of tourists who crowded the streets, bars and restaurants, seeking shade in the narrow streets and retreating into the dark churches and the squares where the giant plane trees gave protection from the sun. In the house in the Rue des Capuchins, Annie closed the shutters, permitting light and air to enter only on the north facing side, whilst the high ceilings and tiled floors helped to create a cool atmosphere. But the days were long and slow. Annie was increasingly absorbed in her pregnancy, the baby kept her awake both day and night and she anticipated the birth with a cheerful optimism that carried them all along. Charlie was admirably kind, eager to assist both Annie and Felix, he provided a distraction that they needed, and the house felt empty on the days when he was out with school friends. Felix struggled. He went through the motions of daily life, getting dressed, though he needed help, and eating the meals which Annie now prepared. He spent long hours in the kitchen watching her and Charlie, unable to do very much, restlessly reading and talking on the phone. He drifted around his study, avoiding the piano, Annie had tactfully closed the lid, but it stood there in the centre of the room, and he touched its smooth surface sadly. He tried very hard not to feel sorry for himself, but was unable to suppress a sense of failure, that he had let Annie down, and was making these last weeks of her pregnancy more difficult. He brooded constantly about the accident, 'Was he to blame? And worst did Annie blame him? Had he been driving too fast? He was overwhelmed with guilt and self doubt. As the days passed, his ribs slowly healed and he could walk and sit with little pain and the scar over his eye became less noticeable. But the wrist and hand were endlessly painful. His plaster was changed and he was told to exercise his fingers regularly. He could not concentrate, was moody and short tempered, whilst trying to do the exercises that the hospital had insisted were the key to his recovery.

*

Annie tried to be patient, hoping that once the pain was easier he would be more cheerful, but tossing uncomfortably at night, hot and thirsty, the baby endlessly disturbing her, she worried about this disruption to their lives. She was very concerned at the injuries to his wrist, there was some discussion about possible future surgery. Marthe wanted to take him to Paris, certain that the very best surgeons were there, no one knew if she was right, and Felix was adamant that if he needed further operations he could have them in Toulouse. Annie tried to put her worries aside and concentrate on looking after him and giving time to Charlie, whose summer holidays were coming to an end. He refused to go to England, despite pressure from Ralph and her mother Claire, replying that he was needed in Toulouse to help with Felix and his mother, whose size now amazed him.

'How big is this baby? He asked with a worried frown, they were eating supper and Felix was trying to clear the table. Annie grinned at him, massaging her stomach, 'Quite big, but a lot of this bump is the fluid around her. She'll be about the size you were I should think. They both stared at her, 'She's so calm! Felix thought, and he put down the plates he was holding and gave her a one sided hug. The baby was the only real distraction now and he was excited every time he looked at her. Annie touched him lightly, she thought he was looking better and had made them laugh at supper, with a description of the family car he was planning to buy. 'Very dull, very grey, very solid, very slow, he had said with a sad face, 'Or maybe not! You can help me choose, Charlie. We'll have a boy's outing, as soon as I can drive.

Annie was relieved to see Felix joking again, he was more like the Felix who she loved, the Felix she wanted back.

*

Claude learnt of the accident several days after it had happened. He had phoned Marthe several times and become frustrated at her failure to respond to his calls. He drove to Les Palmes late one afternoon, having spent most of his day going through the accounts and was looking forward to a quiet drink in her garden, and even supper. Marthe opened the door and said,' You'd better come in. No smile. No welcoming kiss. He hurried down the hall behind her. She told him what had happened whilst standing in the kitchen, Claude listened in silence, the strain on her face told it all. He walked to the fridge and took out a bottle of wine, poured two glasses and said, 'Follow me! They sat beside the fountain and for a while neither spoke. Marthe, Claude realised, was in shock, and he thought of Felix of whom he was very fond, lying in hospital. Marthe's only son, and her only close relative. What if it had been worst? How close had Felix been to…

She turned to him, and tried to speak, but Claude stopped her, 'Just sit here with me quietly, let your fears come out. You've not spoken to anyone have you? It's all bottled up inside you, I know. Let it go Marthe.

And she did, she cried and cried for what felt like hours, he waited, sipping his wine. Finally there was silence. And then she began to speak, describing the car crash and Felix's injuries and all the horrible sights and sounds of the hospital and the endless driving to and from Marciac and her terrible anxieties. He did not interrupt and asked no questions, at the back of his mind thinking of his own two sons, safe at the chateaux. He stood up and put his hand out, 'I'll make us supper shall I?

'There's nothing to eat, I've not felt hungry.

'Let's go and look, there's always something.

Claude stayed all evening, and, for the first time since she had heard the dreadful news, Marthe began to revive. She ate the supper and drank both wine and a small glass of whisky, and even managed to laugh at Claude's descriptions of events at the hotel. He did not stay the night but kissed her gently at the door, 'He'll be fine, he's young and Annie will take good care of him. He just has to get over these next weeks. The injuries may not be as serious as you fear. He needs you to be optimistic and very positive and you can do that.

*

Marthe had put aside the diaries of Bertrand since the accident and so the following morning to distract herself, she took the last diary into the sitting room and began to read. The month of May 1944. Bertrand had received news of the death of his cousin in Strasbourg, and a request from his widow that he should come and be with her. The arrival of the letter was something of a miracle as the postal service, subject to German censorship, was in a state of collapse. It had been posted in Strasbourg some ten days previously. The brick factory outside Strasbourg needed him urgently she wrote. This factory was the heart of the family business, it had been founded by their grandfather in the middle of the previous century and was the source of the wealth that had benefited both families. Bertrand prepared carefully for a journey which would be difficult, requiring the newly imposed travel passes and he anticipated long delays. Marie packed his small case, including a tin of foie gras for the widow and Marthe popped in one of her most loved hankies. It had a border of daisies her favourite flower. He slipped in his book on French philosophers of the 19th Century, it would prove to be the most useful item from his home, and inside the pages, a photo of Marie. It shewed her sitting in the orchard of Les Palmes on a summer's day, her face shaded by a straw hat, and holding some sewing in her hands.

Bertrand left early in the morning after the arrival of the letter, he planned to walk to the local branch line, a short distance from St. Girou and take the train into Toulouse. He turned at the gate of Les Palmes to wave farewell to his wife and his tearful daughter, he hoped, he wrote, to be home again in a couple of weeks. He carried his leather suitcase, as he strode off, but, beneath his calm exterior he was agitated and full of apprehension.

The diary continued with an account of his journey; he arrived from St. Girou at Toulouse, where he planned to take an express train to Lyon and change there for a train to Strasbourg. A simple enough if long journey in peace time, but it was 1944 and, as he feared, the timetables had no meaning at all. The express train out of Toulouse moved slowly North, through the apple and pear orchards of the Garonne valley which gave way to steep limestone hills where cattle grazed and then the vineyards of the Rhone valley. Bertrand noted the empty fields where men should have been at work, in their place he saw women driving the cows into barns and ploughing on ancient tractors, their hair tied up with cotton scarves. Men's work he reflected. It was depressing and deeply disturbing. The train moved slowly into the Zone Nord and was boarded by German troops who demanded to see travel passes and spoke roughly. The soldiers were young and nervous, recently recruited and barely trained, they were as ill fed as his fellow passengers. Everyone appeared tired and anxious, cowed by the soldiers as they held out their passes, avoiding eye contact. No one spoke as the soldiers passed through the train, banging doors and shouting and making coarse comments to the women on board. Bertrand kept to himself, quietly reading his book and eager to be as inconspicuous as possible.

He slept that night at Lyon, in the railway station with many others and was fortunate to buy a stale sandwich made of something which was not bread, and finished the last of the dried sausage that Marie had packed. He was still two hundred miles from his destination. As the dawn light filtered through to the platform where he lay, he opened his diary and wrote, recording the arrogance of the Germans and the humiliation of the French. What had happened to German discipline and the strict morality that he had admired just a few years before?

The sudden death of his cousin, Jean Luc, the uncertainty surrounding the whereabouts of his two sons(who were believed to have joined the Resistance) the emotional collapse of his widow, combined with an atmosphere in the city of fear and panic, made Bertrand's stay an unpleasant experience. His daily record of his life there made difficult reading and Marthe was moved as she read.

*

His low spirits were evident as was his growing anger at the Nazi occupation and its impact on the factory and daily life in Strasbourg. Every man, woman and child was hungry and the long queues for bread and other basic food created a mood of desperation. The American bombers, flying nightly from their bases in England were causing serious damage to the ancient buildings in the heart of the city, though Strasbourg regarded as a 'French' city did not suffer as badly as the German cities to the east. None the less many thousands were killed during the bombing raids of 1944 one of whom had been Jean Luc who had been blasted out of a window at his factory. Rumours of the expected Allied advance after the D Day landings added to the tension and excitement, and Bertrand learnt of French families who had been sympathetic to the German occupation now hiding their valuables and looking for an exit route across the Rhine to the East. It was not clear to Marthe what Bertrand felt about this. He wrote of his exhaustion as he struggled to deal with the problems of the factory which was suffering from lack of fuel and shortage of workers. Jean Luc's widow became increasingly resentful of his presence in her house and his meals with her were meagre. She had taken his ration book and locked away her husband's fine wines in her cellar, Bertrand complained that he was permanently hungry.

*

He left in late June, having been away for more than five weeks, he had not received a single letter from Marie though he knew she would have been writing regularly. He left behind a City in a state of extreme confusion; German troops with mounting desperation were trying to maintain control, marching through the streets with heavy batons whilst armoured trucks were positioned at junctions and outside the government buildings. Bertrand's walk to the station was difficult and he kept to the back streets, holding his case close to his chest observing the cars blocking the roads leading East piled high with luggage, with white faced children staring out. Some had resorted to pushing hand carts, laden with baskets, filled with clothes and food and such valuables as they possessed. There was fallen masonry adding to his difficulties and he briefly lost his way. This is war he wrote later, it was his first real encounter with its realitites.

*

Bertrand's train drew out of Strasburg in the early afternoon, only to stop in a siding, the passengers forced to wait in discomfort. It was very hot. No one spoke. Bertrand noted in his diary later that he watched engines shunting trucks up and down the tracks, he was bemused. A fellow passenger broke the silence, 'Going East. Poor devils.' he commented. 'Soldiers? Bernard asked. The man shrugged, 'Maybe, or French prisoners of war, or Communists, Jews, men linked to the Resistance. Heading East to work in the Polish mines or... worse. His words hung in the air and no one spoke. 'They're cattle trucks surely? Bertrand asked staring at him. The man shrugged again, 'Makes no difference to them. Must be hot though.

Bernard was appalled, these are human beings, he wrote later, such treatment was against all the rules of war and humanity. It was unjustifiable.

His previous support for German values, the discipline of their education, their upholding of family life, and the subsequent occupation of France he now understood was misplaced. It had brought only misery and harsh treatment of civilians and hunger and transportation and forced labour. He felt overwhelmed by his error.

CHAPTER 23

Home in Les Palmes, Bertrand took up his diary, his spirits continued to be low and he complained of head aches and pains in his stomach. Thoughts now poured out of him: he wrote of the fevered atmosphere throughout the Gers, and a growing expectancy that the success of the Allies in the North would prompt long desired changes throughout France. The fall of the Nazis was widely anticipated. There were rumours in St. Girou of growing support for the Resistance and increasing activity, it was met by brutal German responses and atrocities were committed on both sides. Life had become dangerous.

Bertrand kept to himself, rarely going out of his home except to visit the factory, whilst all his earlier hopes for strong government and an ordered society lay in tatters. He received a letter from the widow in Strasbourg, one of

her sons had made his way to England through Holland and had joined the Free French, he was well she wrote. But of the younger son there was no news, she had heard nothing for nearly a year and feared that he was amongst the 'disappeared. Reading this Bertrand turned from his writing and listened to the voice of little Marthe who was helping her mother in the kitchen. 'Safe!' he wrote.

Marthe paused, her sympathy for Bertrand aroused, she could no longer see him in the same light as before. He was disillusioned and unwell she understood, only his daily walks beside the river raised his spirits. As she read into July, it became increasingly sad to read the entries of a man so isolated and unhappy, so disillusioned. As historic events were taking place, as the German army retreated East, and all over Europe there was for the first time a real belief that the war would soon be over, Bertrand sat reading history books in his library and walking his little dog beside the river. All his hopes for a France renewed in the German model were over.

The diary stopped suddenly.

*

Marthe was deeply sad. She sat at the kitchen table, thinking; it seemed apparent to her that Bertrand was not in the summer of 1944 the man that she had understood him to be. She doubted whether he was in anyway now supportive of the Nazi regime, for his diary recorded his dislike of the milice, his hatred of their methods as seen in Toulouse, and his horror at what he had seen sitting in the train outside Strasbourg. Was this a man who would act as an informer? Who would give the names of Jews and members of the local Resistance to the Germans? She did not think so. Also living such a closeted life after his return to Les Palmes how would he have any information to give?

*

She thought of the plaque on the church wall and came to believe that Bertrand had been wrongly held responsible for the arrests and subsequent deaths of the five men. It seemed more than possible that he was a scapegoat seized upon by local hotheads who were eager to blame someone for their losses. She thought of the young Rinaldi brothers, both active in the Resistance. Had they been mistaken? In the febrile atmosphere of that summer it could have happened.

Maybe the information that had led to the drowning of Bertrand, or his murder as she believed, was based not on facts but on suspicion, even prejudice, at a time when law and order were in collapse, and personal vendettas abounded. That it had been a terrible mistake, by the young Rinaldi brothers seemed to her a real possibility.

*

Marthe carefully placed all the diaries in the Salon, beside her mother's desk. She found a small photo of Bertrand in a drawer and looked at it carefully. He was dressed in a well cut suit with a high collared shirt and tie, he stood erect his hair neatly brushed back from his face. Somewhat grave but distinguished. 'Who were you? 'What happened to you? Marthe had no memory of him at all.

And what of her mother? What had Marie known of all this? The old gardener Jacques had spoken of the bonfires she had built in the garden immediately after Bertrand's death, burning papers. Were these evidence of his contacts with the Nazis? Had she realised that his sudden death was suspicious and not an accident? Was she ashamed of him or fearful for her own safety. Marie had packed a single case and taken Marthe from Les Palmes very abruptly and never returned. Why?

She sat at the desk knowing that she would never learn the answers to these questions about her father, her mother and her past.

*

At the end of August, Charlie returned to school and Felix and Annie spent their days quietly in the house. Neither of them was working which felt strange, and their days passed with little routine, apart from meals and Felix's visits from the physiotherapist. Time dragged for both of them. Annie had a check up at the hospital, all was well, the baby was a good weight and the expected date was now mid September. Felix watched the screen and felt a thrill run through him, this baby would be born within a few weeks, and their lives would change for ever. The nurse handed them some images of the foetus, which they could show to Charlie.

Felix and Annie had talked very little about the accident, she felt it was in the past and no longer worried about how or why it had happened. She did not want to explore Felix's role that night, it was easier to look forward to his recovery. He was grateful for that, but it continued to cause him sleepless nights, waking in a cold sweat of fear, his mouth dry and his heart pounding. He was haunted by remorse and regret. Marthe visited regularly; she helped Annie finish the preparation of the nursery and cooked them lunch, bringing treats from the market, a pineapple, and late strawberries and and tall gladioli still in bud. Annie ate enthusiastically, her appetite surprised them both. She saw them watching her and smiled, 'Sorry! I'm just hungry all the time!' She was quite unrepentant. Marthe urged Felix to play the piano, but he shook his head, his wrist would not allow him to use that hand. On a bright morning she arrived early and took Felix out in her car,

'Claude's invited us to lunch, you need a change of scene!' She said firmly. Annie was not sad to see them go, she would have a quiet afternoon and talk to her mother on the phone. Marthe left her some lunch in the fridge, a salad of goat's cheese with walnuts and chicory, and an apple tart.

Marthe took the road towards the Chateau and Felix looked out of the window, it was wonderful to see the countryside after so many weeks not being able to drive a car, confined in the hospital and in Toulouse. It was all so green and peaceful, so unchanging. He began to talk and then couldn't stop: all his feelings of remorse and shame and lack of self worth poured out. Marthe listened and said nothing, until finally there was silence. She stopped the car beside the road on the grass verge, turned off the engine and turned to him,

'Felix listen to me. You've had a traumatic time and the next months may well be challenging. But your injuries will get better and, heaven knows, it could all have been much worse, you could have killed yourself. Next month you'll become a father and Annie needs you to play your part, to support her, help her and celebrate the baby. You have to stop feeling sorry for yourself and obsessing about the accident and think of her! I don't want to see you moping around your lovely house. Get back to work! I don't see why you are not writing for the newspaper or playing the piano. Take Charlie out…there's so much that you are not doing! You'll feel better immediately. This has been hard on all of us, now you can make it easier if we see you trying to enjoy life again. This is a test for you, and it's one you can't fail.

She stopped talking and put the car into gear and drove off, they would be at the Chateau in a few minutes. Felix had not been spoken to so fiercely in a long while and he was shocked. The last sentence resounded 'a test you can't fail'. He knew that his mother had always been slightly disappointed in him, thinking that he had spread his talents too thinly and not applied himself. He couldn't bear to think that she now feared that he would collapse under this new situation, would fail Annie and himself.

'I don't think I can manage lunch. He said.

'Of course you can, Claude will do all the talking and he's a good friend and we can't disappoint him. He's probably been cooking something delicious all morning.

They turned down the drive and parked outside the wing, Felix eased himself out of the car, his face was pale.

'Now, let's try and have a nice time, shall we? Marthe said, taking his good hand and they walked in.

*

Annie ate her lunch, had a rest and spoke to her mother. Claire was eager to come out to Toulouse as soon as the baby was born, an idea that Annie was resisting. After several minutes of argument, Claire agreed to wait at least a month, by which time for Annie and Felix and Charlie, life should have settled down. 'How's Felix? Claire asked. Annie was non committal, brushing off the question as best she could. Claire listened but knew her daughter well enough to realise that it was not a subject that was up for discussion. Putting down the phone shortly afterwards, Claire went to join Tony in the sitting room, 'There's something not quite right in Toulouse, she said. 'Oh? Tony was doing the crossword, the dog Archie tucked under his arm, 'Nothing too much, I'm sure, he replied. 'I think it's Felix, Claire said, 'We never really got the full story of the accident did we? Maybe it was more complicated than we realised.

She sat down next to him, 'I think there's a lot going on that she's not telling me.

'Did you tell your mother everything then? He sucked his pencil as he spoke, 'I guess not! Claire said, 'Still one does worry. Tony filled in a clue, 'She's a very very capable young woman, your daughter, whatever it is, she'll sort it out.

*

Annie was also thinking about the conversation with her mother, but any longer consideration was prevented by the return of Charlie and Felix, who had arrived by chance almost simultaneously at the street door. Marthe had returned home, hoping that her attempt to jolt Felix out of his low spirits would be successful. She heard their voices as they mounted the stairs, laughing and joking. Charlie came in with his usual rush and clatter, heading straight for the fridge, whilst talking to his mother. Felix sat at the table, awkwardly removing his jacket. 'All ok? Did you rest? He asked. She nodded her head, 'And you? How was Claude?

'Oh you know charming and chatty, I think he and my mother are seeing more of each other, much more.

'That's good, Annie said, 'they're well suited. They had a blip in the winter, I could see that, but it's been sorted. They are happier together than apart I think. There was some one else in the spring though, nice woman from Bordeaux, Claude likes female company that's for sure.

'Don't we all! Felix said and Annie realised he was making a real effort to be more cheerful. She kissed him and grinned.

*

Felix turned to Charlie, who had finished a salami sandwich and was wondering what else to eat, 'Would you like a game of chess? Or shall we try a sort of duet on the piano? Me doing the right hand...

Charlie was delighted, both ideas were appealing 'Let's try a duet. We've never done that before. They both got up, Felix waving at Annie as they headed towards the stairs, 'Stay where you are! He called back at her, 'I'll do a risotto for supper, there's lots of mushrooms in the fridge and Claude gave me salad from the garden. Annie was as surprised as Charlie, this was the first time that Felix had shown any interest in doing anything, 'What had caused this change of mood? She wondered.

*

It had of course been Marthe. Felix had been deeply affected by the conversation in the car. Throughout lunch, where, as Marthe predicted, Claude had done most of the talking, he had reflected on her words, knowing that she spoke with all the benefit of age and experience. Marthe too had suffered an unexpected blow, a much greater one, a tragedy, when Xavier, her husband, had died suddenly of a heart attack. But, Felix thought, she had not lingered for long in her grief, but had picked herself up and made a new life at Les Palmes. By comparison his accident was a minor event. He had been quiet in the car, as she drove back to Toulouse and as he climbed out he had said, 'You're right, and I will pull myself together. Thank you.

*

Agathe's time working in the Maison de Retraite was over and she was sad to say farewell to the elderly folk who she regarded as her friends. They gave her a little tea party and a scarf and several hankies, and she presented them with a cake decorated with the last of Gregoire's late raspberries. The manager slipped an envelope into her hand as she handed back her uniform, 'Good luck! Don't forget us! He was genuinely sorry to see her leave. She collected her moped and set off home, diverting to visit Marthe, who she had not seen for a couple of weeks. She was sad, but also very excited, she would start at the hospital in Auch the following week, her training was about to begin.

She found Marthe in the garden, with a man she had not met before, it was Claude. They were deep in discussion and she tried to slip away, but Marthe saw her and called out.' Come in! It was an opportune moment as they had been near to arguing.

Marthe had been talking about her father and his diaries, in particular his account of the year 1944. Claude knew a little of the history of Bertrand du Pont, having become involved in Marthe's family history the previous year when the vendetta against her had resulted in the damage to her garden and the subsequent arrest of Henri Carrere. He now listened carefully to Marthe, silently questioning her renewed attempt to understand Bertrand's role in the deaths of the five men. Claude did not support her new idea of returning to the elderly Jean Jacques Rinaldi to press him on what more he knew, or remembered. He thought it was close to harassment. They had been locked in this disagreement when Agathe surprised them. She was of course herself a Rinaldi, and Marthe, impulsively revealed that to Claude, deliberately introducing her as Mlle. Agathe Rinaldi. He was astonished. It was an extraordinary connection. The present with the past.

She was a pretty girl, he thought, with dark hair and a pleasing smile. She was clearly very fond of Marthe. Agathe described the little party at the Maison and shewed her the scarf.

'And next week I start in Auch! She said, 'I can hardly believe it! Claude listened as she spoke animatedly about the coming months, 'What Marthe has done for this girl, he thought, is really generous. Why is she digging in the past again? She may learn something that could jeopardize her relationship with Agathe and her family. And throw away all her kindness. It was certainly most unfortunate this connection between Bertrand and the family who lived in the Moulin.

Agathe rose to leave and they all stood up, Marthe and Claude returned to the house, but there was slight chill between them and he left soon after. Driving home Claude wondered what, if anything, Felix knew of his mother's visits to Agathe's father and the great uncle in Auch, he decided to take Felix out to lunch.

*

A few days later Claude and Felix were relaxing in one of the better restaurants on the Place du Capitol. Seated at a table away from the street, they talked about the hotel, which was still busy with older people now that the children had returned to school. 'It's quieter, but somehow I quite miss the fun around the swimming pool and the laughter in the dining room, Claude said, he was eating a slice of terrine and waving his hand for more bread. Felix smiled, 'Well, you look well on it! Very tanned and slim! Claude accepted the compliment with a nod of his head, then asked gently about his injured wrist. Felix sighed, 'I'll not know for several months, if I will recover full mobility, the physiotherapist says I have to be patient, wrist bones are slow to mend. I may have to think again, if I can no longer play the piano. I could try some conducting work, though that's a difficult world to break into, and there's my writing… the music criticism. I'm lucky…

'To be alive, Claude said. Felix hesitated, and a silence fell.

The waiter appeared and put a plate of shell fish in front of Claude, Felix had chosen fillets of sole in lemon sauce which was easier to eat with one hand. Several minutes later, Claude dipped his fingers in the little bowl beside him on the table, wiped them carefully, and sat back in his chair. He drank some wine and feeling this was an appropriate moment raised the subject of Marthe. Felix listened in a mixture of surprise and horror. He was immediately angry that his mother hadn't informed him of either of her visits. His face grew flushed as Claude spoke. 'I hope you don't think that I'm being disloyal to your mother, Claude said, but I am concerned. She may find out things that are painful and upsetting. She is perhaps a little naïve.

Felix was too angry to consider that, 'We've disagreed about this whole business before, last year I urged her to put the past behind her, but she insisted on writing to Jean Jacques Rinaldi and finding out as much as she could about her father. They are a complicated family, there were four sons, it was the eldest who died on the train outside Strasbourg, but they use the same name! Jacques. A family thing I suppose. Claude said, 'Well it was a difficult story for her to ignore, be fair! And those diaries turning up was unfortunate. It brought the whole thing back into focus again. I do sympathise with her a little, but I don't think it's wise to embark on this...

'Harassment?

'That's a strong word, Claud said, 'but it might be thought that.

'I'll talk to her, as calmly as I can. Felix said, 'But she can be unpredictable and doesn't like people telling her what to do, or what not to do! I'm still struggling to understand the matter of the twins, though I like them enough.

Claude said, 'I met the girl, Agathe, the other afternoon, she's about to start her training in Auch. I liked her, with your mother's help, she'll do well. Marthe is head strong, we both know that, but you aren't going to change her, and she has a great deal of common sense. It is very generous what she is doing for the two of them. Felix remembered the 'talking to' she had given him on their journey to lunch with Claude, she had really shaken him up, but she had been right on that at least, and he was grateful.

'I'll speak with her once I've calmed down. He promised.

*

Lunch was over and they strolled back together, Felix bought a bouquet of dark red dahlias in the market, and then added impulsively an armful of lilies. They parted at the entrance to the car park in the Place du Capitol, Claude gave Felix a hug, 'Go gently with your mother, you're going to see lots of her, when the baby arrives! And she can't do much harm with her enquiries. Felix walked back to his house, not sure that he agreed with Claude on his last point. He climbed the stairs, 'Annie! I'm back. He put the flowers in the sink, filling it with cold water. The house was quiet and he assumed she was resting, he found her in their bedroom, she was holding onto the bed post, breathing heavily, panting. He was aghast, 'What is it? She looked at him, 'The baby! She's on her way!

'But... you're not due!

'Well, babies are unpredictable! Labour started just as soon as you both left. Felix stared at her, 'What can I do? My God, I should never have left you!

'Don't be silly, there's nothing to be done yet, but a cup of tea would be nice. I'll come downstairs.

They had forgotten Charlie, who could be heard banging about, just back from school. 'Don't look so anxious Felix please! I don't want Charlie to be upset. This labour could take many hours... She went down the stairs, pausing to breathe as a wave of pain ran through her and sat on the sofa as she sipped the tea trying to find a comfortable position.

But she was wrong, the pains grew stronger and stronger, and Annie told Felix to summon the midwife. He was now in an agony of apprehension, pacing about and getting in the way as Annie panted and moaned. Charlie was sent to spend the evening with a friend from school, he left with some reluctance but also a sense of relief, he did not enjoy seeing his mother in distress. She waved him out of the kitchen blowing him a kiss of reassurance. Felix helped her back upstairs and prepared the bedroom, trying not to panic. The door bell rang and he raced back down the stairs throwing the door open. The mid wife had arrived, she made her way upto the bedroom. A few minutes later, Annie suddenly cried out and then again more loudly, she was in the bathroom, and the midwife rushed in, shouted to Felix and within a matter of minutes, delivered the baby on the bathroom floor. It was chaotic and noisy and wonderful and terrifying and the most extraordinary thing that had ever happened to Annie and Felix. The ambulance arrived in the middle of it all and within a few minutes Annie and her baby were taken out by stretcher to be checked over at the maternity hospital. Felix was left behind to pick up Charlie and follow on in a taxi.

They were reunited at Annie's bedside in a small room containing a cot and her bed and two chairs. Charlie stopped at the entrance, then walked slowly forward. Annie watched him, she held the baby tightly wrapped in a hospital shawl, she was smiling. 'Come and see, she urged him, 'you have a sister! Felix held back as Charlie stared in awe at the baby, whose head was covered in dark hair. He hadn't expected that, he didn't know that some babies were born with hair. He touched her head cautiously. 'Come here! Annie said and with some difficulty gave him a hug. 'She came very quickly! I'm fine, she reassured him, Charlie was still very silent. 'Sit down, she said and they brought forward the chairs one on each side of the high bed, and with great care she handed the baby to Felix who took her gingerly, it wasn't easy with his damaged wrist, he gazed at his daughter, she was so small and fragile, he was very tense. 'Sit back! Annie said, slowly he relaxed and smiled at her, 'Wow you gave us all a fright! She looks beautiful, so delicate. I'm bursting with pride and happiness. Annie you are a sensation!

Annie watched as he gently held the baby, she too was bursting with happiness, and relief that it was all over.

*

'What's her name? Charlie asked, they looked at each other, 'Rose, they said together, 'What do you think?' That sound ok with you? She should have two! Charlie said. 'So, as Rose is quite sort of English, maybe Louise I like that name. and it's French. Isn't it? It was agreed the baby would be Rose Louise. Her last name was more problematical and it was left for the moment.

The hospital released Annie and Rose soon after and they returned home, in a somewhat breathless state. Charlie had recovered his poise and helped his mother up the stairs, Felix carried Rose. Annie was settled on the sofa in the kitchen and the baby was given back to her. They all stared at her, 'It seems hardly possible, Felix said, 'This morning it was us three and now we are four!

'I'm hungry! Charlie moved towards the fridge, 'Is there any supper?

'Yes I'm hungry too! Annie said, 'Felix? He jumped up. He had lost all sense of time, it was nearly eight o'clock.

The evening passed in some disorder, and Annie went to bed as soon as supper was over. She was tired but elated. The baby now in her beautiful cot, lay beside the bed asleep. To wake at two in the morning. Life with a baby had begun.

*

The late summer passed in a blur as they settled down to their changed lives; Charlie, hugely proud of his sister, invited his friends to see her, and Annie stood by watching, as they surrounded the cot, and Charlie pointed out her dark eyes and little hands. They stared awkwardly, uncomfortable to be surrounded by all the baby things, the little cloths, the basket of washing, the creams and bottles of lotion, until their fascination wore off, and they backed away, smiling politely. They ran up to Charlie's bedroom, and later she heard them in the kitchen noisily eating biscuits, finally rushing off outside for football in the square. Charlie loved watching Annie as she breast fed, murmuring to herself, stroking Rose's head or playing with her tiny feet, but best of all he enjoyed the weekly bath time, which was a time he shared with Annie; he quickly learnt to pass her little flannel and to support her head, almost holding his breath he was so determined to get everything right.

*

There were visitors: Marthe popped in regularly with gifts of food and little things for the baby, she insisted that Rose looked just like her son when he was a baby, and took endless photos. Annie had to admit that with her dark hair she did resemble Felix. Claude came too, bringing a silver mug with two handles, which Annie feared she would never use, it was engraved with her name. He seemed very relaxed with Rose, cheerfully picking her up and talking to her, rewarded when she opened her eyes and blew a tiny bubble, he was delighted, and Felix almost burst with pride. They were happy if tiring days. Then Claire arrived. Rose was now 5 weeks old and Annie had not enjoyed a single undisturbed night, she was edgy with fatigue.

Annie remembered the difficult months after the birth of Charlie, when she and Ralph had lived in a very disordered state in their cottage. There had been frequent rows with Claire, an almost daily visitor, who believed firmly in order and routine and tidiness, she had reduced Annie to tears with her criticism of what Claire called 'demand feeding. 'You should be firmer! Feed only every four hours, the baby needs to know who's in charge. Routine will help you and him! Annie had looked at Charlie, 'I don't like him crying, it upsets me and he's so small. Claire had shrugged her shoulders,

'Crying is natural for him, it exercises his lungs, she had said. Annie had been defiant, rejecting all her mother's well meaning advice. It had not been an easy time. She prayed that this visit would be a happy one.

The morning of her arrival, she and Felix did a massive tidy up, 'She'll notice everything! Annie warned. Privately Felix looked forward to a little more order in the house, he was fond of Claire and was happy to welcome her. She would at the very least be an extra pair of hands. Claire arrived by taxi from the airport and bustled in with her arms full of packages, Felix followed carrying her case in his good hand. As they came in Rose was crying in her cot in the kitchen, her face screwed up and red, her legs waving in the air, whilst Annie was talking on the phone, her back to Rose, looking out of the window. It was not the ideal start.

Claire tried very hard not to say anything. Ignoring Annie, she threw off her coat, dropped the many parcels and walked across and picked up the fretful baby. Holding her over her shoulder, she patted her and spoke gently, whilst looking at Annie who had put the phone down.

Felix spoke briskly, 'I'll fix lunch shall I? We're all hungry I'm sure. Annie, already anxious, said 'She's hungry too, that's what all the noise is about. Give me a moment and I'll feed her. She took Rose and sat on the sofa, opening up her blouse. Claire watched and her anger subsided, 'She's very pretty! Such beautiful dark eyes. Just like your sister! Annie smiled, 'Marthe thinks she's just like Felix!

'No! Surely not. She's the image of your sister. This little conversation defused the tension and within a few moments they were all at the table eating lunch, though Claire insisted on eating with one hand and holding Rose on her lap and rubbing her back, 'I'm just bringing up the wind, she said, and Annie smiled at her mother, 'Thanks for coming…welcome to the world of babies! Claire gave them news from England: Arthur did not like the hot summer weather and spent all day stretched out on the kitchen tiles getting in her way and Tony had bought a new garden chair. He sent his love she said. Claire suggested that Annie should have a rest, leaving Rose with her for the afternoon. Felix nodded his approval. Annie lay on their bed, 'Why am I so defensive? She means well, but it's like I resent her. Is it because I think that I don't do as good a job as she did? She closed her eyes and tried to relax, listening to the hum of voices in the nursery. The two people she loved most in all the world, apart from Charlie, were here in the house to support her, she must try and enjoy that. 'Let them run the house, that's the thing, she said to herself and with this thought, slowly the tension eased and Annie went into a deep sleep.

*

Claire settled into doing exactly that, she ran the house hold. She rose early and prepared breakfast for Charlie, who found himself eating boiled eggs with hot buttered toast, before being ushered out of the door to school with a hug and a kiss. Felix was given a similar treatment when he appeared half an hour later, the kitchen was tidy and he could smell the coffee brewing as he came down the stairs, 'One egg or two? Claire asked putting the coffee pot in front of him, 'It's like a hotel! He grinned, 'You really are a marvel! Claire joined him at the table watching him eat, 'Good night? Or disturbed? Felix, wishing to be loyal, said, 'Not too bad! I wish I could do more, Annie is getting very tired.

'It won't last for ever. Let her sleep in the mornings, she doesn't need to get up!

A new routine was established and Annie began to look better. Carefully holding a tray with one hand and using the other for balance, Felix took her up a light breakfast, which she ate it in bed, whilst they chatted quietly, it was a much calmer start to the day than for some time. Claire came in, and after watching Annie feed the baby, took her into the nursery, put her down in her cot, and shut the door. Miraculously Rose settled, and though she whimpered a little and cried occasionally, Claire refused to enter the room and Rose slept till midday. Annie remained upstairs, sleeping or enjoying a long bath and came downstairs only in the late morning, feeling rested and ready to start the day. With peace downstairs Felix began to feel less tired and overwrought, it seemed as though normal life was returning. He began thinking of work.

Claire was perfectly happy, she was running the house, caring for her daughter and doing as much as she could to help with Rose. By mid-afternoon she was listening for Charlie's footsteps waiting to see his face as he saw the biscuits that she had made after lunch. Annie and Felix were in the salon and Rose was with her in the kitchen. She phoned Tony, 'Everything is going really well, can I stay another week? Are you managing without me? He laughed, 'Of course stay as long as you are needed, I'm fine. Though Arthur is missing you!

'Don't spoil him! I don't want to come home to a fat dog!

*

Claire stayed for a further ten days which was the longest time that she and Annie had lived together for many years, and amazingly without a single row. Claire avoided commenting on anything that upset her, and Annie held back when she felt her mother's eye on her, she was determined to make the most of her stay with them; Annie slept, rested and cared for the baby. She saw Felix becoming more confident with Rose and encouraged him to spend time with her, lifting her out of the cot and holding her when she cried, he sung to her as he walked about the house and held her as he looked out of the window watching for Charlie. They had begun talking about the future, both life without Claire's help and returning to work, a difficult topic for them both. Felix knew that he had to make some important decisions about his future career, though it was still very unclear how much mobility he would have in his wrist. 'What would you like to happen? Annie asked, she was propped up in bed looking very pretty and finishing her breakfast, brushing bread crumbs carelessly onto the floor. Felix resisted the urge to find a dust pan, that would really irritate Annie, so he stayed at the foot of the bed.

*

'Well, he replied, 'I want to keep up the work at the paper, the reviewing and writing, I enjoy that and it gets me out, meeting people in the music world. Also some teaching, but I'm not sure of that. I'm only interested in really talented pupils, and they're pretty rare.

'So? Annie swung her legs out of the bed and walked over to the window, 'It's sunny! Let's take Rose out later shall we? Felix was taken aback, he thought they were discussing his future. Annie turned and saw his disappointment, 'Sorry Felix! My brain is all over the place, I can't focus on anything. But… go on. You don't really enjoy teaching but you do enjoy writing, yes? He nodded, 'That's not enough for you is it? She probed.

That was his problem, he paused and said, 'What does appeal more and more is conducting, and a bad hand wouldn't matter there. Annie listened she made a real effort to stay in the conversation, this was important, for Felix and for her. Rose shifted and stirred and Felix stood up, 'She's fine, Annie said, keep talking! Felix thought for a moment, 'I haven't explored this, but it's been on my mind, even before the accident, I have spoken to a few people…

'Who? Annie interrupted, 'Well our mutual acquaintance, Charles. Felix answered. Annie looked at him, 'He won't want to share the choir with you! Not Charles. No!

'I realise that, but he has connections in the music world, which is what I need. I don't want to be an amateur. Annie thought about that, there was a great distance between amateur conductors and professional ones who were connected to an orchestra or concert venue. She stared down at the sunny street, there was a street performer doing something with a pack of cards and she was distracted, dragging her thoughts back she said, 'This needs careful thought and planning doesn't it? It may take time, how prepared are you for disappointment? He shrugged, 'I don't know, it's the question I can't answer! Annie put her arms around him, 'You can only try. She said. 'Why not give yourself a year ? You don't need to rush, keep up the writing, perhaps look around to see if you can expand that. You're free lance so there may be other opportunities out there. Maybe in Bordeaux? Or Marseilles? They are both accessible.

'And you? He said, 'We haven't talked about you and your plans have we? She stepped back, this was just as difficult an issue. Before she could answer Rose began to cry and they were prevented from continuing the conversation, Annie relieved, that for the moment, she had held off revealing to Felix what she hoped to do in the coming years.

*

Annie was feeling well, she was deeply grateful to her mother, though she found it difficult to slow Claire down sufficiently for any meaningful conversation. Claire was preoccupied with being Super Gran and if that's what she wanted, then

Annie was content to leave it like that. She worried how they would all cope when her mother went home, though it would be nice to have the house to themselves and not to try and live up to Claire's high standards. But finally it was time for Claire to leave, she would be flying home on the late afternoon flight, and after breakfast she gave Charlie a hug, 'Bye bye! She said, her eyes filling with tears, 'Keep helping your Mum, and give Rose a kiss from me every evening. Charlie was sad to see her go but his mind was on school and after a few seconds, he pulled away, 'I will! Bye Gran! Give my love to Arthur and Tony! And he was off, clattering down the stairs and banging the door onto the street. Claire sighed, and then she thought of Tony and Arthur and home and not being Super Gran, and she was content to be leaving. It had been a busy sometimes exhausting few weeks.

She looked down on the landscape of Gascony from her seat in the plane; the farrowed brown fields ready for the autumn planting, the patches of green woodland, the straight roads and the red brick farm houses, the barns so much bigger than those in Kent. She closed her eyes and slept all the way back to England.

*

It was late September, one of the loveliest months of the year, still warm enough to serve coffee and drinks on the terrace at the Chateau, and though the hotel was no longer full, there were visitors to be fed and rooms to be cleaned. Claude enjoyed this quieter atmosphere; he was able to walk around the garden and even swim in the pool without being stopped by guests who wanted to chat or complain. He was thinking about the coming months. He planned to close the hotel in mid October, but knew that he needed to discuss this with Jerome and Luc, it would affect them more than himself. He had already decided to take a month's holiday, perhaps in Spain, with Marthe, if she would come. He chose his moment carefully, it was Sunday evening and he asked them both to join him in his wing for supper. They knew something was up and as they walked together across Claude's garden, Jerome said, 'What's he want to talk about?

'Money? Luc suggested, 'God, I hope not. I hate figures.

'No. I don't think it's that. More like the hotel itself, what went right and what went wrong.

'It'll be a long evening then, and I'm exhausted already, Luc groaned as

they reached the door and walked in, calling out to Claude. He was cooking roast veal and had a glass of wine in his hand, 'Go and sit down, he said, 'I don't need you to do anything. Put some music on Jerome. He passed them the open bottle of red and Luc looked at the label, 'That's nice, a bit special, he commented and filled two glasses, they went into the big salon and wandered about looking at the books and magazines strewn around on every table. There was a large confit pot of green leaves in the fire place, and another of yellow daisies on the long table which was set out for three. Jerome put on a CD and hummed. Claude had a talent for decorating rooms, and this room was stylish yet homely. They both relaxed, waiting for Claude to join them, glancing at each other from time to time and grinning. 'What did he want to talk about?

Claude served the veal in a mushroom sauce, with a salad from the kitchen garden and the last of the baby carrots, then taking his place, came straight to the point, he was not a man who wasted time on pleasantries. 'I think we should shut in October and take no bookings after the 14th. I've checked the reservations and we do have some guests until that day but then no more. How do you feel about that? They were slow to reply, unprepared for this question. Luc spoke first, 'Maybe we could continue with the restaurant a bit longer? We have to give Marcel a month's notice don't we? I'm sure we could fill a number of tables at least to the end of that month, perhaps doing just lunches, with fewer staff obviously. Claude turned to him, 'Do you want to do that then? Would you be responsible for taking the bookings? Luc was surprised by that, 'Well, I guess so. Where are you going to be?

Before he could answer, Jerome said, 'I think that's a good idea and I'm happy to do the reservations until the end of October and continue as front of house in the restaurant. It seems abrupt to just stop so soon. The hotel side can shut if that's what you want though. He looked at Claude. 'How have we done financially? Are we losing money? We've been nearly full since we opened. Claude replied, 'We've just about broken even, which for a first year is pretty good. Of course I haven't taken a salary, and you two…well you have been underpaid. They said nothing and he went on, 'I think important changes need to be made next year, we need to be better staffed in all areas; a more efficient house keeper, more cleaning and laundry staff, and someone at Reception who is not being pulled away for other tasks. The kitchen has worked well but we could do with another sous chef. He looked at Luc, who nodded. 'We can go into the details in early spring.

'How do you see your role next year Papa? Luc asked, 'Don't you want to be on the Reception at all? I think guests enjoyed seeing you there, chatting and giving out local information. Claude said, 'I have enjoyed that, but I didn't realise how much energy it took, and at times I did get pretty short tempered with the silly demands! I don't think I'm really suited to being on hand all day. It's hard work! He got up from the table and Luc followed him to the kitchen and carried out a large plate of cheeses. Claude followed with a bowl of red grapes and they all began eating again. Jerome had been silent, he had been thinking for some time about the coming months and had formulated a plan for himself which he now revealed. They listened as he spoke with some surprise. Jerome had always been the quiet son, never very confident and inclined to be solitary, running the book shop in Auch had suited him well, though it was hardly challenging. 'I've found a six month hotelier course in Paris, he said, 'It's in hotel management and starts in November. I have enjoyed working in the hotel and now want a more professional training. We're amateurs at the moment, and I want more for myself. Then I'll work in a hotel for four maybe six months to get real experience, and then come back here. Luc gaped at him, and Claude nearly dropped his cheese plate in surprise. 'I've got the money from the book shop so I can finance myself for a year.

'How long have you been planning this? Claude asked, he felt that Jerome should have consulted him. 'In the last month. I heard from the college last week, I was waiting to fix it up before telling you both. If all goes well I should be able to take over the running of the hotel…if that's what you want. He looked at Claude.

'You have caught me by surprise, Claude said, 'I like your idea, and it makes good sense, but it will affect next year, having to replace you. I was hoping to step back, but, well, I may have to think again. Luc said nothing, he was astonished at Jerome's plan, he was used to his brother taking a back seat in life, and here he was intending to live in Paris and train in hotel management. This was Jerome who liked books and jazz and had never had a long term girl friend, studying in

Paris! Jerome said, 'I don't mean to drop a bombshell on you both, but this must be a good idea long term for all of us. The hotel is my future, that's how I see it, that's what I want. And so I must learn how to do it properly and efficiently, how to make money not just 'break even'.

*

'And you Luc? Are you planning to stay? Claude asked. Luc smiled 'As I told you the other day, I'll find chef's work in the Alps, I can now offer some experience, quite a lot in fact. The restaurants and hotels open for the skiing season in mid December and I can work until Easter, or later, then I'll be back here for an opening in May. I may be able to be more than a sous chef by then. Luc smiled at his father who was now looking less shell shocked, 'And for what it's worth, I think Jerome's plan is brilliant, we must run this hotel professionally, if we really want to succeed. This year we did ok, but we could be so much more. I'm going to make the restaurant one of the best in the area! You'll see!

They continued to talk for some time and it was almost midnight when the evening ended, Claude gave Jerome a hug as he left 'I think you've done well, he said, 'Finding a course and planning for the future, it's the right decision. This hotel was always about setting up a family enterprise and you are going to become the key figure. I will hold on until you come back.

*

The next day he phoned Marthe. 'Do you want a holiday? In Spain? With me?

I need to get away for at least a month! Perhaps we might drive down to the South, Seville and Cadiz, it could be part business, buying of course, but also exploring and eating and sitting by the sea. And not thinking about the hotel!

'When?'

'Leaving around the 14th October, the weather will still be warm and lovely, we can wander in the sun and eat all our meals out of doors.'

'I don't even need to think, Marthe was laughing, 'I'd love to! It'll set me up before the winter sets in.'

'No Collioure then?'

'No! I told you, that was a folly. There was a pause and then she added, 'A month? Isn't that rather long?'

'I need a month, it's been a long summer!'

CHAPTER 24

Claude set about the arrangements for the autumn, he would leave Jerome in charge until he left for Paris, then the restaurant would close. Luc planned to go hiking in the Pyrenees before setting off for the winter season in the Alps, he was busy applying for jobs. There was also Gregoire to be considered, he had agreed to work in the kitchen gardens until Christmas, alongside Joel, squeezing a day in once a week, between working his own farm and selling at the markets. Gregoire was doing well, the money from Marthe had enabled him to work more efficiently; the newly acquired tractor and the trailer on which he transported his produce, had transformed his life and he now had plans for extending the farm, bringing more of the abandoned fields into cultivation. He talked to Agathe one evening and she listened as he outlined his vision for the land, 'I'll plough in the further field and get it ready for the spring, he said, 'And perhaps the small area beside the stream. She listened attentively, she loved to hear him talking about the farm and was glad to see that in the evenings he seemed less worn out. He had started going out after their early supper and she wondered where he went, he had never had much of a social life, maybe that too was changing. What a debt they both owed to Marthe.

*

Agathe enjoyed the quiet evenings, she was tired after her long day at the college in Auch. She sat in the sitting room with her grandfather as he dozed by the fire, his head nodding forward and his breathing uneven, he rose unsteadily at about nine and saying goodnight left her to her books. He reminded her of the elderly people in the home in St. Girou and not for the first time, she wondered how many years he still had to live. She hadn't called into see Marthe for a while, it was more difficult now that she was working further from home, and she felt a little guilty. She decided to visit on Saturday, if Gregoire didn't want her to help out on the stall, a job that she found stressful. Agathe was too shy to deal with the banter that was part of the life in the markets, she became flushed and confused when men tried to flirt with her, getting the change wrong and forgetting the prices. 'Come on love! Hurry up! They would say, enjoying her pink cheeks and brown arms, 'Not got all day have I? Gregoire took no notice, he thought it was time that she came out of her shell more, she was so good with old people, it was time that she learnt how to handle younger men. He spoke to her one morning as they were packing vegetables onto the trailer, 'Don't let them worry you. Answer back. It's just harmless chat, he said. Agathe knew he was right, she was experiencing a similar problem at college. She hadn't expected that there would be men training with her, she had thought wrongly that nursing was a female profession. She was getting used to it slowly, but still found herself flushing at some of the remarks made by the male students. Her trouble was that she was a pretty girl and attracted attention.

Agathe tried hard to adapt to the camaraderie but her confidence grew slowly and some days she was glad to jump on her scooter and head for home.

*

On Saturday after helping Gregoire on the market stall, she went to see Marthe. Entering through the garden door as usual, she found Marthe in the kitchen arranging some dark orange flowers in an ochre pot. Marthe was thinking about her trip to southern Spain and planning to go through her summer clothes. Turning round she smiled at Agathe, 'What do you think? More leaves maybe? Take off your coat, I'm nearly finished. She added more green leaves and placed the arrangement on the dresser, standing back to take a careful look. Agathe did as she was told, and seated herself at the table, she liked this room it was so light and airy compared with the dark and smoky kitchen at the Moulin. 'How about some tea? And a slice of cake? Marthe thought that the girl was looking tired, she put the kettle on and opened the cake tin. Agathe watched her. 'How are you? Marthe asked gently, she could tell that Agathe was not in her usual bright mood. Agathe sipped her tea, she felt foolish, her worries seemed so silly and girlish, and anyway why should she burden Marthe? But she could not hide her emotions for long and she slowly spoke of her feelings of being the odd one out at college and not being part of the 'set'. 'I love the work, she added hastily, 'but I don't seem to fit in, it was the same at school. Marthe listened. She knew Agathe to be a shy girl, lacking the social skills of many girls of her age. This was not surprising, she'd led a very isolated life living on a farm with an elderly man and an older brother for company, she had had no mother or sister to learn from. Marthe remembered her own isolated childhood, she had grown up in the home of her grandparents and she had found the outside world of more sophisticated and confident contemporaries difficult. She had however a mother to turn to and had learnt to watch the ways of her friends, she had learnt how to 'blend in', though it was many years before she became a social success. That she owed to her husband, who had encouraged and supported her and brought her into his musical world in Paris. She felt sorry for Agathe and tried to think how she might help.

They talked for some time and Marthe suggested a strategy which might work; she should enlist the help of Gregoire, 'Ask to join him when he goes out, to a bar or café. Watch how other girls behave. Also change your appearance a little, maybe try getting your hair cut and buy some clothes that are a bit, well, younger. I'll take you into Toulouse, if you like, and you can look around. I need to do a little shopping anyway. Maybe try listening to music, everyone talks about that all the time. Agathe, she took her hand, 'you're very pretty make the most of it! Don't jump on the scooter as soon as the afternoon ends, hang around and chat, see what other people are doing.

Agathe listened but her spirits drooped, it sounded so easy, but for her it was a huge challenge. 'But, Marthe concluded, 'be yourself, watch and learn, but remain true to who you are. That is the most important thing. Now come again next weekend and we'll go into Toulouse. And I want to hear that you have tried to make at least one friend.

*

It wasn't so difficult! Agathe forced herself to follow the advice; she stayed in Auch on Monday after college. Parking her scooter in the square near the Cathedral she entered the cobbled streets that were the centre of the shopping area. Wasting no time she went into a hairdresser, the first one she saw. The assistant whose own hair was cut very short, almost like a boy's, hummed to the loud music that filled the salon and chatted to everyone as she first washed then cut Agathe's hair. 'You've got lovely hair, she said, holding it firmly 'but it needs to be much shorter! Agathe sat in the chair watching nervously as the scissors kept cutting. It was too late to stop now and she began to wish that she had not come in. The assistant finished and, still talking loudly, held up the mirror, whilst lifting Agathe's hair and running her hand through it. 'You should use conditioner, she said, 'You can buy some here. And come back at least every six weeks to keep the shape. The girl walked to the till and Agathe followed, she bought the conditioner and made another appointment. The assistant smiled as she opened the door, 'See you again then!

Agathe emerged with a soft fringe and hair that now stopped above her shoulders, she glanced at herself as she walked down the narrow street. It was filled with music stores and clothes shops, she passed Jerome's book shop. She stopped outside a shop which had a bright display of jackets and shirts in the small window, and racks of jeans on the street outside, there were several young girls inside and loud music was playing. She walked in, catching sight of herself in one of the many mirrors and was surprised at how different she looked, she pushed her hand through her hair and as she did an assistant pounced. Several minutes later Agathe was walking back towards the square where she had left her scooter, she was carrying two large bags and wearing a blue denim jacket with lots of pockets. She was surprised to hear her name and turning to her left she saw two of her fellow nurses sitting at a café table, one was waving. 'Agathe!

Returning home two hours later than usual, Agathe reflected on the afternoon; she loved her hair cut and both of the nurses had complimented her on her new look, and 'Where did you get that jacket? It's just what I'm looking for! the one called Anya had asked. They had gossiped about the course and one of the lecturers who everyone fancied apparently, and Anya had asked her where she lived and did she have a boyfriend. Normal easy chat and Agathe did not feel awkward and shy at all. Gregoire immediately noticed her new hair cut, 'Great! You look really nice! He said and gave her a little push. They were eating a late supper, which had prompted a lot of complaint from grandfather. Agathe had shrugged, 'I can't always get home straight after college, she said, 'and I'll be late on Friday.

'Oh? Have you a late lecture? Gregoire was pushing back his chair and he stopped, 'I don't want you coming back on the scooter in the dark.

'I'm meeting some friends that's all, she tried not to sound too pleased, 'and I am quite safe at night you needn't worry.

'Well I hope you'll be able to work on the stall on Saturday.

'Course I will, she said and planned to wear her new jacket and surprise him.

*

That Saturday Agathe determined to enjoy working on the stall and not dreading it as she had been. She wore the new jacket and a pair of jeans, which had frayed ends and stopped above her ankles, she chatted to the girl selling olives and dried apricots and pistachios in the stall to her right, ' How's your week been? She asked. The girl sighed, she had huge red earrings and dyed blond hair and worked the markets every day with her father and saw no end to it. Agathe thought about that, 'Why not try something else? The girl grimaced, 'He needs me, I can't, it's our livelihood. The father shouted at her and she turned away, quickly serving an old man who ogled her as she weighed the olives. Agathe watched her. The morning passed quickly and Gregoire realised that Agathe was enjoying herself more than usual, though she was still inclined to look blank at the risqué comments of some of their customers. She had no gift for repartee but did her best, pleasing most people with her smile and willing manner. She no longer hid at the back of the stall but stood out in the front, inviting people to stop and buy. It was a great improvement.

They packed up at midday and Agathe said goodbye to the olive girl, as she thought of her, 'See you next Saturday, she said, the girl nodded, 'Yes, we could go for a beer after maybe? Overhearing Gregoire was surprised, but what was more normal than two girls having a beer at the end of the morning's work? They chatted in the van on the way back to the Moulin, 'Can I come out one evening with you? Agathe asked, that surprised him even more, 'Yes why not! Maybe Wednesday, after supper. You could meet Loulou. I'd like that. He said no more as they turned into the farm, but Agathe was thinking...Lulu? Lulu? And then she thought, Wednesday and Friday next week, it really wasn't difficult at all. Being social. She hoped that Marthe would be pleased. She didn't really need a shopping expedition into Toulouse anymore.

CHAPTER 25

Claude was looking forward to getting away, and spending time with Marthe. He had not visited the southern part of Spain for many years but had fond memories of Seville and Granada and Ronda; cities famous for their cathedrals and mosques and narrow streets lined with tall houses decorated with wrought iron balconies. He enjoyed the food too, more spicy than French. He would eat paella and baby roast pig and drink the red wines of the region whilst sitting in the autumn sun. He became increasingly cheerful as the day of departure grew closer, he purchased a new straw hat in Toulouse and a linen jacket in pale blue. His two sons watched with amusement as he loaded the car with maps and a thermos and a picnic bag and a tartan rug. 'We'll have lots of picnics, he explained, 'at lunch time.

'Don't drink too much! Driving and alcohol and the sun are not a good combination, Jerome said, 'I am relying on Marthe to keep you in check. Claude grinned, 'She'll do that! He gave them each a hug, and set off, he would not see either of them for several weeks.

*

Marthe too was pleased to get away, she had recently argued with Felix who had forcibly expressed his disapproval of her contacts with the Rinaldi family. It had occurred one morning when she had popped in for a visit, Annie was upstairs feeding Rose, and Felix took the opportunity to raise the subject. They were going over old ground and neither of them had changed their positions. Felix got especially heated, 'You never consult me! How could you harass an old man in his home? And forcing yourself on Agathe's father! How did that help anyone?

Marthe stood her ground, but their differences were apparent; Felix insisting again that she should put the past behind her and Marthe maintaining her right to learn about her father's history.

It was not a happy visit and they remained cool with each other. This was the situation when she left for Spain.

Felix quickly regretted his loss of temper, he knew that he had behaved poorly. He was trying to focus on developing his career, acting on Annie's encouragement. He had written to several music magazines and contacted the more important regional newspapers. He was waiting for responses. He had also approached the local choirs and orchestras, away from Toulouse, sending his career resumes. He was waiting to hear from these also. He had not told Annie yet, hoping for something positive to tell her. In the meanwhile Felix kept his spirits up by helping Annie with the baby and the house and Charlie. He became more confident each day with Rose, taking her out in the stroller, negotiating the streets and squares which previously he had taken for granted; there were so many obstacles! He found it alarming at first; there were uneven cobbles which jolted her as she settled into sleep, high pavements where he had to lift the wheels, there were barking dogs and roaring mopeds. He preferred the squares and if he could find an empty bench, took a seat parking Rose close to him, careful to keep her face out of the sun. He sat and watched the other people who were also enjoying the shade of the plane trees, listening to their chatter as the children played on scooters and little bikes. It did not seem possible that Rose would ever do that, wobble with her feet close to the ground, her face full of concentration. How extraordinary children were, they grew without trying! It just happened! Felix lost all sense of time, unaware of the curious glances of several mothers, who wondered who this father was, until Rose stirred, and he returned home, carefully carrying Rose up the stairs, calling to Annie, 'We're home! She left what she was doing and joined them, taking Rose and removing her little hat, giving her a kiss, 'Did you have a nice time? She would ask, as if the baby could talk! Felix loved it all, and forgot about work and the future and his mother, nothing at the moment was as important as his family.

*

Annie also enjoyed these early months of motherhood, they were so different from the earlier time with Ralph and Charlie. Then there had been multiple anxieties around money, the uncertainty of work, and keeping a cottage warm and a baby fed. She remembered willing Ralph to be more proactive in job applications resenting his careless attitude, she had hated the nagging tone in her voice and her eager anticipation as she waited for a letter offering him employment. They had muddled along but it had not been easy, and she could hear the disappointment in her mother's voice when they spoke on the phone. 'Still not working? Why? Claire asked, 'There must be something out there surely? Annie was forced to defend Ralph from her mother's questions, which she thought unfair. But life was not all bad, Charlie thrived and she fell in love with the cottage garden, it kept her sane, whilst she plotted her return to work. It wasn't just the money, though that was important, it was her career. It was what she had worked so hard for in college, she was not going to let it go.

*

So Annie continued to think about work; there was less urgency this time, her financial position was secure, but she wanted to return to her garden landscaping business whilst there were clients who still remembered her. She raised the subject one evening, they had finished supper, and Charlie was in his room finishing a school project. His education often confused her, he seemed to study such odd topics, the latest was the war in Vietnam, about which Annie knew very little. Felix explained that it was once a French colony, so that gave her some understanding, but she doubted its relevance in the present day. 'It's French history, Felix said, 'That's why he's studying it! Annie was not convinced, silently wondering if Charlie was learning any history that was not French. Her own knowledge of history was poor, she had studied repeatedly the Tudors and Stuarts but apart from that she really knew very little. She had not enjoyed the subject at all.

*

Felix listened as Annie outlined her plans for work, struggling to quell the disappointment he felt. 'So how do you think you can manage this? He asked.

'Well a lot of my work I will do from home; contacting clients, talking over their ideas and drawing up designs etc. I just need a table and a phone. And my reference books of course. I can take Rose with me for the moment on visits to gardens. If I do get a project, fingers crossed, I won't commit to any physical labour, the digging and clearing and planting, that can be contracted out, most landscape gardeners work like that now. But I can get myself back into that world… get myself known.

Felix said, 'This will be a part time sort of work then? Mostly from home?

'Yes. I don't want to work as I did before, I don't have to, thanks to you. So no teaching, no City contract, just me and my ideas. If I get busy, I'll take on a partner perhaps. But that's a long way ahead. She looked at him, she could see the disappointment in his face, but pressed on, 'Felix you know me, you know I need to work, have something outside the home, I had a career, and I want it back. You and Rose and Charlie and this lovely home will always come first, but...it's not enough. That's the way I am! I'm not being selfish or, she paused, 'Is that what you think?

Felix sat silently, he didn't think it was selfish, but he was sad that Annie felt as she did. He had thought she would be happy with her new life in Toulouse, free from worries about money, free to enjoy herself and her family. But no. People don't change, and Annie had always been independent, following her own interests, she liked work and responsibility and meeting new people, having a challenge. It combined with her fear of being, what she called, 'tied down', of not being free to pursue her own passions. He said, 'If that's what you want then I won't stand in your way. Go ahead! See what's out there for you. We can adjust I'm sure. It was not an enthusiastic response.

Annie stood up uncertain as to how this conversation had really gone. She knew that Felix was disappointed at the prospect of her taking up work again, and it was all made more difficult by his own career stalling since the accident. He had had no positive feed back from his many enquiries, though it was still very early days. But she was not prepared to hold back because of that, confident that in time Felix would find his own career taking off, perhaps in a new direction. But she was uneasy and decided to wait a few more months before taking any action for herself.

*

Spain! White washed houses, shuttered and closed against the intrusions of the outside world, wrought iron balconies where women called to each other across the narrow streets, multitudes of pots and urns overflowing with the bright colours of geraniums. Purple, cream and pink bourganvillia pouring down walls and lacing through handrails. Cats hiding in dark corners and scampering through squares, scrabbling for food outside bars. Churches, their heavy wooden doors studded with black iron work, their cold dark interiors suffused with the smell of candles and incense, where silent figures knelt and prayed before ornate baroque altars. And food stalls and street markets and restaurants and tapas bars open till midnight or later. And men gossiping at the tables. And shade from tall lime trees in small parks, their gravel paths dusty and worn. And sunshades and awnings to protect against the heat of the sun which shone endlessly. And dark haired girls flirting with dark haired men. It was intoxicating.

*

Marthe and Claude wandered the streets of Salamanca, their first stopping point, and became familiar with the slow pace of life: lunching at three in the afternoon quickly seemed normal, then resting in their bedroom until six or seven in the evening thus escaping from the heat of the afternoon. Next a shower and fresh clothes, before setting out for a well chilled beer or glass of wine in a bar, accompanied by tapas, as they sat out on the cobbled streets watching the peseo. Dinner finally around ten and bed after midnight. Claude loved it from the first and Marthe too accepted that the French style of regulated dining was perhaps too rigorous. 'It's odd, she commented one evening as they read the menu, 'I like this late eating! Perhaps we should try it at home?

'Hard on the chefs, they have to work so late. Claude replied, 'It does change in the winter, they eat more like nine at night then. It's the climate that has produced these late suppers. But I don't see it catching on at home. imagine if the hotel had to serve dinner at ten at night. No thank you!

Felix phoned in their second week and she was pleased to hear his voice. It appeared that their disagreement had been forgotten. She talked about their holiday, they had reached Toledo, she said. 'Where are you? He asked, 'I can hear lots of voices!

'We're outside a bar eating from little dishes of delicious anchovies and hot almonds and dried figs and having some cold wine. The food is delicious!

'Is that supper then?

'No! Much too early for that, we're trying to decide where to eat. Toledo is fascinating, we've spent the morning exploring; there's a very impressive castle with a huge entrance, perched on a cliff above the city and a cathedral of course, a bit grim inside, dark and cold. And plenty of antiques shops for Claude, he's been digging around and thinking of buying some candlesticks made locally, Toledo is famous for its metal work. We're very busy!

'But it's nearly ten o'clock, isn't that a bit late for supper?

Marthe explained that eating at ten at night was quite normal and then they talked about Rose and Annie.

'That's good. Marthe said putting the phone away.

'Oh?

'We had a bit of a fall out before I came away.

'Oh?

Claude said innocently, he had a pretty good idea what they had fallen out over. 'It's not worth worrying about.

Marthe said crunching a nut between her teeth, 'Goodness these are delicious. Anyway we can't agree on everything can we?

'Don't you have disagreements with Jerome and Luc?

'Oh yes! I try to influence them as subtly as I can. It doesn't always work.

'Has working together at the chateau been difficult?

'We've not seen eye to eye all the time, but on the whole we've drawn closer. Both the boys have impressed me in ways which I had not expected. So for me the experience had been a good one...a very good one.

'So next year more of the same?

Claude hesitated, he had deliberately avoided thinking about the chateau and the coming year and Marthe's question forced his hand. She saw him frown and regretted her question, it had not been tactful she realised.

'Don't answer! It's nothing to do with me!

Claude did answer but he spoke slowly, 'I intend to do less, the boys have shown me that I am more than dispensable! If we can make enough money to pay someone to take over my role, I would prefer that. It'll be tight though. I haven't taken any salary this year, so the hotel needs to bring in more, much more. I suspect we should be advertising more vigorously and attracting wedding parties. There is a lot of money to be made over those weekends. The hotel needs an experienced business manager, in time I think that Jerome will play that role, but for the moment we have to recruit someone. He stretched his legs, and waved at the waiter, and stood up, 'Time for supper ? Marthe nodded and picked up her bag, they waited briefly and Claude spoke again,

'I have rather missed my business this year, I enjoy buying and selling, making deals, and the chateau has prevented that. Your advice I seem to remember: do the one and not the other. And you were right, but next year will be different hopefully.

He did not say anymore, but Marthe, thinking about the conversation later, had a definite feeling that Claude and the running of a hotel were not truly compatible. He had enjoyed too many years of independence to commit to the daily routine of working in a hotel.

Let the boys take over, was her view, they were lucky to have such an opportunity. Even if Claude maintained a watchful eye.

*

They travelled onto Cordoba, which was to become Marthe's favourite Spanish City, smaller and quieter than Seville it had a strong Moorish atmosphere. They stayed for several days. She spent much time in the cathedral, formerly a mosque, its size was extraordinary, with a high vaulted ceiling supported on huge stone columns. It was cool and quiet. There were few religious artefacts to crowd the walls, it felt serene and timeless, and very different from the French Gothic cathedrals that she knew well. Claude prowled the back streets in search of antiques, he found some bargains and spent much time organizing their transport back to France. He found negotiating with the Spanish difficult, a difficulty made worst by their strong southern accents, but with the season now almost at an end the dealers were eager to sell what they could. He hadn't heard from his sons which was fine, and he realised with a start that the chateau was now shut up and empty, it felt like the end of something.

By mid November, they had reached Cadiz, the weather was glorious, cool in the morning, warm by midday and hot in the afternoons. The evenings were mild and they continued to enjoy tapas and wine sitting outside by the harbour. Marthe felt as though she had reached the end of Europe, looking across the empty sea to Africa to the south and the Americas to the west. It was getting dark, suddenly she felt a long way from Les Palmes, a wave of sadness swept through her. Shaken she turned to Claude who was watching some cormorants; they were perched on a fishing boat, flapping their wings and arguing, 'I think I'm ready to go home, she said, 'I feel a little home sick! Can we think about leaving in the next few days?

He turned away from the noisy birds, 'Of course, he said and took her hand, 'We'll leave whenever you want.

As they walked back to their hotel after supper, Marthe said, 'You've had a good time, haven't you? It's been fun, hasn't it?

He stopped walking and enclosed her in his arms, 'I've loved every minute. I would never had had such a happy time on my own. Thank you for coming. She kissed him, and it occurred to her that she might be falling in love with Claude. That and the decision to return home made her deeply content.

CHAPTER 26

December was bright and sunny in Toulouse, and the city prepared for the Christmas holiday and the New year celebrations. A market appeared in the Place du Capitol, selling festive food and gifts and decorations. A strong smell of mulled wine filled the air and Charlie lingered on his way home, enjoying the aromas of nutmeg and cinnamon, pepper and bay. The wine stalls were crowded with people drinking at the high round tables, slick with wine, many held a length of baguette stuffed with the spicy sausage for which Toulouse was famous. It was noisy and lively. Charlie wandered around, he loved this time of year, all the expectation of the coming holiday and the sights and smells of the market. He reached inside his back pack for his wallet, extracting a note, and paused beside a stall selling carved wooden figures. He looked carefully as the man who was watching him waited patiently.

'Combien? He asked pointing at a little roundabout which turned with a handle.

'Vingt cinq.

Charlie pointed at another, it had more figures and was brightly painted.

'Trente.

Charlie thought for a moment, it would be perfect for Rose he decided, he could turn the handle for her and it would be fun. He gave the man thirty euros and the man put it in a box and tied it with a ribbon. Charlie walked away. Returning home he found the kitchen empty and helped himself to some fruit and a slice of cake. There was the sound of music upstairs so he climbed to the top floor and walked into Felix's study. Felix was playing the piano using both hands! Charlie stood and listened. He recognised the piece it was one of Felix's favourites, a Beethoven Sonata but it sounded different. Felix was adapting the left hand, missing out some notes and playing more slowly than usual. But it was still the Sonata. He waited until the piece came to an end whilst Felix sat at the piano his head bent, his hands resting on his lap.

'That was good! Charlie said walking toward the piano, 'What did you think? Felix was taken by surprise, he turned on the stool and stared at the boy. 'How much did you hear?

'From the middle section to the end. Was it hard for you... using your left hand? But you've adapted it haven't you? Felix stood up, 'Yes, he said.

'Shall we play something together? Charlie said, 'maybe I could accompany you on drums. That would be fun. Felix looked at him and paused, 'We could have a go. What do you think we should try?

'Well I've been playing 'Bridge over troubled water' with my school band, do you think you could improvise that?

Felix returned to the piano and waited while Charlie got his drum kit out, he hummed the tune to himself and flexed his left wrist, it was aching a little. 'On a count of three, he said. And they played and then again, each listening to the other.

Annie came in from the street, lugging Rose on her hip and clutching her work case. She put Rose in her bouncy chair and handed her a tiny biscuit. Annie was tired and hungry.

She had been out all afternoon in Toulouse. Her meeting had gone well, the client or clients, a middle aged couple who had bought a large maison with an even larger garden, had shown interest in her dry garden scheme and requested a detailed plan. For which they were prepared to pay. Rose had slept peaceably for much of the visit, fortified by a long feed she had given her in the car. She heard the music and was astonished to hear the piano and drums playing together, she climbed the stairs and waited until they stopped after a loud drum roll from Charlie and then walked in to the study. Felix was standing next to the drum kit as Charlie continued to play with the drum sticks, 'You've a talent for this, he said, 'Tell me more about your band. They had not heard Annie.

'Well, we play together at school in lunch break and at weekends, there's me on drums, Pierre on the electric guitar and Michel who plays bass guitar and sometimes the sax. He's the best of us.

'I'd like to hear you all play. What do you like to play most?

Charlie spotted Annie who had stopped by the door, 'Hi mum. Did you hear us? She nodded, 'It sounded good, was it fun? Felix replied, 'Yes it was, he's very talented. And piano and drums... an unusual combination, but it seemed to work. A wail could be heard from below, 'I'll go! Said Charlie and he ran off and down the stairs.

'You were playing with both hands weren't you. How did it feel? Felix tried not to sigh, 'Difficult but possible. I can improvise. There was a silence, 'I like to hear you play, Annie said, 'It feels normal somehow. You up here again. And playing with Charlie too. There was shout from below 'I think she's hungry! Charlie called out 'Shall I bring her up?

'I'm coming! Annie shouted back. She and Felix went down stairs together, Felix was deep in thought. A quite new idea had entered his head. It might be possible, he was surprised to think.

*

Felix had not had any success in his attempts to find work as a conductor.

He lacked experience in a world that offered few opportunities. He had concealed his disappointment from Annie, whilst continuing to explore the possibility of extending his writing career. He continued to write reviews for the Toulouse paper and was hopeful that there was an opening for him in the Bordeaux regional paper. But as yet there was no offer. Playing with Charlie had aroused a new idea, and he remembered his studies in composition at the Paris conservatoire. He had shown talent, was the view of the professor, but encouraged by his father, Felix had concentrated on a career as a soloist and the composition courses were quietly set aside. He had enjoyed composition was all he could now remember. He still had somewhere some early works for piano, which he had performed for his teacher.

The following morning Felix went up to his study and sat at the piano. On the table beside him were manuscript paper and pencils. He had decided to write a piece for Rose, not exactly a lullaby but something that was gentle and lilting. Something that he or Annie could sing. He ran his right hand up and down the keys and then awkwardly did the same with his left. Felix remained there for the rest of the morning, walking around from time to time flexing his hands and pausing at the window. It was a cold day and leaning out he could see people in the street below bent against the wind as they pushed their way down the narrow road, most were wearing scarves and woolly hats. He wondered what Annie was doing but resolved not to go down stairs until he had something on his manuscript paper. It was lunch time before he reappeared. Annie had passed the morning engrossed in the garden plan, her new commission. The young girl who now helped with Rose every day had kept the apartment quiet, and Rose was sleeping in her room. It had been a good morning for them all.

'Lunch? Felix asked. Annie looked up with a smile, 'It's your day isn't it? She replied. It wasn't but Felix was not in an arguing mood. They ate at the table and Rose, now back in the kitchen, watched from her cot propped up on pillows. She dribbled and sucked a fist and Felix wiped her mouth, 'Is she teething? He asked. 'No not yet, in a month maybe, Annie replied, 'That's when breast feeding becomes more difficult! Felix winced, there was so much to learn about babies he thought, 'What have you been upto? I heard the piano. Annie continued, How's the hand today? Felix stood up 'Coffee? Or are you still not drinking coffee? Annie sighed, 'I just don't like the taste anymore. A tea would be nice though. She wondered if he was avoiding her question and decided not to ask again. They talked of other things and Annie fed Rose. 'I'm going to see Marthe later, now she's back from Spain, Felix said, 'Why don't you come? She hasn't seen Rose for nearly two months. They decided to wait for Charlie and then go as soon as he was back. Felix phoned his mother who offered supper.

*

Marthe was delighted to see them as they trooped in and down the hall. She hugged Charlie and stared at Rose in amazement, 'I wouldn't have recognised her! She's grown so much, she said and Felix tried not to look proud as he carried her into the kitchen, unbuttoning her little jacket. Marthe told them all about her Spanish holiday as they ate an early supper, and Annie thought that Marthe looked particularly well and happy. She wondered if anything had changed in Marthe's life. Charlie talked about school and Annie told them about her hopes for a new and interesting job. 'And you? Marthe turned to Felix, 'How are things with you? Annie flinched, Marthe had put her son on the spot and she feared his response, but to her surprise Felix answered, 'Oh, things are beginning to take shape, thanks. A bit of this and a bit of that, I'm going to be fine. He grinned and Marthe seemed satisfied.

On the way home Rose slept in her chair and Charlie dozed in the seat beside her, Annie turned to Felix and took his left hand, 'Are you ok? Really?

'Well I'm beginning to see my way through. The conducting will come to nothing, I know that. But the writing may expand, and I can still teach.

'And? There's something else isn't there? You seem more positive today.

'Yes, how perceptive of you! I think I am going to try composition. I studied it in Paris and enjoyed it then. I want to try and write some music for Charlie, well, for Charlie and me, and Charlie and his school band. Nothing 'classical' maybe jazz or rock. Annie listened, it seemed a good idea, and would add an entirely new dimension to his life. 'You enjoy jazz, those summer concerts. she said, 'I can see you composing, it's a great idea. Clever you! She stretched across and kissed him on the cheek, 'Certainly give it a try.

'Your mother looked well. She obviously had a lovely trip with Claude, she's positively blooming. Or didn't you notice. He laughed, 'She's had nearly two months of sunshine, rest and fun. She should look well. Annie said, 'I think it's more than that. Just a hunch, but I could be wrong! She didn't say anymore.

*

Felix lay in bed later that night and thought about what he had said about composition, maybe he had said too much, he didn't even know if he could write for piano and drums, they were an unusual combination. And writing for a band, that was something else. He decided to try and meet Charlie and his music friends and hear what sort of sound they made, then he might be able to make a start. He listened to Annie snuffling in her sleep, 'And I'll write something for Rose, he thought. Sleep came.

CHAPTER 27

Small changes were apparent at the Moulin. Gregoire continued to work at the Chateau, using his experience to assist Joel in the kitchen garden. He had agreed with Claude to prepare the area for spring sowing but he refused to commit to more than that. He was concentrating on his own land he explained to Claude and was bringing more of the abandoned fields under cultivation using the tractors and trailers that Marthe had enabled him to purchase. She visited unexpectedly one morning, soon after getting back from her holiday, she found him in one of the barns, greasing the large tractor. They talked about the coming winter and Gregoire spoke enthusiastically about his plans for expansion. 'And the local markets? How are they doing? Marthe asked, she had found a seat on an upturned barrel and was admiring the tidiness around her. 'They're quieter now obviously, but Christmas and New Year will be busy. He replied, wiping the grease from his hands and looking at her. 'I'm buying from an organic supplier in Toulouse, which means a very early start, but the produce is good and I've regular customers at the markets. They help to keep me afloat and I enjoy market work, meeting people and hearing the gossip. It's a lonely life otherwise now that Agathe is up in Auch for much of her time. The winter months will be difficult, he continued, 'it's so easy for people to shop at the supermarket; the young mothers prefer them, everything set out, wrapped in plastic, clearly priced and prepared. The markets don't appeal on a cold wet morning. It's the older people, those who live in outlying farms who want to come to the market, it's their main social event, they meet their friends and the men drink at the bars. The cold doesn't matter to them.

Marthe thought about that realising that she did not go to the market in St.Girou every week, preferring to nip into the local Casino, she resolved to make more effort. Local markets were at the heart of local life.

'Agathe comes when she can, he continued, 'but it's difficult for her to give up a morning. Which is a shame, she really attracted customers!

Marthe looked surprised, 'Oh yes, he continued, 'she's really come out of her shell.

'I haven't seen her for a while, Marthe said, 'Would you ask her to call in and see me sometime soon? Tea time is best when she's on her way home.

'Would you like to see what I've been doing here? Gregoire asked, 'have you time? Marthe stood up and they walked out to the back of the barn and down a narrow path beside the field. It was cold in the wind and Marthe pulled her coat around her. Gregoire pointed towards the South, 'That's all new land brought into cultivation. Marthe saw that the soil was dark brown and shiny, the field was made up of deep troughs and raised banks of earth, it stretched away from them, the lines were very straight. He pointed 'And that field beyond will be the next to be ploughed up. Marthe tried to understand, she was looking at an immense area of rough grass full of docks and thistle and edged with bramble. It seemed an impossible task. 'The new tractor will turn all that over, he said, 'I can't spray because I'm strictly organic. So it will take time before it'll be ready, hopefully within a year or so. 'Organic is what you're sticking with then? Marthe realised the implications.

He nodded, 'Oh yes. Better for the soil and in the long run more profitable. She looked at him, he was wearing an old jacket and thick sweater, his face was deeply tanned and his hands were still greasy, but he looked well and happy. She thought of Felix, 'What different lives they lead, one so rural the other so urban. She hoped that Felix would find work that was as rewarding as Gregoire had found in his fields. They walked back to the farm, his dog Jacques came running out and Gregoire stooped to rub his rough coat. Where are the others? Marthe asked.

'In the barn, they don't come out so much, except for food! Grandfather doesn't like them in the house, under his feet, he says. He's frightened of falling of course. Marthe asked, 'How is he? Is he well?

'Same as ever, though he has a bad cough. He needs to move around more than he does, and he misses Agathe, she used to give him lunch and now it's just us two and I'm busy. He gets irritable!

'Does he keep warm? Gregoire sighed, 'I try. I stoke up the fire before I come out, but he's careless and lets it die down. He sleeps too much!

'Have you seen these new wood burning stoves? Marthe said, 'They stay in for a long time, even overnight. Perhaps you could think of buying one. They burn on dry wood but you've plenty of that. Gregoire shook his head, 'I don't know of those.

'They sell them in Auch, on the road near the golf course. Ask Agathe to take a look, it's not far from the hospital. It might make life easier for him and you.

Marthe left soon after this conversation, she hoped her visit had been helpful.

*

Two days later Agathe found the shop that sold wood burners, she parked her scooter and went in. The assistant was eager to help and explained the principles of a wood burner, its advantages over an open fire. She was impressed but surprised at the cost, 'I'll have to talk to my brother, she said somewhat flustered, 'and there's the lining of the chimney on top of that. 'You'll save in the long run, he assured her, 'burning less wood and keeping the whole house warm too. Sales man talk, she thought but could see that a stove might be a solution to the problem of grandfather. They agreed that she would return with Gregoire. The following day she called in at Les Palmes, it was a miserable rainy afternoon, and Marthe was reading in the sitting room. She was delighted to see Agathe, noting her new haircut, much shorter than before showing off little hoop ear rings. She made tea in the kitchen as Agathe walked around chatting about the hospital and her work on the ward. Her exams were coming up and she expressed some anxiety. 'Of course you're anxious, who wouldn't be? But you've studied hard I'm sure. Marthe assured her. Agathe nodded, 'I hope I do well, I don't just want to pass. I want to come near the top. They sat at the table in the kitchen and Agathe said, 'How was your holiday? Did you get to Cadiz? I've always wanted to go there, it's about as far as you can go isn't it? Marthe was caught by surprise, the question brought back the memory of the evening on the waterfront and looking across the sea towards Africa, and how kind Claude had been when she was overwhelmed with the desire to return home.

'You'll get there one day. She said, 'I had an interesting time in Spain, it's oddly different from France. The

Spanish are a very reserved people, and their history is fascinating, we saw so much that dated back to the time of the Moorish occupation, that's the 15th century and earlier. Agathe sipped her tea and ate a slice of cake, she listened with interest and Marthe got up and found a guide book to Spain that she was still continuing to browse through, and handed it to her. 'Here, take it home and have a look, you might want to travel there next year. It's cheaper than France, both the travel and the food and there are lots of camp sites too. Agathe prepared to leave, she needed to get home and prepare supper, Gregoire was out that evening and grandfather would be waiting impatiently. But Marthe asked her to stay, 'I have something I want to tell you, she said, 'Please sit down for a moment.

Agathe listened silently, not understanding initially why Marthe was telling her this story from the past. Several minutes later Marthe stopped speaking and a long silence followed. Marthe waited, quietly watching Agathe's face. The girl finally spoke, it had been a lot of information to take in and she was astonished by what Marthe had said: the story of the disappearance of the five men, one her great uncle, and their deaths near Strasbourg, she had never heard any of this before and had never seen the commemorating plaque. Then the suggestion that her family had been present at the the death of Bertrand...and Marthe's belief that the Rinaldi brothers. Pierre and Andre had been mistaken, because Bertrand had played no part in their betrayal. 'My family have never spoken of this, Agathe said very slowly, 'I've never heard any account of the disappearance of that uncle or how and why he died. It's my father's family he's never spoken about what the family did in the war. It's a long time ago.

Marthe took the girl's hand, 'I'm sorry. It's a shock I know. I am trying to understand it myself. And this connection between our families…that's been unexpected.

*

'I feel a little overwhelmed! Agathe said, she was pale now. 'I had to tell you, Marthe said, 'There have been too many secrets. Agathe nodded but felt unable to talk anymore, her head was buzzing and she felt exhausted. They said goodbye and Agathe returned home. Grandfather was waiting for her as she expected, he was irritable and the new wood burner was low in the room. But it was still burning and the room felt warm. She quickly put new logs in and hurried to heat up a casserole and they ate together in the almost dark kitchen. Agathe could only think of what she had heard from Marthe and wondered what her grandfather knew of the story. It was not his family, he was not a Rinaldi, but he was a local man and he must have heard of the disappearance and subsequent deaths of the five men. Or maybe not? So much of what had happened during the war years was never spoken of, kept secret or put aside to be forgotten.

Agathe waited up for Gregoire, sitting beside the fire long after her grandfather had retired to bed. She needed to talk to him, to unburden her mind, to share her knowledge. He came in, surprised to find her still up, 'I need to talk, she said quickly, 'I've had an extraordinary conversation with Marthe. I can't sleep till I've told you. Gregoire poured himself a brandy, offering one to Agathe, she shook her head and started to talk. They sat by the fire for a long time. Gregoire knew more about the history of France than his sister, he had studied the events of the two world wars and had found it interesting. But he knew little about the history of the area in which they lived and had never seen the plaque on the wall in the village. He had never heard of the five men who had died and certainly did not know of their connection to him. 'A Rinaldi! He said in surprise. 'There's more, and this is the worst! Agathe was leaning forward, 'And this is where we come in! She recounted the words she remembered as clearly as she could. 'Marthe's father he lived at Les Palmes, his name was Bertrand, he was blamed by the Resistance for these deaths, he was believed to be a supporter of the Germans, some one who helped the Germans, maybe giving them information. And, she took a deep breath, ' after Jacques had disappeared, two of the younger Rinaldi brothers waylaid him on the towpath outside the gate at Les Palmes, there was a struggle and he fell in.

'What? Was he hurt?

'Bertrand drowned! His body was found down river, at the weir at St. Girou, trapped by the wooden piles. Aghast Gregoire began pacing the room, glancing at Agathe who sat pale and silent. 'You mean these two brothers killed him? Agathe answered, 'Marthe did not say that exactly, but they did not try to save him after he fell in the water. So I don't know what that means, legally. Perhaps they thought he would climb out, save himself. He was not an old man.

'How has Marthe learnt all this? Greoire asked.

She has been reading her father's diaries. Felix found them in a chest. They had been there since the end of the war, sort of hidden away. No one knew. Bertrand wrote every day about what he had done, you know, his health and work and such, right up to the day of his death. And Marthe has read them all and thinks he was not responsible for the deaths of the five men. He would not have betrayed them as he no longer supported the Germans, he had come to hate them and so would not have assisted them in that way. Or in any way at all.

'Why? Why had he changed?

'Marthe did not talk about that. I was so shocked that we sort of stopped talking, and I did not think to ask about Bertrand.

Gregoire had finished his brandy and was sitting down, he said, 'I think we should go and look at the plaque to the five men, which I've never heard of before, and also ask Papa what he knows. Would you do that? Would you come with me?

Agathe's agitation had not been diminished as she listened to her brother, he had raised questions that had not occurred to her at all, the fate of Marthe's father and the role of the Rinaldi brothers especially. She stood up, 'Of course I'll come, this is a family thing isn't it. We are both Rinaldis aren't we.

*

Claude was readjusting to life back at home in the wing of the Chateau. It felt peaceful and quiet without the presence of guests, their arrivals and departures, their voices loud in the garden and their cars turning around in the drive. Their endless luggage. He preferred it like this, though he missed his two sons, who had both now left for the winter, Jerome was in Paris, working hard at his hotelier course and Luc was in the Alps, a sous chef in a small hotel. Claude was happy to have the place to himself, though at times it felt empty and he wondered how he would manage during the winter months entirely on his own. He spent time talking to Joel the gardener. They discussed what needed to be done during the winter months and Claude was interested to learn how much preparation went on even during the coldest weather. He knew little about gardening but was interested to learn and he appreciated Joel's enthusiasm. They agreed a budget for the coming months for plants and trees and shrubs and Claude watched with interest as they began to arrive. Joel unloaded them with ease carrying even the heaviest, and moved them around until he had found the perfect site. Staking the trees against the wind, he stood back imagining how they would look in a few years time. He assured Claude that he would soon see the benefits of all the planting.

*

Claude was busy, the full weight of being the owner of the estate, its farms and woods now fell entirely on him and took up more time than he wanted. He took advice from a consulting firm in Auch and, with their help, interviewed a number of potential estate managers, ultimately appointing a middle aged woman who he felt he could work with. She was Dutch, married to a man who had relocated to Toulouse, she agreed to work three days a week initially with the option for more days if needed. He found her an office in the barn next to the pool and put in an electric fire, a phone and internet connection. Her name was Anna and she soon became a familiar figure around the estate, as she got to know the tenants, the land and the work of the farms. She worked hard and was rapidly asked to work a full week and Claude felt able to turn his attention to other matters.

He could now concentrate on his own reclamation business which he had neglected during the long hotel season. He was pleased to return and open it up, walking around his large yard and barns, assessing what he had for sale. The items that he had purchased in Spain had arrived and he watched as they were unloaded; there were lamps and fire grates from Toledo, heavy wooden chests from Salamanca, their lids deeply carved, and paintings and heavy rugs from Cordoba. Most valuable were his Cadiz purchases, a set of chairs originally from Morocco and an oak bed stead with its original drapes. He quietly thought he might offer the latter to Marthe for Les Palmes. He rather fancied waking up in the morning in such a magnificent piece of furniture.

Claude was confident that they would sell and he priced them carefully. He was a well known dealer respected for his experience and knowledge concluding many a deal with a glass of wine in hand. He never rushed a sale or a purchase, and never bought anything that he would not put in his own home or garden. Many people relied on him when they were selling a house for his advice on what they should or should not sell. He gave confidence.

He regularly thought of Marthe. He enjoyed her company more and more and in the absence of the boys he would have liked her to move in with him, his wing felt increasingly empty now, especially when he returned after a long day. She drove up regularly, coming for supper and staying the night and they had been entertained together by several of his local friends. They were seen as a pair, and were popular if unusual in a society where 'living together' was rare. But they weren't living together and that was Claude's problem. She had made it more than clear earlier in the year that she valued her independence, and did not want any new ties, but she seemed to have changed and the holiday in Spain had affirmed that. Or had it? Claude decided to raise the subject again, it was the week before Christmas and all over France, families were planning to be together over the holiday. Luc was not returning, the hotel where he worked was at its busiest, whilst Jerome was staying in Paris. And this rather forced Claude's hand. He did not want to be on his own during a time of festivities nor did he want to go away, he was no longer tempted by Bordeaux and Angelique. He arranged to meet

Marthe in Toulouse, they would have a nice lunch and do some Christmas shopping. They both enjoyed exploring the galleries and antiques shops, and he intended to find something for Felix and Annie. A Christmas gift for the house. He also intended to speak to her about a new arrangement that he had in mind.

*

Their lunch was a success, they ate oysters from Oleron and shared an enormous dish of fried fish, which reminded them of their holiday in southern Spain. Marthe was wearing a new wool suit in heathery colours and for fun a little hat with artificial violets that brought out the blue of her eyes. Claude was delighted with her. She charmed him. They drank their coffee away from the table at a window seat overlooking the river, and he took her hand. 'I want to suggest something to you, which I have been thinking about for some time. She tensed a little but allowed him to continue, 'We both live alone in homes too big for us, I know you fear commitment, but would you consider a new arrangement? I want to be with you and stop all the toing and froing that we're both doing, it's a waste of your time and mine! Let me move into Les Palmes…its big enough for the two of us, and I could settle there I'm sure.

'But what about the Chateau? Marthe said, 'Will you leave it empty? And all your 'stuff': your books and records and lovely things?

'Perhaps I could bring some of it with me…slowly. The Chateau will be fine, I now have the Manager working full time and there's Joel in the garden. I'm not needed!

Marthe sat silently, the idea appealed to her immediately, she would enjoy having Claude in her life on a more permanent basis, and she knew that she was in love with him. But it all sounded rather long term and what if it didn't work?

'Do you really think we could live together happily? I've been on my own now for more than four years and you, well, for ages. What if we quarrelled and came to resent each other? That I couldn't bear.

He leant over and kissed her gently, 'We won't know if we don't try. I can't miss this opportunity, we can be happy I know it! Marthe smiled at him, she knew how lucky she was, 'Well, she paused, then looking at him, she said with a laugh, 'let's give it a try! Perhaps a glass of champagne shall we? And then some shopping?

*

Marthe told Felix her news later in the afternoon as they had tea together in the salon. Claude was downstairs in the kitchen with Annie, they were talking about the garden at the Chateau and Rose was on his knee, he bounced her carefully as she tried to suck his tie. 'You can put her down, Annie said, 'She'll ruin it! Just watch your budget, don't overspend. The garden will absorb all the money that you throw at it! Claude listened, 'I know, but I do enjoy seeing it develop, it's looking good even now in December. Annie enjoyed talking with Claude, and it was easier now that she wasn't an employee, he was looking well, she thought, flourishing really. He had given them a tall vase for the house, Chinese, he said in an off hand way. She hoped that it had not cost too much money, he was always generous. He had positioned it carefully half way up the stairs on a low shelf where it could be seen going up and down. Felix was delighted and had given him a hug, very French Annie thought to herself, wondering if an Englishman would have acted similarly. It made her think of Tony and her mother who she had not spoken to for a few days. They had argued slightly about Christmas, which was normal, it happened every year, as Claire and Tony wanted Annie and her family to join them. Annie had declined, she felt that the cottage in Kent would be too small for all of them especially if the weather was bad and they couldn't get out. 'We'll come at Easter, she had offered, 'Rose will be more interesting by then and we can get out for walks. Would that be nice? Something to look forward to!

Claire had listened, 'What about Charlie? Would he like to come over on his own? Just for a few days. Annie agreed to ask him but the holiday was short and she knew he already had plans. Band plans. She thought Claire was heading for a second disappointment. It was one of the few drawbacks of her living in Toulouse and she felt sad about it.

Upstairs Marthe spoke carefully as she balanced her tea cup in her hand. The salon was as she remembered and she admired it as she looked around, not Rose's territory she presumed. Though that couldn't last for ever, and she wondered how Felix would cope with a toddler with sticky fingers wandering about this room, hauling herself up onto the sofa and dribbling onto the cushions. 'I want to tell you my news. Claude is moving into Les Palmes, we are going to try a new arrangement. Felix, whose attention had wandered, took some time to follow this, 'He's going to live there? With you?

'Well obviously! With me. Marthe felt almost cross, she had hoped for a more supportive response. Felix corrected himself quickly, 'That makes sense, I'm pleased for you. He's great company and it will suit you both well. He bent and gave her a kiss, 'Truly, I'm delighted. The difficult moment was past, but later when the house was quiet Felix passed this news to Annie. She said, 'I thought she liked her independence, I hope she's thought about this carefully. She can be impetuous can't she.

Felix paused, he wanted to defend his mother against this charge of impetuosity, but he shared the view. Recent years had seen Marthe make several unexpected decisions, which had not worked out, and he dreaded another. 'We'll have to hope it's the right thing for both of them, he said 'Claude is independent too, maybe it'll work, if he doesn't try and crowd her. That's what she doesn't like.

'He'll look after her. Annie concluded, 'but it's a big decision!

*

In Toulouse, Gregoire and Agathe were meeting their father at a bar near to where he lived. Gregoire was full of apprehension, he had not seen his father for nearly a year and they had not been on good terms for a long time. He remembered clearly a heated argument following his father's revelation that he intended to leave the farm. His father had been pale and agitated, as he stood in the kitchen whilst his two children sat at the table side by side listening to him in horror, 'I can't live on this farm, now your mother has died! He had said more in sorrow than in kindness, 'There's nothing here for me, I'm not a farmer and never will be. I hate the empty fields and monotonous days and endless dark nights! I can make a new life for us now as a family in Toulouse, I'll find an apartment and you can both go to school and college there. It'll be a fresh start. They had listened, appalled, neither of them wanted to leave the only life that they knew. They had both been born at the Moulin and loved the farm where Gregoire was already taking over much of the work from his grandfather. He saw his future there, and Agathe, a shy girl, lacked the courage to join her father in a City which she had rarely visited, and had not enjoyed when she did. Also there were the grandparents, who would look after them, if she left?

*

Their father greeted them nervously, and they found a table at the back of the bar away from the noisy television. He bought their drinks and they began to talk awkwardly. Gregoire eyed his father. Neither of them asked about his new wife and baby. After a few minutes Gregoire explained why they wanted to meet him, 'We have learnt some thing about your uncles and the war. He said abruptly, 'from a friend, Mme.le Brun.'

He nodded, 'Yes she came to see me, but I couldn't help her. I know nothing of the war or what the family did and I hardly knew my uncles. We weren't a close family, and, he paused looking at Gregoire, 'It was not something people wanted to talk about. He took a mouthful of beer, 'It's in the past. Agathe shifted in her seat and said, 'Had you ever heard of Bertrand du Pont, before she visited you?

'No.

'So there was no connection as far as you knew between our family and Madame's father?

'No. As I said I know nothing about any of this. He was becoming impatient and Gregoire said, 'You are a Rinaldi though aren't you!

'Of course. But I'm not responsible for things done by the family before I was born.

Gregoire saw the logic in that and felt the conversation was getting nowhere. He was already regretting coming to see his father. Agathe was becoming distressed, she had a certain love for her father, though she felt he had abandoned her and Gregoire, still he was her father, and that bound her to him however lightly. She had hoped that the meeting would lead to a certain reconciliation between the three of them and this was not happening. Gregoire maintained his hostile attitude, sitting back in his chair with his arms crossed and avoiding eye contact. Her father looked small beside his son and his somewhat wary look added to the impression that he was in awe of his son, uncomfortable in his presence. They broke up soon after as Gregoire downed his beer and stood up, he strode to the exit and paced up and down outside. Agathe looked at her father sadly, it had not been a happy meeting: they had learnt nothing about the family and the animosity between her brother and father had continued as before. 'Is there anyone else who might be able to help us? She asked standing up and holding her bag close to her chest.

'You have a great uncle in Auch, but he is very elderly and confused. You could try him. I can give you an address if you want. Phone me tonight and I'll find it for you. They embraced, 'Please give my love to your daughter, Agathe said, 'And your wife. He nodded at this and they said goodbye. Agathe joined Gregoire outside, 'There's a great uncle in Auch who may be able to help, so the meeting was not entirely a waste of time! Papa will phone me his address. He looked sad didn't he? Gregoire shrugged and said nothing, and they drove off.

As they headed home Gregoire suddenly took a turn to the right up a narrow lane, 'Let's look at the plaque shall we? Now we're together. The lane continued for several miles, north towards Auch. It was little used, little more than a farm track, passing wide fields and the occasional farm. Gregoire looked around with interest, casting his 'farmer's eye about, Agathe sat silently reflecting on her family; her ageing grandfather and her sad father. She thought about herself too, the new life she was leading, her training at the hospital and her growing social confidence. And Gregoire driving the van beside her, he seemed well and happy. It was not all bad she decided.

In a short while they stood together in front of the plaque. Set into the wall of the church just outside the graveyard it was not hard to find. 'It needs a clean, Gregoire said, rubbing his hand over the surface. As he did the five names became clearer and they read Jean Jacques Rinaldi and his dates. All five men had died on the same day in August 1944 at Strasbourg. Agathe shuddered and bent her head 'Mort pour la France' she said quietly. They were both deeply moved.

'Shall we try and find the great uncle? Agathe asked as they walked back to the van. 'No I don't think so. What's to be gained? We know the story and raking it over…well, I don't think I want to. Gregoire stopped by the driver's door and unlocked it, 'he's an old man, we might revive unhappy memories. I don't want to do that. Agathe climbed in, 'Yes, it's so long ago. But I 'm glad we went to see the plaque.

CHAPTER 28

Felix enjoyed Christmas. Marthe and Claude joined them for the day, weighed down with gifts they struggled noisily up the stairs. Carrying a large quantity of oysters, and expensive chocolates, and a bottle of champagne, a large bunch of lilies, a bottle of Schnapps and a present for Charlie. Felix, who was cooking, turned from the stove, 'Bonne Fete! He said, 'please open the champagne from the fridge, it's well chilled and we can drink yours later! Annie, hearing their voices came down the stairs, and they stood around drinking whilst Charlie opened his presents. Rose slept upstairs in her cot through the lunch celebrations and they all became very merry. Charlie had spent the morning preparing the food with Felix; he was becoming quite a competent cook, enthusiastic to try new things and eager to experiment with spices and herbs from the market. He had not been allowed to open the oysters, but ate them enthusiastically. They were from Oleron, small and sweet. They lingered at the table, chatting over the last dish, an almond tart with thick cream and tiny strawberries, when Rose woke. It was nearly three o'clock. Charlie fetched her down, handed her to Felix and walked to the fridge, bringing out a small bottle of milk. Marthe looked at him in surprise, 'It's her first day, he said putting the milk in a pan of warm water, 'Mum's stopping breast feeding, this is what she's having now. Marthe stopped herself from saying anything and watched as Charlie carefully carried the milk bottle and a teat, handing both to Felix. 'You do it Dad and I can feed her later, he said trying to be casual. The door bell rang and Charlie jumped up, 'It'll be Francois and Philip he said, 'Is it ok to let them in? A further surprise for Marthe. Francois was a tall very thin boy a little older than Charlie, dressed in black carrying a guitar case, the other boy was possibly Algerian, he too had a guitar. They both smiled shyly and stood next to Felix who was carefully feeding Rose. 'You get everything ready. We'll be up once Rose has finished, he said. The boys disappeared up the stairs. Felix, still carefully holding Rose and gently moving the teat in her mouth to encourage her to suck, said, 'A Christmas surprise! We've got a small concert for you all! Upstairs in my music room. Annie was astonished and Marthe and Claude stared at him.

'Yes, Felix continued, we've formed a band and I've written some music, this'll be our first performance! We can go up in a moment, bring the rest of the champagne Claude would you? He tried to sound calm and turning to Annie, he said, 'Didn't you guess? I was up there so often with the boys, you must have wondered. And the noise too! She shrugged, 'This house is very sound proof and when I'm in the kitchen working, I don't really notice anything else at all. How amazing Felix, you and Charlie and those two…piano, drums, and guitars. That's a proper band. She took Rose from him and patting her back rested her on her shoulder, and turned to Marthe and said, 'Shall we go then? A Christmas concert awaits! They walked up the stairs to the top floor together and Claude and Felix followed, Claude carrying the champagne and chuckling to himself. 'You're a man of surprises, he said, 'well done!

*

303

Felix had written two pieces; the first was fast and very rhythmic with solo parts for each of the boys. It was jazz and Charlie on the drums provided a steady beat on the snare drum watching Felix all the time, and performed his solo with the second drum stick held in his right hand improvising some exciting bars. They finished together with a crescendo and an explosion on the cymbals from Charlie. All three kept time tapping their feet on the floor and watching Felix who in turn glanced at them regularly bringing them into the music with a nod of his head and smiling encouragingly. They took a rest and Charlie fetched a large jug of water. Claude had finished the champagne and was wondering whether to bring up the Schnapps, he held Marthe's hand and gave it a squeeze, 'This is really good he said and she smiled. Annie held Rose who turned her head to find Charlie.

*

The second piece had a larger part for the piano and was almost a duet with Charlie, who provided a steady background beat, the melody was a haunting refrain, quite repetitive, in a minor key. Not quite a lullaby, it ended with a series of chords in C major. Annie listened, overwhelmed by what he had written, it was a song for Rose as he had promised her earlier in the year. He stopped playing and Charlie held his drum sticks quietly in his hands, no one spoke, then Felix looked up from the keys and turned to Annie with a hesitant smile. She rose and carrying the baby crossed the room bent to kiss his cheek, 'That's simply lovely Felix, marvellous. I'm amazed. She turned to the others, 'We seem to have a composer in our midst! And an exceptional band! Thank you boys. They stood up holding their instruments and grinned, relaxed now and happy. Marthe and Claude stood up and clapped and Marthe then gave them all a hug as Claude went off in search of a celebratory drink. Felix took Rose, holding her high up above his head, 'Your first concert, he said, 'I hope you enjoyed it! She gazed down at him and dribbled and they all laughed, it had been a memorable afternoon.

*

Marthe and Claude left later, the evening had come in and Felix walked with them to their car. As she prepared to climb in Marthe said, 'Felix, I'm proud and delighted. If you're serious about the composing…that's really exciting. And you play so well despite the wretched wrist, it doesn't stop you at all!

'The thing is I really enjoy it! Felix said, 'and writing for the boys and playing with them, it's magical. The four of us making music, that's what interests me. It's been like discovering a whole new world: not classical but this modern sound. It sits in my head all day and I can't wait to experiment with them. They're inspirational.

He waved as they drove down the cobbled street and stared up at the sky, there were no stars, no moon but it was never dark in the heart of Toulouse; there were lights from the bar opposite, which was still busy with locals celebrating the Fete, and down the street lights filtered from doorways and windows where there were candles burning on sills. He walked in.

*

The first months of the New Year passed slowly, the days were short, the wind cold. The population of Toulouse struggled through the streets their collars turned up and hands thrust deep in their pockets. Few lingered in the outdoor markets and the stall holders sighed and stamped their feet. In their new home Annie and Felix settled back into a routine around Rose and Charlie. Annie continued her attempts to extend her gardening contacts working in the mornings whilst the child carer took charge of Rose, and on the top floor Felix continued with his life, practicing the piano, a little teaching, much composition and writing occasionally for the newspaper. He was happier now and the dark days of the previous year were a thing of the past. He still hoped that Annie would change her mind and marry him but he did not raise the subject much as he yearned to.

The house too had settled into a home. The rooms flowing into each other as doors were left open and possessions drifted carelessly from one room to another. Only the salon retained some order. It was May, a warm sunny morning, Felix came down the stairs from his music room and found Rose there, sitting in the middle of the room gazing about, a look of triumph on her face. He picked her up, automatically feeling her pants, 'So you got in, did you? What do you think then? She pulled his hair, a favourite and annoying trick, 'Shall I show you around? He carried her to the mantel and pointed out the painting, 'That's a mountain, he said, 'And see, there's a red roof and an old barn. The child listened and watched as he pointed with his finger. Annie heard his voice as she came up from the kitchen and walked in, 'What are you doing Felix?

'She found her way in, this amazing wriggling on her bottom, and now I'm giving her a tour. Rose jiggled about in his arms trying to reach her mother, 'Well when you've finished bring her down, will you? Annie said with a smile, 'It's lunch time. We might need to put a gate on the door or she'll be in there all the time.

But Felix thought that a bad idea, he wanted their home to be for all of them, no barriers or special rooms. He decided to shew Rose his music room later and play her something on the piano, a new composition that he was quite pleased with. She could sit on his knee.

They're All Called Jacques

When lunch was over and Rose had been put down for a nap, Felix said 'I've an idea, can you follow me...downstairs. One minute later they stood together in the dark room that led off the entrance hall. It was not quite a basement as there were windows at street level. In past centuries it had been used for storage, in the days when it had been a merchant's house. The room was dusty and airless and had a damp smell. Annie stood in the middle, 'So? she said, 'What do you want me to look at here?

'Use your imagination! Felix replied, he was prowling about, touching the walls and testing the window frames. He reached high above his head, 'It must be at least three and a half metres. To the ceiling. That's splendid.

'Felix! What are you doing? Why am I standing here?

He paused 'Well it's obvious isn't it? This is a music space for the boys. The band. They can't go on using my room upstairs and they need somewhere to practice and play. Here they can make a lot of noise and not upset anyone. This is perfect. It's away from you and me and won't disturb Rose if she's sleeping. They don't need to even come upstairs!

Annie realised that he was serious and she began to take a closer look. What would we have to do? How much work would it need to make it usable? She asked.

'Well I've been thinking a bit. It needs proper wiring, which I can't do. Also proper insulation of the ceiling and the walls which would then have to be plastered. These window frames are rotten, he shewed her with his finger pressing into the soft wood, ' and need replacing and whilst we're doing it, I think, glass with double glazing. The floor is concrete and sound. We need to find a mason, an electrician and a plasterer. In what order I don't know!

307

'That's quite a list. Have you really thought about this? It sounds expensive though I suppose we could decorate it! Annie said.

'Or the boys. It's going to be their space.

'Felix this is such a great idea. Let me give you a hug! When shall we tell Charlie?

'First thing is to get the contractors round, then once it has been agreed... we'll tell the band! It'll be fun and it's making use of the whole house.

'Which I didn't want to live in! God Felix what a fool I can be! Annie looked at him remorsefully.

'We all make mistakes. Felix said softly. 'You don't crash cars.

*

A month later Charlie was surprised to see two vans outside the house. He was walking back from school and planning his weekend, he and the band were going to a gig on Saturday in Auch and he needed to persuade Annie or more likely Felix to pick him up. It would be late. He had stopped at the bakers and bought some éclairs a blatant attempt at persuasion. Annie loved eclairs. A loud banging greeted him in the Hall, there were two heavy sacks of rubble and a large shovel propped against the wall to the room on his left. There was dust everywhere and a radio was playing pop music. As he stood there a dark haired man in blue overalls came through the door and acknowledged Charlie with a wave of his hand. He seemed very much at home.

Bewildered, Charlie gave a smile and holding the éclairs carefully climbed the stairs and found Annie sitting at the table as though nothing unusual was happening.

'What's going on? I met a man in the hall!

'Ooooh! What have you got there? Is it for me?

Charlie handed the little bag over 'Yes. I know you both like them. There's one for Felix too! Annie regarded him with suspicion, 'Do you, perhaps want something?

'Mum! You've not answered my question. What's going on...downstairs.

'You'd better ask Felix. He's teaching for the moment, then you can go and ask him. Charlie sighed, 'Where's Rose?

'She's out with Marthe. In the square I expect. She won't be long either. Annie regarded her son, he's so like me, she thought, impatient. 'Let's share the éclairs, she said kindly and got out a knife.

Felix was delighted to find Charlie at the kitchen table, he had chocolate on his lips.

'Tell me what's going on! Charlie demanded immediately. Felix grinned at him, 'Oh so you've noticed! Come on then we need to go to the cellar.

Annie listened to them going down the stairs, how excited he's going to be, she thought, and how clever of Felix to think of it...a music room where the boys could practice and not bother anyone. Clever and kind she reflected.

Marthe came in, she had Rose in a papoose on her front and was pulling off the baby's hat.

'That was a great success! Carrying her like this is so much easier than the pushchair. We got right down to the river and looked at the boats. It was lovely. Whatever is going on downstairs? Are these men here for long?

It was Charlie who explained it to her. He was very pink and kept looking at Felix as he spoke. Marthe listened in amazement.

'So! A good idea? Felix asked his mother. 'What do you think?

Marthe said 'I think it's brilliant! You're a lucky boy Charlie! You and the band. She smiled at Felix, 'Well done!

309

'It won't be ready for a month or so. Felix said, surprised at how delighted he was to hear his mother's words.

'And I'm going to help as much as I can. Charlie interrupted, 'Me and the band...we'll do all the decorating.

Marthe glanced at Felix, he nodded his head, 'It's their space.

After Marthe had gone and Charlie was in his room, Annie prepared Rose for her bath; Felix joined her in the bathroom and sat on the stool watching the baby who was kicking her legs and sucking a flannel whilst Annie undressed her. 'Is she doing well? he asked pushing up the sleeves of his shirt. Annie was surprised, 'She's doing more than well. She's thriving! Look at her fat little legs! Felix laughed and lowered her carefully into the water, 'That's good then. he said, and and began soaping her tummy.

'Felix. Can I say something? He grunted concentrating on the slippery baby.

'It's just that, well, what you're doing for Charlie is pretty fantastic. And I want to say thank you. You are a kind and thoughtful man and I want you to know that I really don't take all this for granted. Not just the cellar idea but living here in this lovely house and...being cared for, by you. She stopped, oddly she was almost in tears. 'And I love you.

*

Later they made love and Felix drifting into sleep and still a little overwhelmed by what she had said, realised that for the first time for many months he was not hoping for Annie to change her mind about marrying him. He had become reconciled to her position and this realisation took him into a greater contentment than he had previously experienced. He touched her gently and Annie, already nearly asleep, whispered 'Night!

CHAPTER 29

'We're going to be late! Charlie hurry up!' Annie shouted from the foot of the stairs, she was holding Rose. Sophie, the nanny, joined her, she was holding a little cotton jacket, it had arrived that morning from England, a present from Claire. It was embroidered with roses which had made Annie smile, it was just like her mother to choose something like that. Sophie carried a large bag, she took the baby and ignoring a loud wail carried on into the kitchen and sitting on the edge of the sofa began to push Rose's flailing arms into the sleeves. Annie could feel herself getting anxious. She was about to shout again when Charlie appeared jumping down the last of the stairs, 'Gosh! He said, 'You look nice! Really mum, you look...lovely.

Annie softened, 'Do I? I wasn't sure. Felix chose it of course!

'It's such a great colour! Charlie continued, 'Shall we go?

'And you? How do you like a suit and tie?

'I feel as though I'm going to some awful work interview, but, no, it feels ok.

'Bye Sophie! Annie called out, 'Have a good day, hope she behaves!

Annie and Charlie walked down the stairs past the cellar, Charlie couldn't help glancing in,

'It's nearly finished. He said as they turned towards the Place du Capitol, 'We'll be using it next weekend I hope. It's going to be fantastic.

The summer sunshine had brought out the shoppers and tourists and they threaded their way through to the underground car park where Annie always left her car. She felt oddly proud to be walking with her son in his suit and tie, he was nearly as tall as her now and they made a good looking pair. Several people glanced at them.

'Are you nervous? Charlie asked, adjusting his seat belt and finding money for the toll.

'Me? No! I've nothing to be nervous about. I'm looking forward to it. We have to pick up Patricia at the station, so provided she's there, we'll be fine. Not late I mean.

'And what about Gran and Tony? How are they getting there?

'They're coming down from the Chateau. I told you, they're making a bit of a holiday of it.

'I bet Gran can't wait to see Rose! She'll be over every day!

'Probably. Annie drove up the wide avenue which led to the station, 'Look out for Patricia will you, I don't want to park. She's wearing red she told me.

Charlie looked around, 'I can't remember what she looks like!

'Small and smart! In red. Annie slowed right down as she approached the station forecourt, ignoring the angry taxi drivers behind her. 'Oh where are you Patricia?

'There! there! Charlie pointed to the right. 'Thank God! Annie swerved and Patricia stepped off the pavement, waving and smiling and, like any Parisienne, ignoring all the traffic.

*

At the Moulin, Agathe was in a state of great uncertainty, she was standing in her room, a dark badly lit room with only a very poor mirror. She called out to Gregoire, 'Tell me what you think! Please. He came in, 'What's the choice? Agathe held up a pale yellow shirt with pearl buttons down the front and a navy skirt. 'No! you'll look like a waitress. Agathe was too anxious to laugh, 'Well, it would have to be this. 'That! Definitely. He smiled at her, 'And shoes? She pointed at the bed. 'Can you walk in those?

'No! but they're all I've got.

'You've got ten minutes and then we leave. Gregoire was half way out of the door, 'You'll look lovely, he said and ran down the stairs, throwing his jacket over his shoulders.

*

Claude was giving last minute instructions at the Chateau to the staff. The hotel was in full swing and nearly full. The new manager nodded his head impatiently...he was experienced and confident and really did not need to be told what to do. The chef who had worked all the previous year listened briefly and then turned back to his kitchen. Claude sighed. He was joined by Luc as

Jerome brought the car to the front of the hotel and held the keys out to his father. 'Come on! Jerome said. 'Forget all this, we need to get going! Have you got everything? Where's your hat?

Claude held up his hand 'Here! Yes I have 'got everything'! Luc are you really wearing that tie? It's very thin.

'It's leather. It's meant to be thin. Am I on the back seat?

They were finally ready and Claude drove off.

'Nervous? Luc asked leaning forward from his seat in the back and touching Claude's shoulder.

'No! I assume you're teasing! I'm looking forward to the day.

'We all are! Jerome said. But he had noticed his father's hands shaking slightly as he took the car keys. It was most unusual for Claude to be apprehensive of anything. But this was a big day for him...for all of them.

*

At Les Palmes, Marthe and Felix had a last word with the caterers and then prepared to leave. Marthe, elegantly dressed in a blue silk suit and a cream hat with a tiny veil, waited calmly by the door as Felix adjusted his tie and put on the cream linen jacket, newly bought in Toulouse, 'Ready? He asked.

'Oh Yes! I'm as prepared as I'll ever be! The flowers are done, the caterers are here and the garden is almost at its best.

'And it's going to be a sunny day and not too hot! Felix said as he opened the door to the car and helped her in.

*

The Mairie stood on the south side of the old square in St.Girou. There was a small welcome party waiting outside the imposing brick building whose tri color drooped in the sunshine as Claude and his sons arrived. Some older residents of the town whose houses were situated around the square were observing these arrivals, they stood in their doorways. It was the most interesting thing that had happened for a long time and would be a cause for gossip in the coming days. Claude recognised some friends from the antiques world, and others who had known his family for many years, and he smiled as he stepped from the car. In the group that were assembled by the Mairie, a pretty girl caught his eye, she was wearing a short flowery dress with a red belt, and red shoes. Glancing again he recognised her...it was Agathe. Surprised he glanced again,

'Yes, said Jerome who was walking next to him, 'I've seen her too.

'She's Agathe, Gregoire's sister, they're twins, now training to be a nurse. Of course there is Italian blood in the family, Claude said, 'That might explain her dark hair and lovely skin. She'll be a stunner one day. They began walking up the brick steps of the Mairie.

A car hooted. It was Annie, she drove into the square rather fast, parked carelessly, and stepped out followed by Charlie and Patricia. All three waved at Claude and Charlie ran forward, stopping suddenly as he remembered the serious nature of the occasion. He held back and waited for Annie who was carefully crossing the cobbled square in her high heeled shoes. Patricia, in spite of her long early morning journey on the train from Paris was positively brimming with life, looking all around and eager to meet the group on the steps.

'My Lord! She said not so quietly to Annie, 'Claude is gorgeous! Look at that suit. Lucky Marthe! Annie laughed, 'Shush! Everyone will hear you.

'Oh I don't care. She was already on the steps and embracing the three waiting men.

Distracted, Claude missed the arrival of the final car, and Jerome nudged him severely, 'Pay attention for goodness sake. They're here! Claude stepped down and watched as Marthe on Felix's arm came forward, he kissed her lightly on both cheeks, murmuring some words, then taking her hand firmly, he led her into the Mairie. Everyone else followed. Luc walking beside Charlie said, Don't put your hands in your jacket pockets. It's not a cool look! Charlie who had been seized by nerves since emerging from the car, nodded gratefully. 'You're sitting behind me, Luc continued, 'but we can talk afterwards, I want to hear all about your band. Jerome and I listen to lots of jazz.

*

The ceremony did not take long and they came out into the summer sunshine.

'Is that it? Charlie asked Patricia. He felt a little cheated, 'I thought getting married would take longer. 'Church weddings are more protracted, she replied, 'but they couldn't have one, Charlie was puzzled, but before he could ask Patricica what she meant, she said,

'We need to stand here for a while as there will be some photos. Why don't you join your mother for those? Look she's standing next to Felix.

Luc came over and said, 'Come on Charlie, you're family. we need you for the photos.

'Am I? Why? Charlie stared at him.

'Well, Luc started to explain, then realising that technically neither Annie or Charlie were 'family', he stopped talking and putting his hand on the boy's shoulder steered him towards Annie. This idea of 'family' bothered Charlie for the rest of the day and he decided to talk to Felix about it.

*

It was five o'clock and the reception was in full swing; jackets had been taken off and ties loosened. Wine glasses were being filled more slowly and the buffet was over, though the desserts were still waiting for any late comers. Annie walked slowly around the garden with Gregoire pointing out some of the plants that she had chosen for their ability to thrive without constant summer watering, whilst Charlie had led Luc through the garden gate and was showing him the river and the spot where he liked to fish. They stood together under the willow trees watching the slow moving water, it was clear and shallow. 'Do you catch any fish then? Luc asked. 'Not often. No, but it's nice anyway. And I chat to the other fishermen. I like it, he said simply. Luc was surprised it seemed rather dull to him, he picked up a stone and lobbed it into the middle of the stream, 'Come on, he said, 'my glass is empty! They turned back and Charlie felt a little disappointed that Luc had not shown more interest. But Luc had been kind to him earlier so that was all right.

Claire and Tony, who was walking with a stick, had retreated to the shade of the terrace and Tony was enjoying the desserts and admiring the clothes. 'They're all so slim! Claire sighed, 'How do they do it! Tony tapped her on the knee, 'You're just as gorgeous as any of them. He said, 'Have you tried the coffee cake?

Felix, standing under the palm trees, watched with amusement a mild flirtation that was taking place between Jerome and Agathe, who certainly stood out in her flowery yellow dress. They were laughing at something and he was reminded of his flirtation with Annie in the same spot the previous year. Good luck to them he thought and turned away to join his mother who was talking with Patricia near the buffet. Marthe was smiling and Claude caught his breath as he came out from the house and saw her. He came forward tapping his wrist watch. 'Time to go! He said quietly.

Their cases were in the hall and everyone moved in from the garden.

'So where are you going? Jerome asked, 'You've been very secretive! Claude smiled, 'New York tomorrow and Paris tonight. We've a flight from Toulouse at 8. Marthe appeared and Felix opened the entrance door and led his mother out as Claude watched beside the car. Standing beside Annie, and waving at the departing couple, Patricia felt a stab of jealousy then recovered herself, 'Let's go and finish the champagne! She said taking Annie's hand, 'And you can explain to me why you haven't married your handsome man.

*

In Toulouse everyone felt a bit flat on the following day and there were some tetchy moments. Claire and Tony arrived for lunch bringing a chicken pie from the Chateau's kitchens, 'It just needs a quick heat through, Claire said thrusting it at Felix, 'Where's Rose? He pointed her up the stairs, 'And hello to you too! He said quietly to himself. Tony came in looking puffed, 'How are you today? He asked, handing Felix a bottle of white wine. 'From the hotel cellar? Felix said.

'No! We stopped at the wine shop in the Square, terrific choice I could have spent hours there. Why do you ask? Felix blushed 'Sorry Tony, it's been a tiring morning. Let's put it in the fridge now shall we? Thank you.

Tony liked Felix and they stood chatting as Felix cleared the table for lunch. Tony thought that Felix was admirably patient with Annie who, unlike her mother, could be, well he did not like the word, selfish. But he acknowledged that Annie was talented and had done an excellent job rearing Charlie almost singlehanded. He admired her 'drive' and energy. He hoped that living in this lovely house would enable her to enjoy life a little more and that Felix and Rose would help her to appreciate the family that now surrounded her. In his old fashioned way he preferred women to stay at home, cooking and caring for others, it was what had attracted him to Claire who was above all a home maker. He heard her voice as she came down the stairs talking to the child that she held, 'One more step! And we're there!

'Annie looks well! Claire said to Felix, 'and Rose is taking after her. The same colouring. Felix nodded, 'Yes, she is well. Have you seen Charlie?

'He says he has something to show us after lunch, Tony said, 'He wanted to tell us about it at the party yesterday, but then stopped. We are intrigued.

*

They're All Called Jacques

'What have we here? Tony opened he eyes. Charlie had led him and Claire into the converted cellar with their eyes closed, he wanted it to be a real surprise. They now stood in the middle of the room, both looking around unsure as to what they were looking at. 'See! Charlie quickly turned on the spotlights which lit up the room. Claire spotted four music stands that were propped against a wall as she moved cautiously to the window. Feet and legs were passing by which gave her a start.

'It's a room for you isn't it, Charlie! She declared turning round, 'For those drums of yours! Charlie jumped up and down, which gave her another start. 'Yes! Yes! Yes! It was Felix's idea and we've had builders banging away for ages. It's for the band so we can practice without disturbing Mum or Felix.

Tony got the idea more slowly, 'It's rather dark. He said.

Charlie was unperturbed, 'It's not finished Tony. I've discussed it with the others and we are going to decorate it ourselves. To save Felix money. We're going to paint the walls a deep red and the ceiling cream. 'Ah, Tony said, 'moody but not dark.' 'Exactly, Charlie was pleased, 'we do play mostly jazz. Felix composes lots of stuff for us, he agreed to buy the paints as soon as the wedding was over and so we can now get going.

'Well I think it's enormously kind of Felix. Claire was now standing back in the middle of room, 'and I'd like to contribute something.

'No Gran!

'Yes Gran! Claire's voice was firm, 'I'll think of something. A surprise!

*

Claire and Tony had returned to England, it was a week since the wedding.

'Why do people get married? Charlie was helping Felix in the kitchen, he was gently stirring the soup, 'You and Mum aren't. Felix tried to answer calmly, wishing that the boy had asked Annie such a difficult question. He stopped chopping the fennel and turned to answer as Charlie continued stirring,

'Marriage is an important step but not everyone takes it. Your mum took it with your dad, but it didn't work out. She's reluctant to take it again.

'But you love each other, right. And now you've got Rose. So, are we a 'family'?

Felix thought he understood what was really bothering Charlie. He said 'Of course we are. We live together, here, and we all love each other.

'If Mum changed her mind about getting married again, would she have a different name? Yours? And what about me?

'That would be up to her. Lots of women now keep their own name, but most don't. Either way you wouldn't. Change I mean. You have a father and so you have his name, Scott. Charlie Scott...it's a very nice name. Very English! Charlie sighed and came and stood next to Felix, 'But would you like to marry Mum?

'I don't think in the end it makes much difference. Felix said, 'times have changed...

'But Marthe is more old fashioned isn't she? Charlie interrupted, 'And her husband died, so marrying Claude was kind of easy for her.

'That's right, I'm glad that she has married Claude, it feels right for both of them.

Charlie thought about this and said, 'But Claude is divorced isn't he? Like Mum.

'Yes that's why they married in the Mairie, the church doesn't approve of Catholics divorcing. There was a silence, then Charlie said,

'It was a nice day wasn't it. Your Mum looked very happy! And Mum looked terrific!

Felix put his knife down and bending a little gave Charlie a hug. 'Yes, Mum did look lovely and she was very proud of you, in your suit and tie! Married or not married, things are fine with me and Mum, don't you worry. Ok? And if you think about it your Gran and Tony are a 'family' and they're not married. You're part of their family too. You're lucky Charlie, you also have your Dad and Edna. All these people inter linked with you.

Charlie looked up at him, 'Shall we go and play some music? He asked. Felix realised that for the moment the conversation was over.

'Yes. After supper. Go and call your Mum, this is nearly ready. He watched as Charlie walked towards the stairs, he felt the talk had gone as well as it could,

but he wondered whether to tell Annie. Perhaps not he decided, but he could still hear in his head Charlie's question, 'But would you like to marry Mum?' He walked to the fridge and took out a bottle of white wine, poured two glasses and taking one he stood at the window looking down into the courtyard where the urns that Annie had planted earlier were full of colour. He drank from his glass listening for the sound of steps coming down the stairs for the supper that he had enjoyed cooking.

CHAPTER 30

It was early December but the days were sunny and mild. Annie leant on her spade as she scraped the mud off her boots. She felt tired. It was nearly midday and she was ready for lunch. The morning had passed quickly as it always did when she was absorbed and standing upright now she looked around at her morning's work. The garden was walled, and, as with most Toulouse gardens, long and narrow. Her plan was to disguise the straight lines of the beds with planting that would drift and flow, to create a less formal space that would invite one to pause and reflect. She had selected trees that would create a feeling of privacy from the neighbouring houses, which at the moment intruded on the eye. The owners, recently arrived from Paris, had yet to agree to this but Annie, confident of her persuasive presentation was confident that they would give her a free hand. She picked up her hat, which she had thrown onto the ground, gave it a good shake and turned up the path to the street. She would be home in five minutes.

She was hungry and quickly prepared a salad adding some potatoes left over from their supper, then spent some time playing with Rose who was trying to crawl and finding the whole business vexing. They were in the nursery. 'No! Don't push back! Annie said. She was sitting on the floor holding out both hands, 'Come to me! Rose grunted and pushed her bottom in the air struggling to do as Annie asked. Without success. Annie scooped her up and carried her down to the kitchen and put her on the floor there as she made a cup of tea. She glanced at a plant catalogue that had arrived in the post, becoming absorbed as she thought again of her plan for the garden where she was working. She finished her tea and called out to the Nannie who had returned from her lunch for the afternoon shift, she could hear her upstairs. She bent down to kiss Rose goodbye...and she was not where she had been put. A moment of panic followed as she stood up, 'Where was she? Annie rushed around the kitchen, and looked under the table and then ran out into the hall. And saw Rose crawling forwards, her head down. Purposeful. She had almost reached the top of the stairs. 'Rose! Stop! Annie shouted and throwing herself forward grabbed her two feet. She was shaking and felt sick as she stood up, holding a surprised and sobbing Rose to her. The image of the child tumbling head over heels down the stairs was too appalling and Annie was near to tears herself, as she carried Rose back into the kitchen and sat with her on the sofa trying to calm down. The Nannie came in quite unaware of what had so nearly happened and Annie handed Rose over, she was too ashamed to explain why Rose's face was damp with tears, she knew how dreadfully careless she had been.

*

Her afternoon passed in a wave of anxiety as Annie reflected on the image of Rose crawling towards the stairs. Supposing. Just supposing I had not looked up in time, was her constant thought. How could I explain to Felix if she had fallen? How could I live with what might have happened to her? These thoughts were interrupted by the owners who appeared holding her plan as she wheeled the barrow towards the compost area at the far end of the garden.

'We want to discuss this with you please. They smiled as they looked at her. 'We are not so sure.

*

A chastened Annie returned home earlier than she had expected. The conversation had not taken long. The owners would not agree to her plan and were fixed on a more classic design retaining the straight gravel paths and insisting on formal bedding, she had argued vainly and they had, very politely, dismissed her. Annie had lost the only job that she had. It gave her much to think about as she walked home. As she entered the kitchen she was greeted by the Nannie, who was beaming with pleasure,

'The baby can crawl! The Nannie said, 'She has just learnt! She jiggled Rose in her arms, 'Clever, clever baby!

Gulping back the tears that had been building up all afternoon, Annie picked Rose up, 'Oh! She said, 'What a surprise! We'll have to watch her now won't we!

'Of course! Felix must fix some gates immediately please, or we could have an accident. I cannot watch her all the time.

Annie looked hard at the Nannie but her face was entirely innocent.

*

Later, preparing for bed Annie said, 'I've been thinking.

Felix who was folding his shirt carefully turned to her, 'Oh?

'Would you say that Marthe is disappointed...that we're not married?

Felix answered slowly, 'I think she would prefer it if we were. But she's not put any pressure on me if that's what you're worried about.

'But you said once that you felt that you hadn't…

He interrupted, 'Met up to her hopes. Her expectations. Yes I have felt that for a long time, most of my life really, but I think she's more proud of me now. She's more content in her own life and that has helped her see my life in a broader way.

'And you have given her a grand daughter.

'Yes. That has certainly helped.

'And you live in this lovely house. Full of lovely things.

'And with you. She's your greatest fan you know.

Annie thought suddenly of the afternoon and how nearly it could have become the worst disaster possible. I don't deserve all this she thought…so many kind people: Felix and Charlie and my mother and Tony and Marthe and Claude. And Rose.

'I'd like to marry you! She said. It was so unexpected that Felix had to sit down on the bed, he was astonished. Annie, had surprised herself, the words had come out almost involuntarily, but she continued, 'I want to. I've been selfish for too long. All my life really. I've always put myself first! Trying to have it all…a career, a family, a home of my own. And I can't do it any more, and I don't want to. I've lost my job anyway and today I nearly caused a terrible accident. No Felix don't ask. It's too shaming. And I'm tired out. She was sitting on the bed now next to him, 'I want to please you and your mother… and everyone else. Let's get married as soon as we can.

*

The evening fell into tears and love and they were both as surprised as each other, but the decision had been made. The following week as the news spread to Les Palmes and to Claire and Tony and Ralph in England, and congratulations were expressed, Annie and Felix went out to dinner together to celebrate. This was quite a rare event and Felix had planned it carefully, he had selected the restaurant at the hotel du Capitol, very old fashioned and famous for its fin de siècle décor. The chef was renowned and Annie had never eaten there before. She dressed in black and as she came down the stairs looking for her watch, Charlie commented 'Ooh Mum, you look very grown up! But nice!

'Eat your fruit, she replied with a smile, 'and don't forget to look out your stuff for football tomorrow. And go to bed when Sophie tells you. Felix joined them and took her arm, 'Come on, he can look after himself! He's fifteen! They walked together down the stairs.

*

Annie looked at the menu. It was like a book, a large book, cream coloured and covered in black loopy writing. 'We'll start with a white wine of course, Felix took command, he was holding the wine list an equally heavy book. 'And then move onto a Burgundy. Something not too heavy. Annie's stomach lurched, she took a breath, 'And some water, sparkling, she added, and looked at the menu again. The wine waiter brought a bottle of Chablis, pulled out the cork ceremoniously and poured two glasses. 'To us! Felix smiled at her. Annie raised her glass and felt peculiar and nauseous. She tried to take a sip but the smell made her feel worst. Felix was staring at her, 'What? Try it! It's light and not too fruity. You love Chablis!

Annie tried again but this time it was worst, she just hated the smell. She put her glass down. 'Give me a moment. She picked up the other glass and sipped the sparkling water and felt better.

The maitre d' appeared to take their order and shook out her napkin with a flourish, 'And for Madame tonight, we are recommending oysters! Grilled if preferred, or... Annie's stomach lurched again, she felt sweaty and turning from the waiter she said, 'Sorry Felix I feel sick. Very sick! Please I need to get out.

They left quickly and Annie recovered as she stood outside the grand entrance, under the dark green awning, breathing in the night air and holding Felix's arm, she said, 'I don't know what happened in there, it was the smell of the wine and then the thought of eating oysters. I feel better now in the fresh air, can we just walk around a little?

The evening had turned chill and Annie wrapped her coat around her as they walked slowly down the narrow street that led towards the river. Felix was very quiet. As they turned the corner, he stopped suddenly and facing her said, 'Annie, just a moment, do you think that maybe, he paused, 'you might be pregnant? She stared down the street, thinking. People jostled past them on the narrow pavement, Felix waited.

'It's possible, she said slowly, 'Goodness Felix I think that's it. I 've been feeling tired, and... She clutched his hands, 'That explains everything! How surprising!

Felix watched her carefully, 'And are you excited?

Yes! I am! But it is a little much to grasp. Previous pregnancies, I felt anger and disappointment and blamed first Ralph, and then you and myself of course. But at this moment I feel...pure happiness. Felix was overcome with a sense of relief, the joy would come later.

'Can we go and buy some frites? Annie asked, 'And eat them sitting on one of the benches by the river. It's not too cold is it? And I would really like a coke! I'm sorry you missed your lovely dinner and...

He stopped her, 'Pommes frites would be perfect, and then some cheese, if you feel like it, at home with your feet up, you need to eat something more than frites.

'That's what I feel like, sorry. But some cheese sounds nice and fruit, just not oysters and white wine. Felix hugged her, 'Another baby! I can't quite believe it. He picked her up and kissed her as she kicked her feet in the air.

'Put me down, everyone is staring. Go and join the queue at the van, then we can celebrate with frites. Oh and a large cold coke please. Felix joined the queue.

CHAPTER 31

'And how are things in Toulouse? Marthe was talking to Felix on the phone. The previous day she and Claude had decided to invite both their families to join them for Christmas day at Les Palmes, it would be a way of getting everyone together for the first time since their wedding. Claude feared that Jerome and Luc were unlikely to be able to come. Luc was happily working in a small hotel in Meribel, he was a sous chef there and gaining lots of experience and new responsibilities. He phoned erratically and was full of enthusiasm both for the cooking and the skiing and urged Claude to come for a visit when the weather was a little warmer. 'March will be lovely, he said, 'lots of snow and lunch outside at the top! Sunny and not too crowded then. Claude made no promises but was tempted. He had not mentioned it yet to Marthe who had never skied, but surely she would enjoy the scenery and a comfortable hotel in the mountains with log fires and snowy walks. Claude thought that Jerome was more likely to be 'home' for the Christmas break, it was an easy flight from Paris, he had decided to phone him later that day.

*

'Big changes here, Felix replied.

'Tell me.

Felix paused, 'It's difficult to know where to start.

'At the beginning Felix, always start at the beginning, Marthe said.

So Felix recounted the events of the recent days, doctored a little to avoid his mother's questions,

'Oh and Annie's stopping work. He concluded, 'Putting her career on hold. It's all become too much, she says, Rose and Charlie and the house and now the pregnancy!

Marthe was astounded, it was difficult to take it all in... another baby and a wedding and Annie staying at home.

'So I will become a grandmother again! That's just wonderful and...Oh Felix I wish I could give you a hug. And getting married that is almost more exciting! I think I'm going to have to sit down and then drive into Toulouse and give you all that big hug. Can I tell Claude?

Felix smiled, 'Of course! He's family now isn't he. Why don't you? Come over. We're all here, though we haven't told Charlie yet, it's all a bit sudden, he said, but come please.

*

It was evening, Claude and Marthe sat in the salon at Les Palmes, each unwinding after their celebratory trip into Toulouse. Claude sipped a whisky.

'I told Felix, when we were on our own in the kitchen this evening, that I've decided to stop my enquiries into the past, Marthe said unexpectedly. 'He was very pleased.

'All your enquiries?

'Yes. I've put the diaries away, they're now in the chest in the second bedroom. And I'm not going to enquire further into the Rinaldis, any of them, or my father and the events of 1944. I had been thinking about it for some time and then, while we were in New York, being there...well it's such a modern city. No one is in the past, they're all taken up with the NOW. It gave me a real jolt. Claude looked at her, 'I'm glad, he said. 'It's a wise decision. But please stick to it won't you, no slipping back!

'Gregoire said something to me some time ago, it was my first visit to the farm. Marthe continued, 'The dogs had run out to greet me, barking. They're rough coated, guard dogs of course, you see them everywhere. I asked what they were called, there were four, I think. One had been with Agathe when I was lying on the tow path.

'They're all called Jacques, Gregoire said, 'it's easier.

'It was such a simple solution I thought, Marthe said, 'it's a bit of a family name with the Rinaldi's which perhaps explains it. To Gregoire the dogs were all the same, they don't have separate identities. But we're not like that are we? We're all different. And that is what I've come to accept; we each of us have different histories, different family secrets. And we make different mistakes, choosing the wrong paths…She stopped. Claude drained his whisky and looked at her, he smiled gently, 'Well I'm glad you've worked that out, he said, 'of course you're right. We don't always like what we learn about our past, our families what they've done or not done! Nor is it easy to accept our differences, we try to make people into what we want them to be. I know I do with Jerome and Luc, trying to control their careers, their lives really.

'And as I have with Felix.

There was a silence, 'Enough of this philosophising! He said, 'They're all doing all right at the moment. Maybe that's as much as we can hope for, we need to accept their right to go their own ways. As you said, we're individuals. Yes?

Marthe nodded. He reached out and helped her up from her chair, 'And you and I have a great deal to look forward to!

Time for bed I think, and a good night's sleep.

'That sounds good, Marthe said and took his hand.

THE END

ABOUT THE AUTHOR

Hilary Newman now lives in Sussex, the county she called home in her early years.

She started writing late in life as the pressures of home and family receded. She has spent much time in France, on holidays with her parents and then with her husband, children and many friends.